MW01109297

WATERMARK PRESS, INC.
149 North Broadway, Suite 201
Wichita, Kansas 67202

Cover and interior design: Kala Carter
Photo courtesy of: Daryl Moren

FIRST PRINTING

VOLUME ONE

THE WICHITA MYSTERIES

GAYLORD DOLD

UPTOWN WRECK

SNAKE EYES

COLD CASH

Best wishes,
Gaylord Dold

Watermark Press, Inc., 149 North Broadway, Suite 201, Wichita, Kansas 67201

ALSO BY GAYLORD DOLD

UPTOWN WRECK

ONE

It was hot and dead and still. The ceiling fan circled in a futile gesture, casting shadows on the pair of feet I had solidly stacked on my desk. I watched a shiny blue fly do kip-ups and a few twirls from the phone to the phone book and back. Once in twenty minutes it did a pirouette through a smoke ring I drifted between my feet, then settled back on the phone book rubbing its back legs in satisfaction. In the same twenty minutes one beat-up Plymouth cruised past on Lincoln Street and no one went into the barbershop next door. When it was that hot and dead I always drank sweet muscatel and when it got bad enough I thought about my ex-wife, Linda. After five years the memories never got any better.

I don't remember meeting Linda, being introduced to her, or even asking her to a drive-in movie or for a Coke at the drugstore. One day there it was. I was like Gregory Peck in that Hitchcock movie, when he wakes up as the chief honcho in a nuthouse. He can't remember his own

1

name or where he came from or how the hell he got to be chief honcho of a nuthouse. There's just this disquieting feeling that he better string along with the show or turn himself in. So he reads a little psychotherapy. He tap-dances around Adler and looks at the pictures of ids and egos. He is ready to go, and the doctors and nurses can't tell the difference. The patients think he is terrific: he has this natural sympathy and doesn't gum up the works with all that technical jargon which makes them feel sick. Everybody thinks how therapeutic it is that he can be like one of *them*. Well, Ingrid Bergman knows he's not one of them, because she wants in his trousers; Leo G. Carroll knows he's not one of them, because Leo G. Carroll is evil and therefore possesses a clarity of vision. But when it came to the movie version of Linda and me, I played all the parts. That made it harder to wake up.

I know what Linda had for me. In that other summer five years ago she owned an air cooler. It was a green whale beached in a tiny west window, chugging cool damp air and, leaking rusty water. I lived for that air cooler. That summer I was the chief honcho and sole inmate, but there was no Ingrid Bergman wanting in my pants—and no Leo G. Carroll sporting a pencil mustache and toting a gun in his coat pocket. There was nothing to refer to, so I worked and drank muscatel and listened to the Browns on KMOX out of St. Louis. Linda was a ghost who made me fried baloney sandwiches with mustard. I felt bad about all that.

For eight hours a day and four on Saturday I was a thirty-year-old stock boy at the Fox-Vliet drug warehouse at Oliver and Lincoln. I moved streptomycin, Vicks, and Halo shampoo off the loading docks and down the incline ramps, unpacked the crates, and repacked cartons for shipment to drugstores at retail.

I left work every day at four-thirty, my face and arms covered with grimy bits of excelsior, and drove north to Linda through the wasted summer streets of Wichita. I knew what I had to do, how the dream would start, and how it would probably all turn out.

I stopped at the Shoe's for wine. Kenny Shoemaker. The Shoe ran a broken-down liquor store on Hillside. Next door was the Uptown Recreation, a pool hall and hangout for snooker sharks and the boys with peel-off suits. Most of the Shoe's business was guys buying pints to mix with the beer they bought at the Uptown. There was never any trouble with the Shoe. He cashed checks and held on to them for ten days. For a guy with a decent track record, there was credit when he came up a little short. In a pinch, the Shoe would pass a case of Pabst through the back door on Sunday morning, then follow you home and help you drink it. When he got drunk and collapsed into his rocker in the back room, he left a sign by the cash register that said, "Make your own change. Shoe." Shoe stacked all the wine in a sun-scorched window where the labels faded and the wine turned sour. No one cared. Shoe sold mostly whiskey and beer. I had been there the day the Shoe started his "charity fund-raising drive" by putting three quarters in a plastic iron lung on a card with a picture of a crippled kid. There were still three quarters in the iron lung, but the picture of the crippled kid had faded like the wine labels until it was just a crutch and a pair of glasses. The Shoe got up and held the door open for me as I went in.

"Hey, Shoe! How's it goin'?"

"Mitchie, my boy." His mouth was a yellow cave, one teak-colored stalactite incisor holding on for dear life. He was a scrawny gray bird in a string tie and a cowboy shirt, and when he spoke he stuck his beak in my face and looped a bony wing around my neck.

"Mitchie, where you been, how you feelin'?" I was always at Fox-Vliet and I always felt like dropping a Girl Scout on her head.

"Pretty good, pretty good. You?"

"Mitchie, I tellya. I was out at the Rock Castle the other night and some old red-haired bitch got ahold of me. We was out in the parking lot. She was sucking on me, and I thought the fuckin' world was coming to an end. Shit, I was so fucking drunk. Shit!"

"Helluva deal." I looked at the first dollar Shoe ever made taped to the cash register, then at a picture of the Shoe and his wife on their wedding day in 1931, a yellowed clipping from the *Wichita Eagle*. Hands joined, they were holding a knife over an elaborate wedding cake. The Shoe looked about eighteen years old and had a big, wide smile. I realized that the Shoe and I were stumbling through the same darkened charnel house and there was always somebody around to keep score of the bumps and bruises.

I said, "Gimme a fifth of muscatel and a six-pack of Pabst."

"Need some cash?" he asked.

"Thanks, Kenny, not today."

"Whatcha up to tonight, Mitchie?"

I realized I was going to tell the Shoe that I was not up to much tonight—except that I would probably drink some muscatel and listen to the Browns on KMOX.

The Shoe grabbed the glass door and held it open for me. On the way out I passed a pimpled kid with a wispy brown beard. He wore a painter's cap and smelled like he had covered the world.

"Hey, Shoe! How's it goin'?" I heard him say. I fired up the Ford and headed north on Hillside to Linda and the air cooler, choking down the urge to open the muscatel right there.

Linda's place was a brick duplex slapped up during the war for families who came to town to build airplanes at the plant. Square and low. In the summer the place was like a basement and smelled worse. More than anything, though, the joint was cool and Linda's Philco picked up KMOX from St. Louis.

I sat down at one end of the couch, unfolded the evening *Eagle,* and lit a Lucky. Linda nestled beside me. I handed her the crossword and poured myself some muscatel in a glass with a picture of Big John and Sparky on the side. Sparky was a goofy-looking cross between a little kid and a gopher, and I covered his face with muscatel up to his floppy ears. The muscatel always tasted a little like peanut butter.

I never knew whether Linda really loved crossword puzzles, but she worked at them with the dedication of a fisherman at a dry hole. Her face would grow perplexed and she would slowly, thoughtfully, push a red fingernail into her mouth. Her sneaky brown eyes were almond-shaped, her lips luxurious but always pulled tight. In the perpetual dim summertime of the apartment, I thought she looked like Gloria Grahame.

"Mitch, what's ochre? It's a clue."

"A color. Somewhere between umber and sienna."

"No, seriously. Come on."

"All right," I said. "Say it's a vegetable cultivated mainly in the South." This was about the best I could do.

"Fuckhead!"

Usually I would go on for hours free-associating at Linda's expense. Tonight, though, something was up and serious.

"Actually," I said, "it really is a color. How many letters?"

"Six."

"Oh. Well, ochre comes out of the earth and can look like it—the earth. Something like yellow or orange."

"Those both have six letters."

"Well, work around it." God, oh God, I wondered if the wheel was invented by some guy trying to make a raspberry Lifesaver. I took my first big gulp of muscatel.

It was getting to be seven o'clock. I switched on the Philco and watched the yellow light around the dial gradually grow brighter, heard the hum and the buzz, the sound of the radio focusing on St. Louis and, finally, the steamy, faraway voice of Phil Stevens saying how Budweiser was the beer all the Browns drank. They must have drunk a lot of it, because they all played baseball like they were smashed.

The Browns were playing the Indians: the dirty Ohio River and the mighty Muddy in turgid confluence. Linda got up then. If I was lucky, the game would be into the bottom of the fourth before the beer and baloney sandwiches were served.

But something was definitely up. Instead of heading to the kitchen, Linda went to the bathroom and took a long shower. The water ran for an inning and a half. Then there was a frightening, virginal silence. I was sweating and had lost track of the ball game somewhere in the fourth inning.

"Linda? You all right?" Nothing.

The bathroom door opened. In the wedge of light, Linda floated like a blue butterfly. She wore an ankle-length satin kimono sashed at the waist. Her long auburn hair was looped into a single braid down her back. She was trying to swish and glide. A hundred years went by, and I felt circles grow black beneath my eyes.

"Linda?" I wanted to make sure it was her.

"Mitch, sweetheart, dinner is ready."

That night Linda made meat loaf. I sat at the dinette while she swayed around the table, serving corn on the cob, white bread and butter, a jar of dill pickles. Finally, the meat loaf appeared. It looked like a muddy football decked out on a plate of forsythia. The thing weighed a ton. Linda forgot to put catsup and eggs in with the hamburger and it was like eating drywall. I wanted to ask her for some sand to put on top.

Linda talked about her mother's disappearance the week before. Someone found Mom's wallet in the parking lot at Maule Drugs and called Dad who called Linda's brother who called Linda. Suddenly Linda's mother was kidnapped, raped, and murdered. The police were called in to investigate. Actually, the police was some twenty-two-year-old kid who probably played fullback once at North

High. He looked me up and down and smelled muscatel and a rat. An hour later I was no longer a suspect. Linda's mother turned up at home complaining about her lost wallet. But there were still several hours in there somewhere that remained unexplained and everybody in the family had a theory. Linda thought her mother was in a religious crisis, though I could not figure out what kind of crisis a Southern Baptist could possibly have.

Linda stopped. Then: "Mitch, you don't have to go home tonight." I always went home after the Browns finished, played through a few chess games, and went to bed. By then the night was cooling down and, half drunk, I could sleep.

"Okay," I said. I saw myself chained for life to a meat loaf.

"Then come along to bed." She left.

The Browns and the Indians were tied in the ninth. I gulped the last of the muscatel. I followed a gulfstream of perfume into the bedroom, thinking about the bottom of the ninth and the good old days of fried baloney and Pabst.

In the faint light I saw Linda lying on her side covered by a sheet and two blankets. The bedroom air was a motionless, murky syrup. I undressed slowly, straining to hear Phil Stevens above the steady din of cicadas, the chug and clank of the air cooler. By the time I was naked, the Browns were threatening with two men on and none out.

"Linda, could we put on that little lamp in the corner?" If it was going to happen, I wanted to see it.

Linda said, "No, I'd rather we didn't."

"What?" I said.

"I'd rather we didn't put on the lamp."

"Why?" Perched on the scaffold, the condemned man discusses any topic whatsoever with his executioner.

"I don't want you to see my face." I felt the shame and fear in Linda's voice and felt sorry for both of us, for the loneliness she wrapped herself in, for the advantage I took of her weakness. I wanted to make things right by her.

I curled up behind her question-mark shape and lightly kissed her cheek, feeling with my lips how she held her jaw clamped shut, seeing in the streetlight and shadow the lines etched around her tightly closed eyes. She clutched the sheet and two blankets in a bunch beneath her chin. In the living room the Browns pushed a man to third, sending the Indians's manager, Billie Joe Walker, to the mound.

If Billie Joe could go to the mound, so could I. I touched her shoulder gently, rolled her over onto her back, and with my left hand pulled down the sheet and blankets before she could protest. She still wore her kimono, sash done up in a double half-hitch, her ankles locked. I knelt over Linda like a catcher behind the plate and jammed a sweaty right knee between her legs at the thigh. She relaxed, then tensed again. We were like those love bugs you see in the summer, wedded at the butt in a perpetually lewd embrace, the monster with two backs, an embellishment on the world's absurdity. Billie Joe Walker was at the mound again, the fans screaming for a walk. A Browns fan knew both limit and potential.

With the grim determination of Tamerlaine, I braced myself with two hands against an outcropping of pelvic bone around Linda's hips, raised my left knee, and brought it down between her ankles, working it in like a corkscrew and, at the same time, walked my right knee northward toward her crotch. I wondered if Linda heard the fans bellow at ball one. I used my right leg as a church key, prying at her thighs, gradually inching my left leg between her calves, then on until I felt my left knee between her own knees. I pressured her hips, pushing down and slightly out. The dangerous operation required speed and grace, power and finesse. Phil Stevens's beery voice rasped out ball two.

Suddenly, Linda's ankles popped loose and her legs flew open like a pair of scissors. She hissed like a cornered cat. With my knees delicately balanced on her thighs, my hands still grasping her hips, I bounced her twice against the bed with my whole weight and when we left the sheets for a brief second, I jerked the kimono all the way up around her belly. Before she could rally, I swallowed a quart of syrupy air and pushed myself backward and down, sliding on sweat, until my nose came to rest in her hillock and my shoulders were firmly entrenched between her thighs. I wrapped my arms underneath her legs and dug my hands into her bum. I curled an eyebrow up over the tree line and took a look around.

Linda still grimaced.

"You're not going to do *that?*" she said. There in Linda's bedroom, buried in the hooting and yelping of cicadas, buried in the misty depths of Linda herself, I did what Linda couldn't bring herself to say.

The Browns won the game on a wild pitch with the bases loaded. Later that summer the Giants caught the Bums and went around them on the miracle of Bobby Thomson's home run. It stayed hot in Wichita and, one dead Friday evening, Linda and I drove the Fairlane down to Nowata, Oklahoma, and were married in a little drive-in chapel. The Reverend Bob Smart officiated. The good reverend ran a mortuary in the basement and, as we left, he gave me his card. "We marry 'em and bury 'em."

Fall brought cooler weather and a divorce. The Shoe loaned me a grand for my investigator's license and a few months' rent on a little office along Lincoln Street. Mine was a small life, skip-chasing, repossessing Pontiacs, and trailing boozy husbands to their unholy nests. But it was a private life and I made my own hours. When it got hot and dead still, I felt bad about Linda. But not much.

TWO

My office edges up against downtown, an area of mom-and-pop shops, hardware and shoe stores, lawn and garden emporiums, and the always-empty beauty parlor. There are vacant lots full of weeds, tin cans, discarded tires, and leftover houses with tumbled porches and dirt yards, old couples out front in the swing, all cancer and Social Security and no place to go. I like Lincoln Street though, elm-shaded and red-brick. I'm the end suite of three in a single-story, mud-colored row of offices set back off the street. Two blocks east on Lincoln looms Thomas Jefferson Elementary, built in 1929—stately, made of red brick like the street, a spidery silver fire escape trailing around the pointed roof and on down between the rows of tall, shimmering windows. In autumn, when the air sharpened and the elms glistened red and orange, I often contemplated the shining school windows, imagining paste and erasers and chalk smelling just as enviably fresh and clean as linen or apples. It was good then, or in early spring on a blustery

10

mid-morning in March, blue and gray clouds bumping along in the chilly air, to stroll the long block west down Lincoln to Betty's Coffee Pot, and there, in the white neon glare, to drink coffee and eat warm cinnamon rolls. I had the time these days and I was trying to be quiet, to gain something from being small and paying attention to detail.

I was next door to Jake Singleton's barbershop. Jake's nose looked like a roadmap of the Weller's distillery and he was the only guy I ever saw who really had Popeye forearms. "Bowling and jerking off," he told me, "and hell, that's what happens when yer damn dick weighs sixteen pounds." Jake cut my hair every two weeks, cigar ash and grayish-brown hair disappearing down my collar. He talked and I read *Field and Stream.* We both worried a lot about the rent on our places and I generally agreed with him that the potholes in the gravel parking lot were worse than ever this year. Jake said he wanted to try his concoction of HA Hair Arranger and lilac water on my head. "What the hell, HA finds out about this, we make a million." I liked Jake and he liked me, though he said he could never figure how a snoop could make an honest living.

It was the snipe end of a weary August, ten o'clock in the morning, when I skidded the Fairlane to a stop in front of the plate-glass window: MITCH ROBERTS INVESTIGATIONS. No staring eye or deerstalker hat, just a come in and venetian blinds. I waved at Jake and flashed him a grin. He was patiently cutting the hair of a fat guy who hardly had any, carressing the few strands of pasted-down black hair around the guy's crown, tilting his shiny head gently back and forth with steady hands, generally making the guy think he was really getting a haircut. For the bald guy it was like having a smart, good-looking whore ask to feel his muscles. A buck and a quarter and he got to hear what Jake had to say, read his *Field and Stream,* and look at the girl's ass on the calendar. Jake stuck his scissors in the pocket of his smock and returned a salute.

It was going to be hot again. In powdery sunlight, I

opened the office door and walked past Gertie's desk, around the wood-and-glass divider, and sat down behind the oak desk I got at Razook Furniture for $12.50. Gertie would be late again, home with female trouble, or maybe just weary and demoralized from my last shoot-out in the office. Maybe she was out on an undercover assignment for the boss. Hell, it didn't matter. Gertie had been born two years before, when I went to the Kress store downtown and bought a suede purse in blue, a cherry lipstick and powder kit, and a three-by-five picture frame. I left the paper photograph of Donald O'Connor in the picture frame and set the stuff in a lifelike disarray. My regular clients— the junior bank managers, the half dozen lawyers, the handful of insurance adjusters—were mostly beyond kidding me about Gertie and her Donald O'Connor look-alike husband. As for the rest, what few there were, I hoped they would become regular clients before they found out I didn't have a secretary and never would. Gertie saved me a lot of shit.

I made some coffee on the hot plate and leafed through title documents to my repossessions. One guy owned a Hudson Hornet. I mean he and the bank owned the Hornet. He had bought the thing two years ago and was now three months shy on the payments, and the bank was feeling insecure. The slob worked the last shift at Boeing, so he got home about an hour after daybreak and probably started drinking whiskey, chasing it with beer. I figured he was on the run from the wife and kids, but couldn't get away from the job that quick because he needed the dough. I also figured that by ten he would be asleep on the couch in his dirty efficiency at the Matthewson Apartments, bundled in a white T-shirt with burp stains on the belly, a copy of *Modern Detective* straddling his broken-down face. I had to think about the guy that way. If I thought long enough about the eight hours this guy spent burring rough edges from metal pieces down at the plant, his wife's mother-in-law on the back porch chewing tobacco, and the radio blaring Don McNeil's *Breakfast Club* at eight in the morning when he was trying to sleep, I would think about tipping the guy to scram. Hanging on the way I was, I couldn't afford social theory. To me it was an easy daytime snatch, the owner dead on the couch. No guns, no fights, no hollering.

I was still matching car keys and title documents when the phone rang.

I answered in a tough-guy voice, adding a little: *My secretary didn't show this morning and I'm annoyed about that.* "Mitch Roberts."

The voice on the other end was Okie, about twenty years out of the hog thicket, slow and drooling, with an undertow of calculation. It was an ole-boy voice backed up by a little money.

"This here the private investigator?" This voice was definitely connected with a sneer. I could picture this voice shooting neighbor dogs, maybe setting a barn fire.

"Speaking," I said.

The voice said, "This here is Carl Plummer." I never heard of Carl Plummer, but the voice presumed I had. I decided to call the voice *Mr.* Plummer, see what happened and whether I was going to get some of that money.

"Well, Mr. Plummer, what can I do for you?"

"Do you find people? People who up and run off?"

"Mr. Plummer," I said, "I go and look for people who run off and sometimes I find them. Sometimes I don't."

"I say you do your job kinda half-assed then, boy." There was nothing in the tone to make me think I was being kidded.

"What's on your mind, Mr. Plummer?"

"I got a job fer you."

"If I take it."

"You can afford to sit around there with yer feet up waiting fer yer rich uncle to get his head sucked into the mowin' machine?"

"Mr. Plummer, I'd like to dance this two-step with you

for most of the rest of the night, but the widda Jones and her scrawny sisters are waiting out at the Tucker place for their bull. Now why don't we get down to business before my new blue seersucker suit plumb melts away?" I didn't trust the voice and I didn't like the Mr. Plummer it said it was, but so far this conversation was more fun than going over title documents with the junior assistant manager for credit compliance at Union National.

Mr. Plummer said, "Boy, you think you can find South Broadway?"

"I got a compass, a sack of sandwiches, and the Boy Scout Handbook right out in the car. It might take a week, but I'll find it." South Broadway was the main truck drag running north and south through Wichita. On Mr. Plummer's end, Broadway was Highway 81 running down to Oklahoma City and Dallas.

"Well now," Plummer said, "why don't you make a run at my place this afternoon. We'll see if you make er. I got some business where I need someone who can nose my son down. You shape up right to me, we might make some kinda deal." I knew being specific was not trump to an Okie no matter how long he was out of the hog thicket. "You know my place? Salvage yard down across the bridge."

"I'll find it, Mr. Plummer."

"I hope so. I surely de do hope so." He hung up.

I leaned back and lit a Lucky. I flipped the Yellow Pages through until I found "Salvage." Plummer's Salvage Yard was at Broadway and Thirty-ninth Street South, no high-priced ad, no slogan, no picture of a tow truck, just the name and phone number. I dialed the number. Plummer answered, "Salvage." And I hung up.

I dialed Andy Lanham. Andy was the lieutenant of detectives down at the WPD, a friend, and good for pulling license tags and running spot checks in return for french-fried cauliflower and a night at the ballpark. Sometimes Andy dropped by my place on Sycamore and we would sit beside the open window, play chess, and drink beer. Since the birth of his third kid, Andy dropped by less. We hadn't been to the ballpark together all summer. I was on hold at the switchboard for a minute, then Andy picked up his phone and said hello.

"Hello, Andy. How the heck are you?"

"Great, Mitch. Good to hear from you. You playing any chess these days? Those fucking Braves."

"Yes—and those Braves are the greatest." I was following the Botvinnik and Smyslov championship match pretty closely, at least until I got a little drunk in the evening and walked over to the park to watch the Braves for five innings. I lived across the street from Lawrence Stadium where the Braves played Triple-A ball.

"What can I do for you, Mitch?"

"Listen, Andy, I need a short favor."

"Shoot."

"Are you guys working any missing-persons case on a kid named Plummer? Don't know the first name. If so, what kind of action? Second, you got any record on Carl Plummer—arrests anywhere, any other beefs?"

Andy said, "Hold on. I'll be back." I lit another Lucky and waited.

Five minutes later Andy came back on the line. "No open case on any Plummer missing person. Also no reports. No arrests, wants, or beefs on Carl Plummer." I heard him drag a cigarette. In a sharp, serious way he added, "What's the action Mitch? You gone inquisitive?"

"Thanks a million, Andy. Drop by soon and we'll catch Indianapolis and play over some old Alekhine games."

Andy eased, disappointed. "Take it easy Mitch." He hung up.

I hung the BACK AT FIVE O'CLOCK sign on the glass door, put the top down on the Fairlane, and drove east on Lincoln through a cavern of dusty elms. I had done some missing-persons work in the past, mostly teenagers on a toot. Those were cases the police worked on, but the client was willing to spring the thirty-five a day for personal service. Three times a year I went looking for Mrs. Richard Donahue, whose idea of a really good time was a shack job in Kansas City with an ex-con or truck driver. Mr. Richard Donahue paid me fifty a day and left the police out.

Something bothered me about Carl Plummer and his missing son. There was no police beef, no missing money, no hint of alarm in Carl Plummer's voice. If anything, Plummer was mad as hell. I pulled up in a bus stop in front of the Uptown Recreation and hopped out. If there was anything out on the streets about Plummer, the Gar—bartender and small-time grifter—would know.

The decorator who appointed the Wreck was fond of sepia and blue neon. Saloon bar in front backed by a mirror, line of booths along one wall, and four snooker tables to the back door. Beaming, Tony Garcia stood with both hands on the bar. Above his head the Hamm's bear kept hitting a lighted golf ball over a forest and into a placid mountain lake.

"Roberts. Starting kinda early?"

"No thanks, Tony. How about some coffee?"

At the back snooker table two gas-and-electric guys clicked snooker balls around a perfect green felt table. They belonged to the G & E truck parked on Douglas. Taking a break.

"Sure thing. Just a minute," he said.

Tony owed me. One Saturday night I shot a fat woman in the foot. The fat woman had a butcher's knife in the Gar's belly and was about to butterfly his spleen. The Gar went down for two months, but he wasn't out.

Tony came out of the back room with my coffee. "So, Mitch," he said, "it is not Saturday night, there is no loose girls at the bar, you are wearing a suit. You are wanting information." Tony was doing Joel Cairo.

"Tony, you are a very wise man." I sipped the coffee. My eyes were getting used to the dark. Tony was a huge man with olive skin and black hair. His face was round, his left eye a sightless white. A rainbow scar ran from the corner of his white eye to his mouth.

"Does the name Carl Plummer mean anything to you, Tony?" I asked.

He looked over my shoulder at the pinball machine. "Carl Plummer. No, Mitch, it means nothing to me."

"Ask around a little for me would you, Tony? It is not an unimportant matter. Also, it would be best if it was not known that I am interested."

Tony laughed. "The word is as good as out."

I finished my coffee and left Tony with a promise to be back Saturday night for some snooker. The G & E guys were still on break when I hopped into the Fairlane and drove south on Hillside, like always, sticking to the shady tunnels on Wichita's old brick streets.

I spent a couple of hours doing my repos. The Hudson Hornet showed forty thousand miles and a ripped headliner, all in two years. The junior assistant manager for credit compliance was not amused with his collateral. After a Nu-Way burger, bowl of chili with onions, and a glass of beer, I was ready to go dancing with Carl Plummer.

South Broadway is the crawl space of Wichita. Hill people from Arkansas and Oklahoma, Ma and Pa and four or five kids jammed into broken-down jalopies, come north looking for jobs at aircraft plants, packing houses, or refineries. They make it to South Broadway. They are all along there, sitting on buckets and stumps in front of the Moon Motel, rooming by the week in hot little cubicles, the vacant-eyed scruffy kids throwing rocks at stray dogs. The street is littered with used-car lots, salvage yards, greasy spoons, and nightclubs. Every Sunday morning in the back pages of the *Eagle* you read about the guy kicked, stabbed, or shot to death in the parking lot of Cal's Lightning Lounge. It just means some hill family goes home to the hills without Pa.

I worked a lot of skip chases along there, sometimes Honest Al, other times Buck's. It happened that Honest Al used more oily sawdust in his transmissions than most, which meant that when I found the guy who owed Al money I towed the man and the car both. It was unpleasant work.

I drove across the WPA bridge over the Arkansas River, through the intersection at Twenty-ninth Street and past Honest Al's. Carl Plummer's salvage yard was on the right, surrounded on three sides by a ramshackle corrugated-metal fence, the back boundary the river levee. Five or six old cottonwoods with great gnarled trunks shaded the heaps of rusted wrecks, and seedpods filled the air with cotton balls. Dust enveloped the Ford.

When I pulled off the brick street I was in sand and loose dirt three inches deep, fine and silty. I drove through a portal of rusted truck frames and into a fiery wilderness of wrecked cars and trucks, windows smashed, seats torn out. Under one of the cottonwoods squatted a tar-paper shack about fifteen feet square, the walls covered with hubcaps, a sign over the screen door saying OFFICE. I parked, and thought about how long it was going to take to get my white oxfords white again.

A yellow mongrel lay in a wet, sandy hole by the screen door. He arched his back. Without lifting his head, the mutt curled his lips over a row of sharp teeth and let out a constant, unsettling growl, low and mean.

A voice called, "Who is that?" It was Plummer.

"Mitch Roberts."

Plummer snapped, "Abraham!" The dog stopped his growl. I opened the screen and went in.

Plummer sat behind a metal desk, picking his teeth with a small pocketknife. He was wiry, and from what I could see he was tall. His long arms were muscled and brown from working in the sun. Short sandy hair, narrow eyes and a gray, shaggy beard—he looked leathery and lean. He didn't move when I came in, just sat in the wind from a fan stuck in a window behind him.

"Mr. Plummer."

"You eat all yer sandwiches?"

"Not quite." I wondered if the patter was permanent.

"You want the job looking for my boy?"

"That depends," I said.

Plummer looked up. He folded the knife slowly and put it in his pocket. "Depends on what?"

I was standing. There were no chairs in the shack. The whole greasy place was filled with generators, radios, drive shafts. "Now why don't you tell me what you want and why? Then I'll tell you whether it's possible, and if it is whether or not I'll do it for you. If I say it's possible and I'll do it for you, then we'll talk about how much you're going to pay me and when. Then if I agree to the arrangement I'll get to work. Up to now, Mr. Plummer, I don't like the dance and I don't think much of my partner. That's how it is." Plummer leaned back.

"All right," he said. He was smiling now, but it was sinister. "It's like this. My boy is Frank. Frankie Plummer. He's been gone three, four days. Supposed to be working for me around here. What I want is that you go looking for him, find him, and bring him back here. Put him in a goddamn basket if you have to. The why is—he just run off. That's all."

"Why don't you go find him yourself?"

"I ain't got the time."

"How old is he?"

"Old enough." In the corner of my eye I saw a figure outside the screen, just standing.

"Well, Mr. Plummer," I said, "if he's old enough, then he's entitled to leave home and not be dragged back. Suppose, if I go looking for him and find him, that I just tell you where he is and you can take your own basket and bring him back. Kidnapping is a beef I don't need."

Plummer thought for a moment. "All right," he said again.

"I need something to go on," I said, "like photographs of Frankie, some idea of his friends, a line on his car, where he hangs out, what kind of money he has. If he drinks, I want to know where. If he's fucking someone, I want to know who." Plummer was getting mad. I went on. "I get fifty a day and reasonable expenses."

Plummer didn't like any of this. His ears reddened. "I get yer picture," he said. "Frankie has money, he drives a blue '55 Pontiac. He don't stick to one bar more'n another, he ain't got no friends." Empty silence. Lower now. "You try talking to someone named Carmen Granger, lives up in Riverside. She may tell you something." Plummer nodded at the figure at the screen door. He went on. "Frankie stays down at that trailer on the levee. There's a picture from his high school in there somewhere, probably the desk drawer. I'll pay the fifty."

I didn't flinch at the name Carmen Granger. "I'll work for you, Mr. Plummer. Give me a few days. If I don't turn anything, I'll let you know and get off. If I do, you'll hear from me." I turned, then looked back. "Frankie ever been in trouble with the police?"

Plummer said, "No." He barked. "Gomez! Take Mr. Roberts down to the trailer." For the first time, he put his blue eyes directly in mine. "You be in touch. You try Carmen Granger and you be in touch. I expect that." Carl Plummer was making certain where I started.

It turns out Gomez was the lurker at the screen door, a dark-eyed punk about twenty, greasy and trying to act tough. He wore overalls with the name "Tomas" over the heart. Gomez was trying to grow a mustache, but for now it was just a few black hairs looking very lonely above his lip.

"This way," he said. I followed Gomez through the wreckage and back to the levee where the small, twelve-foot travel trailer was parked. It had seen better days. I looked at the ground around the trailer. There were no tire tracks, no oil spots. The trailer stood in direct sunlight, surely over ninety-five. I was thinking that if I lived in a tin can I would park it in the shade. I would also park my car next door. Gomez stood aside and I stepped up on a cinder block and went inside.

It was an airless oven. There were dishes in the little aluminum sink and a calendar on the wall. No phone. I walked to the rear and saw that the bunk bed was unmade. I looked inside the tiny closet. It was empty. Gomez stuck his head inside and said, "Come on. The picture is in that drawer." He pointed to the counter next to the sink.

I opened the drawer Gomez pointed to. In a mess of rags, tools, kitchen utensils, and matches, Frankie Plummer stared up. The picture had been scissored out of a yearbook. The kid looked a lot like his father. I reached with my left hand and casually turned the cold-water tap. Nothing. Gomez snapped, "What you doing, man? Come on." I went outside.

I held the picture up to Gomez. "Is this Frankie Plummer?"

"Yeah."

"How long ago?"

"Five, maybe six years."

"He change anything?"

"Hair's longer. That's all. Kind of ducktail. You know." That made Frankie twenty-three and pretty. But he didn't live in any trailer down by the levee at the junkyard. He had money and drove a new blue Pontiac. Carmen Granger knew where he might be. Frankie just didn't sound like a hill boy with his thumb up his ass.

Gomez followed me all the way to my car, saying nothing. I got in and started the engine. "So long, sonny," I said and smiled. Gomez was saying something, but I was already pulling away, digging through sand, gunning the engine.

I was in traffic, settled behind a Texaco tanker. I lit a Lucky and took a deep drag, thinking. Carl Plummer was not a fool, so he would never expect me to believe that he was just a worried old dad missing his sweet little boy. For some reason he wanted me to believe that Frankie lived in the trailer down by the levee, but didn't have the time or savvy to make it look convincing. Carl also wanted me to think that Frankie boy broke down front ends and scrounged parts. Maybe he did. But it didn't seem likely somehow. What got me was the part about Carmen Granger, Carl tossing off her name like it was supposed to be nothing, just another girlfriend. Hell.

I got under the shady elms on Harry Street and went west.

In the green, cool mountains of north Pakistan, brown bears abound. Natives from Lahore go up to the foothills in summer, stun a little bear out of his tree with a rock or club, stick a ring through his wet nose, and cart him down to steamy, tropical Lahore. You see the bears all over there, matted scabrous skin, watery eyes, dancing in endless circles, standing on hind legs in garbage, surrounded by a laughing mass of toothless, turbaned people. The little bears bleed from their paws. They live five or six years.

I got thirty-five a day, but if Carl Plummer was willing to pay fifty, he could have me for a while. I could feel the ring, hear the toothless laughter.

THREE

It was almost five when I got back to the office. Jake was closed, already home with his wife, Katherine, TV blaring Deputy Dusty and the grill boiling charcoal. There was a letter waiting for me from Jack Graybul, one of the half-dozen shysters who sometimes spoon me work. Jack laconically offered one of those take-it-or-leave-it, twenty-dollar-a-day "injury scouts" he sometimes got the insurance company to spring. It seems some poor bastard was riding his kid's pogo stick down the basement stairs, showing off, when the thing fell apart and sent the guy bouncing down the steps on his forehead and eyebrows. The guy claimed he couldn't walk, talk, or fuck, and was suing Duckwall's five-and-dime, Mattel Toys, a metal manufacturer in New Jersey, and J. Edgar Hoover for fifty million bucks. Graybul wanted me to hang around the guy's house for a couple of days to see if the aggrieved party started doing hundred-yard dashes. If he did, I got fifty for testifying. Graybul was not beyond offering me three hundred for testifying anyway, but he did it half-hearted.

Graybul was the kind of guy who smoked constantly and had bad dandruff: his cheap serge suits looked polka-dotted. He French-inhaled without taking the cigarette out of his mouth, and could argue a case and eat lunch that way too. Once another shyster hired me to tail Graybul around town on an adultery caper filed by his wife. It turned out he was seeing a cashier at Brown's Grill on Central Street across from the hospital. She had braces on her legs from having polio. Jack would see her sometimes at lunch hour, buy her a gardenia at the flower shop next door, and then they would go across to a little park and sit and talk and look at the tulips. Jack never touched her except to kiss her cheek. I turned in a report giving Jack a clean bill of health and never bothered to find out whether he stayed with her at night or not.

Jack loves the trumpet. He sits for hours in his eighth-floor office facing a blank brick wall, playing flourishes and trills. When I give my reports to him he plays while I talk, making the song fit the report. The time I recovered a stolen Persian cat for an old lady out in Eastborough, Jack played "Hold That Tiger," wrote out my fifty-buck check, and never missed a beat. His secretary was going nuts, and Jack was going broke. He was tawdry and tired, but he always paid on time even if it killed him at home. I figured to be finished with Plummer in a couple of days and decided to call Jack Monday morning and start earning my twenty a day watching some guy force himself to hobble around.

I walked through the office, pulled a Pabst out of the refrigerator in the storeroom, and went through the back door. I sat in my rocker and rocked under a mimosa tree, cracked the beer, and lit a smoke. Somewhere behind me the sun was setting, sending dusty rays of orange and gold through the mimosa flowers, lighting the green elms that swayed in the breeze. It was getting cooler. Heat lightning-showed on the prairie to the north of town and thunder-heads, black and yellow and purple, were building far away. It smelled like rain.

I couldn't figure out the part about Carmen Granger and Frankie-boy Plummer. If Carl wanted Frankie to marry or fuck his way into money, he couldn't do better than Carmen Granger, and from what I heard, she was a knockout to boot. So it figured that Carl didn't want me to put Frankie in a basket. What he probably wanted was to find out what was going on and how. But I didn't have a clue as to why. I finished the beer and the cigarette and decided to stake out the Granger house in Riverside. It's better to cop a feel of the merchandise before buying. I locked up and drove home.

I live on Sycamore in the bottom half of an old shingle house. I've got two big rooms and a walk-in kitchen, brass doorknobs, and a stained-glass window through to the backyard. Mrs. Thompson lives upstairs with her cat, Francis, and parakeet, Tweeter. Francis sits all day and stares at Tweeter while Mrs. Thompson listens to the radio. She is real quiet. Once in a while she shuffles downstairs in her tattered housecoat to ask what day it is in case her son is coming with the week's groceries or to take her to the doctor. Mrs. Thompson thinks I'm a real nice young man because I don't make noise and chase women. I don't know what she thinks about the boxes and sacks full of muscatel bottles.

All I own in the world is in the apartment: rolltop desk, teak Staunton chess set, brass bed and Grandma's quilt, two Hopper prints, a set of Hegel, one 9mm Browning automatic. I thought of buying an air cooler, but couldn't bring myself to do it. I decided to save a dollar a week for a bamboo fly rod and I had fifty bucks squirreled in a pair of brogues. I kept figuring that in another two years I would have the fly rod, but every time I looked in the Bean

catalogue the price went up thirty dollars. It looked like I
would be casting for Dolly Varden from a wheelchair at the
old folks' home.

I parked the Ford around back in a shed beside the
neighbors' chicken coop and scuffled my way through the
fallen catalpa beans to the front porch. Francis was perched
on one of the eaves above, watching while I got the mail
out of the box on the wall. The mail was a cardboard roll
from England, the poster-size photograph of Carl
Schlecter, one of my heroes—a pale, callow ghost with
piercing black eyes and disheveled hair. Schlecter played
the great Lasker for the world chess championship in Berlin, 1910. In the twentieth and last game Schlecter led
Lasker by a full game and needed only a draw to become
champion at age twenty-one. He played ruthlessly, and
midway through the game had a winning position. Most of
the burghers in that baroque pavilion thought Schlecter
would encase himself in an impregnable shell, play cau-
tiously, and lock up the championship. Schlecter attacked.
He remained himself. The wily Lasker defended patiently,
then ensnared Schlecter in an invisible iron net. Finally,
Schlecter resigned. The match was drawn, and Lasker re-
tained his championship. Four years later Schlecter died of
starvation that first cold winter of World War I. There was
something romantic and sad and courageous in all that and,
except for baseball, life didn't seem to offer much in the
way of romance and courage. So I added Carl Schlecter to
the Hopper prints.

I stripped to my shorts and poured a tall muscatel with
ice cubes. I got out a piece of veal, pounded on it for a
while with a serrated hammer, breaded it, and stuck it in
the ice box. Then I made a big salad, adding a couple of
tomatoes from my plot out in the backyard. I heated a pan
of peanut oil and dropped the veal into it. I made gravy
from bacon grease, flour, and milk, and added a little
lemon juice. By the time I was ready to eat I had downed
three glasses of muscatel, the fireflies were making circles

in the quiet evening air, and the heat lightning was coming closer to town.

I ate dinner, my feet propped in the front window. I looked through my toes over the left-field wall of the ball-park, past two rows of orange boxcars, to the slow Arkansas River and downtown, twinkling in the hazy twilight. As I sopped the last tomato in olive oil and lemon, a dusty blue Plymouth pulled up in front. Andy Lanham, smoking a cigar, got out, waved, and walked through the shadows and fireflies to the front porch.

Andy was all angles and bones, the kind of fellow you call "Red" when you're a kid. He came into the house smiling and said, "Hello, Mitch. I figured it was about time to drink a beer and try out a new opening. Your phone call reminded me that we hadn't played for a while. What the hell, you up for it?" The Dutch Masters he puffed smelled like a wet dog. I lit a Lucky and puffed back.

"Andy," I said, "my heart goes out to the cops, eternally clad in wrinkled suits and serving the undeserving public. How are you?"

"Fine, Mitch, really fine. When the public is as slovenly and hopeless as you, this job is a pain in the ass." He saw Schlecter on the wall over my rolltop. "Ah, Schlecter." There seemed nothing more to say.

"What has the lieutenant been working on lately?"

"You know, Mitch, the usual. Two guys are drinking beer and shooting pool down on South Broadway. Someone starts to lose and things get nasty. Out in the parking lot a .22 comes out and one guy gets gut-shot, takes him thirty minutes to fucking die. The uniformeds show first, later Andy Lanham interviews witnesses, and it takes an hour to straighten everybody out. The crime is solved. Everybody but the dead guy goes home." Andy shook his head and shrugged.

"You mean you don't get too many hound of the Baskerville murders with a dollop of gold bug capers?"

"You got it. It's just three yards and a cloud of dust."

"Well," I said, "sit." Andy took off his wrinkled jacket and showed me the blue knit shirt with sweat rings around the underarms. He wore a shoulder holster and a police special. He looked tired as hell.

"How about a beer, a game of chess, and some decent conversation?"

"That's fine," Andy said, "just fine." I went to the refrigerator and got a can of Pabst, pulled the Staunton board to the window, and handed the beer to Andy. He was quiet, setting up his pieces. I thought he was nervous, kind of fidgety. He chose white.

We played for a while; then, when I asked him how things were going at home, he told me about his new kid. Andy wasn't saying much, just sitting hunched over and tired-looking in the open window. I tried talking about Eisenhower, about the Braves, about the gob of pigeon shit on the hood of the Fairlane. Nothing moved him, and so after a while I just sat quietly drinking muscatel and playing chess. I used a Caro-Kann to his king-pawn opening, a strategy I new fairly well from following Botvinnik in the latest championship matches. Andy was a good player, but tonight his moves were disconnected and pointless. After ten moves he was down a pawn with no development and no organization.

Andy sat crouched over, his head in his hands. He asked quietly, "You been working on anything special lately?"

"Nothing special."

"Anything going down on your search for Frankie Plummer?"

"Nothing yet."

"Say, who is this guy Plummer anyway? You were pretty tight-lipped about it. It sounds interesting." Andy studied the board, then moved a knight he had moved before, wasting tempo.

"I told you," I said. "He may be missing. I'm not sure yet." Andy had let his cigar go out. "How about another beer, Andy?" He told me thanks but no and made an aimless pawn move. I cleared out the black squares for my bishop and doubled rooks on the knight file against his king. Andy turned and looked out the window. Thunder rumbled far away.

"It must be good to get something meaty for a change, instead of repos and that stuff, huh?" he said. "I mean, a real live missing person out of the textbooks. What is the first move on a deal like this anyway?" There was no conviction in his voice. He picked up his cigar and stuffed the wet, chewed end in his mouth. I drank some muscatel. I was thinking about a knight sacrifice on the bishop file. I said nothing, letting the silence and the distant thunder build.

Andy was getting more nervous. "Huh?" he said. "You gonna just go out and start looking for this kid Plummer from scratch? You got any leads?"

I took a large slug of muscatel and with my right hand swept all the pieces to the side of the board. The game was over. "What the fuck is this? What the fuck is going on?" I thought I sounded angry. "You come around here and expect me to spill my guts about Carl Plummer and Frankieboy. You called him Frankie. I never said anything about that. What the hell? You drop by on Friday night about seven just to play some chess and drink beer? Is that it? Bullshit! If you're off duty, then you go home and put a kid on each knee and play pablum patsy, you talk to the wife, maybe watch the fights. Mow the fucking lawn. You don't come over here and play chess and drink beer. If you're on the clock, then what the fuck do you want with me and why are you nosing around? I don't like it, so tell me or get the hell out."

Andy was looking at me now, his face scarlet. He said nothing.

"Well?" I waited. "My guess is Bull Granger pulled the puppet string and sent old Andy over to find out what I know. What I don't know is why. But if Colonel Granger says stick a hot poker up your friend's ass, Lanham, then

you stick a hot poker up my ass and go back and report.
So, you got Colonel Granger and his little daughter Carmen to look out for. And me—I got a poker up my ass."

"I'm sorry you feel that way, Mitch."

"What's the answer, Andy? Did Bull Granger send you
here?"

Andy stood up and put on his jacket. "I'll be going," he
said, turned, walked out the door and through the gathering
night to his unmarked Plymouth. He paused, then got in
and drove away.

It was hard to figure why a hill man like Carl Plummer
would spring fifty a day to have me check up on his son
Frankie, especially since the kid was sniffing the pants leg
of someone like Carmen Granger. It was even harder to
figure why old Bull Granger, Mr. W. P. Granger—colonel
in the Wichita Police Department, head of Vice, adviser to
the Chief—would assign a lieutenant to ferret information
out of a small-time gumshoe like me. If Bull Granger
didn't like the idea of Frankie Plummer running his daughter, then the Bull Granger I had read about would waddle
up to Frankie Plummer and break his arm. Nothing explained why Granger would send Andy Lanham over here.
I knew Andy well enough to know that he was busted up
about doing it, and that hangdog look on his face when he
turned and drove off proved it. So I was stuck with a police
colonel and a junk hill man both interested in Frankie
Plummer, but not able to walk right up to him and lay their
cards on the table. To me, that meant that Frankie Plummer
had something on these two clowns besides an interest in
Carmen Granger. But if Frankie Plummer had something
besides Carmen Granger, how did she fit in?

There was one thing I knew. I'd made a mistake talking
to Andy that way. The story of my blowup was going to get
back to Bull Granger sooner or later. I should have played
dumb. Muscatel and friendship had got in the way of my
judgment.

A cool east wind blew the catalpas and elms around

outside the front windows. Night crickets clattered. I laughed softly at myself, at how smart and tough I believed I was, realizing I had made a beginner's mistake. It was like the time at Carlsbad in 1929 when Nimzowitch lost a game to a *patzer*, jumped on his chair in the quiet tournament hall, and fired a heavily weighted rook through an open window. He shouted, "How can I lose to such a fool?" Nimzowitch and I should have kept quiet. The way it was, I might as well have sent a telegram to Bull Granger.

By the time I finished the muscatel and a last cigarette it was after ten. I took a cool shower and dressed in jeans, flannel shirt, Red Wing boots, and windbreaker. I got a rain hat out of my chest of drawers and put a fancy blackjack in my back pocket. I took thirty dollars out of my wallet, put the wallet under my pillow, then put the thirty dollars and my investigator's license in the heel of my left boot. I locked up and went out to the Fairlane and put the top up. The night was dark. Arcturus glimmered pale red on the black horizon and a misty wedge of moon hovered in the cottonwood along the riverbank. I could smell fall in the air. I remembered that tomorrow it would be September.

Carmen Granger lived on Nims across from Riverside Park and the zoo. I drove down Central in the fog, across the river, then circled the park. I parked in dense shadow by the Murdock Bridge. The three-story gabled place she lived in was two hundred yards away, obscured by elms and cottonwoods and the lion house. It was one of those Victorian gingerbreads, porch wrapped around three sides, carriage house, and gazebo, all on a corner lot surrounded by a black iron fence. Abbott and Costello met the Wolf Man in a house like that. I took my binoculars from the glove box and strung them around my neck. I walked slowly through the park, looking for a perch.

I found a wooden bench in the dark near the open-air bear exhibit. The bears had a rock pile and swimming hole, but they mostly slept and ate and swatted flies. They moved around more than the alligators, but not much. Owl hoots. Two macaws conducted an auction. I sat in the dark, fired up a Lucky, and waited. I had a half-pint of Old Overholt and hit it. There was no porch light at the Granger house, but a dim glow showed in the main room downstairs. I saw a white stripe on the grounds of the house where a night-light burned in the pantry. There was no motion. Maybe the people were asleep. I smoked, drank rye whiskey, and traded winks with an ostrich.

An hour went by, then two. At midnight a blue Pontiac roared over the bridge on Nims, pulled into the driveway of the Granger house, and stopped. A woman got out, opened the carriage-house door, returned to the Pontiac, then drove the big car into the dark shed. Through the binoculars I watched her walk up the porch steps and disappear through the front door and into the dim interior. The door shut. I was pretty sure it was Carmen Granger. She was tall and slim and wore a white pants suit, light gray raincoat. From what I could see in the foggy night she had a terrific figure; she walked erect, swiftly, holding an umbrella. She wore a straw panama. I thought she was smoking, but I couldn't be sure. One thing I was sure of: the car Carmen Granger drove was a '55 Pontiac, blue, clean, and in tune, a car that belonged to Frankie Plummer, at least according to Carl Plummer. I sat tight. In an hour the Overholt and Luckys would be gone and maybe I would have earned fifty bucks.

Behind me the bears snored dully. Then on the path leading through the trees to Nims two figures appeared, walking briskly my way. Both wore trenchcoats and felt hats. The guy on the left was built like a coal barge—thick neck, heavy occipital ridges, and bushy eyebrows. His buddy was shorter, left hand hidden in his coat pocket. It looked to me like these goons were trolling for shit and I was a turd. There was no use running, and after the Overholt I didn't feel like it anyway.

Coal Barge and his buddy got close enough to let their thick shadows fall either side of me on the bench.

"Looks like we got us a bird-watcher," Coal Barge said. The binoculars around my neck weighed fifty pounds.

Buddy put his other hand in his pocket. "The queers are sucking dick over at the shelter in Oak Park. Or didn't you know?" he said. He snickered. I went to high school with these kinds of guys and now they were cops, using the same lines they used after study hall. Okay, I'll meet you after school kind of stuff. I could act tough, innocent, or scared. It was always better to act tough.

"Your parents know where you are?" I said.

"Funny." Coal Barge.

"Actually, I'm bird-watching. Looking for yellow-backed flatfeet. Travel in pairs. Late-nighters. They're called yellow-backed because they travel in pairs, but they're harmless really. Their call is the wisecrack." It was the whiskey talking, but me that was getting rousted.

Coal Barge took a step forward. Buddy put a hand on his arm. Buddy was in charge, and it was Buddy who I had to deal with.

"You have a date downtown, slick," Buddy said. "Get up." I had been downtown before.

"Suppose you tell me the beef," I said.

"Suppose we cut the crap," Buddy said, "or we'll put some of your teeth in our pockets. We can roll you downtown in a tin can or you can get the fuck up and come around like a good little man. Right now I don't give a goddamn. You got a choice."

"Gosh oh golly," I said, "since you put it like that I think I'll come along. Let's go."

Coal Barge looked disappointed. We walked in silence to the blue Plymouth parked on Nims, down the block from Carmen Granger's house. I was not surprised to see it after Andy's visit earlier. Coal Barge drove. Only one thing bothered me. Carrying a blackjack in Kansas was good for six months in the city jail. And when I got out I would be back at Fox-Vliet packing crates of streptomycin.

The Wichita Police Department occupied all six stories of a sandstone rococo palace downtown. The building looked like it was built by a mad Ludwig of the prairie— gables, cornices, archways, and clock tower. Inside, though, it had that dreary look all police departments dredge up out of a collective unconscious. The walls were green up to shoulder level, then puce. The place stank of disinfectant and sweat. In the distance someone was cry-ing. My playmates and I went up the elevator to the third floor. A Negro woman sat on a metal chair outside the Bull's door, her nose bleeding. No one paid any attention at all.

Coal Barge opened the door and I saw Bull Granger sitting behind a gray metal desk. He was a big man with a sandy crew cut, a flat face, and a neck the size of a stove-pipe. I could tell he was mad, because the veins in that neck stuck out like ropes. I counted his heart rate and it was high.

Coal Barge pulled a chair in front of the desk and said, "Sit down, scumbag." They didn't check the back pocket. I sat.

Bull spoke in a growl, his voice as flat as his face. "You tell me what you are doing outside my daughter's house. Then you tell me it won't happen again." Bull had that south Wichita drawl that bordered on a whine. Nasal and sharp.

"Well, Colonel, I tell ya. I've never seen ostriches fuck. They didn't tonight."

"Maybe you don't know it," the Bull said, "but Detec-tive Sergeant Davis here is aching to put yer dick ina pencil sharpener. I'll see it happens, then I'll see you sit in jail till yer mother forgets you exist."

"You got a charge, Colonel?"

"We'll think of something."

"You better get busy thinking. It's not your strong suit."

The Bull got up and walked in front of the desk and sat

on the edge. He was about two feet in front of me. He smelled like Lysol and sweat and his heart rate was way up there. The Bull slapped me full across the face. I didn't move.

"You get it, fuckface. You're a little turd in a big cistern. What yer doing I want it stopped. Yer out of yer league. I won't tell you again. Leave my daughter alone. Don't hang around, don't peep. Call Carl Plummer and resign. You'll last longer." At least I knew I was right about Andy Lanham. He had been in to see the Bull about me. I still didn't know why.

I moved my feet apart. If this got worse I figured to kick Coal Barge in the knee and give myself fifteen seconds with the Bull. A blackjack can even things out real fast.

"Colonel," I said, "you mind telling me why?"

"Don't think. Crawl back into your slime hole. You get it?" I really didn't like the Bull.

"I get it," I said.

The Bull looked at Coal Barge. "Escort this fried peckerwood out to the street."

At the door I turned and looked back at the Bull, still sitting on the edge of his metal desk. He wore a rumpled blue suit with an American flag on the lapel.

"Colonel," I said, holding my voice down and calm, "you touch me again and you better kill me."

As I turned to leave he said, "You got a deal, peckerwood." I walked the two miles home and thought things over. It was a cinch I wouldn't give up on Frankie Plummer.

When I got home the eastern sky was pink and gold. The goddamn birds twittered wildly. My mouth tasted of Overholt and Luckys and my jaw hurt. I decided I had earned my fifty for that day.

FOUR

Finally, the birds gave up their stupid twitter. I got a solid three hours of sleep.

Then Mrs. Thompson was pounding at my back door, as insistent as a seventy-six-year-old can get. A lovely morning.

"Mr. Mitch, Mr. Mitch!" Her voice was one part hysteria, one part simple panic. "Mr. Mitch, Mr. Mitch!" I loved being called Mr. Mitch, seeing myself in a Frank Capra movie about small-town America before things got complicated.

"I'll be right there, Mrs. Thompson," I shouted. It wouldn't do any good to shout at Mrs. Thompson. She could barely hear. But everybody shouts at deaf people. I wrapped myself in a dirty bathrobe and creaked to the back door. My jaw hurt, my ankles were stiff, and my eyes burned. On the way past the bathroom mirror I sneaked a look. I was not a pretty picture. Mrs. Thompson pounded and shouted, shouted and pounded. Everybody in the neighborhood was used to Mrs. Thompson except the Aleys next door who thought she was a witch. The Aleys also thought Truman was a Communist and Mitch Miller a musician.

I opened the back door and put a hand on Mrs. Thompson's quaking shoulder. She was wringing her hands. The cotton lining of her housecoat showed through the rips.

"Is my son coming today? Is my son coming today?" she screamed.

"What day do you expect him?" I shouted, then caught myself and picked up the pad and pencil on the counter by the sink. I wrote on the pad: WHAT DAY IS YOUR SON SUPPOSED TO COME?

Mrs. Thompson cradled the precious message in her trembling fingers, panicked, and shouted twice as loud as before. "Oh, is it today? I just can't remember!" I wrote on the pad again: WHAT DAY DID HE SAY HE WAS COMING? Mrs. Thompson thought a moment, still shaking. "Wednesday," she barked. I wrote TODAY IS ONLY SATURDAY, HE WILL COME IN FOUR DAYS.

Mrs. Thompson smiled sheepishly, feeling helpless and ashamed. I didn't like that part of our visits. I patted her on the back. From the pocket of her housecoat Mrs. Thompson pulled a scurrilous-looking apple and held it out to me. I mouthed "thank you" and accepted it. She turned and climbed the treacherous stairs to her place.

Well, I was up. I put some coffee on to perk and started a frying pan full of link sausage. I broke eggs into a bowl, added cinnamon and cream, then sopped three slices of bread in the egg. While the sausage and French toast and coffee cooked, I got the sports page of the *Eagle* and checked the scores. The Browns had left St. Louis for Baltimore, so now I followed the Cards. They always came in second or third, sometimes worse. Last night they beat the Cubbies, the McDaniel brothers pitching a combined seven-hitter, with Stan the Man cracking a game-winning double in the seventh. Phil Stevens was gone forever. He

went down with his mike. But for an announcer the Cards
had Harry Caray intoning his breathless, maniacal, "It
might be, it could be, it might be, *it is. A home run!*" Myth
transformed into magic. I'd have to miss the afternoon
game from Chicago if I wanted to go have a talk with
Carmen Granger. Colonel Bull or no Colonel Bull, there
were fifty simoleons at stake. Besides, I hoped that broad
daylight would make a difference to my night-creeping
friends Coal Barge and Buddy.

I sat down with the coffee, sausages, and French toast. I
poured Vermont maple syrup over the toast. My Grandpa
Roberts sent me the syrup in one of those little souvenir
packing crates, the only present he ever gave me. No one
knew why he sent it and my Grandma Roberts was
stunned. Then, two years ago, Grandma found Grandpa
face down on a gravel road, stone dead from a heart attack.
When I poured the syrup, I felt I was using up Grandpa's
secret, trading the magic beans for a cow. When it was
gone it would be gone forever. I ate the sausage and toast
and thought about Grandpa Roberts.

Grandpa flimflammed his way through the 1930s. He
found a farmhouse or a shack at the edge of a little Kansas
hamlet, then disappeared for a year, maybe two. Grandpa
also sold Bibles, which was legit. He sold magic pills,
which was probably not. He talked to anybody who'd listen about flower gardens. "Them roses look a little pun-
ish," he'd say. Friends and neighbors would explain how
they ordered the bushes from the catalogue and they came
all dried up and limp and they put them in the ground and
nothing was growing pretty. At that point, Grandpa would
tell about a miracle pill he had that made roses—flori-
bundas, hybrids, and all—grow strong and pretty and
bloom twice a year. June and September.

"Now," Grandpa would say, "you put this pill in a
bucket of water, dissolve it, and pour the water on the
rosebush every third day during the summer. You water

roses every third day and they're gonna bloom like a dang virgin at a barn dance."

But Grandpa made his real living cheating the big land-owner, banker, and capitalist. He would put an advertise-ment in the local rag of some hick county seat—offering oil leases for sale to the highest bidder. Make it look offi-cial and important. In small print he stuck something about all sales subject to credit checks and cash deposits. That kind of thing appealed to folks, to their greed and vanity. Then he showed up in town a couple of days before the auction driving a swell car, acting all business and secrecy. Before long he had the local banker trying to jump the gun on the auction. Grandpa would hold out a long time, "set-ting the hook." He wasn't anxious to get involved in any-thing shady. The night before the auction, the banker would fairly force the money into Grandpa's pocket, and Grandpa would give him a frilly paper full of legalese, describing the leases and the rights of the parties. Then Grandpa would leave town—driving all night across the state line to Cherryvale to get drunk and look for a woman.

Finally, electricity and telephones came to almost all the farmhouses, run-down or not. The dirt roads turned to gravel, then asphalt, then became county roads and U.S. highways. Maybe the county clerks got smarter. They even put radios in the police cars. "There's just too goddamn much information," Grandpa said when they put him in Lansing for five years, drawling the word *information*, saying each syllable like a separate word. He was in the slammer for only two years. For eight years after that, Grandpa stayed home and cut hair in a barber chair out back on the porch of the farm. He didn't ever look very happy. Then one day Grandma found his corpse on the gravel road. Grandma got a barber chair, a tweed suit, a set of scissors and combs, and six sons and daughters. Me, I had half a jug of maple syrup.

After breakfast I took a long, cool shower. My heart started beating again so I decided it was time to deal the hand, to visit the Granger house. I wore my blue seer-sucker suit, white cotton shirt, pale blue tie with white puffy-cloud design, white oxfords, and a touch of Old Spice. I felt like a slave to a barbershop quartet. I copped a last look at myself in the mirror, wrapped some aviator sunglasses around my eyes to calm the sun, then stuck that fancy blackjack in my rear pocket to calm my nerves. I could get through the day imagining a blackjack looped hard up onto the septum of Bull Granger's nose.

I retrieved the Fairlane and drove up Sycamore to Douglas and went east across the Broadview Bridge into downtown. The sky sparkled clear and blue; the cold front that had moved through last night left the air clean and mild and ready for fall. It was a good day in Wichita. I turned north and parked next to the boathouse, about three blocks across the park and zoo from Carmen Granger's house.

I walked the shady side of Nims without bringing any gorillas out of the jungle. When the door opened, Carmen Granger froze me with her pale sapphire eyes. "Yes, what is it?"

She looked about twenty and wore a white cotton frock that set off her copper skin. On her feet were rope sandals. She smelled like the dew on a daffodil. I smelled like Old Spice and Lucky Strike Red.

"My name is Mitch Roberts. If you're Carmen Granger, I'd like to talk to you. It won't take long."

She stared at me with her sapphire eyes. She had a thin, young face and high cheekbones, pure black hair falling around her shoulders. The only makeup she had on was a touch of eye shadow and some peach lipstick. I wished I had big muscles and a tan.

"What is it you want?" she asked.

"I want to talk about Frankie Plummer." Behind her a staircase rose and abruptly disappeared into the second floor darkness. She stood in an entryway, sunlight pouring through a window on her left. I couldn't see the blue Pontiac anywhere in the drive, but a pink Thunderbird was parked by the carriage-house shed. I could also see the outline of Carmen Granger's body through her white frock. She stepped back slightly.

"I see," she said coolly. "In that case you had better come in."

Double mahogany doors opened onto the main room downstairs. It was large, airy, and high-ceilinged, a set of bay windows catching the light and green of the park. The parquet floors smelled of wax. A mug of yellow roses stood on a shiny black grand piano. Through one of the windows I saw a woman digging with a trowel in the garden. The yellow roses were her work.

"Please sit down," she said. "May I get you something to drink? Something cool?"

"Have you any Earl Grey with a sprig of fresh mint?" She laughed at that one, a nice small laugh, very authentic.

"I'm having gin and grapefruit juice, lots of ice. But I can get you a cup of instant Folger's if you like."

"Gin and grapefruit juice, then," I said. It was hard to see any Bull Granger in Carmen. She walked past me to the rear of the house, her sandals scraping the parquet.

"May I smoke?" I said.

Quietly: "Of course."

The kitchen and pantry were behind me. I could hear her humming softly to herself. I figured four rooms upstairs, probably bedrooms and a study or den, another attic bedroom above them. I smoked beside the fireplace and flicked ashes into it. I didn't see any ashtrays. I was tempted to open the drawers of a big desk in the corner, but fought it off. On the desk was a picture of a dark-haired woman with black, limpid eyes. She looked about fifty and wore a lace mantilla. Her face bore an expression of unbearable sadness. By the time Carmen came back into the big room carrying a silver tray and two drinks, I had finished my Lucky.

I sipped the gin and grapefruit juice.

"You have a lovely home," I said. One of Elgar's symphonies floated into the room. "I didn't think Elgar penetrated the prairie past Peoria."

She sipped her gin. "I don't want to be rude, Mr. Roberts, but you mentioned the name Frankie Plummer and said it would only take a minute. We are working on several minutes already."

"All right," I said. "A kid named Frank Plummer needs someone to find him. Me. I have reason to believe you know where he is. If you do, then you could help by telling me what you know."

"What is your interest in this matter?" She didn't sound rude or anxious, just businesslike and short. I strained to hear sounds upstairs—footfalls, doors creaking. I heard nothing. "I'm a detective, Miss Granger." I couldn't keep my mind off the picture of the woman.

"I see. Then will you tell me who is looking for Frank Plummer and what his interest in this person is?" Still business.

I needed a Lucky and some Overholt. This conversation was giving me a pain. "Look, Miss Granger," I said, "detectives are supposed to come around and ask questions and push people up against doors and tear their lapels and finally find out everything they want to know. Well, it's really not like that. I don't push people around. With my credit I couldn't get an apple ring down at the Spudnut. I paused to let the effect set in. "My client is someone who cares about Frank Plummer and pays me to keep his little secret, but he doesn't pay much. I don't want to hurt you, upset you, threaten you, or make you angry. It's just a question I have to ask, and you are the first person I asked on this bright Saturday morning. Give me a break?" I gave this sob speech once before at the door of a motel in El Dorado. That time I had a fistfight with the guy in 16B.

Carmen Granger laughed gently. I joined her. "All right," she said, giving me a smile. "I suppose I can help a poor fellow who can't even get an apple ring at the Spudnut." Still no creaking floorboards upstairs. The woman outside the bay windows continued to dig and mulch. "I've met Frank Plummer and gone out on dates with him. He's a nice boy but a little wild for my somewhat refined taste." She laughed again. "Actually, he really is too wild for me. It doesn't amount to much beyond a family dispute and I would rather not discuss that part of it with you."

"I see. When is the last time you saw him?"

"Yesterday evening. No, perhaps late yesterday afternoon." Last evening when I was dancing with Carl Plummer.

"Do you know where he is now?" I asked.

"I really couldn't say."

"Do you mean you couldn't say because you don't know, or because you know, but you won't say? I get a little snarled by these semantic pythons."

I saw a fire in the sapphire eyes. She glanced out the window at the woman gardening, then back at me. "Mr. Roberts, I have seen Frank Plummer. He has been my escort in the past and it has caused some embarrassment to me and my family. I spoke with him yesterday evening about nothing consequential and he went away. I really don't know where he is at this moment and am unwilling to discuss my personal affairs with you further." Carmen Granger at twenty could negotiate Jack Graybul out of his trumpet.

"Do you know where I might start to look for him?" I asked.

"His father owns a salvage yard, I believe."

"You mind telling me if Frank has any other friends who might be of help in locating him?"

We sat there sipping gin and grapefruit juice. The Elgar stopped. I really hate Elgar and was hoping that Ellington or Basie would drop onto the invisible turntable. The day outside was clouding over, turning gray and cooler. The elms in the park danced in reflection on the parquet.

Carmen stuck her peachy lips against the frosted glass of

gin. "Please, Mr. Roberts. This is a simple matter between Frank and me. I don't know where he is. I don't know his friends and probably wouldn't sic you onto them if I did. I appreciate the fact that you have a job to do. But, you must appreciate my privacy and my need to conduct my affairs without interference."

I was thinking that now we had both delivered our prepared speeches and the score was tied.

I got up and put my glass on the silver tray. "Okay, Miss Granger, I'll lay off you for a while. But if I have to, I'll be back and you'll have to come off the Little Miss Muffet routine."

More fire in the sapphire.

"I'm sorry I forgot to wear lapels today," she said. "Now, please leave."

She walked me to the front door. I stood in the wind, turned, and said, "If you change your mind about this, for any reason, call me at my office. I'm on Lincoln. Roberts."

She said, "Good-bye," and closed the door. I stayed on the porch for a minute, then went around to the side of the house.

The woman kneeling in the rose garden watched me walk toward her. Then she stood, her blue sarong with pink water hyacinths billowing in the wind. She was taller than Carmen and older, a fuller figure, but with the same copper skin and deep sapphire eyes. She wore a white sweater. Her face was sculptured, not young and thin like Carmen's. I didn't think muscles and a good tan would mean a thing to her.

"Hello," I said, feeling the modulation in my voice that meant I was scared. Her neck was long and dreamy and she was high-waisted.

"Hello." Melodic.

I looked at the roses. "Hybrid polyantha?"

"Why, yes. Actually there is very little tea rose in this

one. It is beautiful, isn't it?" I shot a look at the upstairs windows of the house. No movement, no shadows.

"Yes," I said, "especially the yellow. What do you call them?"

"Texas Beautiful." She looked down at the rosebush. She had a pruning tool and trowel in her hands, gardening gloves. "Are you a rose lover?" She took off her straw gardener's hat. Her hair fell down her back, shining. I had expected it to be black, but it was auburn.

"Yes. My grandpa taught me a lot about roses. Water them every third day." I smiled. "Actually, my specialty runs to potatoes and squash. How is it you can nurse these by the heat of summer?"

She looked straight through me. I realized her eyes were deep green, not sapphire at all. Maybe they changed color in the light. I couldn't tell.

"I make a point of covering these special roses with cheesecloth during the hottest part of the day. I keep the cheesecloth damp. You mustn't let water touch the leaves. They will rust, and then one gets mites and mildew." She knew exactly how to hold her hands. I didn't. "Knowing how to prune in spring and fall is the secret to large flowers—and, of course, the water and nutrients."

"I guess it's a matter of care, then?"

"Of course."

I held out my hand. "I'm Mitch Roberts. I've just been visiting Carmen Granger in the house and saw the roses and thought I would find out their secret."

"My name is Carlotta. Carlotta Granger." We shook hands. She laughed. "Excuse the gloves," she said.

She went on. "The Texas Beautiful is my creation. If you look closely they are a very deep yellow and the petals are wide and strong. I registered the hybrid with the Rose Society."

I bent over and smelled the roses.

"No, there will be little or no fragrance. The more beautiful and cultivated the rose, the less its fragrance." She shook her hair free. "Don't worry," she said, "there are always lots of ramblers and climbers to make the air smell pretty in spring." She had seen a feigned worried look on my face. Our little joke. "Are you a friend of Carmen's?" I couldn't get over how she said the cultivated and beautiful roses didn't have a fragrance.

"No, Miss Granger," I said. "I'm a private detective looking for Frank Plummer."

"I see." That was what Carmen had said. "Did you have any luck?"

There was mystical intensity in Carlotta. She stood perfectly still in the wind, her sarong flapping. Concealed everything she was thinking. She was smart and beautiful and strong.

"Not exactly," I said.

"Then you didn't come over here to talk about my roses." She made it a statement and not a question.

"Yes and no." I answerred anyway. "I'm finished talking about roses, but they are still very beautiful."

"And now you want to talk about Frank Plummer?"

"Yes," I said, "and perhaps about your sister." It was getting too cool for seersucker. "Why don't we talk about this over lunch? If you don't have anything to say, at least you snatch a free lunch and get to be seen with me."

There was silence. A lion across the street yawned a roar. I felt Old Spice collecting in my white oxfords.

"Why not?" Thank God, she was smiling. "Let me clean up and change clothes. I'll pick you up in thirty minutes in front of the alligators. Wait for me there?" She disappeared around the back of the house. I heard a screen door shut.

I walked across the street and up Nims to the bird house. There were rows of cages out in the open. I leaned on the railing looking at the ring-necked pheasant and smoked a cigarette. There must have been five hundred thousand ring-necked pheasants in the stubble fields of western Kansas and this poor bastard ends up in the zoo. No fucking, no flying, no eating corn. When I was a kid I used to come down to the pheasant cage and eat peanuts and try to get the pheasant to make his noise. It sounded like, "Ugh-OOOH, ugh-OOOH." I burned my throat making that noise until the pheasant ruffed his neck up and responded. It usually took an hour or so.

I thought about Carlotta Granger and about trying to get the pheasant to make his noise. A little girl in a blue sundress held a balloon next to my ear. She stared at me. It would have been too easy to put my Lucky out against the balloon and start her bawling. I walked over to where the alligators snoozed on wet sand and waited for Carlotta to pick me up in her pink Thunderbird. At least I hoped she belonged to the pink Thunderbird.

I was smoking and looking at the alligators sleep. Through the wire gondola over the alligator pit I saw Coal Barge and Buddy walking fast up the path. They looked mad. I knew another trip downtown meant I could collect my mail at the city dump. Behind me Carlotta pulled up in the little Thunderbird and gave a beep. Coal Barge and Buddy stopped and stood still. I walked to the Thunderbird and got in beside Carlotta.

"We're off," she said and smiled.

We drove down Murdock toward the bridge. I gave Coal Barge the finger and my best Sunday grin.

FIVE

Behind us Coal Barge was a rictus and snap-brim hat steadily receding. Paddleboats in the river churned the muddy yellow water and a few canoeists glided their canoes under the bridge. It was all dragonflies and hoptoads. It was that time between summer and fall when the old man finally agrees to a picnic and loads the battered DeSoto with kids, some sandwiches, and a mushy watermelon. It was that time of afternoon at that time of year when the old man wishes he was home with a beer and a ball game. The clouds kicked themselves around enough to let some sunshine dapple the water and the red-brick street. Cottonwoods down by the riverbank flapped leaves in the wind like a field of wet silver sheets.

"Friends of yours?" Carlotta said, half smiling.

"Old bowling buddies. Guy on the left is Joe Joseph. On the right is his cousin, Pat Patterson. Parents blessed with lots of imagination."

"Funny," Carlotta said. "One of those gentlemen looks

very much like Detective Sergeant Davis. Perhaps just one of those silly coincidences."

"No way. Could not be. I met those guys years ago at the Civic Bowl at a marathon onion-ring-eating contest. No mistake, sure thing."

Carlotta kept her eyes on the road, glancing in the rearview mirror, but I could see she enjoyed the way things had started out, kind of a perverse sense of poking a finger in authority's eye.

Her hair curled up behind her in the open air, but strands of it came loose and wandered in the rush of wind. It was auburn when the sun glanced past it, shaded henna. She wore a shiny, ocean-green skirt that fit her like a steam bath, pale green high heels with a strap around her ankles. She showed enough long, nylon-wrapped leg to make a boy quit the church. Her laugh was nice and neat and very authentic. Still, there was tension in her, and she drove too fast, cutting in and out of traffic, beating lights to the punch. In Wichita, there is just no place to get to that fast.

Before long Carlotta was driving ten miles an hour over the speed limit. She changed lanes smoothly, always in control. Finally I asked her if she was hungry and she said, "I'm starved." I offered her a choice between Ralph Baum's Burger Bar on Kellogg Street or the Madrid Supper Club south of town out by the air base. By the time we got to the Madrid we called each other by our first names.

The Madrid isn't much more than a joint. It's a square box with a flat roof and flamenco dancers painted on the walls by some local sign painter. Three rows of tables clutter the floor, all set with candles and imitation roses in vases, a raised platform in one corner for the local cowboy bands on Friday nights, and a horseshoe bar in the middle of the room. We got a table and sat down. We were almost alone in the place.

"Is this what you call a roadhouse?" she asked as we picked up our menus.

"This is a true-blue roadhouse."

"It's kind of low."

"I know what you mean. Even the mice are hunchbacked."

She laughed and looked at the menu. "I'm having a good time. I haven't laughed like this in a long while. You don't know."

"Good," I said. "It suits you. I tell you. The steak sandwiches are great, or a big rib eye and enchiladas. Maybe some guacamole and fried cauliflower. The fries are greasy enough to lube a double trailer. What do you say?"

"It sounds so eclectic. What about steak and enchiladas and some guacamole?"

"Sold."

We ordered a pitcher of Hamm's, too. When it came I lit a Lucky, offered Carlotta one, and she took it. She asked me about myself and I told her about my mom who lived on a farm down in southeast Kansas and my Grandma Roberts who still rooted for the wrestlers on TV out of Pittsburgh and Joplin. I told Carlotta to dip some cauliflower in hot sauce and put vinegar on the fries. She was like a kid at Christmas. We finished the enchiladas over our second pitcher of cold brew.

"It's funny," I said, "but you don't particularly look or act like Bull Granger. Christ, you don't look like Bull Granger at all."

She stayed quiet for a while. Finally, she said, "He's not my father. He's my stepfather. He married my mother when I was in my early twenties. Carmen was quite a lot younger then."

"Your father?"

"My father died during the war. Carmen knew him only a little."

"I'm sorry," I said.

"It's all right. My father was a wonderful man. A doctor in the Navy. He was older and working on a hospital ship outside what was supposed to be the zone of action. Off

Okinawa in the last days. His ship was hit by kamikazes. He was lost with lots of other men."

"Your mother is the woman on the desk?"

"Yes."

"She is very beautiful."

"Yes, she was very beautiful. And gentle."

"Her daughters have the same quality."

Carlotta smiled, but without much heart. She looked at the bubbles in her glass of beer. I had been with her a couple of hours now and didn't want to get around to Frank Plummer and Bull Granger.

"Your mother is dead, too?" I asked. For fifty bucks a day I was turning gold to lead.

"Yes. She died five years ago in June." I was trying to think back to the headlines or the obituaries. Five years of muscatel was a lot of muscatel.

"I'm not sure I can see Bull Granger with your mother either. Perhaps I'm prying into things I shouldn't?" I tried to get it through my head that it was my fucking job to pry.

"No. It's all right. My mother met Bull in San Antonio. He was just Sergeant William Granger then. We lived there in the hills outside of town. A little ranch my father built. Bull was in training at the army base, doing something with the military police. Believe it or not, he was somewhat earnest and impressive. My mother was lonely and confused. She married him and brought us to Wichita. The rest is history, as they say."

I gave Carlotta another cigarette. She went on.

"It was hard for us. Bull turned out—well, perhaps you know."

"I think I do. The last time we chatted he called me a peckerwood and offered to make a necklace of my teeth."

"Yes. That's his style."

"I'm sorry, Carlotta," I said. "I like you a lot. I like being around you. But sometime soon we have to talk about Frank Plummer."

Carlotta said quietly, "Maybe we could drive a bit? Or just sit outside? I need some fresh air."

"I know just the place. I've got a mimosa tree, a rocker, and a refrigerator full of cold beer. What do you say?"

I paid the check. On the way out I saw a few airmen leaning on the horseshoe bar drinking. It would be six or seven hours before the serious fistfights started.

When we got outside, the sun slanted low through coral clouds bunched on the western horizon. Everything bathed in a silky glow. Carlotta drove the shady streets and told me about bringing up Carmen and about how Bull kept them both on a short string. The Hamm's was working on me, and as Carlotta drove through the crystal evening I fantasized my way from her knee on north. I directed Carlotta to my office and she parked in the gravel lot in front. We got out and went through the office to the backyard. I showed Carlotta the rocker and pulled up a paint bucket for myself. I got two cans of cold beer and sat down beside her.

We sat still, listening to the elms swishing and a couple of doves cooing. A red squirrel stood in the shaggy grass eating an acorn. We might have been alone on the face of the prairie. I liked that thought. Andy used to tell me that private detectives were better off in L.A. or Chicago because there was more action. After my divorce from Linda I decided I wanted quiet more than action. So far I had the quiet, all right.

We drank. The squirrel ate his acorn.

"How is it you can make it with the Bull? There doesn't seem any percentage in your trying to wait him out. I mean, it must be terribly difficult for you."

Something kept me from asking the questions that needed asking. Some of it was the way I saw the same lamentable look in Carlotta that I had seen in that picture on the desk. I sat on my paint bucket with my elbows on my knees and let smoke from my Lucky curl up in the breeze and fade. A train north of town, out by the grain elevators and refineries, blew an A minor seventh, the mournful sound gradually growing smaller and sadder.

"You know," she said, never taking her eyes off the motionless squirrel, "once I was standing with my mother across from police headquarters. I must have been in Wichita only about six months. Carmen was still a kid in school." She paused and gave me a little smile. "Anyway, my mother took me downtown that day to shop. We were going to meet Bull for lunch. There was something wrong with Mother then, some dreadful sadness. She kept to her room upstairs, hardly coming down. She cried. Wept, actually. We talked and she said she was homesick. But I knew a lot better. Bull was terrible. He bullied. He lied. He scared her with his violence and drinking. I heard them quarrel. Not quarrel really, just Bull and his terrible voice accusing Mother of things. Slut. Whore. Then, of course, he could be contrite, beg her forgiveness. When he was angry there was violence in the air that stopped everything. Time stopped.

"Well, anyway, I stood across the street from police headquarters with my mother after shopping. I remember she bought me some new white gloves. I wore this blue summer dress with big white polka dots and she wanted me to have some light white gloves for summer. I remember the day. Big puffy clouds and bright sunshine."

She stopped and took a drink of beer. Her voice was failing her a little bit. The squirrel sprinted up the mimosa, hopped a telephone wire, and disappeared in the bulky swirl of elms across the back fence.

She went on. "Bull wasn't Bull then. He was Detective Lieutenant Granger. Just like Davis outside today. A detective. We saw him pull up that day in an unmarked car followed by a squad car. In the backseat of the squad car one uniformed officer sat with a Negro woman. Another officer drove. Bull got out of the unmarked car and walked back to the squad car and opened the back door. The officers left the squad car and walked to the station-house door. Bull stayed. My mother and I just watched. We could hear everything. Bull leaned in the window, bent over with his forearms on the body of the door. 'Okay, bitch. Whore, out.' That's the way Bull talked to her. She moved to the door. Then he slapped her a little. Not too bad. Just a swipe with his hand across her face. She had this crazy red light in her eyes. I remember the hate in those eyes. The woman said something like 'Get off my case, you honky.' At that, Bull quickly kicked her leg in the open door and shut the door on her ankle. At first he shut it just tight enough to trap her foot. She stopped talking and leaned back with her elbows on the back seat. She was just waiting, breathing hard from her cursing, a look of concern creeping inside all that hate. Then Bull leaned on the door. The woman was terrified.

"Bull bent his knees then and worked on the door. The woman screamed. Oh, Mitch. You could hear her ankle break. A grisly pop. 'You gonna be fine now, bitch,' Bull said. I know he said that. The uniformed officers stayed by the door to headquarters, looking, not saying anything. Bull grabbed the woman by her bloody ankle. It was bent at a strange angle. He pulled her hard in one jerk out of the backseat and onto the pavement. She bounced on the edge of the car frame and then on the ground. She was lying there, crying.

"Bull made a sign to the officers at the door. They picked up the woman and dragged her into the station. When I looked at my mother, she had her fingers in her mouth and one hand on her forehead. Her face was terrible —paralyzed with hurt and fear. We left. I had to help her walk away."

"I'm sorry," I said. There wasn't a helluva lot to say.

I went into the storeroom and cracked two Pabsts and tore off a handful of Kleenex from the box on Gertie's desk. Gertie, I could tell, wouldn't mind at all. I came and sat down on my paint bucket. Carlotta held out her hand for the tissues but I reached over and dabbed at the tears on her cheeks myself.

"What if I get tipsy?" she asked.

"It's okay. I know this guy in Vice who can get you off a public drunkenness charge." We looked at each other for a moment and then laughed out loud. She was laughing and crying at the same time. I thought she looked beautiful.

"What about you? How is it you can make it?"

"Oh, shit, Carlotta, I make it on muscatel, chess, and baseball. Sometimes I get down my Hegel and go in for the master-slave dynamic. Sometimes I don't think about it. When I do, I don't see a helluva lot of formal order in the world. Things sort of jumble together. Once in a while something good falls out of the dumpster, but mostly it's just other people's garbage and your own. Lots of ruined crap. Discarded dolls, broken-backed books, glue bottles, women's hose, that kind of stuff. Then there is the guy in Hoboken who finds a thousand-dollar bill wadded up inside a scumbag. Me, I look for Hanebrink or Matthews to dive for a screamer down the third-base line and snag it over the bag, come up throwing, and beat the guy at first by half a step. I give a shit if the rest of the game nothing happens. The catcher falls asleep. The vendors disappear. They give away all the hot dogs. The beer goes flat. But there will be one play Matthews made at third you can talk about in the bar for the next six months."

"What about girls?" Carlotta said.

"I like 'em."

She said, "Haven't you married?"

"I got married once a long time ago," I said. "I was drunk when I asked, I was drunk when I bought the ring, and I was drunk when I said yes. I meant it at the time, though."

"What happened?" She paused. "You don't seem that way to me now. Here."

I ducked the question. "How old was your father when he went in?"

She frowned. "He was fifty-three. He was fifty-seven when he died. He was in the Reserves for a long time. He wanted to go in even though we all told him he could stay in San Antonio and work at the hospitals there and do just as much good. He told us that doctors never got killed in wars. He said that a lot. In all his letters, Doctors don't get killed in wars. Don't worry. In his last letter, it was in the summer, he said that we were beating them badly now. The war wasn't over yet because the fat lady hadn't sung yet. He'd be home when he could hear the fat lady singing. He could hear her warming up in the wings. Then he died."

She looked down. "I'm sorry. Please. Why did you want to know?"

"I was in the same war. Different part. I was just a kid when I went in. Twenty-two. I was gonna be a flier. Sit around pubs and drink whiskey and smoke English cigarettes. Wear a black leather jacket with a skull on the back. Maybe a blue silk scarf. I got to England and found out every kid who joined the Army applied for the Air Corps. Five thousand airplanes and fifty thousand hotshots looking for jobs flying them, all sitting around in their dreams in a black jacket drinking whiskey. I went into the Engineers because that's what they told me I volunteered to do. One day I woke up and I was strapping dynamite to tank traps on a French beach, machine-gun bullets whizzing around, and mortars exploding on the beach. It was before dawn and the water was cold as hell and there were guys screaming and dying everywhere. I was scared. But, then I made it through and things got better. When we got across the Rhine, all the guys started talking about home like it was a real place. No one dies anymore, we all go home.

"Then one day my four buddies and I found this old house on the outskirts of a little Alsatian town, kind of a villa with a little pond, a couple of sheds for tools and cheese and meat, a big mountain house with a veranda. We got into the wine cellar and there must have been a hundred bottles of champagne, vermouth, and old French brandy.

We found meerschaums with carved figures on the bowls. Tobacco that smelled like apples. This one scrawny goose wandering around the pond we caught and stuck him on a spit over a fire we built. It was April and the pear trees were in bloom and the bees were buzzing their heads off. In this one closet I found a trunk full of hats. There were four or five opera hats, you know, shiny black top hats that pop up when you hit the bottom. Hey! Top hats. Yeah! So my buddy Joe Smith gets the other guys together and they put on these top hats and pass brandy and tobacco. Joe and I, we had been on the beach together and we looked for land mines all the way from Calais to the Rhine. I had this old box camera with me that I took pictures with. Bridges we built. Bridges we blew up. The Eiffel Tower. Bullet holes in the art museum. Anyway, I got the guys bunched together and snapped their picture. When I snapped I heard a sharp crack behind me. I put the camera down. There was an echo in the valley. It was the report of a bullet. When I looked around, I saw the guys bunched around Joe. His legs twitched once. One hand was in a fist. I walked over and looked at him. There was a pure blue bullet hole in his forehead. As they say, he never knew what hit him. I've still got the goddamn picture. Four guys in tops smoking pipes. A brandy bottle at one guy's lips. Joe had a big smile. The guy next to him had his arm draped in a Vee over Joe's shoulder. I look at that picture and know that the bullet is in that picture, stopped forever. The goddamn bullet is in the picture."

I looked at Carlotta. She was serene in the dusk. A few early stars twinkled overhead. To the east between the elms I could see a bank of lights glowing. At the stadium the guys in left field would be warming up, catching flies over their shoulders and chewing tobacco, not giving a thought to invisible bullets in tangible photographs, not to speak of crushed ankles and Bull Granger.

"Why don't you just make a break for it?" I asked. "Get out of this crummy little town and leave old Bull behind?"

"Yes, why not?" Her face got hard and her eyes narrowed. "You see, old Bull took my mother for every penny she had. Sold the ranch and put the money in the house in Riverside and in College Hill where he lives now. Dear old Bull lets us live in the Riverside house, but he owns it. Owns everything now. Do you think I should go to work down at Woolworth's? My stepfather threatens us both with such things. And worse."

"How about some legal action?"

"It won't work. I've checked."

She put her face close to me.

"I hate him so terribly, so desperately. For what he did to my mother. For how he changed my life. And for Carmen."

"What does Carmen feel?"

"She feels the same." She straightened up and shook her auburn hair. There were tears in her eyes. I couldn't tell if she was laughing or crying.

I got up and went to the storeroom to get more Kleenex. When I got back I reached over and dabbed the corners of her eyes. I was looking at Carlotta and then I kissed her and she kissed back. She tasted like beer and salt. I moved back a bit to look her over, but when I did she grabbed me and held on and kissed me some more. Then we came out of the clinch, the bell rang, and we went to the corners to get worked on by cut men and managers.

"Can I trust you, Mitch?" Carlotta whispered.

"Why not? Now that we've gone all the way."

Carlotta smiled at my little joke. "Frankie Plummer is crazy. He's got something on the Bull, something that lets Frankie get away with things no one else could. He comes and goes at the Riverside house. He terrifies Carmen and the Bull won't stop it. Usually, the Bull reserves that honor for himself. I think Frankie is blackmailing the Bull."

Carlotta stared at me with frightened eyes. She was wringing her hands.

"You don't have any idea what it's all about?" I asked.

"No, but the Bull is capable of anything."

Carlotta brushed the hair away from the corner of her mouth and sighed again deeply.

"Will you try and get Frankie away from us? Talk to the Bull? I can take it myself, but I can't stand to see Carmen dragged into this terrible mess. She's such a kid."

"I already have a client, you know."

"Can't you do it anyway?"

"Well, I guess there is nothing to the International Code of Ethics for private detectives to prevent me doing a favor for a friend. I'll check around. See what there is."

Carlotta smiled and put her hands on my shoulders. She put her cheek on mine.

"God, thank you," she said.

We left the office and Carlotta drove slowly back to Riverside and the park. We crossed the Murdock Bridge. There were just a few canoes left in the water. The old boathouse dock creaked as waves lapped its side. It wasn't dark yet, but the street lamps in the park cast hesitant halos in the dusk. We stopped beside my Ford and Carlotta leaned over and kissed me hard. I kissed back. Somehow, I was doing it against my better judgment. I got out and stood in the street watching Carlotta turn the T-bird and disappear behind the bears, then appear between the ostriches, and drive into the driveway of the old house on Nims.

I got in my car and dug the binoculars from under the front seat. I put them on Carlotta. She drove up to the carriage house, got out, opened the doors to the shed, lit a cigarette, and went up the porch steps to the front door. Carmen opened the door, they embraced, and both were swallowed by the shadows in the front room.

There was no blue Pontiac. Carlotta parked in the shed like there wouldn't be a blue Pontiac in the near future.

I started the Fairlane and drove around the neighborhood

for about five minutes looking for dusty blue Plymouths. I didn't find any. I drove out of Riverside wondering where all the blue cars filled with blackmailers and cops had gone. Just yesterday they were a big deal.

And then there were Carlotta's lies to think about.

SIX

It was growing dark as I drove out of the wooded park and across the Nims Street Bridge. Light from the copper lamps on the bridge danced in the river water, mingled with the reflection of lighted buildings from downtown. My head buzzed from the two pitchers of beer and several salty, hard kisses. I let the smoke from my Lucky drift out of my mouth and rush past my ear. There was a softness in the air, a feel of the heat breaking down; I could sense summer losing its legs in the middle rounds and starting to sag against the ropes. The cicadas no longer gave out a raucous uproar and the squirrels were intent and purposeful, not dallying and chattering anymore. I reminded myself to check the fuzz on caterpillars to see if winter was going to be a bitch or not.

I drove down a nearly deserted Central Street, past the closed stores, avoiding the crowds of teenagers who flock to the main drag to drive their new Chevys and Fords, looking for some kind of excitement from a town that goes to sleep at ten. What I needed was a piss and some time to think.

Carlotta expected me to believe that Carmen was terrified of Frankie Plummer and walked around the big house in Riverside like a zombie in distress, or maybe like an unraveling mummy. But I had taken a pretty good look at Carmen and she was fresh and cool as a gherkin on ice. I tried to remember a ruffle in her come-on, some sort of crack in that lacy and dignified demeanor, but couldn't. She seemed in control. It was my guess that unless she was a pretty good actress there wasn't anything on her mind that involved being held hostage against her will by some ducktailed punk like Frankie Plummer.

I was in and around the house for about an hour and there was no sign of Frankie. No cigarette butts, girlie magazines, creaking floorboards. No smell of lilac water. If Frankie Plummer was in that house it looked to me like he was the one being held hostage. If he was upstairs in that strange old house, then he was holding his hill-boy breath.

For some reason, I had let it pass with Carlotta that I had seen Carmen driving Frankie's big blue Pontiac at midnight on Friday night. The way Carmen roared over the Nims Bridge and into the carriage house, it was clear she was coming and going in a hurry. It didn't make sense that she was being held against her will and terrorized when she had taken the kid's wheels and scooted around town like a pasha. Somebody was bullshitting me. When I started making a list of the people talking crap, it turned out that almost everybody I spent any time with in the last two days was spreading it around for the flies. Carl Plummer. Andy Lanham. Carmen and Carlotta. Even the Bull just slapped me around a little when he and the boys could have served my bones for dinner to the guys doing sixty days on the p-farm.

This thing was getting to be the hall of screwy mirrors at the State Fair. Carl Plummer hires me to find his kid and then tells me where to go to put a finger on him. So Plummer the Elder probably wants me just to flush the kid out of his hiding place and keep track of his movements. Why? The cops are interested in the same information, so Coal Barge and Buddy hang around like buzzards on a rail. They try to run me off before I steal a bite of the skunk they have spotted in the road.

The tea leaves said that Bull Granger and Carl Plummer had the same interest in Frankie, but worked the opposite sides of the street. Carl hires me to hang around and peep; Bull runs me off.

I flipped on the Philco and got Nat King Cole singing "Tangerine." The porch sitters were out and I could see them rocking on the swing and smoking. When Nat finished with "Tangerine," Jimmy Fiddler came on with some strident nonsense about Linda Darnell and Cornel Wilde. I'd rather hear the farm report.

What got me was the fact that I was stooging for Carlotta. She wanted free of Bull and she wanted revenge. She was deeply damaged by the knockout Bull gave her mother, but how she expected to get free—and get her money and her revenge—was still obscure. But if Carlotta and Carmen had on their boxing gloves, I had no way of knowing what their best punch could be. In that case it's always best to watch the guy's navel. Come to think of it, I wouldn't mind watching Carlotta's navel for a while anyway. Carl Plummer was giving me fifty a day and Carlotta was sticking hard kisses on my mouth and old Mitch just shucked corn down at the crib. It was time to start tying my own shoes and catching the school bus on my own. It was time to get some answers and play the game for keeps.

I got across town to the Uptown Recreation about seven o'clock and pulled up in the bus stop. The door to the Wreck was open and from inside came the jukebox sound of Johnnie Ray and the muffled blather common to joints all over the country. Cheap conversation and watered beer.

I flipped off the ignition and sniffed at the stale odor of

beer and nuts flooding from the open door. It was a hell of a way to make a living, prowling grimy bars, rubbing elbows with thugs and grifters. I should have been upside down at the third level of Carlsbad Caverns.

The answer I needed most was why the cops weren't interested in Frankie Plummer anymore. On Friday he's the crown jewels; on Saturday he's a dandelion in a wheat field. Whatever made Frankie interesting to the cops on Friday was gone.

The inside of the Wreck was deep in neon and sepia. Johnnie Ray gave way to the Platters. There were a couple of guys shooting snooker on the first table by the bar. A sign on the wall said NO GAMBLING. There was a ten-spot by the corner pocket and the two guys walked around the table silently, shooting snooker for the ten-spot. At the end of the bar Kenny Shoemaker sat sucking on a draft and smoking a Camel.

"Mitch!" he boomed.

"Hi, Shoe, how are you?" Without waiting for an answer I said, "Shoe, you know where Tony might be?"

"Back room," he said. "Hey, by the way, did I tell you what happened to me the other night out at the Moose Club. The fucking dime slots. I got this girl shacked down in Haysville and we were out at the Moose playing the fucking dime slots."

I interrupted. "I'll be back, Shoe. Keep it in your pants for a while. I gotta talk to Tony right now."

"Okay, Mitch," Shoe said.

I skirted the snooker tables and went into the back room. Tony was lifting a case of Budweiser bottles. He saw me and smiled.

"Be right with you, Mitch," he said. He got his case stacked up on the top of a pile of empties and turned around.

"I figgered I'd be seeing you."

"Well, here I am. You know why I'm here."

Tony said, "Let's go out in the alley."

We went through the back door and into a dark alley that separated the snooker hall from the Uptown movie theatre. The current show was *Wichita* with Joel McCrea. The goddamn world premiere. Tony cracked a Pabst and held it out to me.

"Tony," I said, "you and me, we've known each other for a long time, right?"

Tony fidgeted and nodded yes.

"I figure if it wasn't for me that fat lady would have made your liver a little drafty. I figure a couple of times I bail your dumb kid out of his speeding rap because I go talk to Andy at headquarters. Half a dozen times the cops out of Vice come down here and ask you why you are sitting around blowing reefer and drinking beer with the customers at three in the morning when closing time is midnight and reefer is against the law. The goddamn pinball machines pay off. I call Andy, he talks to a couple of the boys, and you are still sitting pretty instead of doing ten up in Lansing. Your old lady has a husband, your kids still got a father."

I looked at Tony. "How'm I doing so far?" I asked.

"I can't wait for the fucking punch line," Tony said.

"So, anyway, I been knocking around the gutters of this village for quite a few years. Nothing big, mind you. Then all of a sudden I hear about this guy Frankie Plummer. The cops don't know nothing about him. Sure. I don't know nothing about him. Even the kid's old man don't know nothing about him. So, old Mitch here, he's pissing in the wind. Getting it on his trousers. He comes to his old buddy Tony for some information. He figures Tony is good for the truth because Tony is Tony. You tell me this morning you don't know shit about Frankie Plummer. I say you and everybody else I talk to about this fucker are liars and scumbags."

I hit the Pabst. "That's the punch line, Tony," I said.

"It ain't like that, Mitch. Really it ain't."

"Let me explain something," I said. "Make it clear so even a dumb fuck like Tony Garcia can understand it."

Tony weighed in at two-thirty-five and I was hoping he wouldn't get mad. If he did, I would have to go for the blackjack in a big hurry.

I went on. "Bull Granger wants this Frankie Plummer for some reason I don't know why. Frankie's old man, this junkyard hill man, wants his kid, but not bad enough to go right on in and get him out of his hole, wherever that is. I get a feeling even the goddamn newsboy down on Douglas and Main knows what the fuck is going on. Not me, Tony. I don't know shit. You sit there and tell me you don't know either, you're a goddamn liar."

Tony was quiet. I washed my anger down with a gulp of suds. "Tony, you owe me a goddamn honest fucking answer."

The last of sunset smoldered on the horizon.

"Mitch, I know you're shitting me a little bit. But you make me feel bad too." Tony looked at the ground and dug a pack of Pall Malls out of the back of his jeans.

"Look, I know we gone down some miles with each other. You done some nice things for my kid. We had some good times," he said.

I waited. There was something on Tony's mind and I was gong to hold on and let it come out in its own sweet time.

"You got a punch line for this?" I asked.

"I got a punch line, but you ain't gonna like it."

"Try me."

"What if," Tony said, "there's some kind of shit going down around here that's bigger than we can handle. Bigger than we want to handle. The kind of shit, you can get in but you can't get out. I ain't talking about sitting around blowing reefer, no fucking speeding ticket for the kid. No shitting around and drinking a few beers and being buddies."

Tony stopped talking while some guy in a dusty Stude-

baker pulled into the alley and turned around. From the
theatre there was a sound of a gunfight in the cow-town
streets of Wichita, then a crescendo of music that meant
the bad guy was dead and Joel McCrea was getting a big
hug from Vera Miles.

"Hey, man, you know there's only one thing worse than
anything else, right?" Tony said.

"You mean like waking up on Sunday with no private
stash of muscatel and finding Kenny is out of town?"

"No, man," Tony said. "I mean being dead. Fucking
dead. No more muscatel, no more nooky, no nothing."

"What're you saying, Tony?"

"I'm saying, man, if we mess around in this shit we
gonna wind up in half a tuxedo down at Maple Grove.
Dancing with the fucking worms. I can't deal with it, man.
I cannot fucking deal with it."

"I can," I said. "I'm the one who has to deal with it.
Right?"

"No, man, that ain't right. I tell you. This shit you are
into. I think you get in far enough some guy is gonna come
around and he's gonna have some pals behind him. They're
gonna get you in a corner somewhere and kick the shit out
of you. Then one of these guys is gonna ask who you been
talking to. Where you get your information. You know? It
didn't just fall out of the sky like pigeon shit. Then one guy
pulls out an acetylene torch. They ask you again, where
you get the information. These guys hold you down and
put that fucking torch to your hand and you tell them: Tony
Garcia, he told me everything. It was Tony Garcia. And
hey, man, I would do the same fucking thing. So then these
guys come looking for me. You dig?"

It wasn't Aristotle or Maimonides, but it was pretty
tight.

"Hey, let's start out slow," I said. "Let's take one thing
at a time. You come to a place you can't tell me then we
talk it over and see if we can figure a way around your
problem. Okay? Here we go."

Tony stomped his Pall Mall out with the heel of his work boot. He rubbed his eyes wearily.

"Bull Granger had a wife. Five, six years ago. Maybe more. She died. You know her?"

"Man," Tony said, "you shoulda let that fat lady do me in. Yeah. Where you been? Old lady Granger took a dive, couple of twists, maybe a gainer. But, you know, she missed the pool."

"How? When?"

"Late Forties. Dove out of the sixth floor of police headquarters. Shit, that ain't far enough to really kill you right off. Not her anyway. Lived for a while."

"Suicide?"

"Well," Tony said, "if I was married to the Bull I'd give it up too. Except I'd take the fucker with me when I went. Maybe it's possible that Bull drove her out the window. Nobody said much and the coroner came back real quick. How'm I doing?"

"Great," I said. "Now, what about Frankie Plummer?"

"Here is where we got a problem," Tony said. "You got the answer like you said?"

"All right. You say some big guy is gonna put the flame on my mitts. Suppose I give them somebody else. Maybe I got somebody else's name to scream out and scream it loud enough they're gonna let up a little."

"I don't know," Tony said.

"Say we give them the Toddler."

"Oh, man, who's gonna believe the Toddler knows shit?"

The Toddler was a small-timer who lived in the basement of one of the old pastel-colored apartment houses on Oakland Street just behind the Uptown Recreation. Oakland wound downhill for about two blocks. The street was overrun with drifters, runaway kids, and beatniks.

"Hey, Tony, what do they know? The Toddler runs a little reefer, does some hot cars. Right? Maybe he heard it from somebody else."

"I don't know," Tony said.

I waited. I didn't say anything.

The Shoe stuck his head out the back door.

"Hey, you guys. What is this shit?" he said. "I'm a customer and I'm taking snooker money, drawing beers, and making change. You guys getting married out here in the alley or something?"

Tony stepped toward the door. I put my hand on his chest and pushed him back a little.

"Hey, Shoe," Tony said, "take care of the bar for me for a little while, willya?"

"Uh, yeah, sure, I guess so," Shoe said. He ducked back inside.

"Hey, look," Tony said. "I tell you what I know and we're even, right?"

"We'll see. We're friends no matter what. You tell me the truth, that's all. That's my main fucking interest."

Tony leaned back.

"It's like this," he said. "Maybe a little heroin gets into this town. Not much but a little. There ain't much here to stay, but maybe a lot moves through. You follow, right?"

"So far, Tony, I can follow this real good."

"Yeah, well," he continued. "You know there's a man here in town who has the corner on that kind of shit. Well, this man has the shit trucked to the big boys in Chicago and Kansas City, but he keeps a little for his trouble and he makes some pocket change. You know, he keeps himself in Packards and blondes."

"Like Johnny Rossiter," I said.

"Like maybe," Tony said.

"Well, this man here he has his helpers and his assistants. Sometimes he needs a little executive cover just to oil the bearings and keep things running smooth."

"Will you cut the crap," I said. "Granger provides the executive cover."

"Hey, man," Tony said, "this is hard for me. Okay, so let's say there's an old junkyard hill man who is one of the assistants. He has this business connection with the main man. So the junkyard man sees to it that the shipment gets into town and gets to the main man. The junkyard man ain't nothing but a messenger, a middleman, but he is handling some very hot shit for the main man. That makes this main man very interested in the junkyard man because he pays the junkyard man to see that the shit arrives and gets to the main man so the main man can get it to Chicago. Say something goes wrong. The shit comes to town, the junkyard man takes delivery, and something goes wrong. Then the junkyard man has lots of trouble. But, hell, nothing ever goes wrong. The shit comes into town, the junkyard man takes the shit to the main man who takes a cut and sends it along to the boys in Chicago and Kansas City. A nice working arrangement for everybody, right?"

"I follow," I said, "but I could use some subtitles."

"All right. So the junkyard man has this kid. This kid is definitely bad. Wild. One day, say, the kid takes the shipment that the main man is supposed to get and holds everybody up for some bread. Nobody knows where the shit is except for the kid. Hell, maybe they don't know where the kid is. The kid wants to take his old man out of the play, take over the business sorta. You can see how this makes the junkyard man feel. Of course, the main man is most upset."

"So," I said, "why don't the junkyard man and the main man move in on the kid and put a blue flame to his fingers?"

"Yeah, well, that's a neat one, that one is. You know, Mitch, I don't the fuck know the answer. I just don't."

"One thing more, Tony," I said. "You know how sometimes Vice will come around and find some reefer in the corner pocket of the third snooker table and somebody gives the Vice guys twenty and it will just not turn into a major problem?"

"Yeah."

"So, like I said before. Granger provides cover for the main man? For Rossiter?"

"Listen, I don't know. How do you figger Granger owns a couple of houses and drives a Packard? I don't know."

Tony took a deep breath. "Hey, man," he said, "what do you think? You think that shit comes into this town and out to Kansas City and Bull Granger doesn't get a cut for keeping the guys off the main man's ass? How the fuck do I run the nickel machine, play slots out at the fucking Moose? Fuck, yes, man. Bull Granger and a couple of his stooges protect the main man. That's how it works, it always has worked, and always will."

"Okay, Tony," I said. "Thanks."

Tony walked around me and got half inside the back door. He stopped and turned.

"Stay out, Mitch. I don't know any of these guys. You know I don't mess with heroin and I don't mess with the main man and I don't mess with Plummer. Hell, I don't even know these guys. But some heavy shit is coming down now that the kid has jumped with a delivery. Hell, I don't even know where the kid could go to hide. But look, there is a lot of dough riding on this one and these guys get very upset and play rough."

Tony went inside. I could only see the red glow of his Pall Mall. He said, "You know I don't think they would put the flame to you anyway, Mitch. I think they might just kill your ass right off, you know?"

"Then the Toddler's got no problems. Right, Tony?"

He laughed. "Yeah. The Toddler's got no problems. See ya, Mitch. Be careful."

Then Tony was inside. I walked out of the alley and around to Hillside.

I drove slow uphill on Douglas and into College Hill toward Bull Granger's house. Three-story houses, big lawns, elm trees, and fancy cars. If you got to be rich you got to be here.

So Frankie Plummer copped a shipment of heroin from

Carl and Johnny Rossiter and split. He was trying to muscle in on the heroin-delivery business his old man ran for Rossiter. And Tony couldn't figure out where Frankie was hiding. Carmen and Carlotta and Frankie—what a happy family. Nothing made sense unless Carlotta fit in somewhere. She had to.

I had it figured that Carmen meets Frankie and they hatch a plot together. Frankie wants the heroin and the heroin-delivery business, and Carmen wants money and revenge on the Bull. As a team they are dynamite. They hide the heroin and hold the Bull up. The main man is steamed. He wants his heroin and the Bull's daughter knows where it is. But the main man can't squeeze Bull's daughter, and the Bull can't squeeze anybody because if he squeezes his own step-daughter the whole world finds out about it and Bull is out of business. The main man can't move on anybody because the Bull is in a spot. So Carmen and Carlotta and Frankie are standing off Carl and Rossiter and the Bull. Altogether, it is a very delicate situation.

One thing I couldn't figure exactly. Carlotta wanted me to roust the Bull and she lied about her involvement with Frankie. Maybe she just wanted me to horn in and make the Bull even more nervous. Maybe make him come across with some dough a little faster. But the heroin was missing and Carmen and Carlotta and Frankie knew where it was. Things didn't fit any other way.

I remembered I hadn't eaten anything since that rib eye and guacamole. I decided to cruise Bull's house in College Hill and then head home for a shower, some grub, and maybe the last four innings of the Braves game.

I thought about kissing Carlotta. Then two and two started making four and I knew how Mitch was going to cut himself in on this deal.

SEVEN

College Hill doesn't have a college, and only if you were a myopic spider from somewhere around Lubbock would you think it was a hill. There is just an oblong clay mound that rises slightly above the plains where the Arkansas River runs through plum thickets and where the deer and the antelope used to play before the white man shot them all to death. Just after the deer and the antelope disappeared, the city fathers convened and decided the mound would be a good place for the local emporium for higher education, so they planted elms and cottonwoods and redbuds and platted streets with names like Vassar and Yale. It turns out the center for higher education became a modestly unimportant private university on the other side of town. The mound turned out to be College Hill, where modestly important bankers, businessmen, and doctors pursue modestly banal lives.

Driving up a tree-lined Douglas Avenue from Hillside and into the heart of College Hill you can see the elms and cottonwoods wax brawnier, the lawns grow bluer and more expansive, the cars longer and more glittery. The driveways in this part of town on Sunday morning look like a Lincoln-Mercury showroom where guys in pink bow ties and buckteeth wait with a handshake and a finger puzzle for the kiddies. On the hill's leeward slope the lawyers and college teachers hang on with their wives and house payments and one and a half bathrooms. On the flats, near the Catholic elementary school, a few Boeing engineers, high school counselors, and dentists are keelhauled in the invidious social wake.

College Hill was a beehive for the white middle class, the class that elected Eisenhower over Stevenson. If you got all the way up to Belmont Street on College Hill, you stopped being a worker and became a drone. Bull had made it to Belmont.

I cruised with the top down, trying to clear my head. I hadn't taken a piss back at the Uptown Wreck and my back teeth needed life jackets.

The entrance to Belmont off Douglas is embraced on either side of the street by two imposing stone pillars engraved with the name BELMONT. A grill fretwork arch connects the two pillars. A medieval copper lamp swings from the fretwork and the dancing light from its single bulb casts eerie shadows.

Bull Granger lived in the middle of the block on the east side of the street. I had decided earlier today that the best policy was to know the enemy on his own ground before making any definite moves. So I decided to get to know Bull Granger and Carl Plummer before cutting myself in on this heroin deal. It was an instinct for caution I picked up one starry night in a foxhole near Cherbourg.

Bull Granger lived in a Tudor mansion wrapped in a cocoon of lilacs, redbuds, and elms. A circular front porch was surrounded by a low stone wall, where ivy grew in profusion. In back was a double garage built like the house and separated from it by fifteen feet. Stairs wound up to the second floor of the garage, some sort of quarters for a servant if there was such a thing, or maybe a half-wit demented brother nobody wants to see.

I drove past Bull's house, around the corner, and parked in deep shadow under a cedar.

I took off my seersucker coat and tie and threw them in the backseat. Then I slid the blackjack under the front seat and strapped on an old pair of sneakers in place of my oxfords. I strolled up First Street in the dark and turned down Belmont toward Bull's, whistling "Jimmy Crack Corn" and trying to look for all the world like a weary real-estate entrepreneur on his evening perambulation.

Four conspiratorial tykes huddled at the base of an elm tree and put their eyes on me.

"Hello, men," I said. They stood there like a herd of zebra sniffing a lion in the bush. "Playing a little football, huh? Getting to be that time of year, I guess."

There were four boys, two of them either brothers or built from the same Erector set. They had the usual complement of towheads, cowlicks, missing teeth, scrapes, torn jeans knees, and ripped elbow patches. They wore Wichita Braves hats.

"Hello, mister," the tallest said. He was blond and had a voice like Froggy on Andy Devine's show.

I looked at Bull's Tudor mansion. There were no lights in any of the windows, but a gaslight burned in the front yard and there was a single bulb glowing over the garage doors. No cars in the driveway, and from what I could see no cars in the garage either. From the rest of the houses on the block a deadly blue glow reflected on the lawns. The people were inside somewhere numbing their brains on Two for the Money and George Gobel.

"You boys live around here?" I asked.

"Sure, right here," Froggy said.

"You gents know old Mr. Granger?"

"We might. Huh, fellas?" Froggy said. He was established as the spokesman for the guys. The two shrimpy redheaded brothers scurried in an effort to hide behind each other and the elm tree that served as a goalpost. The fourth kid was a fatty. He picked his nose and pretended to examine the results. The three of them nodded in unison when Froggy looked their way.

"Listen, you guys, I'm a detective on a case." Froggy looked at Fatty and they all giggled.

"Sure," Froggy drawled. "You can't fool us."

"Hey, this is no kidding. I'm a detective on a case and I'm trying to get some information on Mr. Granger. You kids could be of help on the case. You know, like the Hardy boys. It's a big mystery and I can't trust just anyone. Anyone I trust I gotta know is square and won't rat on me or tell me lies. That's the way it is in the detective business where you're into a big mystery."

"What do you want?" Froggy asked. The two tadpoles behind the elm-tree goalpost edged their way out when they heard the Hardy boys mentioned.

"You guys be my helpers and I'll let you in on the mystery and there will be a little cash in it for you. Only you gotta promise not to tell anybody, especially your folks or Mr. Granger. It's part of the deal."

"Yeah, so what else?" Froggy.

I paused for the dramatic effect. "You guys like Mr. Granger?" I asked in my best conspiratorial tone.

Froggy shrugged and looked at the ground. The tadpoles wriggled out and stood behind Froggy and Fatty like shadows.

"Nah," Fatty said. "He's kind of a squirrel."

"Yeah, a real drip," said Froggy. So I had established that Bull was a squirrel and a drip. This was real progress.

"What seems to be the problem?" I asked.

"My dad says he doesn't belong here," Fatty whined.

"He's just a mean tub," said Froggy. Between the social explanation from Fatty and the metaethical one from Froggy, I preferred the latter.

"See," I said, "I don't like Mr. Granger either. I want you guys to keep watch of the house tonight. Stay up as late as you can and when I come back around here tomorrow tell me what time Mr. Granger comes in and if he sees anyone. It might be as late as eleven or twelve o'clock."

"We stayed up that late before," Froggy said eagerly.

I dug into my wallet and got out four ones.

"Here's four dollars for you guys. When I come back, let me know when Mr. Granger comes in tonight, and keep an eye on him tomorrow. Kind of see who he's with and where he goes and when he comes home. There's another dollar in it for each of you tomorrow. That is, if you can keep a secret and do a good job. I'll come back here around five o'clock before supper. You guys be around?"

"Sure, mister," Froggy croaked. The gang checked their new dollar bills.

"I'll be here," Fatty said. The tadpoles were speechless.

"I'll see ya then."

I walked down the block and around onto Douglas where an alley split the block, turned up the alley back toward Bull's house, and stood behind the trash cans and rose trellises. The mansion looked about the same, dark and forlorn. But there wasn't any vicious mastiff with razor teeth and a spike collar.

By the time I drove home, my molars were being used as life vests on the SS *Hamm*'s. I made my way slowly around the side of the house. It was when I got to the porch that I saw the two-tone tan and brown DeSoto parked in front, a ghostly outline in the haze of left-field lights at Lawrence Stadium. A youthful smirk that looked like it might belong to Gomez leaked from the passenger window. The shadow behind the wheel probably belonged to someone who would back Gomez if it came down to brass tacks. I shuffled over, feeling rather ridiculous in seersucker pants and sneakers.

"Señor Gomez. What a pleasant surprise. And you come with your friend Cantinflas, no doubt."

Gomez called me a name, a series of them actually, in Spanish. My guess was that mother, my dog, and a dozen sailors from the *Arizona* could all take offense.

Finally, he added, "I have been sent here by Mr. Plummer."

"Which Mr. Plummer?" I asked. "I mean a guy like you Frankie Plummer probably pushes around easy."

"Hey, fuck you, shit! He don't push nobody around now."

Gomez stopped short. The shadow spoke in Spanish and there was a rondo and then a volley that echoed from here to El Paso. I figured I might force Gomez into a quick mistake and he had let one slip. Get a punk hot like that and his mouth runs by itself. They were trying to put the slip straight. Too bad Gomez didn't speak German. *That* I could understand.

"It's hard to tell about Frankie, right? I mean, I been looking for the handsome devil all day and he just won't turn up. You seen him, Gomez?"

Gomez stuck his greasy overalled arm over the door frame and growled, "The boss don't need you anymore. He says for you to get off the case."

"Did Frankie climb back into his plush trailer out behind the cottonwoods? You know, Gomez. The tin can that sits in the sun and doesn't have any running water?"

"All I know is Mr. Plummer he says he knows where Frankie got to and he don't need you no more. You get the fuck off and stay off. He don't like you anyway. I don't either." I remembered my blackjack under the front seat and wondered if I could handle two kids and two knives and a set of tire chains. It would have been easier if I didn't need a piss quite so badly.

"When did Frankie come home?" I asked.

"Today," Gomez said. There was another Spanish cadenza. "I mean Mr. Plummer told me today he didn't need you anymore. I don't know where Frankie is. I ain't seen him." Gomez was mad and making another mistake. He had told me why Plummer wanted me off the case and that he had seen Frankie. Turn on the boy's temper and his smarts drained out of his asshole.

"What time does Carl Plummer want me to come and report to him the results of this investigation?" The longer I kept this jackrabbit on the spit, the more mistakes he was bound to make. It was a working hypothesis, anyway.

"You don't come out to the salvage lot." Gomez was tough again. He blew his nose by pressing a thumb against one nostril and letting go with the other. His droppings landed by my sneakers. I was too tired to draw a line and dare him to step over.

"Doesn't he want to know what I found out about the game being run by Carlotta? And the stuff?" When this got back to Carl it would make the same kind of hit Gypsy Rose Lee made in Chicago.

"What are you talking about, man?"

"What are you Gomez, some kind of a numbnuts or something?"

"You better watch out."

"That's what I *have* been doing. Watching out."

"Say," Gomez sneered, "they gonna be eating that skinny white dick of yours for sausage down at the Masonic Home."

"So long, punk," I said softly. "You been very helpful."

"I will see you again," Gomez replied. The DeSoto jerked into gear and began to roll.

"Tell Carl I'll be along to collect my fee," I said.

"No need, fucker," Gomez said. He threw a wadded bill onto the grass at my feet. It lolled there in the catalpa beans and scruffy crabgrass. When I unrolled it there was a picture of U. S. Grant staring me in the face. Carl paid me the fifty for my day.

Wearily, I scaled the front porch and unlocked the

door I had walked out of over a hundred years ago. My neck and back ached and the Rockettes tap-danced inside my head. I stripped off my clothes and stuffed them in the laundry bag hanging behind the bathroom door, turned on the shower, and let the bathroom fill with steam. After a number one, a shower, a shave, and a tall glass of muscatel with ice, I felt the blood begin to circulate. It was too late to catch the last few innings across the street, so I decided to fix a good meal, relax, and play through a few games from the great New York tournament of 1928. Capablanca, Alekhine, Lasker, Nimzowitch. That's the one where a sixty-five-year-old Lasker faces all the hotshot kids and comes out on top. In the last game he plays Capablanca, the young classical Cuban, slicked-back hair and diplomatically balanced world champion. Everybody expects the Cuban to slice the old guy like a ripe banana. After all, Capablanca took the title from Lasker in 1927, the year before, and was at the height of his power and grace. Lasker opens with the exchange variation of the Lopez, a slow and quiet, rather plodding and drawish opening. With subtlety and finesse, the old man wore the temple-dweller down, and in the end crushed him like a bug. I enjoy that game as much as any other: Plato teaching Aristotle.

I cored half a dozen ripe tomatoes from my garden and while garlic sizzled in some olive oil, I diced fresh onion and green pepper and added them to the oil. Then I added the tomatoes, some cumin and fennel, fresh bay leaf, salt, pepper, lots of brown sugar, and a liberal handful of oregano. Under the cupboard was the last of a decent dago red; I dumped it in the pot with some water, and then covered the sauce to heat it. Then I made a salad and washed some apples and grapes. I uncovered the pan and let the delicious steam invade the kitchen. Francis must have sneaked in the front door with me because he was doing curlicues around my leg and purring like a naked Bardot on leopard skin. I leaned down and fed Francis a slab of mozzarella. He seemed to like it just fine.

"Francis," I said, "it would seem that Frankie Plummer put in an appearance at the junkyard this afternoon or evening. What do you think? Any theories, old man? How about this? Frankie and Carlotta and Carmen hold up Carl and Bull—and, indirectly, Rossiter—for a shipment of heroin. Frankie needs Carlotta because he can hide from Bull and Rossiter at her house for a while during the time it takes the opposition to get organized. Hell, Bull can't just move in and wipe out his own step-daughter. Bad, bad press. Right? Carlotta and Carmen need Frankie to cop the heroin in the first place, right?"

Francis purred and scarfed down another mouthful of mozzarella.

"So I figure Carl, the old man, hires me because he needs an independent agent to spook Frankie while he stays at Carlotta's place in Riverside. Carl figures Frankie sees someone hanging around he doesn't know, he might panic and run, then Bull and Carl can pick him off. Bull's men don't like me coming around, though. They figure Carl is trying to play the game by himself and leave Bull with the blame that Johnny Rossiter is looking to dish out. Bull's men run me off and the Bull threatens me in order to run the show himself. Bull figures he doesn't want any strange detectives lurking around his daughters when they are holding him up for such high stakes. Maybe there is just no communication between Carl and Bull yet. They both got a big problem."

Cheers erupted from the stadium across the street. Wes Covington probably smashed another rocket against the boxcars past the right-field wall. They should put a sign out by the river: DANGER. WES COVINGTON AT BAT. Have it flash when he gets up to the plate.

"And then there's Carlotta and Carmen. They are lying to cover their involvement in a heroin snatch. I can't blame them there. But, old man, I can't figure out why Carlotta should want me involved with the Bull. To make him nervous? Throw up a smokescreen? Maybe Carlotta plans to use me to make the drop and get her the bread. She needs a go-between, someone both sides don't trust. Therefore, someone like me, neutral. I figure Carlotta and Frankie are holding up Bull and Carl. They probably wouldn't do it to Johnny Rossiter if they want to play ball with him in the future. That explains the sob stories and the kisses."

Francis jumped on the countertop by the sink and sniffed the salad. He found particular interest in the anchovies. I grabbed his yellow bottom and held him under my arm while I poured a saucer of half and half. He lapped it, purring. I poured myself another muscatel and ice. We both lapped, purring.

I stirred the spaghetti sauce with a wooden spoon and watched the red elixir thicken and bubble. Then the screen door in the front room banged and rattled.

A voice said, "Mitch. Are you there, Mitch?" It was a woman's voice and I thought I recognized it.

"Be right there."

Through the screen I saw Carlotta. She had a paper bag in her arms and some kind of plea on her face. I opened the door and she came in.

Carlotta wore blue jeans and a soft white cotton blouse open at the neck. Her middle was sashed with a belt hung with turquoise. Her neck was an exquisite Caravaggio, long and slender and mannerist. She had tied a brown ribbon in her hair, and the broad ponytail fell in an auburn landslide down her back. She was the Rose Parade and Mardi Gras rolled up into one big ball. I realized I stood there in a blue bathrobe with a mustard stain on the tattered lapel, a steaming wooden spoon in my right hand.

"Excuse me," I said. "I expected to get drunk alone, study the Ruy Lopez, and eat some luscious spaghetti and a salad."

"Ruy Lopez was Spanish," she said softly.

"He was," I said.

"He taught that the experienced and efficient chess player should always situate his opponent so that the sun shines directly in his eyes at all times."

"He did," I said drunkenly.

"Was he not also a man of the cloth? A bishop, in fact?"

"He was."

"Did he not also teach that knight to bishop three and bishop to knight five following a king-pawn opening was a most delicate and aggressive opening sally?"

"He took the game right out of the Middle Ages and into the modern era. And Carlotta, sweetheart, if I don't get out of this flimsy bathrobe, I'll make an entirely involuntary and most aggressive opening sally myself." There was an embarrassed silence. "Shit, Carlotta, I'm sorry. I'm getting a little drunk."

She laughed. "I brought some wine. I'm worried, upset, and I need to talk. Have you got some time?"

"Nothing but. I'll be right back," I said.

In the bathroom I put on jeans and a flannel shirt. I combed what was left of my hair and took a look in the mirror. Better than an hour ago, but still a little fuzzy around the edges.

"It smells wonderful," Carlotta piped from the kitchen.

I stepped out of the bathroom. Carlotta stirred the sauce and hummed lightly to herself. Like Carmen.

"There's just enough for two," I said.

I put dishes out on an old round oak table wedged in an alcove between the kitchen and what served as my living room and bedroom. When the spaghetti was al dente and the sauce thick, I finished shredding the mozzarella and grating the Parmesan. We sat across from each other and ate for a while in silence.

The wine was a Bardolino, deep and fine. Even though I was tired and hungry, I was anxious to hear why Carlotta was upset and nervous. Funny, she didn't show it. Cool, like her sister Carmen. That afternoon seemed a million light years across the galaxy from where I sat in the dim yellow light of my alcove, staring across at the silky image of Carlotta.

She looked up. "Have you ever been in love, Mitch? I know you were married once, but it didn't sound like love."

"No."

"That's strange. Why?" She sipped her wine. "You really should, you know."

"Maybe I never met the right girl. Maybe I don't give a goddamn. Maybe it's a question I don't think has much validity in the first place." I was being touchy, trying to keep from digging into her about the lies she was telling about Frankie. Then I decided that she had big problems and it wouldn't do any good to be a rough guy about them. "I'm sorry, Carlotta. It's a question I've been asked before by my aunts and uncles. Every Christmas. Oh, poor Mitch, he's going to wind up like Uncle Vern, living in a little trailer out behind the milking machine. All alone. Never married. I guess it gets me. Sure, sometimes I think about women, about a particular woman, but I just like the way I do things now. It was a while ago that I decided that I would live without the frills that some guys need. Insurance policy, annuity, money in the bank. The hell of it is, I've learned to live with myself. It's not selfish. Just the way it is. I owe nobody, nobody owes me."

"You had love once, in your family. Then you just decided against it? Does it work that way?"

"I never decided against love. Just one kind. Yeah, I had love in my family. It doesn't mean that I decided against a whole lot of other values, you know, like friends, fun, honesty, and the others. It just means I probably can't buy young love and teddy bears and this is forever."

"It's not the same for me, Mitch."

The ball game was over and the ground crew burned just one bank of lights over first base. In that dim reflected light, Carlotta was breathtakingly beautiful.

"You see, I never chose anything. My father was taken away from me, then my mother, and in their place came hatred and evil and there wasn't anything I could do about it. Nothing I could do to stop it or get away. Those values you say you have. They went away."

Carlotta was obsessed. It was making me uneasy. There was a dreadful intensity in her and a hatred that threatened to consume all her beauty and goodness.

Suddenly, she said, "I've sent Carmen away. She left this afternoon and I hope neither Bull nor anyone from the police department is able to trace her. I pray she's hidden."

I finished the Bardolino and poured myself another big tumbler of muscatel. Pretty soon, Francis would have some fuzzy rabbits to play with, maybe some pink elephants.

"Why? For God's sake, Carlotta, can't you tell me what's going on?"

"Not now," she said. "Please." She hesitated. "But Frankie is gone too, disappeared from the house, and I don't think he is coming back."

"When?"

"He was gone when I got back this afternoon. Carmen told me when I came into the house that he was gone. Took all of his things and drove away. I don't know where he went, don't know why. But before he left, he threatened Carmen that he would be back and would hurt her if she spoke to anyone about his stay at our house. For some reason he wants it to be a secret."

"Carlotta, if I'm going to help you, you have got to tell me the honest-to-God truth. Did you ever stop to think I might understand your motives and be willing to help?"

A horrible thought crossed my mind. I wondered if Frankie Plummer had struck out on his own with the heroin, double-crossing Carmen and Carlotta after using their place as a safe house to cut a deal with Bull and Carl. If that was the case, then Carmen and Carlotta had burned a lot of bridges with nothing to show for it. It could explain why Carlotta was so worried now, and why she had sent

Carmen into hiding. And why she was desperate for my help, anyone's help.

"Where is Carmen?" I asked her.

"No," she cried. "Can't you understand? I can't tell anyone. She's my sister and she's in danger." The tears came then. "Why is Frankie threatening us?"

I was beginning to wonder if Tony had his story straight. It was just possible that Frankie copped the heroin and was using Carmen as a shield until he got a deal cut. Maybe he had Carlotta so frightened she found it impossible to confide in me. Then what the hell had I done to deserve confidence?

"Can't you make Frankie and Bull leave us alone?" She sobbed and put one lean hand at the base of her neck. "I'm sorry," she said at last, "I'll stop crying. Then I'll be fine."

"When did Frankie come around?"

"Friday evening. Afternoon. Late."

"What did he say?"

"He threatened to expose us, to harm Carmen unless we hid him." She sighed. "Then Bull told us to put up with him when we talked to him. He demanded it."

"And you discovered him gone Saturday afternoon and made Carmen leave then. Is that right?"

"Yes. And it was lonely and frightening in the old house. So I came here with a bottle of wine, like everything was all right. It's not. Not at all."

I got my chair next to hers and put an arm around her slender shoulders. They felt good. She looked up at my face.

"I just wanted you to know," Carlotta said, "I got Carmen out of the way, away from Frankie's awful taunts and threats and I'm free to deal with this on my own. I just want to see if you can find out why this is happening to us, and do something about it."

"I said I would. Remember?"

"Yes," she whispered, "but I need some reassurance."

She put her arms around my neck and kissed me. "God, I'm so alone," she said.

Feeling her need was like being lost in the jungle, hearing drums. When I carried her to my bed I could feel the darkness opening to swallow me, the whir of a blackened room full of ticking clocks.

In the morning Francis lay curled in the question mark of my legs. But Carlotta was gone.

EIGHT

I sat on the back-porch rail in my dirty blue bathrobe and smoked the first Lucky of the morning. After the little death Carlotta and I had suffered through last night, I was feeling the kind of wistful sadness that would have made Havelock Ellis wet his pencil. The hound of Mr. Baskerville had camped inside my mouth and done his job—the taste of swill and cigarettes filtered through watery beer, an aftertaste drifting daintily in the Ms, between mendacity and murder.

During the night a grim-sounding south wind had gathered and now rattled and rushed stiffly through the cottonwoods behind me down by the river. A few catalpa beans clattered to the ground. Above the soft and rollicking sea of elms and above the clock tower of old Friends' University, the sky boiled in dirty clouds. It wasn't hot and it wasn't cold, just dry and dusty and windy and the kind of empty only Sunday morning in Wichita can be.

In a couple of months, when the corn and milo fields lay

stripped of grain and drowsy brown in the autumn sun, the crows would come back and roost in the barren elms, transforming them into a strange feathered necropolis. And maybe I'd still be here on the rail. Roosting, just like the crows.

Carlotta made love desperately, in a bubbling and fever-ish silence that threatened to burst. It never did. "I need you," she said, and I wondered what she meant. If Carlotta had been double-crossed by Frankie and had sent Carmen away hoping to avoid the revenge that Johnny Rossiter would surely inflict, she needed me to fall for her and maybe act as some sort of protection. But protection wasn't my racket and never would be. If Frankie had taken the heroin and cut a deal with Carl and the Bull, it was a sure thing he would be back at the junkyard acting like the only rooster in a bawdy henhouse full of love-starved cluckers. Maybe Frankie had turned over the heroin and split town with a large hunk of change. Maybe he had thrown Carl over and was running the courier business on his own. If you cut the deck like this, then Carlotta came out with a deuce and a death's-head.

One thing was certain. I had been on the case for one day, earned fifty dollars for my trouble, and found a trail that led to heroin, money, and graft. I lit another Lucky and listened to "String of Pearls," which Mrs. Thompson had on the radio upstairs. The wind howled like one of Glenn Miller's trombones. I had been slapped, pushed around, made love to, and threatened. I wanted what every private eye wanted: my freedom and my cut.

I put the coffee on to perk, took a long hot shower, and scrubbed yesterday out of my teeth. I shaved. While I drank a cup of strong coffee I put on a work shirt, old Army fatigues, and my Red Wing work boots. I cleared a space on the kitchen table, pushing aside the spaghetti-stained plates, cigarette butts, and wineglasses. It was hard to believe that eight hours earlier I had picked Carlotta up and carried her to bed. It was something that happened to guys like Spade and Archer, not to Marlowe and me.

I took the Browning automatic apart and cleaned each piece with gun oil and a soft cloth, reamed and cleaned the barrel. I put the gun back together, wiped it down, then loaded two clips. I jacked one round into the chamber, put the gun in a cloth bag, and closed the drawstring. In one of the big, baggy pockets down my thigh I stuck the spare clip and my blackjack. I meant to use the Browning if I had to. When I told the Bull never to touch me again it was one of those childish epithets that a guy better back. Otherwise he looks silly and the guys will push him around on the merry-go-round over at Joyland.

I rummaged through the old streamer trunk at the foot of my bed and fished out a day pack. I put the Browning in the pack, along with a flashlight, two decks of cigarettes and three books of matches, an old bayonet I brought back from France after V-E day, and a dog-eared copy of *In Our Time*. Stakeouts were a boring necessity, so I decided to bring along my plastic pocket chess set and work on my King's Indian defense while I sat and smoked and watched the junkyard. Watched long enough, the spider's nest out at Carl Plummer's might turn up some heroin, and I wanted my share of the action. I also wanted to give Bull Granger a bad day. It was my civic and professional duty.

On the way downtown I stopped by a grocery and bought four sandwiches. I put my sandwiches in the day pack and drove over to skid row to have breakfast. Skid row is two city blocks of bars, beaneries, late-night movie houses, and run-down hotels. The big, red-brick Salvation Army building rises at one end of the row like a Gothic cathedral. Next door, across the tracks, is the ruined marble train station where bums and drifters sleep on benches and mingle with the pigeons. Like all skid rows, this one was bounded by the Continental bus station, the railroad tracks, a Union rescue mission, and City Hall. It was eyed by the police and disdained by the citizens. Drifters—old and young, grizzled and red-faced—leaned in the filthy doorways or hung their heads out the dirty curtained windows along East Douglas. The main goal was sixty cents for a quart of wine and a bowl of chili. The main diversions were dominoes and conversation. That summed up the human condition in the lower depths. I liked skid row and always had the feeling that a streak of bad luck was all that stood between the guys in patched jackets and ragged felt hats who slept in doorways and the fat cats in suede coats with clean fingernails who bunked with blondes out in Eastborough.

I sometimes drank in the Hotel Eaton Tap Room, the dark boozy place where Carry Nation and her gals took hatchets to the bar. I never saw a fight. Down at the other end, the Corral Theatre presented double features for seventy-five cents and if a guy fell asleep they let him snore until they closed around midnight. It was sometimes the only place those guys got to grab a little shut-eye. The Corral had rats and a heart.

I pulled up in front of the Great White Way, bought a Sunday paper from a machine out front, and strolled inside through the big glass doors with gilt lettering. White Way. Snooker. If the Salvation Army building across the street, brick, six-storied, spired, and gabled, with a gleaming white roof, is the Chartres of skid row, then the Great White Way is Les Halles. It's where the locals go for social and political sustenance. A bar and restaurant with the soul of a Fauve.

The Way was a mammoth Victorian hall with a high tin ceiling made of little squares; flowered designs had been worked into the tin by hand and ceiling fans, dangling at intervals, turned slowly both summer and winter. Bright fluorescent bulbs glowed constantly in long banks, illuminating each detail in bone-jarring white and green and brown and gold. Twelve green felt snooker tables and a disheveled row of black domino tables stood in surreal relief against the shiny mahogany bar, the acre of polished mirror behind it. The place smelled of beer, chili beans, coffee, peanuts, horseradish, and cabbage. Take the green felt, the black and brown leather, the gold and silver, cover it with a white glow, add a constant murmur and hum of male voices talking politics, police, snooker, and women, mix in the click of ivory against ivory and slate, and you have the Great White Way.

I sat down at one end of the mahogany bar and ordered chili, eggs, potatoes, and coffee. There just isn't any beer in Wichita on the Lord's day.

Halfway through my first coffee the front door opened and the wind blew in a scruffy old guy dressed in baggy cords and a frazzled work shirt. He was somewhere between fifty and eighty and wore the sunburned, beaten look of a man who did a lot of time on railroads and highways with his stuff tied to a stick in a red bandanna. With a white beard and red suit he would have looked like a proletarian Kris Kringle and when he ordered coffee his voice cracked like the Mojave in August. I watched him over the top edge of the sports page as he dumped six or seven scoops of sugar into his coffee and sat staring straight ahead into the big bar mirror, stirring his coffee. The ear that pointed my way from two bar stools over was covered with hair. The old guy had a straight back and wore a blue bandanna around his neck. He looked at me.

"Howdy," he said. He didn't smile and he didn't pout. He took a brief look at the chili and eggs, then buried his nose in the coffee cup.

"Want some of the paper?" I asked.

He laughed good-naturedly. It was robust and honest. "What the hell would I want a newspaper for, mister?" he said. "I ain't read one in twenty years. The last one I read talked about there ain't no jobs and the land is blowing away from the roots and there's gonna be a war and some Chinese are getting themselves killed."

"Yeah," I said. "I usually toss the front page myself. Stick mostly to the funnies and the sports."

The old guy put his nose back into his coffee. Maybe he had exhausted his fund of conversation in that one-shot social comment. I liked his laugh. I wondered if he would let me buy him breakfast with some of Carl Plummer's fifty bucks and wondered also how to bring the subject to a head without hurting his feelings. I took a gurgling slurp of hot coffee and a mouthful of catchupy eggs.

"You from here or just passing through?"

He turned his head. "I ain't from nowhere. Not since I was twenty-five years old. I left my farm then and ain't been back. Damn bank had it anyhow."

"I was kind of raised around the farm myself. Left as soon as I could, though." The old guy didn't respond. He leaned over his coffee and shoveled some more sugar in. He was eating two or three meals in that one cup. Making it last. "Well," I went on, "if you don't want any paper, how about me buying some breakfast. Hell, I just came into a windfall kind of, and there's no use me keeping it to myself. Need someone to celebrate with before I gamble the shit away. You know?"

It was the best I could do on short notice and I thought he probably wouldn't go for it. The old guy sat in silence, the sound of the south wind rattling the big plate windows, dust spitting against the shiny panes of glass.

Then he said, "I ain't no bum. I don't take no handouts. I'm a hobo."

"I'm sure you're not a bum," I said.

"You say?"

"Well," I responded, "if you were a bum you would have hit me for the coffee right away. Grabbed the section of the paper."

"Well, that's right," he said. "Now a hobo, he don't mind working, but it's just that he don't like being tied down to one particular job in one particular place. He likes to take some time off to think about things and be with his buddies and let the fruit of his labor kind of ooze all over him."

"You want to earn some breakfast and ten bucks?" I asked.

"You serious?"

"I'm serious."

The old guy was Myron Kendall from outside Iowa City, and he left a wife and kid in 1934 to hit the road. He never went home and he never knew his kid. Myron spent some time with the Wobblies up in the state of Washington, but they were dying out then and it was a scramble just trying to make enough to contribute to the stew in the jungles along the Columbia River valley. I ordered a short stack, scrambled eggs, hash browns, and a bowl of chili, and watched while Myron gobbled the mess down. Over coffee I told him I wanted him to watch a house over in Riverside for me and tell me who came and went and approximately what time. He didn't ask me why; he just agreed to do the job.

I said I would pick him up around five-thirty or six and talk it over and give him the ten bucks. He said it was the first time in his life he would ever get ten bucks for sitting on a park bench.

Myron waved contentedly when I deposited him on the bench across from Carlotta's house, the same bench I used Friday night when I met up with Coal Barge and Buddy. As I drove south toward the junkyard along Maclean, past the ballpark, the dairy and lumberyards, then the old county p-farm, I realized I had my own agency now. One old hobo and four little kids on stakeouts. Pinkerton probably started this way.

It was my hope that by plotting the movements of the characters in this melodrama, I could get a line on the heroin. If Frankie Plummer had double-crossed Carlotta, as I suspected, then perhaps I could help her recover the heroin and stick it to the Bull. I had decided to deal myself in on the play. One way to do that was to get information and run a bluff. If Bull or Carl thought I knew where the heroin was, I became an instant big man. Maybe Carlotta trusted me, or needed me enough to deal through me. But the one thing was, I might end up with a handful of acetylene torch flame.

At ten-thirty I parked the Ford on a dusty lane under the shadow of the levee. A scruffy brown mongrel on a tether jumped against a tattered wire fence and yapped at me. I was about a mile north of the junkyard in a clapboard-and-tar-paper neighborhood where the squalor and the chicken crap and the dirty-faced kids get hidden from the general ebb and flow of suburban goodness and light. The levee wall rose about eight feet on a gentle slope and beyond was a ditch about a hundred yards wide that ran north and south around the city to carry flood water from the Arkansas River. It was mostly a kids' playground and unofficial city dump. The Plummer junkyard ran up to the levee wall. it was from the wall that I decided to put the spyglass on Plummer's operation in hopes of finding the heroin and Frankie.

I got the day pack and an army shovel out of the trunk and strung the binoculars around my neck. A couple of shy Mexican kids stared at me from across the fence and I gave them fifty cents to watch the Fairlane. They grinned and took up their posts. I scrambled up the levee wall, down the weedy embankment on the other side, and walked south toward the junkyard. The ditch was dusty and full of blowing tumbleweeds. When I had gone about a mile I climbed the bank and looked over. The junkyard was three hundred yards south and I saw the shack that Plummer called his office. A cottonwood grove hovered above it in the wind and dust. The yard itself was rectangular, full of weeds, sunflowers, and six acres of rusted metal, maybe a hundred yards wide and three or four hundred yards long. The hubcap-encrusted shack huddled near the Broadway entrance, and in the corner nearest to where I crouched on the levee, an old red barn with a mansard roof stood in disrepair. Two old Chevy trucks were parked near the double barn door and each Chevy carried a load of smashed wrecks ready for the scrap heap. Behind Plummer's shack the trailer was parked in the open. When I put the glasses on the shack I could see Abraham the watchdog sleeping in his wet, sandy hole by the front door. I had forgotten about Abraham. I scanned the junkyard but didn't see any signs of life. I didn't see the two-tone Dodge either, and figured that Gomez and his playmate were saying Mass.

I ducked back over the levee and crawled another fifty yards to a grove of huge old cottonwoods surrounded by scrub thicket and thistle. I peeked over the levee, then crawled into the thicket and opened the army shovel. I dug a small hole and sat down in it on the levee bank in soft sand and loam. I placed the day pack beside me and took out my copy of *In Our Time.* I opened the pocket chess set. From where I was dug in on the levee bank I could see the whole junkyard. I was relatively certain that only by accident could I be seen by anyone down in the yard. In another couple of hours the brown basketball of sun would be completely behind me. Then anyone looking up into the cottonwoods and brush would be squinting hard to spot a herd of circus elephants, much less a cleverly disguised private detective.

In two hours I read about Nick Adams getting shot and coming home to disillusionment and discontent, played through three Alekhine games from the Capablanca match, and smoked enough Luckys to make an ugly little pile of butts in the dust. Ten moves into a gemlike four-knights defense played by Rubenstein against Tartakower in Riga and an intense daydream about licking muscatel from Carlotta's knees, I spotted a black Kaiser roaring through the front gate of the junkyard, followed by the two-tone Dodge. The cars stopped in front of the hubcap shack and Carl Plummer got out of the Kaiser and walked back to the other car. He stood talking for a moment. In the binoculars I could see Carl's thin, cruel mouth working. He gestured to Gomez and his playmate and the two drove to the old barn, parked, and went inside. Plummer entered his office, reappeared moments later, then walked to the barn and went inside. I put down Alekhine and Hemingway and stuck the glass on the barn and smoked. Abraham slept in his wet hole. There was no sign of Frankie Plummer.

I waited tensely, not thinking. By now the tumbleweeds blew through the junkyard in clots and the sky was turning darker with dust and topsoil. The sun cut slanting rays through the bubbling air. Then a cream-colored Packard roared past the front gate of the junkyard and skidded to a halt behind the Kaiser. Bull Granger got out. He walked hurriedly to the barn, holding his hat with his left hand and leaning into the wind and the dust. He disappeared inside.

Whatever this troop of Boy Scouts had to talk about took only a few minutes. All four came out of the barn, Gomez closed the big red doors, and they drove back to the hubcap shed. Granger sat with Plummer in the backseat of the Dodge and went with him into the office. They made a nice couple in the binoculars.

Gomez and his boyfriend sat in the Dodge and smoked. Dust swirled around the car and the hubcap shed. A flock of battered crows threaded through the wind and settled into the cottonwoods above the shed. Their feathers ruffled. The cawing and the steady howling of the wind increased the tension I felt. After a few minutes, I put the chess set and book back in the day pack and moved the Browning to the top of the pack, where it would be handy. I took the binoculars off my neck and put them in the pack as well. Where I was going I wouldn't need binoculars. If the heroin was in that mansard-roofed barn, I would see it close enough to put my hands on it. Then I'd have the joker, the ace, and the one-eyed jack.

I got down in the thicket and moved on hands and knees through the sand and scrub. Stickers jabbed my hands. The wind moved the rising dust quickly. At the bottom of the levee slope there was enough of the corrugated metal fence to hide me from the boys inside. I crept along the fence and peered through the gaps. There was no action from the

shed. I saw a brown arm popping out of the driver's side of
the Dodge where Gomez and his pal were waiting. Evi-
dently Bull and Carl were still talking inside the shed.

I stuck my head through another gap in the fence and
pushed aside some sunflowers and buffalo grass. On my
left, about seventy yards down, were the old barn and the
two Chevy trucks parked out front. Gomez and the boys
were maybe two hundred yards away through weeds and
rusted wrecks. If they gave me ten minutes I could be in
the barn and out with the heroin. It crossed my mind that if
Frankie were still holding out on Bull and Carl, they might
have him in there too. If so, I would take the heroin and
leave Frankie with his tail in the ice machine.

When I'd made it to a hole in the fence just behind the
barn, I squatted and held my breath and listened for any
sound from inside. There was the howl of the wind and the
caw of the crows. There was a squeak and a clang, rusted
metal banging against wood. It was steady in the wind and
I decided it was nothing holding a gun. I crept down the
fence another ten yards and looked at the barn from the
other side. I found what I was looking for.

On the side of the barn away from the hubcap shed was
a small door latched from outside, the kind of barn door
split across the middle and used for livestock and horses
instead of machinery. If I could get inside the barn that
way, there would be no need to run the risk of using the
double front doors and being seen by Gomez. I held my
breath and sprinted the ten dusty yards to the livestock
door, crouched beside it and flicked the latch. The bottom
door gave way easily and I slithered inside, pulling the
half-door shut behind me.

The dusty black air inside the barn smelled of hay and
oil and paint. Bars of sunlight split the place into black and
yellow wedges. I slid the Browning out of the day pack
and clicked the safety off. I held it in my sweaty hand.
Except for the clanging metal there was an absolute silence. Everything inside seemed cut away from the wind

and the tumbleweeds and crows, as if it existed in its own dreadful world. In the dark, I heard something alive and small scurry through the straw and become quiet. My skin crawled after it. My own breathing became stertorous and sweat collected on my chin and dropped to the oily dirt at my feet. If someone opened the big doors, I might have to use the Browning.

Gradually, my eyes adjusted to the murky light. I was crouched next to a row of dilapidated horse stalls stretched along one wall of the barn. Above me, a platform that had once been used to store hay and grain was now filled with engines and transmissions pulled from wrecks. Light from a small, dirty window opposite me illuminated a workbench and a torn-down motorcycle. What got me was the car parked in front of the double doors about halfway to the back of the barn. Unless I missed my guess, it was a dark blue 1955 Pontiac with the trunk and hood and all four doors wide open. I put the Browning on safety and stood up. I dug the flashlight out of the day pack and turned a dancing ray on the car.

It was Frankie's Pontiac. Someone had torn the guts out of it. I walked slowly toward it, keeping the beam of light pointed low and into the ground below the frame of the Pontiac so no one from the shed would see a flash crossing the chinks in the barn walls. The door panels were ripped out and torn to shreds, the seats slashed and pulled from their moorings. Inside the hood, insulation hung like stalactites. The air cleaner and carburetor lay scattered. The same people had gutted the dashboard, and parts from the radio and heater littered the barn floor. The trunk was torn to the metal, and carpeting was stuffed under the rear wheel. It was no use looking for the heroin in the Pontiac because Carl and the boys had already done a good job of that. There was no heroin, no Frankie, and no deal to cut myself in on. I felt the brooding disappointment, the same feeling I had when I thought about the ball I threw into the dugout from third in the bottom of the ninth during the American Legion finals.

I turned from the Pontiac and walked to the double doors and put my eye to a crack. A tumbleweed had blown underneath the Dodge and Gomez was on his hands and knees trying to clear it out. Sand spread like a sheet in the wind and collected in the doorway of the shed. My hands froze against the door. I pressed closer to the crack. Abraham was gone.

It was time to head for the livestock door and make a gracious exit before the torch got too close to my hand. I turned off the flashlight and backed nervously away. Suddenly, I was on my back in the dust and darkness. I gave a small cry. From one of the horse stalls a pair of legs protruded. I had fallen over them. I put the beam on the legs. They wore dark black cotton slacks and white socks stuffed inside black alligator shoes with a gold buckle. I moved the beam up the legs to the torso. Yellow dress shirt and white tie lying askew along the outstretched right arm. Very nice. My light reached the head that belonged to the legs. There was a smooth and untroubled face, a shock of black hair slicked back into a ducktail. Oil and dust smeared the forehead and sand stuck to the pomade in the rich, wavy hair. It was a young face I had seen before, in a photograph of Frankie Plummer taken in high school. Just older and dead.

I took a closer look. Under Frankie's chin a long blue and black crevasse ran from ear to ear, through veins and muscle in the open neck, through the main artery on the side of the throat, severing the gaping windpipe. Someone had butchered Frankie like a pig, and it hadn't taken him long to die his nasty, messy death.

NINE

I finally stopped breathing like the battleship *Maine,*
scrambled to my hands and knees in the dust and oil, and
put the flashlight on wide beam. Frankie was still dead.
There was a metal water bucket hanging on a nail about
three feet over his limp head, and when the the wind gusted
through a chink in the wall behind it the bucket rocked and
rolled against the splintery wall in a clanking and forlorn
funeral dirge. Frankie's shirt was a flashy yellow silk all
right, but when I leaned in to take a closer look I saw that
the shiny silk became a crusted mess of black on his chest.
Shock and fear had pushed blood through the severed veins
and major artery in a gush. From the neck down Frankie
looked like a Halloween jack-o'-lantern that had up-
chucked a load of holiday licorice. Under cow manure,
grease from a thousand transmission jobs, and the nameless
crud pigeons leave behind, floated the delicate smell of
death. Frankie was fermenting. When I touched his hand it
was ice cold and limber. I had touched guys like that on

Omaha Beach and I was sure Frankie had been dead for at least one whole Saturday night. It started me thinking.

I checked the car again, this time looking for blood and a razor, not for heroin. There was nothing on the seats or carpets inside the Pontiac, but when I dragged out the carpeting that covered the trunk I thought I could see some stains in the hazy light. It made sense to me that Frankie rode to the barn in the trunk, because I didn't think he had been killed in the barn. At least there weren't bloodstains in the dirt around the car or the stalls that would lead me to believe a grown man got his throat cut nearby, bled four or five pints, then lay down nicely on his back with his legs crossed without leaving anything for the maid to clean up. I crawled back to Frankie and slapped a hand on his rear pocket to check for a wallet. My hand came away cold and sticky and in the intense beam of the flashlight I could see the same crusty mess that was on Frankie's silk shirt. Frankie stood up long enough after his throat was cut to let the blood pulse down his chest and collect in his trouser pockets. It didn't seem possible.

With my left hand on Frankie's forehead I lifted his neck just a little so I could take a look at the damage. The slit in his neck was the color of day-old liver, the kind of smelly stuff I used to take down to the creek on hot summer days to catch catfish with. The path of the wound slanted from beneath the left ear, coursed through the Adam's apple, and wound off and over the right shoulder blade. Part of Frankie's left earlobe was severed by the murderer and the wound was deeper under the left ear and down the left side of the throat. It was a wound made from behind by someone wrapping his right hand around Frankie and slicing him across his throat and down his back. I figured it was someone much shorter than Frankie because the path of the wound indicated that the murderer probably stood on tiptoe and then leaned into his work. When I let Frankie's head down, all the parts didn't fit back together quite right. The coroner could worry about that.

Then I got the shakes. I didn't need Bull and Carl and Gomez waltzing into the barn while I was nosing around in their messy little murder. And if they waltzed in, I didn't want to be on their dance card. Stuff like that is hard to explain down at the sixth floor of the police department while rubber hoses do the doodlebug up and down your kidneys.

I crawled toward the livestock door. Before I got to the door I saw a green Army duffel bag wadded and thrown into the corner of the same stall Frankie had rented for the fall season. It looked out of place, like Frankie himself. I got it open, stuck my hand in, and pulled back a gob of stuff that stuck like wet enamel. It was another five ounces of Frankie's blood. He had been murdered, trussed in the duffel bag, then thrown into the trunk of his own Pontiac. The usual questions came to mind.

I finished sleuthing and crawled closer to the livestock door. Then I heard it. Old Abraham growled a low staccato and pushed his drooling nose and lips into a crack between the lower door and the barn wall. My heart started playing taps in two-four time. A row of white teeth flashed into a bar of sunlight, then disappeared. A nose, a set of teeth again, bumping and pushing against the door. At the other end of the teeth ninety pounds of junkyard dog bristled. I imagined a tackling dummy doused with Old Spice and Lucky Strike tobacco being torn to shreds by Abraham when he was just a puppy learning how to kill snoopers. Abraham left the staccato and started his mean legato, a low growl he kept suspended just above the roasting fires of hell. Then the door buckled, which meant that Abraham had his front paws against the barn. If Abraham decided to bark I would have Bull in front and Abraham behind.

"Abraham," I whispered. "Good doggie." I thought perhaps I heard Abraham modulate his growl into circumspect hatred. "Abraham, it's me. You remember my voice? The guy who works for the guy who feeds you?"

I stuck my palm up the crack in the door.

"Here you go, old buddy. Smell me. It's just old me."
Abraham thrashed himself against the barn door and tore
out an inch of splinters with his teeth. The flurry reminded
me of an old Buster Crabbe short where the cows get stuck
in the Zambesi and the killer fish descend. Then I remembered the Old Spice and the dummy and junkyard dog
training school.

"Goddamn it, Abraham. I can't shoot you." I would
rather shoot a man than a dog, and besides, if I shot Abraham the boys would be down to the barn in fifteen seconds
with their own guns out. It was no way for a slick detective
to make his getaway. "Come on, Abe, Jesus Christ." I
amused myself with the biblical connective. But Abraham
didn't like his nickname, because I could see him through
the crack backing away from the door a few feet, setting
his legs, and throwing himself at the wall. On my hands
and knees I braced myself against the bottom of the livestock door and took the shock. Abraham landed on his feet
and growled.

I got the pack off my back and dug down past the gun
and the copy of *In Our Time* and pulled out the sack of
sandwiches. The top sandwich was boiled ham and Swiss
cheese. I tore the sandwich in half, then slowly unlatched
the wooden bolt that held the door shut from inside. Abraham growled more sullenly. Quickly, I pulled open the bottom door and threw out the boiled ham and cheese.
Abraham pulled backward and thrashed his big triangle
head, then put his wet flared nose down in the dirt and
smelled. Then in one jerk of his bristled neck he took the
sandwich down the hatch.

"Oh, boy, Abraham. Nice dog. You like that sandwich?
Mmmm, boy. Swiss cheese, your favorite. You want another bit, boy?" Abraham growled on, but he had his nose
to the spot in the dust where the aroma lingered.

"Here, boy," I said. I threw out the other half of the
sandwich. Abraham didn't jump this time. He gulped the
sandwich. Abraham and I were having lunch together.

"All right, Abraham. Just for being such a good boy, I'm going to give you another ham and Swiss." I tossed a whole sandwich through the door. Abraham wagged his tail and picked the bread and meat and cheese out of the dirt. He wagged steadily with the sandwich lodged in his mouth. Tilting his head, Abe gave the sandwich a quick *harrumph* and it disappeared into his gullet. I stayed quiet for a minute. Abraham followed his mustard-covered nose to the door and stuck one nostril in the dust. A half inch of weathered wood separated my boot from Abe's nose.

My beloved corned beef and sauerkraut on rye was next. I took it out of the wax paper and held it next to Abe's nose. If Abraham hated sauerkraut, my goose was cooked. I chuckled and shivered at the same time.

"Now, Abraham, my pooch, we're going to try a little more Pavlov. You know Pavlov? Lovable Russian dude." For the first time in two sandwiches Abraham stopped his steady growl and squeaked. It was a sign he had been a puppy before he started tearing dummies to shreds. We were playing. I hoped that *speak* was a command they left out of the junkyard-dog course. I let the bottom door fall against me as Abraham pushed with his head. When the door was open wide enough for Abraham to stick his head inside, I caught his jaws with my knee and held him there. I had the corned beef in my right hand, broke off a piece of fatty meat, and let Abe catch it with his sloppy tongue. He whimpered. Like all junkyard dogs, Abraham was hungry. And I had provided a just and suitable alternative to the Mitch Roberts club-and-bacon sandwich.

"Okay, when I say so, we're going to play a little game of fetch." Abraham was silent. "This fetch game is going to be built on mutual trust and friendship. I feed you corned beef; you don't tear my arm out of its socket, right? Here we go."

I put the day pack around my shoulders again and tore the corned beef in half. In a squat, I pulled the bottom livestock door open and whizzed the corned beef by Abe's nose and twenty yards into the brush and twisted metal wrecks. It came apart and bread and meat and sauerkraut splattered everywhere. Abraham wheeled and dashed after the exploding sandwich. While he played tag with the pieces of my corned-beef sandwich, I strode quickly to the metal perimeter of the junkyard and ducked through a gaping crack. Abraham spotted me and became alert, growling.

"It's okay, boy. I wasn't bullshitting you about the trust. Here." I threw the rest of the sandwich over Abraham's shoulder and into the backseat of a rusted Studebaker. While Abe collected the beef and slurped the sauerkraut, I slithered north along the levee embankment through dust and sand. When I finally saw my car and its two Mexican hood ornaments, I sat in a plum thicket and lit my first Lucky in an hour. I took the smoke down deep.

When I thought about it, what I had in my skull was a theory about hidden heroin that was on a par with electric snowshoes. I flirted once with the idea of Frankie Plummer as a double-crosser, but even that was starting to wilt. What I knew was, I had a guy who steals some heroin from his old man and Johnny Rossiter, then shows up murdered in Carl's barn. The murderer gets behind Frankie without raising any suspicion. This murderer was short, right-handed, and very determined. I smoked a second Lucky thinking about all that, then got into the Fairlane and drove down Broadway toward the junkyard, wondering whether a woman could cut a guy's throat like that.

The sky boiled. I drove Broadway with the top up and the radio tuned to Reverend Theobald Miller of Metro Baptist and his sermon on the power of prayer. The car lots were full of Mom and Dad looking over the new models for next year, already out in September. When I went past Twenty-ninth Street I waved at Joe Stanberry, who ran a motor-car company and sold the only honest used car in town. Joe carried a 198 average in the Wednesday scratch league at Sky Bowl. It didn't matter to me that he made up for his honest cars by cheating at lowball every Monday night in the back room of the Moose Club. I flipped my burning Lucky out the window and wheeled into the junkyard. Under the semicircle of welded metal, I pulled up behind Carl's black Kaiser and parked. Abraham got out of his wet hole and pushed the fur up along his backbone. I wasn't looking for any more trouble from him, just some answers from the Vatican Council inside Carl's hubcap shack. Abraham let me cruise softly past his best low growl and push my way inside the fly-specked screen door.

Carl slumped behind his metal desk, one elbow propped on a knee, his grizzled, gray head nestled in his left hand. His other arm draped over the desk listlessly. The fan in the window behind him whirred and a squadron of flies practiced landings and takeoffs in the dust-riddled air. It was hot and dry inside the shack and the blowing sand and dirt collected in drifts in the corners. Except for Bull Granger, standing with his back turned in a neat blue pinstripe suit, the shack was the same as it had been on Friday when I put in my first appearance. I let the screen slam. Bull swiveled. Carl's head popped up.

Carl spoke slowly. "I told you what for, didn't I?" He snuck a look at the Bull. There was cold finality in his voice, but a speck of pain as well. His eyes were red-rimmed.

"Now Mr. Plummer, sir," I said, "the way I see it you didn't tell me what for. Not at all. You send me out to take a crack at finding your boy and the city's finest run me off. Then I find out it was all a big mistake."

"You been paid," he said. I took the shoulder pack off and cradled it over my left arm. The Bull glowered and the rolls of fat on his neck turned scarlet. His gun would be a police special tucked around the right hip. He'd have to swing open his coat and unbuckle the strap before drawing it. With the day pack over my left arm, I could stick my hand in and grab the butt of the Browning and let the pack fall. In this variation I gave myself odds of knight and first move on the Bull.

"I been paid, yeah," I said. "But I'm a little curious why Frankie would be hanging around Carmen Granger. That's pretty far uptown for a boy like him to go, isn't it?" I was stabbing in the dark, taking swings, trying to make something happen. There isn't a fight unless some guy takes the first punch.

"He was a good boy," Carl said. His voice broke.

Bull said, "Shut up, you fool." Then Bull looked at me. "I think I gave you one warning, didn't I, peckerwood?"

"Now, let's see. Wasn't that down at police headquarters in a small room with two goons leaning over my shoulder?"

"It don't make no difference to me," Bull said. "I'll sit on your shit whenever and wherever I feel like. Now get out of here."

"Not until we have a little talk. Nice and friendly."

Carl spoke. "Abraham," he said.

Abraham came into the shack through a square of screen that was ripped from the flimsy frame. He curled his lips back over his yellow teeth.

"Sit down, Roberts," Carl said. "I'll have this dog rip you wide open if you don't."

"Fine," I said. "Don't mind if I do." I sat in the chair behind me, one not around two days before. Abraham glued his green-and-black eyes to my throat. I had my hand curled around the grip of the Browning, but to get the gun out and to fire a shot that counted while ninety pounds of teeth and fur flew at me through the air would make me slightly better than Annie Oakley's rifle instructor. Abraham sounded like he remembered nothing about a ham and Swiss on wheat, or the lovely time we'd spent over sauerkraut and corned beef.

"Now," Bull hissed, "it's me that wants answers." While Bull spoke I unwrapped sandwich number four, the grand finale: a pepper loaf and jalapeño pepper cheese. I pulled it out of the day pack and tossed it to Abraham. He bounced in the air wagging his tail and got the sandwich into his mouth. He jerked it back. Hot pepper cheese, jalapeño peppers, hot pepper loaf, and Grandma's hottest relish. I've seen grown men cry eating that sandwich.

Abraham wobbled and staggered two steps back toward the screen door while his eyes emptied of hate. He got to his water dish in the corner and lapped at it with his tongue. I could have told him that water on a jalapeño burn was no good. Abraham whimpered and howled and rubbed his nose with both his front paws, finally getting down on the rough floor of the shack and rolling over and over, rubbing his nose and wailing like a baby.

Carl stood. "You poisoned my goddamn dog, you son of a bitch."

"Sit down. Don't worry about your damn dog."

Abraham dashed out the slash in the screen and headed yelping past the cottonwoods for the river. I still had the gun held out of sight.

"Now," I said smiling, "which one is Boswell and which one is Johnson?"

"I told you before what would happen if you kept nosing around, didn't I?" bellowed Bull. He was sweating and the red from his neck swept up to his chin.

"Let's can the tough shit. I want to know what you expected me to find out at Carlotta's house. I want to know what you expected me to learn by tailing Frankie and why you put me off the case before I even got started, before things heated up." Carl broke a little. His face caved in like a coal mine and I couldn't tell the sweat from the tears. Maybe the old man was crying.

"What's going on, Carl?" I asked.

"They didn't have to," he said.

"Shut up, fool," Bull said.

"I don't care," said Carl. Bull spun and backhanded Carl across the cheek. He went over backward in his metal chair, then slowly righted the chair and sat back down, his head in his hands.

"Now, boys. This séance is getting out of hand. But we are getting someplace." I waited in silence. The flies buzzed and the fan whirred. Through the smudged window over Bull's shoulder I could see tumbleweeds flying through sand and rusted metal, cottonwoods waving wildly, the sky blackening.

"All right, boys. Here's how it is," I said. "I got a new client. I want you to listen to me. I don't care that you got a badge and a couple of stooges in the wings. What you really got is trouble with Rossiter and I think I can fix it, but it's gonna cost you."

"Shut up, peckerwood. You don't fix nothing for me," Bull said. "I fix my shit myself."

Carl sat quietly, his head still in his hands. Then the screen screeched open and Gomez appeared. He held a straight razor in his right hand and wore a big grin. I dropped the day pack and let the nose of the Browning rest on his chest.

"First, you," I said. "Then it's your bag of shit Colonel. I promise. What do you say, fuckface?"

Gomez and the Bull shot messages at each other. Bull nodded and Gomez dropped the razor. It hit with a dull thud on the wooden floor.

"Fine, just fine," I said. "Now here it is. You guys got a problem with your last shipment. I really don't care that much, but I know you are having a problem making a deal with the party that is holding you up. Maybe you both need a middleman. Boys, I think I can deal for your stuff, whereas you can't. If I get it, get paid, and get out, I figure I could take a little for my trouble. Then everybody is happy and nobody gets hurt. Well, nobody else." Carl looked up. "I'll say this once. I know your game and I don't care a damn. What I want is for you to let Carlotta and Carmen go. You go back to pushing trash around like a

cop, I make a few bucks, and Carlotta and Carmen take off
with what's theirs."

"No deal, peckerwood," Bull said. "I make my own
way. And you go down. Way down."

"Okay," I said. "You change your mind, you get in
touch. I think you guys need help on this deal. More help
than Carl there can give you. You need someone with
brains because you sure as shit ain't got any."

Bull clenched his fists. They were like hams. I put the
pack over my shoulder and edged toward the screen, then
pushed my way out into the blowing dust.

Along Broadway the day was over for the used-car
dealers. The black sky and whipping wind had driven Mom
and Dad and the kids home to their dinners of roast beef,
mashed potatoes, and butterscotch pudding. I flicked on
the headlights and fired up a Lucky. It was clear to me that
Carl was hit hard by Frankie's death, that the game was
now rougher than he had wanted it. That left me with the
grim feeling that Frankie hadn't double-crossed anyone,
that he had been a clown in a production put on by a major
showman and had gotten himself killed during the first act.
I imagined Carmen's slim fingers and sapphire eyes and
thought how a kid could let himself be sucked into darkness for a lot less. Then I saw a maelstrom of slim fingers
and sapphire eyes. If Carmen and Carlotta were out to destroy the Bull, they were taking along anyone who got in
the way. It worried me to be in the way.

One big raindrop plopped on my windshield and ran in a
grimy rivulet down to the hood, then three or four more
splashed on the dirty glass. I saw plenty of rain like this on
the prairie. Ten minutes of big drops wetting the dust, the
sky turning green and yellow, then nothing. Just a hint of
cool, and a promise of wet. I drove north across the WPA
bridge and looked down at the collection of rusted refrigerators, used tires, and automobile hulks lining the river
bank. I felt tired, cheap, and used myself. It took me an-

other fifteen minutes to get back into College Hill and park under the cedar tree on First Street.

When I walked around to Belmont Street I saw Fatso standing by the big elm tree those kids used a a goalpost. He picked his nose and wiped the leftovers on his sweatshirt sleeve. His sneakers were untied and the strings dangled in the grass.

I walked up to him. "Hello, there," I said in an avuncular tone.

"Hello, mister."

"How did things go last night and today?"

"Okay, I guess," he said. "Except those small fry couldn't stay out and they couldn't come back either."

"Well, they're pretty little. Where's your other friend, the guy with the Froggy voice?"

"He gotta go to church on Sunday evenings."

"So you're the last of my operatives on the job?"

"What's that?" Fatty said.

"Well, it's not important. Operative means a guy who works for me. Anyway, you been out here most of the time?"

"Most of the time, I guess," he said.

"Well, what does most of the time mean?" I started to smell four pint-sized rats.

"You know," Fatty whined. "Most of the time."

"Look," I said. "I'm getting dizzy on this ride. Why don't you start from yesterday evening, and tell me how much attention you guys paid to the scene across the street and whether you saw anybody come around."

Fatty backed a step or two. He looked at the ground, drew a lemon-colored booger out of his nose, inspected it, then wiped it on his sleeve. My boat got a little drunk, then the wave of nausea passed it by. I smiled.

"Hey, you're my investigator now. I gotta trust you, see?"

Fatty looked up. "You gonna pay me?" he asked. We now flirted with ultimate issues.

"Of course. Don't you trust me? I already paid you guys four dollars and said I'd be back tonight. Here I am."

"You gonna give me the four dollars more like you promised?"

Fatty put his hands on his gelatinous waist and stared at me cockeyed. For a second I thought about backhanding the twerp. Instead, I dug in my wallet and fished out four crinkled Washingtons. I held one dollar in front of Fatty's snout.

"Here. Take it." His greasy hand snapped the buck. "Now let's start this conversation again. When were you around last night?"

Fatty scowled. "What about the other three bucks?"

"You mean for the other guys?" I asked.

"Yeah. Sure."

"You talk, then I give you the three. You're into me for two already. I'm not gonna cheat you now."

Fatty thought it over. The three dollars ruffled in the breeze like crow feathers. Finally he said, "All right. I was here for a while last night. The other guys had to go in. I didn't see nothing. Now give me the three dollars."

"Wait, wait, wait. You didn't see nothing?"

"Well," Fatty said, "I didn't really see Mr. Granger talking to nobody. That's what you wanted us to look out for."

"Didn't anything go on around here last night? Anything? Anyone go up to the door, stop by, honk? Come on."

"Well, I did see a couple of cars come by like they was just looking for Mr. Granger, but they went away real fast. Mostly anyway."

I decided I hated this little tub. Zits collected in the creases between his nose and cheek and he had the round stupid eyes of a hog. He wore his ball cap all wrong. That was what really got me. His ball cap wasn't broken in right: there was no good break in the bill and the peak was straight instead of rounded. There was no sweat in the liner. Fatty didn't play ball, he just wore the damn cap around.

I said, "What do you mean by mostly?"

"Last night, after you left, we were still playing pass and keepaway."

I interrupted. "You mean you and Froggy played keep-away from those four-year-olds?"

"Yes."

"Terrific."

Fatty took the rag-end of a Baby Ruth out of his jeans pocket and poked the whole thing into his billowing mouth. The nuts and nougat wedged between his pointy teeth and floundered there in a sea of slobber.

"So anyway," he said, "these two cars come up and one drives into the driveway. This lady gets out and gets in the other car, and then the other car drives away. That's it. How about my three dollars?"

"These cars," I said. "What did they look like?"

"You know. Cars. I don't know."

"What color?"

"This one that drove off, I guess was real funny-looking. It was kind of small."

"Pink?"

"Oh. Yeah. Pink. It was small, you know?"

"What about the other car? Big or small?"

"Big, I guess."

"What color?" I asked. Fatty evacuated his brain. His eyes flattened. "Dark or light?"

"Dark," he answered. He was losing interest. I folded and refolded the three dollars. He perked up a little.

"So what did this lady look like?"

"Gosh, mister. I told you everything I know. Give me my money."

"Three bucks for one answer. That's asking very little."

I could see the one unbalanced flywheel in Fatty's brain spinning wildly.

"She had real long hair. She was kinda tall. Oh yeah. In

the pink car there was this lady too, but I couldn't see her too well. Oh yeah. Some truck came later and took away the car they left."

I smiled and patted Fatty on the shoulder. He jerked his porky finger away and grabbed at the three bills. He missed.

"My money," he whined. "You said you'd give me my money!"

"Hold on." I stuffed the three bills in my shirt pocket, pulled out a Lucky and got it started in the wind. "Let me give you some advice. Now, see, yesterday you and I made a deal. You come out here and look around for me, then report what you see when I get back. I promise to give you two bucks, half now, half later. Simple. Now you want to hold me up for four bucks. Maybe you don't plan to give your buddies any. Even if you do, see, they didn't do anything to earn it. They took the buck, then did nothing. You gotta keep your word. Do what you say, and if you don't want to do more, then don't. But if you do more than you say, don't come sucking around whining about doing more than your share. You do more than you say, just shut the heck up, and somebody will eventually notice. You get me?"

"You promised me four bucks."

"I'm charging you three bucks for advice."

Fatty stomped his legs. "I'll tell my dad." He turned, then looked back.

My neck caught fire. "Hey, you fat sack," I said. "Go get your greasy old man and bring him out here and we can fry him up for breakfast. Yeah, go get him." Jesus, I thought, what am I doing getting in an argument with some upper-crust ten-year-old on Belmont Street?

Fatty waddled toward his red front door. I turned and walked quickly around the corner to the car and got in. I gunned the engine and sped downtown along Second Street. I could see the headlines: DETECTIVE BEATS FAT KID'S FATHER IN ARGUMENT OVER THREE DOLLARS.

TEN-YEAR-OLD SUFFERS CUT LIP IN ALTERCATION WITH
SLEAZY WICHITA DETECTIVE. Cripes!

By the time I got to the park, a limp sun peeked through
the elms. The house where Carlotta and Carmen lived was
dark and sad. I could see the back of Myron Kendall's head
as he sat slouched on the bench where I had parked him
this morning. I stopped the Fairlane by the Murdock
Bridge and walked through the park listening to the squirrels making their ratcheting noise. Because of the wind,
dust, and threat of rain, the park was empty. Normally
there would be herds of families eating watermelon and
listening to the waterskiers race by on the river. I flopped
beside Myron.

"Hi," I said.

"Howdy, Mr. Roberts."

"How'd it go today?"

"Well, it was pretty quiet for the most part, I guess. We
did have a little action in the forenoon. Otherwise not
much."

"You get anything to eat?"

Myron said, "I ate some peanuts. That breakfast you
bought me is more than I eat all day sometimes."

I offered him a Lucky. He took one and lit it.

"Tell me about it," I said.

"Well, about ten this here tan DeSoto pulls up. There are
three gents inside. It looked like there was a couple of
Mexicans. This one old guy gets out of the passenger side.
Tall, kind of thin, but tough-looking. Flat gray hair. Lots
of wrinkles. He goes up to the door with one of the Mexicans and pounds. I thought that was kind of funny. He
didn't ring the bell or just knock. He pounded and yelled.
Then this young woman comes to the door and opens it but
keeps it on the latch. They start shouting. It was a knockdown, drag-out mess. She slams the door. The gents go
away. I thought that was a strange Sunday morning hoe-
down. Nothing else happens all day. About an hour ago the
woman comes outside, gets a little pink job out of that shed

there, and drives away. That ain't much for twenty bucks, I'm afraid."

"Nothing else? Nobody else?"

"Nope," Myron said. I folded a twenty and gave it to him.

"How about tomorrow? You want to make another twenty on this stakeout?"

"No, thanks, Mr. Roberts. I really appreciate the offer. I feel kinda strange making twenty dollars spying on somebody. Then, I been working the harvest all August, and I gotta get on with the apples and pears this month. Working too much is bad and that's what I been doing."

"Philosophical differences, huh?"

"Yeah, you could say that."

I shook his hand. "You need a ride downtown?"

"No," he said. "I'll just walk there. Need to get off my can for a little."

"Thanks, Myron. I'm in the book if you're ever in a jam. You come into the Way, we'll shoot a game and swim through a bowl of chili."

He strolled away with his hands in his pockets, kicking his feet at twigs and pebbles. He turned. "I'll count on that," he said and kept walking.

On the way back to the car, I thought things over. Jesus! Carmen and Carlotta delivered Frankie and his Pontiac right to Bull's front door last night. A wrecker dragged the Pontiac to the junkyard where all the boys went through it. That prompted Carl and Gomez to visit Carlotta this morning. I looked back at the big house, dark and somber and gray. The windows rattled and the yellow roses in the yard swirled.

I'd slept with a murderess. Somehow, I thought, it didn't matter at all.

TEN

On the way home I stopped at Ralph Baum's Burger Bar on Seneca Street and ordered a double chili cheeseburger, an order of greasy fries, and a vanilla malt. They were gone by the time I let myself in through the back door. Francis followed me through a crack in the screen, jumped onto the kitchen sink, and got himself a fresh drink of water from the faucet, which dripped steadily. The south wind had died to an impatient rush from this morning's determined howl.

I looked at Saturday night's dirty dishes piled in a lambent chiaroscuro on the oak table in the alcove, then at the disheveled sheets piled on the brass bed, and felt the sudden desolation and disillusionment of every man who lives alone and goes about the sullen business of making beds, preparing meals, washing dishes, and keeping clean—in the stark face of his own loneliness and despair. Above the rosewood Staunton set, the stern and youthful visage of

118

Carl Schlecter looked down through dusky wedges of sunlight.

I put my hand on Francis' big yellow head. One of his ears had an inch-long burr knocked out of it and his left eye showed a deep scar.

"Oh, Jesus Christ, Francis," I said aloud. I marveled at another biblical juxtaposition. "I'm feeling sorry for myself again." Francis purred and rubbed his side against my pointy elbow. Then he reversed his ground and rubbed again and purred.

I made a bet with myself that I could persuade Carl and the Bull to deal through me for the heroin I didn't have. I didn't even have an idea where it was hidden. Maybe it was gone. With Carmen. But then, I thought, Carmen was driving the Pontiac just last night when she and Carlotta showed up at Bull's house to deliver their nice surprise package. That meant there was a chance Carmen was still in town and that the heroin was hidden nearby. That gave me some hope that I could convince Carlotta to work through me. If she trusted me. If I could make her trust me.

God, I thought. Carlotta committed a murder in order to promote a fantastic plot to revenge herself on her stepfather and to get what she believes is hers. Bull can't touch her because too many people know about his protection scheme and would put two and two together. Besides, as long as one of them stays hidden to blow the whistle if Bull makes a move, the Bull stays trussed tighter than Johnny Weismuller in a close-up love scene. But I had the sick feeling that the Bull had enough evil in him to pull his own double-cross when it came to exchanging the heroin for money. I could see the Bull arranging an exchange with Carlotta, then killing her when he had his hands on the stuff. When I considered it, my involvement in this mess was intended to prevent Carlotta from destroying herself with her own hatred.

Francis dug his claws into the sleeve of my flannel shirt.
"Sure, old boy," I said. I poured Francis a saucer of milk
and tuna juice.

After a hot shower, I dug out the phone book and called
Carlotta. The phone rang ten times before I hung up, wondering if she was out trying to make her own deal for the
heroin right now. Maybe she was up at the Rock Castle
talking to Johnny Rossiter. Whether she made the deal with
Rossiter or Bull, she was going to need some backup when
she made the switch. I couldn't see a guy like Rossiter
sitting still for thievery and blackmail while he was supposed to be king of the coop.

When I had the knapsack unpacked and the Browning
safely tucked back into my sea locker, I poured myself a
tall muscatel and went to the front porch and sat down in
the rocker. There had been a day game at Lawrence Stadium and attendants and ushers walked silently in the parking lot picking up Coke cups and hot-dog wrappers. From
the players' clubhouse behind a wire fence a tall, gangly,
bowlegged kid appeared and ambled to a black '36 Chevy,
got a kiss from the summery girl in the passenger's seat,
and drove north on Sycamore. The Chevy rattled like a bag
of bolts. The kid looked like a lefty to me, some young
Warren Spahn dreaming about the big leagues, the glory,
and the money. It gave me a bad case of the minor-league
blues. The muscatel, the french fries, and the chili gave me
heartburn.

After twenty minutes, three smokes, and another glass
of muscatel, I called Carlotta. There was no answer.

The wind blew a Braves program over the curb and into
my yard. It startled a scruffy black crow, which hopped
sideways to avoid the flapping pages. It flapped its own
wings in return and cawed, then pecked at the picture of
Joey Jay, the Braves's ace. The crow pecking the Jay.

In the middle of peck and a caw I remembered Joe Stanberry standing in the wind and tumbleweeds waving back
at me on Broadway. Suddenly I realized what that knowing

wave meant. The week before I had promised Joe to repossess a couple of clunkers he sold these two factory types in time to offer them for resale on Labor Day afternoon. It seems he had some end-of-the-season sale going and wanted to offer these two cars at special get-acquainted prices. He offered me twelve bucks a car, and ten bucks for trying.

It seemed like a snap when I said yes because snatching a repo on a holiday is usually pretty simple unless the guy goes out of town. You hit a guy about six o'clock on a holiday morning while he is in the sack. By the time he gets up, he thinks his car is stolen and calls the cops. The cops don't care about a missing junker on Labor Day morning. Sure, a Cadillac is a different story. But not some junker a union man uses to get to work in. By the time Tuesday rolls around, he figures that the bank is probably upset about the three payments he is behind. Stanberry is hoping that the cars are sold on the same day the cops give the guy the bum's rush. When the guy finally makes it over to Stanberry's by cab, Joe says it's the bank's fault. The bank says it's Joe's fault. Then the guy's foreman out at the plant calls and tells him to get his ass to work or he will be scratching fleas at the fucking zoo for a living. He writes the car off and maybe he goes back to Stanberry Motors after two or three paydays and buys the same car all over again. By then Joe has it repainted and the odometer turned back.

I got out of the rocker and headed to the office to review title documents and get the keys to the cars. Joe had left them in the mail slot on Saturday night.

Kellogg Street was deserted. An exhilarating dose of desolation bubbled through my veins. When I reached the top of the Kellogg viaduct overpass, I got out of the car and stepped to the cement guardrail. Below me, fives sets of railroad tracks snaked north through a waste of warehouses, ripped and rusted boilers, abandoned cars and trucks, and heaps of nameless refuge. I blew a ragged plume of blue cigarette smoke into the orange air and looked at the fat setting sun behind the ragged buildings downtown. I thought that Wichita was a goddamn heartbreaker, a shameless woman with her hose rolled around her calves, makeup melted. I turned and leaned my back against the guardrail, arms akimbo, surveying the expanse of clapboard-and-tar-paper squares people lived in, finally to where the elms quit and the broad wheat and cornfields began. God, such a town, laid out in back-and-forth certitude that mirrored the belabored nothingness upon which it was originally built. Religion, family, and profit.

I was losing my friends and growing tired. Reason and luck and sentimentality were no more important than a broken ankle some black woman didn't deserve. It had been six months since I had been to dinner with Andy at his home, and just as long since we shared beer and tobacco over the chessboard and talked about politics and life.

The last time I was there we all sat around the walnut dinner table and found an embarrassed distance encrusting us like cement. The children buzzed like flies at a picnic, upsetting a milk carton, refusing to eat the carrots. Midway into the dinner, the in-laws, stooped and gray-faced, slouched into the room and sat down at the table without a word of greeting. The father stuck his face into my plate and inquired, "What is it?" "Salmon," I answered, annoyed at the question and at the drool that preceded it onto my plate. "Don't like fish," he said, plucking a morsel from my plate and thrusting it in his mouth. "Ugh," he grunted. He extracted the wet wad of salmon, looked it over with the concern of the proctologist, and deposited it on the tabletop. "Don't like fish." The doorbell rang and in swept a frowsy blonde carrying a bushel basket of Tupperware. Andy's wife leaped to her feet and disappeared into the next room with the Tupperware lady. The kids ran away to play. A beaten-down factory couple in cloth coats came in the front door and sulked in the parlor until Andy left the table to discuss a broken toilet in one of his rental apart-

ments. Suddenly the room was empty. The salmon, potatoes, carrots, and biscuits grew cold. I left by the back
door.

I threw my Lucky into the swirling evening, watching
its red glow disappear into weeds and tin cans. I would
help Carlotta make her heroin deal if she would let me.

By the time I pulled the Ford into the lot in front of my
office, evening was in full swing. Thin purple wisps and
blue velvet hung in cloudy fingers in the east and the wind
had died to a whisper. A few eager crickets and cicadas
rubbed legs and cackled.

When I opened the door a smell of dust and ink erupted.
I opened the venetian blinds and let in some hazy light and
looked around. The title documents and keys lay piled on
the floor under the mail slot in the front door and there was
a note from Jake wanting to know if I could go fishing at a
half-dry farm pond east of town on Labor Day. The walls
were covered in stripes of shadow and light. Wispy
mounds of dust collected in corners. Some office, I
thought. Maybe I would do the repos early on Monday and
take Jake up on his offer to fish. No thrill like the thrill of
pulling a five-inch baby largemouth out of a withered farm
pond in the sweltering heat and washing the thrill down
with an ice-cold beer. Maybe even better than sitting alone
drinking muscatel until the game was six innings old and
you could walk across the street to sit in the stands for free.

For ten or fifteen minutes I sat at my desk matching title
documents with keys, taping the keys to the title, making
some notes. The back room was dark and quiet, just the
hum of the refrigerator and the slight wavering rattle of the
screen door in the wind. I got a bottle of Pabst and opened
it, then went out into the backyard.

I put a hand on the rocker to swing it farther under the
trees and away from the sunlight. I saw it. There was a
swish and a sickeningly loud crack, then an emptiness full
of revolving and exploding stars, a demented galaxy of gas
and pure white light. In my forehead one bright flash im-

ploded past my eyes and sped down the ridges of my cheeks. Then a sudden pain expanded and pulsed in my neck. I was on my knees, looking at the blades of blue-grass. The tiny black antennae of a cricket loomed huge in my eyesight. My head and neck burned. Suddenly, another blow shocked my head down. Consciousness lapsed into nauseated darkness. There was nothing left but hooded, episodic dreams.

An enchanted road. Dust spiraling into a pure, royal blue sky. Nuggets in the road the color of shining onyx, the sky as thick and tangible as oil paint. I walked for hours, then days, with a febrile anxiety growing in my chest. I floated, disembodied. Cornfields extended in all directions. Vivid yellow stalks rose straight into the blue sky; green corn sheaths hung down like swollen thumbs. I walked through an impenetrably thick silence. In one fleeting en-counter, two magpies perched on an irregular pole fence, their black bodies and orange beaks wildly contrasted with the yellow and green fields behind them. Goddamn Heckel and Jeckel. They eyed me suspiciously and looked at each other with a mild disapproval. They drooped their malevo-lent eyelids.

In another vision I fished in a sparklingly clear lake. Fireflies danced; willows bent into the turquoise stillness in a sheltered cove. I held an old cane pole and watched a red and white cork bob peacefully on the water's surface, then waver and finally plunge beneath the water. I jerked to the surface a monstrous, growling bulldog, baring its teeth. Its eyes glowed red. Steaming saliva dripped from its vile nostrils. I screamed and felt a human hand on my neck. It was Jake, the barber from next door, and his face was twisted with fear.

"Jesus, Mitch." Jake said with a quivering, tremulous quality. He lifted my head gently and peered into my eyes. I could see the round outline of his face. "Mitch! Oh Jesus, Mitch. What happened?" Then I heard him say, "Harvey, get on next door and bring me some cold towels, the bottle of Listerine under the comb dispenser, and that bottle of brandy behind the cash register." Harvey grunted approval. I heard myself groan.

"Okay, boy, you're gonna make it. What happened? Who did this? This ain't no goddamn accident." I swam in nausea. My body boiled with pain. I heard a screen slam and Harvey was back with the missionary supplies.

"Here, drink this," Jake said and tipped my head to the neck of the bottle. I felt hot brandy in my throat and gagged and coughed. "All right, just take it easy."

Jake swathed my forehead and neck in cold towels and wiped them across my face. He carefully dabbed at my eyelids, then gave me another gulp of brandy. I was coming back to life, but the nausea and pain overwhelmed me. My head felt like one of those pancake heads in a cartoon where Wile E. Coyote gets flattened by a truck.

Like in the movies, I managed to say, "Where am I?"

"You're out in back of your place. I got to the shop this morning and thought you were up kind of early for a holiday. Hell, I just came down to clean up Saturday's clippings; otherwise you coulda laid here forever. Shit, I saw your car but didn't see you inside. I came on in and here you are, laying like some goddamn squashed turtle out on Highway 54. How long you been here? Who did this to you? What the sam hill have you got yourself into, you dumb shit?"

Silvery sunlight danced above me in the mimosa. The air felt cool. "What the hell day is it?" I asked.

"Early Monday morning. Hell, it's Labor Day. You want me to get you a doctor? An ambulance? I think we should, Mitch. You look hurt real bad." He threw the towels over his shoulder. They were covered with blood.

"No ambulance. No doctor. I'll be okay."

"Harvey," Jake said. "Get some more towels. Here, Mitch, take another slug. What happened?" He poured brandy down my throat. The pictures swam, but the outlines cleared.

Harvey returned with clean towels and stood with his hands on his knees and a terrified expression on his face. He was one of the old guys who sat around the barbershop all day. This blood was giving him palpitations. Jake doused the clean towels in Listerine and dabbed at the top of my head. "My God," he said. "You got a damn crack in the top of yer head you could stick a dick into." He dabbed some more. "Christ, Mitch. Here's another crack. You need some stitches real bad, and somebody better look you over. They damn busted yer head open."

I tried to move and couldn't. "Just lay still," Jake said. He rubbed the towel over my face again and I saw it come away red and wet. "You bled a lot," he said.

"Raise me up a little, Jake," I said.

"You sure?"

"Yeah."

Jake put his thick forearm around my shoulders and got me halfway off the ground. Warm blood dripped from my eyelid to my nose. Jake put me down right away. I groaned and felt the pain explode in my head again.

"Here," Jake said. He slid a cold towel under my head and took off my shoes. He loosened my belt and felt my pulse.

"Barbers, you know," he said. "Surgeons of the Middle Ages. Hell, that's what you are: middle-aged. I think I got me some fresh leeches around here somewhere." He laughed.

"Oh, shit," I said. "It hurts like hell when I laugh."

Jake unbuttoned my shirt. He peeled it away from the skin and hair around my neck and when he did I saw it crusted with blackened blood. Just like Frankie's yellow silk. I turned my head into the grass and lost a double chili cheese burger, greasy fries, and vanilla malt. When the retching stopped, I felt cold.

"Get me some hot towels, Harvey." Jake had a cold towel around my neck and wiped the crusted blood away in globs. He shook the towel and bloody flecks detached themselves. When Harvey came back, Jake rubbed my arms with hot towels.

"Oh, goddamn, Mitch. Jesus Christ!"

"What?" I said. "What the hell is it, Jake?" Jake took away his right hand and stuffed the heel of his palm into his mouth. There was a sickened look of fear on his face. "What the hell is it, Jake?" I asked again.

"Your finger, Mitch." Jake spoke in a flat monotone. There was no emotion in his voice.

"My finger?"

"Look," Jake said. He held my left hand in a hot towel and swabbed the top of my palm. I looked. My little finger ended before the first joint and what was left was an ugly sore with a white piece of bone broken and extended beyond the jagged, blue flesh. Blood oozed from the wound.

"Goddamn, Mitch," Jake said. "They cut off your goddamn finger. Jesus H. Fucking Christ!"

I let my head drop into the wet towel. So, I thought, this is what it's like to play hardball with the boys in the big leagues. Mitch Roberts, boy detective. Tries to play with the guys down the block and clucks around in his own blood and loses a little finger. Then I felt a line of pain shoot up my arm and clatter around the elbow. Now that I knew, my left hand throbbed.

"Mitch, I better call the police and an ambulance. This is too much for a barber. You need help."

"No, please," I said. "No police. No ambulance. Just get me up on my feet."

Harvey looked stupefied while Jake and I struggled together. Finally, I was up and we went into my office in a slow-motion shuffle.

"Drive me home, Jake? You keep my car and I'll pick it up when I'm up and about."

"No deal," he said. "First I drive to the emergency room. We make up some bullshit story about how you had an accident, then I drive you home. Otherwise, I call the police."

"Yeah, sure," I said. I had lost a lot of my pluck and didn't feel like arguing.

Around noon I got out of the emergency room with a head full of stitches and a handful of bandages. It seems I was climbing a ladder behind Jake when he let slip a full bucket of paint which hit me on the head on its way down. I fell and grabbed for the gutter but got snagged by the ring on my pinkie. Tore the damn finger off.

"Where's the finger?" the doctor asked. "Dogs ate the damn thing," we said, practically in unison. "What took you so long to get here?" the doctor asked. Jake and I shrugged. The doctor sewed.

That day I stayed in bed, sleeping fitfully, letting the concussion tire itself out. My thoughts whirled in a confused kaleidoscope, but mostly I thought about Carl and the Bull and how they looked at me when I invaded their sanctum and held a gun on them. Then I thought about Gomez and the knife he flashed. It could cut a man's finger clean off. On Tuesday I was up and mad.

It was Tuesday night when my mother and grandma called from the farm. They were hysterical, crying. When I got them calmed down, they told me. A small package came in the mail. They opened it together because the return address was mine. They figured it was a little present. They got the brown-paper wrapping undone and searched the cotton inside. They found a bloody, severed finger wrapped in a note. NEXT TIME IT WILL BE YOUR PECKER-WOOD SON'S FUCKING HEAD.

ELEVEN

That night I sat rocking and smoking. Empty and full of dull anger. It was ponderously hot again and my sweat collected in the folds of the old blue bathrobe. The smoke I blew shimmered in unmoving clouds in the still air. The Braves were winning the championship, and the roar from the stands across the street hovered over the cries of the vendors. "African hamburgers, get 'em now." "Cold beeeeeeeer, getcha cold beeeeeer." At midnight I turned on the Philco to Fred Huddleston's KFH police report and listened to the tin litany of minor disturbances, robberies, assaults, and burglaries.

"At 8:38 P.M. police were called to the Ozell Liquor Store at 3906 West Thirty-third Street South by the clerk on duty, Miss Mildred Sawyer. Some minutes earlier two men entered the store and chose a six-pack of beer from the cooler. When they approached Miss Sawyer one of the men pulled out a small-caliber black revolver and pointed the weapon at Miss Sawyer. She was instructed to empty the cash register and lie down on the floor. The men fled and the clerk called police. She described the men as of normal weight and height, Caucasian. One of the men wore his hair in a pompadour; the other had long sideburns and a tattoo on his hand in the shape of a snake. Miss Sawyer was not hurt. She could not describe the getaway vehicle. The estimated loss is one hundred and five dollars. Police are investigating.

"Thirty-eight-year-old Amos Reedle of 1336 South Emporia reported the entry into his locked garage sometime yesterday during the daylight hours and the theft of a radial saw, two fishing poles, a pair of steel-toed construction boots, and three bottles of whiskey.

"Owners of the Terrace Drive-In Theatre reported a disturbance during the second feature showing of *Teen-Age Crime Wave* at approximately 10:05 P.M. last night. Rocks and bottles were thrown when two cars of high school students engaged in a dispute. Police report that the students had been drinking beer. Police officer Kerry Riggs took seventeen-year-old Milo Weaver into custody. He was released to his parents. . . ."

In the middle of an assault and battery at the Tropics Lounge on South Broadway, it came to me. I knew where the goddamn heroin was being hidden. I knew what Carlotta had done with it. I went to bed then, and slept soundly for the first time in four, long days.

I woke at noon, rolled over in the wet, crumpled sheets, and finally opened and focused my eyes. I stayed in bed, reading the paper, catching up on the pennant races, drinking coffee, thinking about how to keep my anger in bounds long enough to do a workmanlike job on Bull Granger. Heat danced on the venetian blinds and the room was filled with an airless, dusty silence. Then I could hear Mrs. Thompson shuffling around upstairs, changing stations on the radio, humming "Wabash Cannonball" and "Nearer My God to Thee." Tonight, I thought, the Braves played the last game of the season and then the good players went to

Milwaukee to finish September. The stadium would remain empty except for the numb meaninglessness of high school football in the fall. I wanted to do what I had to do in time to catch a few innings of the last game. But that was up to Johnny Rossiter and the Bull.

Just before six, when the sun ducked behind the elms and the air burned less violently, I took a shower and put on a blue silk shirt and my best white linen planter's suit. I looked a little like Dr. Cyclops on Pago Pago. After stuffing the Browning into the day pack, I went out into the plodding late summer heat. I put the Browning in the trunk, started the Fairlane, and drove slowly up Broadway to where the Rock Castle nestled in a grove of hedge and maple.

The Castle hugged Broadway like a hooker hugs a fat man. It was a square limestone fortress in various russet shades topped by two turrets flanking either side of the square. Behind the nightclub a motel court circled a gravel parking lot. A Skelly station flanked the court. The castle, the court motel rooms and their semiattached garages, and the Skelly station were built from the same limestone and took up most of the block of Thirty-ninth Street North. The motel catered to truckers who plied the highway between Nebraska and Texas on their way to nowhere and getting there fast. The castle catered to characters, wheeler-dealers, investors, and men and women on the make. There were plenty of each category to go around.

When it was built in the Thirties the Castle was a speak. When the age of illegal liquor ended it became a roadhouse and gambling den where you could get a steak and a game of craps along with dance-band music. You could still get the steak and the dance-band music, but the gambling had simmered down to a very expensive nightly poker game. I was a nickel, dime, quarter man myself and never sat around the green felt in the back room with the drunken doctors and bankers and professional hustlers. The game was straight, except that Rossiter took five percent of every pot.

I parked and walked through the double mahogany doors. Inside it was dark and cool, and a tingly piano version of "Misty" wafted in the dimness. A tall, thin, and indelibly handsome man with a pencil mustache said, "Good evening, sir." I nodded.

"Will you be dining?"

"Yes."

"Will you be joined this evening?"

"No."

"Very good, sir," he said.

"I'll eat at the bar. Over here with Tom if you don't mind."

"Very good, sir."

Double bars stretched on either side of the entryway. Mr. Pencil led me to the right. I perched on a stool and looked around. Behind me a brass rail divided the bar area from the dining room and dance floor. Square white tables surrounded the polished wooden floor. Brass lamps glowed yellow on each table. There was the inevitable single red rose in a slender glass vase. The room ended in a raised bandstand. Behind the bandstand was Rossiter's office and the room where expensive poker was played. It was early and only a few couples were eating. The place tinkled with silverware sounds and the hiss of silk. The piano in the corner was big and black and played by a woman with icy features and red lips who never went home with the customers. She was very, very good.

"How are you this evening, Mr. Roberts?" said a ruddy voice from behind the bar.

I swiveled. "Fine, Tom. Thanks."

"It's been a while. I trust you are well?"

"Yes. Fine." There was a bloody patch on the top of my head and bandages on the back of my neck where the doctor took stitches. My left hand carried two pounds of tape and gauze. I could imagine how I looked.

Tom Silver's big red and white face swam in an ocean of bar glasses hanging from a rack above the bar. He was the perfect bartender. He spoke when spoken to and otherwise stood leaning against the counter with his arms folded across the massive pad of his enormous gut. The drinks he made were clean and when you ordered call-booze you got what you called. When some woman you were with ordered a gin fizz or a Gold Cadillac Tom made it quickly, correctly, and without the condescending leer of the bartender whose only desire is to stir a jigger of whiskey into a six-ounce tumbler with Seven-Up.

"Waddle it be, Mr. Roberts?"

"Old Grandad with water back, please, Tom."

"Yes, sir."

While Tom poured the Grandad into a shot glass and the ice water into a tumbler, I let my eyes adjust to the dark. Tom sat the drink down in front of me and retreated to the counter, where he leaned back. When my waiter came by I ordered chateaubriand medium rare, sautéed mushrooms, baked potato with sour cream, Caesar salad and French bread.

"Is the boss around tonight, Tom?" I asked.

"Do you mean Mr. Rossiter?" Tom said.

"Yes."

"I'll check for you, Mr. Roberts," Tom said. He walked to the entryway and spoke to Mr. Pencil in a whisper. Mr. Pencil strode deliberately to the bandstand and disappeared into the darkened hallway which ran around the stage. Tom planted himself in his spot. I sipped the Grandad and watched the beautiful ice-woman while she played a very low-down version of "Tangerine." Mr. Pencil reappeared and walked to my side.

"We will speak to you in a moment about your inquiry," Mr. Pencil said. I wondered who *we* were and what *we* were to speak about. A waiter in black brought me my salad and I ate it and finished the whiskey. I felt better and ordered German beer to go with the steak. When it came I drank the beer and listened to music and melted the steak on my tongue.

I was nibbling the tag end of a dish of spumoni when a bruiser the size of Mount Rushmore leaned over the bar. He wore a loose black suit and white tie with a diamond stickpin. You could shave your face in his black patent shoes. He had a thick, sandy-colored face and his eyes were covered by shaggy eyebrows. He looked like Mike Mazurki.

"You the guy wants to see the boss?" he asked. His voice was four miles of highway under repair.

"My name is Mitch Roberts. Yeah. I'd like to see Mr. Rossiter for a few minutes." Tom the bartender walked to the other end of the bar and around the corner. The perfect bartender.

"What about?" Rushmore asked.

"Business," I said. Rushmore blinked and ran a thick finger along the south side of his nose.

"Mr. Rossiter, he's kind of busy. What kind of business you got to talk to him about?" His tone was hollow with no hint of cynicism or impatience. I was not inclined to be flip with this guy for fear he would snap off my arm and use it as a backscratcher. I slurped another gob of spumoni, took the whiskey and swirled it in front of my eyes. I looked at Rushmore through the liquor.

"This business," I said, "is private. Very private. Mr. Rossiter gives me one minute and I guarantee he will want another fifteen on top of it."

"Whadda you selling? Encyclopedias?" Mr. Pencil peered around the corner from his spot near the front door. Tom edged back. Three tables over there was laughter and the ice-woman played "Take the A-Train."

"Tom," I said, "please get me a pen." Tom reached in his white jacket pocket and produced a gold fountain pen. I took it and wrote on my cocktail napkin: *I know where the shit is hidden. Mitch Roberts.* I folded the napkin and handed it to Rushmore. He unfolded it, read it carefully, then returned and walked into the darkness behind the stage.

The waiter cleared my dishes and Tom returned to his spot. "Will there be anything else?" he asked.

"How about some plaster of Paris?" Tom smiled. I finished my whiskey and waited. In five minutes Rushmore walked briskly from the darkness. He was followed by a dark little man in blue pinstripes with a white carnation at his lapel. His ears looked like kites. The two men got up to the bar and stood around me in a half circle of quiet stares. The dark man had a big hook nose.

Finally Hook Nose said, "Come on." I got up and the three of us walked through the gate in the brass rail and back to the darkness behind the bandstand and into a narrow, heavily draped corridor. I knew the poker room was at the end of the corridor. Halfway down was another door on the left. Probably Rossiter's office. Rushmore put his hand on my shoulder.

"Hold on, cowboy," he said. He shoved me gently and I stopped with my back to the draped wall. "We're just gonna check you over. No problem with that, is there?"

"No problem," I said. Rushmore stood two steps back while Hook Nose patted me under the arms and down the legs. He turned me and went over my back pockets and down the back of my calf.

"Let's go," Hook Nose said. Rushmore knocked on the door. A voice inside said, "Yeah," and we all went in.

Rossiter's office was a fifteen-foot square carpeted in white shag. The only light came from a lamp that cast a circle of yellow on the glass top of the steel and glass desk. Rushmore sat in a beige couch against one wall and Hook Nose leaned against a shiny wet bar on the other side of the room.

Johnny Rossiter sat behind the glass and steel in a black tuxedo. He had the body of Fred Astaire and the high forehead and slicked-back hair of Valentino. His hands were graceful, the fingers delicately small. He was eating a small filet and green salad. Rossiter didn't look up or speak. He just ate his filet and sipped at a goblet of wine. When he had finished, he carefully wiped his mouth and hands with a monogrammed linen napkin, lit an English Oval, and raised his limpid eyes.

"Sit down," he said. His voice was precise. I sat in a leather chair at an off-angle to the front of the desk. Hook Nose removed the dishes from the desk and piled them on the wet bar.

"You've had an accident," Rossiter said.

"You could say that," I responded. "It's been a very tough few days."

"You're Mitch Roberts. You're a private detective with not a lot on the ball and you send me a note like this." I stayed quiet.

"Wine?" he continued. Hook Nose gave me a goblet and splashed Margaux into it. It had more nose than the muscatel. I was tempted to make a joke about nose for the little guy's benefit.

Rossiter pasted his droopy eyes on mine. "You'll want to explain in certain terms the meaning of the note and the purpose of your visit. Don't embellish and don't lie. Come to the point and I will make some kind of judgment."

I sipped the wine. "A few days ago Carl Plummer hired me to tail his son and gave me directions on how to find him. It seemed odd at the time and the deal fell through when Plummer took me off the case right away. By accident I found out that Frankie Plummer stole something that belonged by rights to Johnny Rossiter and that Carl was upset. Lots of people were upset. It didn't mean much to me at the time. But then I ran into a pair of young women who interested me and I learned that these two might have some knowledge of where the stolen merchandise might be. By that time the principals were anxious to discourage me from making further inquiries, from learning any more professional secrets. I can't blame them. I would have felt the same way. So these people arranged for me to have an accident. But I'm not discouraged. On the contrary. I am mad as hell. Now, I sat around for a few days letting the knots on my head unravel and something came to me. What came to me was where the merchandise was hidden. Just deduced the goddamn answer out of thin air. But I'm sure I know and I'm sure I'm right."

"What do you propose?" Rossiter said.

"I return the merchandise to you. You pay me a finder's fee."

"You think I should buy merchandise that belongs to me already? Merchandise I bought and paid for? What kind of businessman would that make me, Mr. Roberts?"

"I'm a businessman too. I want ten thousand. If you don't like it, get the ten thousand from the people who lost the merchandise in the first place."

"What assurance do you have that I won't simply have you killed when you return the merchandise?"

I raised my glass. "I'm not worth it," I said.

Rossiter leaned back in his chair and smiled. "When can you deliver this merchandise?"

"Tonight." I paused. "There's one other thing. These two women. When I return the merchandise, they have to be left out clean."

Rossiter inhaled some English Oval. "I see," he said. We sat in silence. I knew I was taking a chance trying to sell Rossiter on the idea of paying for the return of heroin he considered his own. But I decided that if I made the price tag low enough he just might do it to avoid problems. And if I made the price tag high enough he would feel my services were valuable.

"We close at three A.M., Mr. Roberts. I'll expect to see you before that time. There is enough cash in this room to cover your expenses. If you show up with the merchandise, I'll pay you and send you on your way. I'll even ignore the women of whom you speak. You will be away clean, as you say."

"All right," I said.

"On the other hand . . . Should you fail to keep your appointment with me I will have you tortured and then killed. Is that clear?"

"What if I'm wrong?"

"Then," Rossiter said, "you will be dead wrong. Is it clear?"

"Clear."

"Good then." Rossiter stood and extended his narrow hand. I shook it. Rushmore and Hook Nose joined me for the walk down the corridor. They left me at the bandstand and headed back down the darkened passage. Hook Nose turned. "Good fucking luck, punk," he said.

I walked back to the bar. Tom leaned in his spot. There were more couples at the tables. Tom stepped forward. "It's been taken care of, Mr. Roberts. Thank you very much."

"All right, Tom. Good." I dug in my wallet and got a five and put it in the tip bowl.

"Thank you, Mr. Roberts," Tom said. I walked past Mr. Pencil and through the mahogany door.

Outside, a few whimsical stars dusted the eastern horizon, already streaked cerulean blue. A slow freight chugged north. The fireman waved a red lantern.

In the wavering twilight I drove south on Broadway, past secondhand stores, junk shops, Mexican diners, and used-car lots. When I got home to Sycamore I changed into a pair of blue jeans and a dark, lightweight turtleneck. I put the blackjack in my back pocket and the Browning in the front seat. Then I drove over to College Hill and parked under my trusty cedar tree. I felt grim as a Goya.

The night was blowsy and the elms paraded in a sibilant rush, waving their leafy arms and creaking in the steady south wind. Light from the copper lamps on Belmont streaked the darkness, the rays and shadows colliding in an eerie embrace on the lush, dark lawns of the rich. Across First Street the door to a two-story Ozzie-and-Harriet stood open, and the blue light of television oozed onto the sidewalk. Then the sound of canned laughter broke the windy silence. A dog barked. My heart did the tango and I sat smoking, thinking with cruel remorse about the night I spent with Carlotta and about the sad-faced lady on the desk in her house in Riverside. I suddenly felt a longing for the life of quiet and anonymity I had lived for so long. It was funny. I started thinking that tonight was the last night of the minor-league season. Guys like Joe Torre, Juan Pizarro, Joey Jay, Hammering Harry Hanebrink, and Carl Willey and Wes Covington would be gone forever from this square, brown prairie town. They would make it to the bigs. Shit, I thought, I should be there to watch them go.

I felt anger and fear and despair and when I finished my smoke, I locked the Ford and crept into the alley that ran along the back of Colonel Granger's Tudor outhouse. Somebody's idea of a ragman scarecrow startled me in the gloomy shadows and I shivered respectfully at what went through my mind.

Bull's big house was dark and empty-looking. I huddled behind the garage, away from the thin mist of light that escaped from the bulb over the double doors. Through a dusty window in the back wall of the garage I could see that Bull's creamy Packard was gone. I held my breath and peered into the windswept ink of the backyard. There was an empty birdbath, a couple of lounge chairs, a row of thick cedar hedge shielding the yard from the neighbors, and no sign of a snarling Doberman. I picked up a stone from the alley and tossed it toward the back porch. It clattered against the flat stones. No barking, no snarling, no lights, and no sirens. The alley was a jungle of hedge, vine, and mulberry, and I didn't think any of the neighbors could see me from their kitchen windows. Out on Douglas only a few cars passed. I hopped the picket fence and silently pushed my way through the side door of the garage and went inside to wait for the Bull. It was hot inside and sweat soaked my clothes.

With the door shut behind me, I stood still and looked

around, adjusting my eyes to the new darkness. The garage was empty. Silent and sterile as a Southern Baptist dance hall. There was none of the usual suburban stuff like scattered tools, hoes and rakes, toys, old barbecue sets, coils of hose, and bicycles. Neat rows of pasteboard boxes rose at the back end; along the south wall at my elbow a neat squirrel cage held ordered arrays of hoes, rakes, trimmers and mowers. There was a gardener at work. Maybe a servant or two. Certainly no evidence of some harried Dagwood in a holey woolen sweater raking the lawn, throwing his tools in a scattered pile in the corner before playing catch with his bucktoothed kids. A faint oil spot marked where Bull parked the Packard. From the position of the spot I could tell that Bull pulled his car into the north side of the two-car garage and got out with only a few feet to spare between himself and the north wall. I sat in a dark corner to the left and behind where Bull would stand when he got out of the driver's door. If there was a passenger with the Bull when he came home, my plan wouldn't work. But that didn't seem likely.

I squatted in that dim corner for thirty minutes. When bright car lights broke the plane of darkness, I pulled the blackjack out of my back pocket and pushed the Browning deeper into my belt. The Packard idled. My heart accelerated.

The Bull grunted, then heaved up the double garage doors and got back into the Packard. The big car rolled into the dark garage past where I squatted in the corner. It purred and puffed carbon monoxide into my face. I could see the outline of Bull's big neck where it bunched up in rolls under his felt hat. He was alone. After a pause, he shut off the motor and opened the door. When he got the door open and one leg out I was up from the darkness taking two quick strides toward him. He said something like, "Whaaaa..." before I clipped him behind the right ear with the fat end of the blackjack. He yowled and grabbed at the spot.

He swooned and his hat dropped to the floor. I pushed his face down and back until he was prone on the front seat of the Packard, an abandoned whale on the camel-hair beach. The car's yellow overhead light revealed a fat, obscene face, floppy jowls hanging in arches around the chin, bushy eyebrows growing like radioactive lichens above his piggy eyes. His chest heaved and I could see that he was conscious, but barely hanging onto the edge of a whirling galaxy. He held one porky hand below his right ear and groaned.

"Goddamn it," he said in a bewildered growl. "What the fuck is this?"

I got his thick left leg untangled from his suit coat and draped it over the right leg and under the ivory steering wheel. Then I grabbed the heavy car door with my left hand and shut it gently on the ankle of Bull's right leg. He eased up on his elbows and looked at me with a confused scowl. The window was down and I could see a look of hatred and sickness simmering in the dim light.

"You," he said.

"Hi." My hands shook. I stuffed the blackjack into my rear pocket and hauled out the Browning. My bandaged left hand did nothing but hurt.

"This bullshit is your last trick, son of a bitch," the Bull said. He was up off his elbows and had one hand on the steering wheel desperately trying to get his balance. I poked the nose of the Browning inside.

"Get back down." The Bull glared at me, then looked the Browning up and down with an air of modest disrespect.

"You won't," he said. "You ain't got the fucking guts."

"Try me," I said. The fear was gone from me and now I operated in the airless region of pure hatred. I lodged one foot against the garage wall and gave the car door a quick shove against Bull's trapped ankle.

"*Aaagghhh,* Jesus Christ!" I pressed my full weight against the door and bounced it with my shoulder. The Bull gurgled fish sounds and dropped back to his elbows, then onto his back and put his right forearm over his eyes. In an instant he was up, lashing out with his right hand for my face. He missed as I ducked and levered the door against his ankle. Bull disappeared back down to the seat.

When I looked over the window edge the Bull struggled with the gun at his hip.

"Don't," I said. I leaned inside the car and pointed the Browning at his bloated belly. "Unhook the belt buckle and keep both hands in front. Then let the ends of the belt go free and slide the belt away from you and hand me one end. Do it slow and easy. If you don't I'll shoot you someplace and stop you and maybe I'll kill you by accident."

"You won't get away with this. You're a dead son of a bitch." The Bull finished his promise, then slowly unbuckled his belt. It came away and he leaned up and I got one end of the belt in my bloody bandage and pulled belt and gun away from the Bull.

He leaned back on his elbows. "What the fuck is this?" he asked again. There was a hint of vulnerability seeping through the hard guy.

"Listen," I said. "Be quiet and listen. You make any sound and I shoot you. Fucking breathe like you're gonna yell and I'll put a bullet in your goddamn forehead." The Bull started to speak, then relaxed. "You and your goons gave me a hard time last week. I told you then. Do it again and I'd kill you." While I spoke I increased the pressure against the car door. Bull broke a heavy sweat and his face contorted. He made no sound. "What it is, Colonel, is a fucked-up hand and a bashed-in head and the finger you sent my old lady."

"Hey, what are you talking about? I don't know about any of this. What I know is you got your nose in deep, coming around making deals like you're trying to make. I don't know who burned you. It wasn't me. I will next fucking time."

"Fine," I said. "You're taking the fall for Carl or Gomez

or his chicken-taco buddy." That was when I backed off the door and relaxed. Quickly, I slammed it shut again as Bull tried to pull his ankle out. There was a sharp crack and Bull croaked in pain. I bounced the door against the ankle. I heard skin tear and two or three more cracks.

"Oh God. Oh God. Damn it." Bull pounded a meaty fist on the dashboard. I jammed a foot on the top of Bull's instep and pushed on it with all my weight. The ankle gave with a shrill pop and waved at a demented angle. Bull gasped. He stared up out of the yellow mist.

I said, "That one wasn't for me. That was for the black lady down at police headquarters."

"Look," Bull rasped, "you want to make a deal, you got it. I'll give you part of the action. Frankie's dead. You know that? You can take his place. We need a tough guy. There's some dough in it." Bull's face was red and twisted.

"No deal. Let me tell you what's happening to you. I'm snapped out, see? Wacko. Psycho. Fucking crazy. I see guys like you shove people around all the time, guys in big fancy cars and felt hats and heavy coats. They got the dough and they got the diamond rings. Hell, maybe that's okay. I don't give much of a shit about that. But you. You just gotta push people around for the hell of it. Maybe everybody pushes somebody around once in a while. But it's guys like you got no excuse to exist. You make everything smell like shit."

"You fucking asshole," Bull said. "Shit like you is made to be pushed. You think you're any better? I know about you. Fucking repossessing some guy's car, sucking up cheap jobs and booze. You're in the same shit we're all in, gunsel. You just ain't got as much of the action."

"Then," I said, "there's Carlotta and Carmen and the woman you forced out of the police station window without out a net. That's something extra that works on me."

The Bull was tough. I had to hand it to him. He didn't beg and he didn't whine.

"Fuck it then. Maybe you're right. It's just revenge,

Colonel. That's all. It's for me because I hate your fucking guts and you backed me into a corner and slapped me around, then cut off my goddamn finger."

"You're crazy," Bull said.

The bullet went into the middle of Bull's zipper just below where his belt had been. It made a sickening thud and Bull's body convulsed with shock, then shuddered. Then I heard the explosion of powder. Bull lay spread-eagled on the camel-hair seat of the Packard, a circle of dark blood radiating from the small blue bullet wound, soaking his pants. His right hand quaked like a wet sparrow on the floorboard and his eyes twitched shut. A blue swath of cordite rose to the tan headliner and hovered there.

If any of the neighbors had heard the gunshot they would be talking it over right now, trying to decide whether it was a backfire, a firecracker, or a 9mm Browning automatic. There was a fifty-fifty chance that some housewife in mudpack and curlers was dialing the cops to report a strange noise. But there was an equal chance that some husband was saying shut up and go back to watching TV. To me it was worth the gamble to watch Bull die.

"Oh God, help me. Help me." Bull's voice trembled. "Oh please," he said. I watched the red circle expand and collect on the rich camel-hair front seat. Bull grabbed his stomach in both hands and tried to hold the blood and guts inside. Somewhere down there a slug had ripped into his intestines and rattled around. Bull had his head down and his chin back. "Get me a doctor. Get me a doctor. Call ambulance," he whispered. Blood bubbled from his nose and the corners of his mouth. "Why?" he said.

The Bull coughed wildly. He brought his hands away from the wound. They were covered with slick blood. "It hurts," he said. I stuck the Browning into my pants and closed the car door. When I looked back inside I saw clots of blood on Bull's chest where it erupted from his mouth and nose. Bull held his legs in a V, the broken ankle swollen grotesquely out of his wingtips. Then he seemed to relax, and with one soft cough he was quiet.

I got out quick and walked through the alley. It was a zombie who drove west into Riverside Park, under the black wavery shadows of the crow-shrouded elms. And when I stopped, I saw that Carlotta's Victorian was dark.

TWELVE

I sat on my park bench and watched Arcturus shimmer red through a purple cirrus web. Behind me, the bears paced and got up on their hind legs to stick their noses through the black iron bars of their cages, sniffing patiently for the popcorn and crackerjacks that kids threw. Well, I knew how they felt. A frightened dancing bear with cracked skin and a short life expectancy. But I was emptied out. The sweat and the trembling and the adrenaline disappeared down a hole of relief and fatality. I had killed a man in cold blood for my own reasons and there was nothing left of the panic and anxiety, nothing left of the pride and vanity that made me point the Browning at Bull's fat gut and pull the trigger and feel damn happy about it.

I relaxed and took a lungful of smoke and looked at Carlotta's house, thinking about her body and the way it felt Saturday night when I made love with her. She was a beautiful woman and I wanted her, but that was all behind me. I was going to walk across the street and get the heroin

146

and sell it back to Johnny Rossiter. I figured that Carlotta would get what was coming to her and I would too. So had the Bull. If the heroin was gone, then I would wait and let Rossiter take his best shot. It was a gamble with larger stakes than I wanted. But it was my gamble and I had to see what the cards said.

I got my Army shovel out and walked in the wind and darkness across Nims. I jumped the curb, then hopped over the picket fence and landed in the peonies and roses. In front of me was the Texas Beautiful, full of blooms with no scent, lovely and dimensionless. On my hands and knees I felt the loose earth beneath the rose. It had been turned. When I put the shovel down the blade went in easily. I scooped out three shovelfuls, then dug with my hands until I struck hard earth. My heart raced. If the heroin wasn't under the bush I might as well reserve a plot at Maple Grove and start composing an epitaph. HERE LIES A STU-PID, VAIN PRIVATE DETECTIVE WHO MEDDLED IN SHIT LARGER THAN HIMSELF.

The wind was hot. The elms waved wildly. From the darkness of the old porch I heard her voice.

"It's not there," she said. The sound was lost in the filmy whooshing wind. I gazed into the shadows, then stood up and dropped the shovel. By the time I got halfway to the porch I saw her in the wavering shadows by the old swing. She wore something white. She looked like a ghost.

"No," I said to the shadows. "I really didn't suppose it would be."

"I'm sorry, Mitch," she said in a whisper. I walked up the porch steps, letting the surprise and disappointment sink in. Jesus, I thought, what am I going to do? Am I going to let Rossiter and his muscle push my face in the dirt and pour cement in my shoes? Will the fish start with my eyes and work my asshole for desert?

I got to Carlotta, stopped, and watched the wind blow her hair in a stream around her shoulder. Her cotton blouse was open at the throat and revealed her long, brown neck.

She had on jeans and sandals and she smelled faintly of musk. When she stepped from the shadows I saw she had been crying.

"Are you hurt badly, Mitch?" she asked. She put her hand on my cheek, then wrapped both hands around my neck and held me silently. She cried. I could feel her tears on my neck.

"No, not badly."

"You'll be all right?" She put her cool cheek against mine and kissed me, then led me to the swing. We sat down and stayed quiet. She put her head on my shoulder. The wind blew her hair across my forehead.

"I'll be all right. He got my hand pretty bad, put a couple of knots on my head. He didn't figure on that being my least vulnerable territory."

"I'm so sorry. I'm so sorry, Mitch," Carlotta said. She sniffled. The streets were empty and the park deserted. I kissed her mouth.

"Do you know?" she asked me after the kiss.

"I do. I think I do." Carlotta wiped the last tears away from her eyes with the back of her hand. She gave me a halfhearted smile.

"You don't hate me?"

"God, no, Carlotta. I don't know you very well. But I don't hate you. What you did, well, I can understand it. Maybe I can't judge you or anybody else for feeling like you do, for wanting to hurt somebody badly enough to kill in the name of the feeling. For revenge. In the name of some principle or other." Carlotta had her head on my shoulder again. As I spoke I watched the bears pace in their cage.

"How? How did you find out?" she asked me at last.

I kissed her. "I got into the barn out at Plummer's junkyard. They had the Pontiac towed there when you left it at Bull's house on Saturday."

"You know about that too?"

"Professional stakeout. Operatives under the pillows, in

the pantry. Operatives to the left, behind the hour hand, in your hubcaps."

"We had to. We had to kill him."

"I know. Which one of you did it? How did you manage?"

"Oh God," she said. "You won't hate me?"

"No, of course not."

"He was hideous. He pranced and preened and he was such a child. He was vain and arrogant and we decided we could use him. It wasn't hard because he never questioned his power over women, his attractiveness. He really thought he was irresistible. We never intended to kill him. You believe that, don't you?"

"Yes, I believe you."

She shook her hair free. "He wanted to get away from being just a gofer for his father. He wanted to get some real action. It wasn't until he approached Carmen at a party Bull gave that we had any idea that Bull provided protection for Rossiter. We knew he was crooked, that he got money from some source, but we both thought he just protected pinball-machine owners, bartenders who stayed open late, poker games, prostitutes. We knew he was capable of any sort of evil, but we didn't know about Rossiter." She stopped and took a deep breath. She ran her fingers over my bandaged hand. "Are you in pain?"

"Some. Not much." I got out a Lucky and sat smoking.

"It was Frankie's attention that started us thinking. We were desperate. He came to the house and hounded us, making ugly remarks, swaggering. The Bull enjoyed our suffering. He knew Frankie did it, knew how we hated him. Bull enjoys pain, though, enjoys other people's pain, he enjoys watching, being responsible. And so he encouraged Frankie. Carmen was terrified, of course. One night Frankie was drunk and started talking about his business. He called it that. His business. We could tell that his business involved Bull and Johnny Rossiter, and finally, when he was very drunk, and making just a little sense, he told the whole story. How Carl ran heroin in from Mexico. He did it by hiding it in shipments of scrap metal loaded on trucks and driven from Mexico to Wichita. The junkyard was a good cover and Rossiter used it well. The Bull protected these people and was well paid. I suppose Frankie thought that the Plummers should have more for what they did. He kept saying he was going to crack Rossiter. He had a scheme. It was then he told us he was planning to hold Carl up by disappearing with a shipment, then muscle his way into the business. That's all it was to him. Just a way in his drunken dreams to become bigger than he was. It never would have worked. Rossiter and his people would have broken him, made him talk, and that would have been the end of Frankie's dreams. The whole scheme was probably just drunken talk. He could have gotten up in the morning and the idea would have been gone and he would have stayed Frankie Plummer. He kept saying he was no small fry. They couldn't keep treating him that way."

"So," I said, "you showed him a way to make his scheme to steal the heroin possible."

"Yes." A quarter moon danced in the elms, its light silver. "We calmed him down and showed him a way to make his dream come true. We told him he could steal the heroin and use us for protection. The Bull can't allow his own stepchildren to become involved in a thing like this. It becomes perilous for him. What if the papers find out? What if the Chief and all the boys who know about this protection racket all of the sudden won't stand behind Bull anymore? No, we made Frankie see that if we all participated in the deal Bull would have his hands tied, that Rossiter wouldn't just barge in and start hurting people. Frankie liked it."

"What would you do? Did you know?"

"Ruin Bull. It's all we ever wanted. We wanted him ruined the way he ruined our mother. We hated him. I don't think we knew exactly what we were going to do when Frankie decided to steal the heroin and come here to hide.

We knew we had a few days before Carl and the Bull and Rossiter all got together to plan something. We knew we had to do something in that time. In a week, maybe less, things would start to fall apart. And then we didn't trust Frankie. It turned out that he planned to sell Rossiter the heroin and cut us out. If he did that, our idea for ruining the Bull would be meaningless. We decided to kill him. It seemed the only thing to do. You understand?"

I nodded.

"We were desperate. At our end. And we were frightened of the Bull. Afraid he would make some decision to burst in and terrorize us. To throw things over. And so we decided to kill Frankie. He was already dead when you came here on Saturday. He was upstairs, dead."

"How? How did you do it?" Carlotta closed her eyes. "I'm sorry. I want to know. I can tell you why if you want."

"No. It's all right. You should know everything." Carlotta stood and walked to the porch rail and looked into the night. She turned, sat on the rail, and put her hand to her forehead. "It's so hot," she said. "The wind and the heat, it makes me feel restless." I leaned back in the swing.

"He was shaving," she said. "That's funny, isn't it? He was shaving and he cut himself badly." There was nervous hysteria in her voice. I got up and held her and stroked her hair.

"It's all right. Don't say anymore."

"I want to." She gathered herself. "Carmen got behind him. He was singing. She cut his throat with a straight razor. It was horrible. There was a hideous gurgle. The blood was awful." I felt her tremble.

"He stood," I said. "How could you handle him?"

"I was there. In the next room. I watched while Carmen went to him and watched while she put her arm around him. When it was done I helped Carmen hold him up while he died."

"You bled him into the sink?"

"Does that make it worse?" Somehow the thought of an act so ruthless surprised me. Then I thought about the bullet ripping into Bull's gut and it didn't seem so ruthless anymore.

"No, of course not. Never mind. I'm not thinking very well. It takes me by surprise. Then you put the duffel bag around him and stored him in the Pontiac."

"Don't, please," Carlotta said. "Yes, of course. We wanted to put him in Bull's lap and let him deal with it. We knew he couldn't do much. We made the dirty work for him. He could never expose us without ruining himself." The wind rose and fell around us.

Finally Carlotta said, "What would you have done with the heroin?"

"I told Rossiter I would return it to him," I said.

"For a price?"

"Yes." Carlotta looked at me.

"How did you know where it was hidden?" Carlotta turned and stood with her back to me, looking out at the park. The white cotton ruffled in the breeze. Her back was very straight.

"Oh, that. Well, I had a few days to think after I got my brains caved in and a finger lopped off. I started thinking about you, about Saturday night, and about how quickly things were happening around me. Then I remembered you there on Saturday in the sunlight, kneeling in the roses, working the earth. Then it didn't make sense anymore after talking to you about roses. You were mulching and pretending to prune. You had a trowel and pruning knife. But you don't mulch and prune roses on the last day of August. Sure, maybe you do a watering, spray for hairy bugs. But you don't mulch. So, I decided you probably buried the heroin under the Texas Beautiful."

"I forgot about your grandfather and his rose pills."

"It doesn't matter," I said. It didn't.

"Why take the heroin this way?" she asked. Her voice was gentle, almost diaphanous.

"Because I killed the Bull tonight. Shot him. Right in the gut, too. Didn't give him a chance. So I wanted something for myself."

Carlotta said nothing. There were worlds moving behind her eyes. She took a long, deep breath. "He's dead?"

"If he's not, I'm in a world of shit. When he gets out of the hospital, he's gonna come after me and he's gonna be mad."

"No, please," Carlotta said in a trembling voice. "Please, not now."

"I'm sorry. You're right. I killed him tonight, Carlotta. He's dead and I'm glad as hell."

"Oh," she said. Then she held me and I could feel her shake. She gulped tears back. "No, I won't. I've wanted this for so long." After a while she said, "I have to go. What about the heroin?"

"I don't know," I said. "It doesn't matter much to me now. I expect the cops. I expect Rossiter. Whoever gets to me second is going to find bleached bones anyhow. Carlotta, I only made the deal with Rossiter because I thought I could make some money without hurting you. I didn't give a damn about anything else. It was Mitch Roberts I was thinking about. I figured if you could get what you wanted, so could I. So I shot the son of a bitch in his fat belly and came looking for the heroin. Now, go on."

She kissed me and it felt like the last one forever. "I have to go. I have to take care of Carmen. Maybe," she said, then stopped.

"Yeah, maybe. Get on." I smiled at her.

She got halfway down the porch steps. "What will happen?" she said.

"I don't know. I'm glad you're getting out. Go. Quick." Carlotta came back up the steps and kissed me. I was not going to tell her my problems with Rossiter. They were mine; I made them. Then she was gone into the darkness. I heard her open the shed doors and start the Thunderbird. I got out my last Lucky and watched the red taillights disap-

pear down Nims and across the bridge. A feeling of enormous weariness settled over me then. Tired of greasy
spoons, easy friendship, and the casual drunkenness that
passed for sociability. Tired of the bruised summer days
when you couldn't get your breath and the sterile winter
when the clapboard and the dirt showed through. Tired of
this helpless, brutal town lived in by helpless, brutal people
with a knack of overlooking the obvious. I knew why I
hadn't told Carlotta about Rossiter's threats. I didn't give a
damn. Let him come. I would take him out if I could. It
was a helpless, brutal idea.

I drove past the old Southwest Grease Factory and along
the right field wall of the ballpark. I stopped for muscatel
and cigarettes, then went home to a warm shower and a
smoke.

I rocked on the porch. Across the street banks of lights
glowed above the stadium and the sound of the organ
bounced around the stands. People filed out of the gates
with their hats and pennants and souvenir bats and drifted
to their cars. It was the last game of the season and the
public-address announcer thanked the fans and the players
in that strong, confident echo that fills ballparks everywhere. Moths circled in the wavy currents of air and light,
and there was one last, wistful cheer for little Joe Koppe
who got player of the month. When the parking lot was
empty and the ground crew had turned off all but one last
bank of lights over the left-field wall, I sat in red-striped
shorts and Marlon Brando T-shirt, rocking and pouring
back tumblers of muscatel from a green gallon jug. I had
the Browning tucked next to me beneath a spaghetti-stained
tea towel. My feet balanced on the porch rail and pointed
east. Between my toes I could see a sign that said Pepsi in
red and blue. If a guy hit the Pepsi sign on the nose, he got
a free dinner at Marvin Gardens on Harry Street. The
sweet-and-sour at Marvin Gardens was like pancake dough
sopped in lemonade, and to get that unlucky you had to hit
a ball 378 feet on a dead line to left center. I think Coving-

ton did it once that season. I wondered if he ate the soggy chow mein.

I didn't think about Rossiter and his pals Hook Nose and Rushmore. I slid muscatel down and felt the warmth and freedom descend from my neck to my hands. I studied the plastic chess set, then got out a collection of games played by Steinitz in Germany during the 1890s. I was ten moves into a baroque queen's gambit when a dusty Plymouth braked hard and squealed around the corner onto Sycamore, finally coming to rest against the front curb. The headlights stayed lit and a rumpled man in a squashed linen suit staggered out the passenger door. In the dim light, I saw Andy's face, flushed and twisted. He stumbled when he got to the porch steps, then stopped and collected himself.

"Mitch," he said. "It's me." He took a couple of deep breaths.

"Come on up. I been expecting cops. You count as one of those. You here on business?"

Andy scaled the last two porch steps and held onto an edge of fusty white railing. "Sit?" he asked. When I said yes he collapsed into a slag heap with his back to a peeling post and his hands cupped between his legs. He looked beat and soused. "Business," he said. "Well, I don't know. I just don't goddamn know."

"What you need is some muscatel and a cigar. I got the muscatel, you got the cigars in your front pocket."

"Sure," he said. "That's what I need." I poured muscatel into a tumbler and put in some ice from a baking dish I had stashed full of cubes underneath the rocker. When I handed him the glass he took a big tug at it, then took five minutes to get his cheap Corona going with some soggy matches. He looked better when he had it under control.

"Business?" I asked again. There was a long silence while Andy looked at the darkened ballpark.

"You know," he said, "we didn't get to one doubleheader all goddamn season. That's a goddamn shame." He puffed the Corona. "I guess that's not the question." More Corona smoke.

He put his eyes on the floor between my knees. "I just came from over at the Bull's house. Some old lady puts in a call about two hours ago. She thinks she hears some-thing. So a couple of boys run out that way. The old dame says she thinks she heard a shot but she can't be sure. Her old man says it's a backfire. Says she's crazy. Our boys look around and notice that Bull's Packard is nestled in its bunk, but there isn't any lights up in the palace. Well, it's pretty early for the Bull to be beddy-bye. They pound on his door. Nothing. Finally, they get out to the garage and what do you think they fucking find?" Andy lifted his eyes to mine and smiled a disconnected smile. His eyes floated like beach balls in the surf.

"Armadillos," I said. "Goddamn armadillos."

"Yeah, that's right. And you know what else?" I shook my head. "They found old Bull. Colonel Granger, head of fucking Vice. But he was one dead son of a bitch. He was so dead he'll never be the same again. And you know, Mitch, some bastard put a slug between his legs and let him bleed to death. Whole damn front seat full of blood. Buckets and buckets of it. Jesus!" Andy took a long drink of muscatel and we both sat quietly.

"So you had a few belts."

"Yeah," he said. "So I talked to the doctor. Then I had a few belts. He was a cop, you know. Like me." I put the chess set down beside the rocker. There was nothing to say.

"Doc said he hadn't been dead two or three hours. Had a big slug in his belly. What I hear, it's a 9mm. Must have hurt like hell for a while. It's like those guys I find down in the parking lots on Broadway with their guts spilled out like a busted watermelon. Uglier than shit." Andy had so-bered. He pulled his tie off his shoulder and sucked at the stubby cigar he clenched in his teeth. There was look of sudden thoughtfulness on his face. He ran his stubby fingers through the shock of red hair sprouting on his head. "You own a Browning, don't you, Mitch?" he asked.

"Oh, that's fine. That's just fucking fine. You come around again. Sucking. You got something to say, for God's sake, say it. Say it." Andy drained his muscatel and held the tumbler out. I poured it full. I took a drink myself.

"I can't help the way it comes out, Mitch. I'm a cop. Okay."

Francis poked his triangle head around one of the porch posts. He meowed and jumped into my lap. "Yeah, I own a Browning," I said. "The Bull was a son of a bitch, Andy."

"He was a son of a bitch and he was a cop. Jesus, I got it bad, Mitch. I tell you something. I started looking over the body. Out of reflex, doing the stuff a cop does. There were things that didn't make sense." Andy put his back against a post and relit the Corona. He talked to the sky, letting smoke drift away from his freckled face.

Francis purred. I covered a finger with muscatel and let him lick it. He preferred Montrachet.

"I'm talking to the doctor," Andy said, "and he says come over and look at this. So, he shows me the Bull's ankle. Damn thing broke in half. And I say, so what? And the doc rolls up Bull's pants leg. Four, five, maybe six big bruises, a couple of deep lacerations. Cuts and bruises. The fucking guy is playing the *Tell* overture on this ankle. Cuts and bruises on top of a jagged break. Then I get to thinking. Some guy is bouncing that fucking door up and down on Bull's ankle and it was a Ping-Pong game. Mashed the son of a bitch, then torqued it and broke it. Now why would a guy do something like that?" Andy stopped.

"I don't know. You tell me, Andy," I said.

"Oh, yeah," Andy said, "Bull had money on him and a big watch. No robbery."

"Maybe the guy gets scared. Loses his head."

"Right, sure," Andy said. "He gets so scared he hangs around bouncing a door up and down on Bull's ankle. Scared as a fucking snake." I poured muscatel. Andy had his tumbler out. I filled it. "I'm looking at the doc and he's looking at me. So we are thinking the same thing. Some guy hides in the garage and catches the Bull from behind and pops him on the ear, but not enough to really hurt him. Just a tap. Bop. Then the Bull is down and has his ankle in the door, or maybe the guy puts it in there for him. Then he shoots the Bull, or maybe he plays a game and breaks an ankle while the Bull is alive. Probably that, says the doctor. By the bleeding and bruising he can tell, he says. So we got some psycho? Or we got a guy with a bad grudge, some guy out of stir with a crease in his balls? I don't know, the doc says. I think we got somebody very cool here who knew just what he was doing and why. That, he says, is just what we don't know. We got the how. Now, he says, go home and make a list of people who hate Colonel Bull Granger enough to kill him. He snickers. Take a couple of pencils, he says. And he laughs."

The left-field lights went out suddenly, leaving Andy and me silhouetted by the yellow light smeared on the dirty blinds behind us. Francis rolled onto his back and put his feet out. I scratched and he purred and I drank muscatel and Andy smoked his cigar and the old guy who chalks the baselines came out of the press gate and got in his pickup and drove slowly up Sycamore and into the neon haze of West Douglas.

We were well into the gallon. "So...you made the list?"

"Maybe," he said. "I took a pint of rye on a ride around town anyway. You see, Mitch, there's something bothering me that makes sense, but I don't want it to. So I drink some rye, but it still makes sense no matter how hard I try. You want to know?"

"Sure," I said. "Spill it."

"Gimme another one first." I filled his tumbler and put some fresh ice on top. He shook it and looked through the glass with one eye shut. "I tell you a story," he said finally. He slurred a little. Not much. "I'm a kid, see. Pretty new on the force. I got this shiny tail and a nice, shiny new badge and a shiny new wife and a shiny new house and I figure I'm gonna make the whole fucking world safe for fucking Joe Citizen."

Andy gulped muscatel. He was getting shaky. He didn't drink much rye or muscatel and it was hitting him like a sledge on the forehead. "So I get on Vice. Hell, that's pretty good duty, they told me. You don't sit around a desk all day, and there's some action and a chance to make stripes and get somebody's attention. That's when I get hooked up with Bull. He's a detective. Real hotshot. We're all supposed to kiss his ass, I guess, and learn how to be tough. After a while, it's not so hot. He pushes people. He does it for kicks. For fucking fun. He's got us licking his boots and after a couple of years it's no fun being a cop anymore because we just sneak around town taking bribes and pushing people in the goddamn face. But I do it, goddamn it. I got kids and a new house and I'm making stripes and I'm getting to be a rotten cop. Something happens and I'm no fucking good anymore. I'm standing outside that Packard and there's blood everywhere and I realize it's been ten goddamn years and I'm rotten as he was because everywhere he went, there I was to pick up his shitass garbage. It makes me sick."

"Take it easy, Andy," I said.

"You know something, Mitch? I don't talk to Elaine. Come and go and go and come and go. Jesus, she can't even look me in the eye. I don't goddamn blame her." Andy pulled a rag end of coat from under himself and leaned back against the post. "I tell you another story. Another one. This one is a real beaut."

"Okay."

"I'm still in uniform. It's late in the Forties sometime. I'm either driving for the Bull or doing his backup work. Me and this other guy. So one day we are out cruising when the Bull spots this colored chick pays him protection. Hooker. She works down Grove Street and she's been up

and down more times than a yo-yo. You run her in and she
bounces back. But she don't get in any brushes, not in any
cons or heavy push=arounds. She just works her shit and
lays the bread on her pimp and the Bull. But the Bull
hassles her. This chick breaks a honky off in Bull's ear. It
hit him wrong, and he runs her in. We get down to the
station house and the Bull is in the lead car. Me and this
other guy are driving the chick. We don't know what to tell
her. So I get out and walk over to the station-house door
and wait. Bull opens the door of the squad car and yanks
this chick partway out. He gets her ankle in the fucking
door. She's screaming. And I'm standing there and the Bull
breaks her ankle. It makes me sick. And I just stand there.
I don't do anything. Nothing. Bull drags her upstairs and
beats the shit out of her and charges her with soliciting and
resisting. Jesus! I didn't say anything. But, you know, that
ain't really the story. All the time I'm standing there by the
station-house door, I can see Bull's wife and stepdaughter
on the sidewalk across the street going nuts. Carlotta and
Bull's wife. I forget her name. Anyway, they are crying
and carrying on, watching this whole scene. Now, you can
probably understand that when I see Bull's ankle busted off
in that car door, it leads me to think about Carlotta
Granger. How she stood there watching the Bull pull this
number on that colored chick and how her old lady took a
dive out that sixth-floor window. You see how I would start
thinking about that?"

"Andy, I can see how you would start thinking. You got
any official-type thoughts?"

"For starters, I don't figure a woman the size of Carlotta
Granger can hold that door shut and bounce on it hard
enough to break the Bull's ankle. I don't figure she can
handle a big 9mm automatic and shoot a man like that. I
could be wrong, but I don't think so." Then he said, "Hell
of a deal, we won the goddamn pennant. You know that?"

"Ten games," I said. I rocked back. "I killed the son of a

bitch. I got in the garage and broke his damn ankle and killed him."

"Jesus! You killed him for her? I mean you got in there and shot Bull because of Carlotta?"

"No," I said. "Not because of her. Because of this shit." I picked up my left hand and held out the bandage. Andy took hold of my forearm and ran his fat hand along my thumb.

"I wasn't paying any attention."

I leaned forward and bent my head down.

"He did that to you?" Andy said.

"Him or his buddies. You know about being pushed in the face, how there were all those nameless bastards pushed in the face? Hell, I was one of them. Only I pushed back."

"That's it? You pushed back."

"That's it. The fucking historical dialectic got the son of a bitch. Fucker ran head-on into the world historical spirit. And the world historical spirit was in a fucking bad mood." Andy laughed. "So what are you going to do, Andy?"

Andy shook his red head and stuck the wet cigar in his mouth. He picked up the pocket chess set and studied it. I handed him the book of Steinitz games.

"Yeah," he said. "Fucking Viennese Jew, right?" Steinitz was world champion for twenty years. Maybe the first you could really pick out who beat everybody in sight and didn't give a shit about anything except chess.

"Of course," Andy said, "I remember this game. It's the one where that son of a bitch moves his major pieces around for sixteen or eighteen moves and then gets them all back on the first row, except in different positions. His damn knights are on the wrong squares and the bishops are shitting their pants in the corners. His opponent didn't know what the hell to think. You remember what he said about all that?"

"Sure," I said. "'Why do you move that way?' the opponent asked. Steinitz glowered in unutterable contempt.

'You've seen a monkey observe a man wind a watch, I presume?'" Then Steinitz crushed his confused opponent, stalked from the club room in disgust, and wound up his old age in an insane asylum on Long Island, forgotten and abused. He bore bad, new ideas.

"Hell, I'm gonna go home," Andy said, "and kiss my wife. I'm gonna take a shower and see if I can't untangle all those goddamn pieces from the back row." He drained the muscatel from his tumbler and put it down on the railing. He scratched Francis on the back. "I feel like shit," he said. "I don't know what the hell to do with myself." He dropped the Corona in the catalpa beans and started down the stairs. "How did those guys get you anyway, you dumb shit?"

"Sunday evening," I said. "Out back of the office. I wasn't paying attention. Thought I had the world on a string, sitting on a rainbow. You know?"

"Sunday evening?" Andy said. He stepped back on the porch and stopped. He pushed a red wave from his eye. "Hey, Mitch. Jesus!" he said.

"Yeah?"

"Sunday evening. All evening. I was with those guys. Bull and Carl over at his place, playing poker like we do on the first Sunday of every month. This time they were talking about Frankie and one of their shipments and what the hell to do. They'd go in the other room and have these confabs, then come back and play some poker and drink. They didn't go anywhere. Gomez was driving a scrap truck to Texas. He left town Sunday afternoon."

I stopped thinking and let the pain and surprise settle. I felt drained and ugly. Carlotta. Jesus! On that Saturday afternoon we spent drinking, I told her about my life on the farm and about my mother and grandmother there. She knew I spent the early evening in the back of my office, sitting under the mimosa, smoking and relaxing. She knew about my run-in with Bull and about the threat I made to kill him if he touched me. When I phoned her Sunday evening she was out. She waited for me. Carlotta killed Frankie and she had killed the Bull and I was the puppet.

"You okay, Mitch?" Andy said.

"I'm just fine. I'm tired. I feel like the monkey who looks at a guy winding a watch."

"I know what you're thinking," he said. "It might not be."

"Yeah, it might not."

Andy started for his Plymouth. "We gotta get off the goddamn back row," he said. "You know, I got a feeling the cops are going to be stumped on this cop-killing deal." He got in the Plymouth and started the engine and drove slowly back to Maple and disappeared around the corner.

The night was finally still. I rocked and drank and smoked and played chess. At midnight Orion rose in the east above the gray outfield walls, above the line of boxcars on the Santa Fe tracks. I tensed when a white Cadillac stopped in front. There were two figures in the front seat and I could see the outline of Hook Nose on the passenger side. I pulled the Browning onto my lap and covered it with the dirty tea towel. I was drunk enough to believe that I could take Hook Nose out before he got up the steps.

Hook Nose had on the same pinstripe suit and white flower at the lapel. When he got to the steps he stopped and said, "You are a lucky punk." He threw two white envelopes my way. "Here," he said. "Count it."

I leaned down and picked up the envelopes. Inside was ten thousand in crisp hundred-dollar bills. Carlotta, I thought again.

Hook Nose turned. "The boss says this is your first and last adventure. You turn up again, anytime, anyplace, we put your fucking lights out, no questions." Hook Nose got back in the Cadillac. The car sped into the night.

I sat there all night, drinking muscatel. Just before dawn the Steffen's milkman strode briskly onto the porch with his rack of bottles and load of cottage cheese. He looked me over once and hurried away. Green gallon of muscatel, red-striped shorts, sweaty T-shirt, and Browning 9mm automatic pistol. The birds twittered for half an hour. The sun broke out. People went to work. Around ten, Mrs. Thompson poked her frazzled head around the corner of the porch. She saw me and hobbled up the steps. She wore the same dirty housecoat as always and her white hair stuck out in all directions. Her head bobbed nervously. Like a poor sparrow.

"Mr. Mitch! Mr. Mitch!" she screamed. Her eyes were halos of uncertainty. "Oh, Mr. Mitch!"

She handed me a pad and pencil. "What day is it?" she yelled.

I wrote: THURSDAY. DON'T WORRY. I'LL TAKE CARE OF YOU. SIT WITH ME?

Mrs. Thompson took the note, read it, and smiled. From a fold of her housecoat she took a big red apple and held it out to me with her withered, wrinkled hand. I took the apple, stood up, and pulled another rocker up next to mine. I got Mrs. Thompson to sit down and we rocked and I smoked and she looked serenely happy.

While we rocked the day became hot and dead still. I thought about a little piece of land for sale up by Thompson Falls, Montana, where a guy could fish for trout even with nine fingers. Then I thought about the bamboo fly rod I could finally afford. Last of all I thought about my ex-wife, Linda. When it was that hot and dead still, I always did.

SNAKE EYES

ONE

The first Saturday of May mamboed into my musty office and sashayed around the place, curvy and luscious as Rita Hayworth in a terry robe. I put some coffee on the hotplate to perk, then reclined in my captain's chair to let Rita walk her milky hands through my hair. I'd been away from the office for more than a week, and it felt wonderful to close my eyes as the scent of lilac, sunshine, and fresh coffee shoved aside the winter smell of disuse. Outside, robins rhapsodized, a few Fords and Chevys tooted and chugged, and Rita slid a hand around my wallet. When I opened my eyes, I stared at a stack of bills and collection notices piled neatly on my desk. The bills and collection notices stared back. I poured myself a hot cup of coffee and started feeling not-so-wonderful.

I sat back in the blackoak chair and slid a fingernail under the flap of the gaudiest notice. Inside the envelope cringed a flimsy slip of onionskin bordered in black, accoutered with nice, red letters, demure as a dame along the Pigalle. FINAL NOTICE, it screamed. I folded the slip and shoved it back into its cheap envelope with the window on the side. I closed one eye and shuffled the deck of notices and peeked at the top letter. The top letter was another cheap envelope with a window. I riffled the deck and cut to another cheap envelope with a window. When you're

1

thirty-seven years old and live all alone, you begin to think
of two-stepping with collection notices as a segue to Social
Security. I hurled the stack of notices to the back edge of
my desk and unfurled the sports page. The Bums and the
Yanks made me forget about Social Security.

Just then a voice boomed, "It's a matter of life or
death." I looked through the wavering coffee steam and
followed the sound of the voice to a velvety shadow hidden
behind the gauze of the screen door. The velvety shadow
merged finally into the oafish head and neck of Jake the
barber. Jake owned a two-chair shop next door to my office.

"Well, come on in," I said. I hadn't seen Jake in a
month, just the amount of time it had taken to grease the
wheels of my latest squeaky murder case and unravel the
bonds of a mucky trial at the county courthouse. The murder solved itself, as murders will, but the murder trial itself
had evolved into a nasty evil cavern. In the end, a crusty,
alcoholic D.A. had stumbled out of the cavern with a conviction in the buttonhole of his gabardine suit, saving my
own noodle from the soup. It had meant weeks on the
witness stand, a gun under the pillow at night. In the end,
a bad guy went to prison for thirty years. By the time he
got out we'd both be too old to make a fuss. In the meantime my pal Andy Lanham in Homicide still circled the
house late at night, and I hadn't seen Jake.

Jake tossed aside the screen and staggered in, trailing a
wake of cigar smoke. He wore a white barber's smock
above plaid pants and white orthopedic shoes. The shoes
were broken at the heels. His red face glistened with sweat
and turmoil. "I'm foiled," he said sadly. "I'm flat foiled."

"Someone run off with your Nat Cole collection?" I
asked.

"Worse."

"Leper take a bath with your wife?"

"Worse. Much, much worse." Jake rubbed a meaty

hand across his face, unlocked his knees, and fell straight down into a leather chair tipped against the wall. He focused his eyes and unholstered a pint of Overholt rye from his hip.

Jake and I went way, way back. We'd met five years before, when I was moving into my offices, deerstalker, magnifying glass, and all. We both toured the economic countryside sniping for rent payments, and we shared an interest in whiskey and baseball. Once in a while, we snuck out to fish for cats in a farm pond north of town. We were suitably philosophical and good-natured about misfortune. Each of us had killed Germans in the war and now dreamed about it at night. We talked a lot about baseball. We never talked about the war.

Jake proffered a glug of rye. I refused.

"You been sober lately, I hear," he said.

"Couple or three weeks. The trial."

"I hear there was some news about a gal with black hair, figure cute as a goldfish."

"News travels fast in a town like this," I said. I pushed a cigarette into my mouth and stoked. Jake smashed into the rye and grimaced as he swallowed, then ran a white arm of smock across his lips. There had been a black-haired gal, but there wasn't anymore.

"What the hell is that like? Being sober, I mean," he asked.

"Rough." I laughed. "Rough as hell. I see things clearly. Fuzz on a woman's leg, warts, harelips. I wake up before eleven. I talk to the mailman, change the oil in the car. Senses too sharp." I wanted to let the melodrama unfold in its own time, with its own internal force, the way the villain ties the heroine to the railroad tracks, the way the story unfolds every time. I smoked. Jake gulped the rye. In the rectangle of sky outside the screen door, a cobalt patch floated, one white cloud suspended in the patch. A green frieze of elm slanted into the cobalt patch. The green frieze danced in the breeze. Two cardinals played on silvered limbs of the elms, each bird chipping a staccato song into the wind. Time washed up on the sand.

Finally I said, "Okay, Jake, spill it. What's so bad it has you by the Overholt on a beautiful Saturday morning?"

"My boys are going to college," he said.

I nodded sympathetically. Jake relaxed. He possessed two sons, each a lopsided version of a rural lumberyard. They wrestled at East High, and I knew Jake wanted them to join the army like their old man had.

From his slouch, Jake dragged the Overholt to his mouth and sucked. "You been gone," he said. "I found out a week ago about this college thing. I know I gotta have some extra money. See, I can't send two dopes to college on what a barber makes in a two-hole crapper. No sir."

I smoked. Jake sat back to tell his tale. "Anyway, I find this ad in the newspaper. The state wants a barber to cut the hair of crazy people up in the state hospital. I figure this is going to be a way to make some easy money every Friday night. I check around, see. I gotta bid for the contract, so I get ahold of some guys I know down at the Moose Lodge and they tell me I can probably get the contract for forty cents a head. They got about two hundred crazies up there that need whacking every Friday. That ain't bad money for putting clippers to a wacko's head, right? I figure it'll take me about two minutes each. I'm up there a few hours and back home with the wife, no problem. So, I get the contract."

Jake shook free of the chair and stood in spiraling shafts of sunlight, touching a match to his wet, dead cigar, then chugging a dense smoke ring into Rita's lovely visage. Outside, a robin coughed. I listened and smoked.

"Anyway, I drive to the hospital last night after I close the shop. A matron who looks like Bela Lugosi meets me and takes me into the basement of a redbrick bunker and there they are, two hundred crazies lined up like ducks. Bellowing and slobbering like ducks, too, they were."

"It's only a haircut, right?" I said. My encouragement stumbled and fell into the gutter.

"Yeah," said Jake. "We got pinheads, cretins, freaks, dwarfs. Old ladies acting like flies without wings. The matron sets me up with a cane chair and a bottle of alcohol. What's the alcohol for, I ask. The matron grins and buzzes away. I start shaving. The third pinhead down the line, I shave through a wart and the blood starts to fly. Dwarfs and pinheads and cretins screaming bloody murder. The old dames spin like dervishes and shout. Me, I grab the alcohol and splash it on the wart on the pinhead. Rest of the night I'm burring heads and throwing alcohol. Took me twelve hours to earn eighty bucks. Knock off ten bucks for gas, ten bucks for whiskey, ten bucks for two pairs of scissors someone stole, and two hours lost at the shop. Some deal."

"How long does the contract last?" I asked.

Jake shoved the Overholt into the hip of his smock. He tossed me a wan smile. "Two years," he said. "Two long years."

"What happens if you don't show?"

"Not show up for the state contract?" Jake shook his head knowingly. "State license board sneezes on me and I'm covered with snot."

In the parking lot outside a muffled rumble pushed itself through the breeze. What seemed to be a cream and beige Packard crunched the gravel and stopped. A shawl of dust drifted into the sun. Somewhere, a sweet motor churned like the Gulf Stream off Cornwall.

"I gotta get back to the shop," Jake said. He stood with his back to me.

"You know, Mitch. The last guy had the state haircut contract was named Snively. I knew him. Had a shop down on Broadway. Couldn't ever figure what happened to the guy. I hadn't seen him at the lodge in a year." Jake went to the screen door and stood, exhaling smoke into the clear, blue atmosphere. He puffed dramatically, then leaned his head against the mesh. "That guy Snively. I saw him last night. I swear he was in line waiting for a shave." Jake went out. He pushed his head against the screen again, his face a Halloween mush of disillusionment.

"You believe this shit?" He laughed.

I settled back, thinking again about collection notices and black-haired women. A melodic creak of elm came in the spring breeze, then I heard, unmistakably, two thumps of very solid steel. Another velvety shadow appeared at the screen. This time the shadow was dark and narrow. Sunlight streamed around the shadow, lending form to the gestalt of an exclamation mark on a field of daisies. The door opened.

"Yes?" I said. It was a formal yes, out of place as a showgirl at the senior prom.

"Mr. Roberts?"

"You got it, pal. Come on in."

The exclamation point entered, wary and alert. The guy wasn't quite tall enough for oxygen at sea level, but he was tall. Everything about his form was trim and well-done, but there was nothing skinny about it. He wore a dark blue windbreaker and wool slacks. The slacks were expensive and held a crease that would have sliced sirloin. Half moons of sunlight danced diamond shapes on alligator shoes. The guy stared at a spot on the wall behind my left shoulder. I shrugged, trying to shake the stare away from the wall. The stare stayed put.

"You sure you got the right place?" My office was no place for wool slacks and alligator shoes. If the guy belonged to the Packard, then he didn't know that Packards didn't slum.

"You're Mitch Roberts, aren't you?"

"Yeah."

"Then I've got the right place." The guy stood. I sat. Then I saw the dog, motionless as malice aforethought. The dog didn't say anything, he just sat. One of the guy's thin hands held a leather circle. At the end of the circle a spike collar wound around the dog's neck. The dog was pure Doberman, brainy, sleek, and inscrutable. A brown wedge of fur melted from his chest into a sea of silky black, shiny as his master's alligator shoes. Two frozen eyes drilled from the dog's head into my throat. It was a short ride in the country, imagining several hundred sharp teeth tearing chunks of detective.

"You've got me at a disadvantage," I said. The guy gazed illogically. The dog did not.

"I'm Jules Reynard," he said.

His voice was all alto, calm and solid. Reynard stood unwavering as a taproot. He had square shoulders, a line of jaw shaped like a horseshoe. Beneath olive skin you could imagine fine, white bone. His hair was an ebony shell, gray at the ear. For the life of me the guy looked like Gary Cooper.

"Have a seat, Mr. Reynard."

He did, shuffling slowly with purpose. Reynard swished the leash. The dog moved with him like a disembodied shade. My throat began to sweat. From the barbershop erupted morning radio. Reynard sat and the dog descended to his haunches, two ears like radar spikes.

"What can I do for you, Mr. Reynard?"

"Have you made your decision?"

Reynard reached into the windbreaker and extracted a flashy gold case. He opened the case and took out a cigar the size of a poison dart. He lit the cigar, waiting for a reply. A reply didn't present itself.

"I trust your answer is yes, Mr. Roberts. I don't detect any reluctance in your demeanor."

"Forgive me, Mr. Reynard. My demeanor is confused

right now. Suppose you circle the bases, wave to the crowd, and step back to the plate.''

Reynard inhaled smoke with deliberation. A faint five o'clock shadow dusted his jaw. I supposed it was a permanent fixture. "I don't believe I understand," he said. His stare grew its own whiskers.

"Look, Mr. Reynard. I really don't know who you are, what you want, or where we go from here. Maybe we'd better get in step before we scuff up our new shoes.'' Next door, I heard Jake singing to a Nat Cole number.

"You didn't get my letter, then?'' Reynard asked.

I leaned over the desk and shuffled the collection notices again. A second shuffle produced a rag-weave envelope without a window. Serious swirls of black ink had melted into the rag weave, letters the size and shape of King John's signature on the Magna Carta.

I put the letter down carefully. The return address read *Black Fox Ranch. Augusta, Kansas.* "What does it say?'' I asked.

Reynard relaxed. The dog stayed put. "The letter tells you I'll be by on Saturday. It says something important is bothering me and that I want to discuss retaining your confidential services. It asks you to call me if the time is inconvenient.'' Reynard stabbed an ironic period to the words.

"Why me?'' I asked.

"I've been in the hospital during the past weeks. There has been little to do save play chess and think. I recall an article in the local newspaper that mentioned your name as a detective and a witness in a local murder case. There was mention of your competence, but little else. It seemed enough to go on for the meantime.'' A faint smile snared the edge of Reynard's mouth and tugged. "Perhaps there is more than one Mitch Roberts in Wichita. Perhaps you don't read your mail.''

"I've taken some time off,'' I said.

"I don't blame you. A six-week murder trial is withering fire. I must say, it looks as if you hold up well."

"I've been in withering fire plenty. I never hold up, particularly not well. I was lucky."

"Nevertheless," Reynard said.

"Nevertheless," I said back. Reynard sat, thinking. Uncertainty blundered around the room.

"Mr. Roberts," Reynard said at last. "I've lived a long time not needing a private detective. Most people do. Under those conditions of life, there are no criteria for choosing one when it comes up. I saw your name, and it stuck. Do you have any objections?"

"I'm sorry, Mr. Reynard. I don't object if you read every newspaper in Duluth. It's just that right now I can't take on any cases. I'm worn down and tired and behind in every category from repossessing a Dodge to serving an eviction notice. I haven't washed my dishes in six weeks and the moths have subdivided my wardrobe. Whatever problems you have, Mr. Reynard, you'll have to take them down the block. I can recommend some good people."

I felt bad saying the words. I'd stared into the gullet of a fat lawyer. The gullet called me liar and two-bit. At the end of the trial a black-haired woman had folded the deal and sold her seat. Any day I expected Satan to follow suit. It was no excuse to snap at Reynard.

"Look, Mr. Reynard," I said. "You may have a problem I could help with, I don't know. I know I've got half a dozen steady clients. These guys keep me in white bread and cheap beer. I serve their papers, repossess their cars, find their wives. They send me a check, small and comforting. If I didn't have those clients, I wouldn't make enough money to spit at a crippled newsie."

Reynard jerked the leash. The dog went on to its belly. For a while we sat surrounded by sunlight, hearing the cardinals and the Chevys, Jake caterwauling in his barbershop. Reynard seemed to look at the floor.

"Please hear me out," he said. The quiet drowned his voice.

"You want some coffee?" I said. Reynard nodded slowly. I handed him a cup and he handled it unsteadily. "All right, Mr. Reynard. Shoot."

He sipped the coffee. "Have you ever had your life come apart?" he asked.

"But yes," I said. "Three or four times if you don't count finding out I couldn't hit a curveball."

"I'm fifty-four years old. I've just spent two weeks in the hospital. I've been ill for six months. I may regain my strength, but the doctors say it will take some time. Maybe never, they say." Reynard waited for me to speak. It didn't seem necessary. "You see, I've controlled my own life, achieved a measure of success, made some money. But in the last year I've lost some bets. I don't mind losing on a square table and right dice."

"One dot short on the dice these days?"

"One short, one too many. What is the difference?"

I lit a Lucky. "Go on," I said.

"One of my businesses is out of hand. I want you to find out why."

"I know a good accountant," I said. "I imagine you do, too."

"It's gone beyond that point," Reynard said. He rested his hand on the dog's ear. A fly buzzed around the dog's snout, but there was no flinch. "There's more."

"Deal it up," I said.

"The illness was arsenic."

"Someone tried to kill you?"

"Possible. Probable, moving to likely. Arsenic is hard to pick up from a dish of strawberries."

"I understand the best recipes leave it out."

Ash drifted from Reynard's cigar. A wad of it dropped to the floor. It was a curious display for a guy in creased wool pants and alligator shoes. Reynard puffed gently, savoring the smoke. I sat thinking, not savoring a thing.

Finally, Reynard said, "There've been some personal problems. Problems of the kind one doesn't admit. Contorted things. You remember, Mr. Roberts, I asked you if your life had ever come apart?"

"I remember."

"I need some patchwork on my life."

I sighed. The sigh hit bottom. I poured some coffee and motioned to Reynard for a refill. Nothing budged, not even the drizzly stare he had affixed to the wall. A vague weariness wiggled to the surface of the past six weeks and poked its head above the slime. In six weeks I'd spent sixteen dollars on bad courthouse coffee and earned half that in fees. At this point, life's problems were bad breath on a first date and the only mouthwash was real money.

"Let's see," I said. "Skip tracing is twenty-five a day. Repossession without a gun, twenty-five a day. Service of process, ten bucks a pop, plus gas. Let's just say I haven't put a price on human patchwork."

"Ten thousand dollars," said Reynard. "Ten thousand now, a bonus of ten thousand when you're done. I cover all expenses, no questions asked. I've got the money."

I relaxed into a surprised clump. Rita swished my way and rubbed the fuzzy, cashmere curves of her sweater against my forehead. Her breasts thumped inside the fuzz. She roped her long red hair around my neck, giving me a good, long whiff of perfume. Four shiny nails scratched my chin, then lifted it toward two lips the color of sweetheart roses. We kissed. Rita struggled with the wallet. I devoured her next twenty thousand kisses. Reynard stood and switched the dog's leash. The dog rose.

"What's a life worth, anyway?" I said.

"Precisely," said Reynard. "Perhaps you can work mine into your fee schedule."

"I see your point." A man could fit plenty of white bread and bad beer into twenty thousand dollars.

Reynard walked slowly to the screen door. "I'd like you to come out to the ranch tonight. Black Fox Ranch—east of Rose Hill, south of Augusta. It's easy to find, check a county map. About eight o'clock?"

"I'm not making any promises."

"Fine," Reynard said. "We'll have dinner, play a game of chess, perhaps." Reynard pushed clumsily through the door. There was a solid, steel thud, then the sound of the Packard toiling in gravel.

Saturday devolved into repossessions. I paid some bills. Later, I drove through deserted streets to my rooms in an old Victorian on Sycamore. I waltzed with the dirty dishes and took a nap. In one dream, Rita cooed a siren song, washed whirling to a rocky deep.

TWO

Magenta sun swept my three rooms, shafts and streaks breaking through stained glass, glass shimmering like bloodstone. I lay on an old brass bed looking past the V-shape of my feet at the rough, triangular head of Francis the cat, who sat preening himself for an evening on the town. Francis stroked his tongue along a gray flank, then pecked at a hairy slab of right ear. Beyond my feet, beyond the gray head of Francis, wind and sun played tag in an elm current. Limbs bumped rhythmically like a steady, green symphony. The dust in the air vibrated. Except for the sound of children far away, the silence itself seemed deep as the green symphony outside. Francis rolled onto his back, stretched his stomach, and yawned.

I pushed a pillow against the bedstead and sat upright. My rooms wound through the bottom of an old Victorian on Sycamore Street, across from a minor league ballpark. I'd lived here since coming home from the war. The unconcern of a Kansas City slumlord made it appear as if I could live here until Yorick himself won the Irish Sweepstakes. Or at least until the Athletics won the pennant. My kitchen was full of muscatel empties; the main sitting room and bedroom was divided from the kitchen by an oak bookcase and stained glass window. The room itself was airy, full of the disheveled remnants of chess games, ball scores,

and fishing tackle. Late at night I enconced myself in a
gray overstuffed chair haloed in the aromatic gleam of a
brass lamp, smoking Latakia in a calabash, playing the
games of Alekhine or Capablanca. The large room let into
an alcove, with an antique oak table and my unique collection of dead cacti. Bay windows encircled the alcove. It
was through the bay windows that the green symphony
leaked.

Time, dense as regret, passed through these rooms. I
dozed and dreamed, trying to suffocate the memory of the
murder trial and the black-haired woman. Nothing seemed
to work.

After a while, I rose and poured a glass of muscatel from
the last gallon in the refrigerator. I stared through the back
screen, watching the wind in the weedy backyard, the
chickens and the rabbits in the hutches, looking down the
tangled alley that disappeared down a row of Victorians
like mine. A rickety staircase ascended from my porch to
the rooms of Mrs. Thompson, an old lady who lived upstairs.

I finished the muscatel. While I showered, the memory
of the black-haired woman revealed a soft line of throat,
mahogany hair lying against a white sheet, fibrous as an
exotic plant at the bottom of the sea. The steam cleared.
I shaved and washed behind my ears, then took a look
inside the bathroom closet. There were a few pairs of
cords, some shiny dress pants, half a dozen wool shirts,
Red Wing boots, hiking vests, and a few tweed coats.
Little enough. I put on a clean flannel shirt, a pair of
brown cords, and a tweed coat. There wasn't much
choice. I brushed my teeth and combed the ash-blond
mop that passed for hair.

I was ready for dinner with Jules Reynard. Save for
the lack of a tulip in my lapel, I thought I deserved a
C+ at least. I went through the back door, leaving the

ghostly woman with the black hair and the murder trial behind.

I went down the steps to the rabbit hutch. Mrs. Thompson huddled by it, covered by her gray housecoat, her white hair rippled by wind as if an electric current had passed through it. She was short, hunched, and her movements were sparrowlike, stuttered, and cluttered by indecision.

"Mr. Mitch," she screamed. "Oh, Mr. Mitch!" Mrs. Thompson was nearly deaf. "They've got two new babies!"

Two small rabbits slept in the hutch, patched white and black both. I held Mrs. Thompson by the shoulders, then put my mouth to her ear.

"What are their names?" I yelled.

Mrs. Thompson recoiled. She stood, seeming almost to fall. Finally she said, "Faith and Hope."

I winked, got into the Fairlane, and started the engine. I waved to the old lady. She poked slices of carrot at the noses of the sleeping babies.

I rumbled through alley chuckholes and drove east on Maple Street, away from the setting sun. The Black Fox covered six hundred acres on the near edge of the Flint Hills, twenty miles southeast of Wichita. I fished the creeks and farm ponds in that country, and knew a country lane that I used as a shortcut. The lane wound through dense hedges along a river bottom. Five miles from town I rolled into farmland crowded by oak and elm scrub. The road descended through a series of creek bridges, iron monuments built by the CCC during the Depression. The thicket thickened gradually, until the spark of spring stars dwindled to scattered streaks obscured by shade. Frogs and crickets clattered. Puffy clouds darkened. In the deep, the lane bordered a meandering river surrounded by sycamore and oak. In that place there was no light or sound, save for the frogs and the crunch of tires on gravel. I flicked on the radio, filling the Fairlane with yellow glow and Artie Shaw. Washington Irving disappeared into the fog. Then the road ascended, turned south, and at the same time became a black macadam strip.

The strip sped past widening swales of green winter wheat. The wheat drifted in the wind. I let cigarette smoke into the evening, thinking about Jules Reynard and the curious problems he had announced. He spoke of his own murder in the calmest terms, approaching it like a chessboard. I had felt uncomfortable in his presence. The sound of his money had made me feel worse. It was the sound of money seeping into the crevices of a man's soul, corroding it like poison. In the detective business, there is money that obliges a good job and money that obliges a good cry. But Reynard's money obliged too much.

Wheat fields evolved into pasture. Pasture rolled and fell, and in the declivities cattle grazed. Spring stars—Regulus, Leo, Spica, and Pollux—popped into focus, becoming points on a field of cobalt and mauve. Lights flickered in the distance at the Black Fox. I swung the car into a cute lane and drove along more pasture. A three-strand white fence separated the lane from manicured farm buildings. Quarter horses munched prairie grass. The lane wove around a horseshoe lake that wrapped around a large house. The house was L-shaped, brick and wood. I parked in a copse of Scotch pine and jumped out of the car. I lit a Lucky. The front door was big and heavy. There was a knocker, and I knocked.

A cowboy opened the door. He was average size, with striking, angular features. His arms and hands were big. He wore a blue work shirt, chinos, cowboy boots, and a dark blue vest. He stood there in the Scotch pine shadow.

"I'm Mitch Roberts," I said. "Here to see Mr. Reynard."

"Right," he said. "Come on in." The cowboy flicked

a hand at a Doberman. Wind creased the cowboy's blond hair.

I went into a room the size of Cleveland. One whole wall was glass. Past the glass was the horseshoe lake. The lake glowed, lamplight dancing on the surface. Behind the lake, pasture waded uphill into a purple sunset. A Hogan three-iron away from me, carpeted stairs descended to a sunken area. In the sunken area were two zebra couches and a few stiff chairs, a mahogany table, decanters, and a chess set in onyx. On one wall was a well-stocked bar, the bar snaking along to what looked like a conservatory. The conservatory was dark, but the darkness emitted a smell of damp palm. Silver-barreled lamps cast a dim glow. In one cool circle of lamplight sat a black Doberman, head on paws, eyes alert and focused. Except for the Doberman, the place looked like Rick's Café American.

I followed the cowboy and the Doberman to a glass door. The cowboy opened the glass, and I went out onto a flagstone patio littered by iron tables, lounges, and deck chairs. The patio followed the lake's contour, five feet above the surface.

The cowboy said, "You'll find Mr. Reynard at the end. Follow the blue lights." The cowboy went inside. I walked to the edge of the patio, followed the blue deck lights, and stood at the last iron table. Reynard sat, hands placed calmly. He wore a black turtleneck and the same wool slacks. A mild breeze ruffled his black hair. In the evening light, he made an articulate form. The smoke from his black cigar leaked into the wind.

"Good evening, Mr. Roberts," he said.

I sat down. "How long have you been blind?" I asked.

Reynard's free hand fell to the flank of the Doberman. The Doberman crouched, the leash tangled at his neck.

"I wondered how long you'd take," Reynard said. "Tell me about the evening. What does it look like?"

"It's lovely," I said. A whippoorwill sang.

"No," Reynard said. "What do you see?"

"The wheat is liquid jade. The lake is black, wheat reflections and the wheat itself rising up from the pasture into a sunset gone gold and mauve. Then a line of elm in the west, a few stars twinking."

I smoked. Reynard was quiet.

"You're good. Why the game?" I asked.

"I pretend," Reynard said. "When others know, it twists things out of shape. When did you figure it out?"

"Two doors slammed when you drove up to my office. I thought it odd that only one person came in. Your stare just missed my face. It got to me after a while. You let cigar ash drop."

Reynard smiled as if the smile escaped from somewhere deep. He faced the receding sun, one purple gash illuminating the square set of his face. I gathered the empty liquidity of his sight. There was no injury or disease in the eyes, just cold pales of brown. Each movement for him was a measured volume of uncertainty and dread. He poured the volume into a beaker of his own needs. Whippoorwills hid in the prairie grass, singing sadly.

Reynard spoke. "I concentrate on your voice. I direct my own movement to the sound. It's not perfect, of course. You detected it quite quickly."

"It wasn't that easy. How did you do the chair?"

"My secret."

"Anyway, Mr. Reynard, it wasn't that easy. The gaze and the dog and the car doors made me wonder. Nothing special. I offered you a cup of coffee and you didn't move a muscle."

"Oh," Reynard said. "Something small always spoils the game. I can't tell if you don't apologize and fumble. Most people do. Why not you?"

"No reason."

The cowboy moved behind us. He set down two glasses of beer. He went away.

"I trust you're a beer drinker," Reynard said.

"Cheap beer and white bread," I answered. Reynard held his glass. I clinked it, and we drank.

"I've been blind for a few years. At first shapes and now just shapes of shapes. Diabetes. It's been part of my problem lately."

I pulled at the beer. Going down, it was like silk along a woman's leg, slick and shiny. Jeweled rays played in the glass, reflecting an evening sky itself silken; lapis lazuli edged by black elms; mauve rays snaking along a ragged lee of horizon; fireflies blinking above the lake. A single damask swath hovered above the treeline. The barrel lamps inside the house threw a burning shaft into the fluid night.

"You remember being sighted?" I asked.

"No," he said. That was it. A "No" welled up from the pit, a maelstrom of an answer. Reynard drank his beer.

"Well, you do fine. You had me fooled."

"Tiresias keeps me headed in the right direction." Reynard patted the dog's head. "I've blind eyes. He, a blind soul, blind to the world. He leads, I follow. Blind and sighted leading the sighted and blind. That's my secret of the chair."

Reynard ran a hand through the dog's ears. The dog flicked his head, ears perked.

"You saw Creon inside," Reynard said. "They're killers."

"They roam the place?"

"At night," answered Reynard. He restarted his cigar. I smoked a cigarette.

"I hope you're hungry," Reynard said. "I'm serving a small fillet, mushrooms, green salad. I'm afraid it's nothing fancy. I've got some good whiskey." I nodded, thinking how stupid that was.

The cowboy served with a tray. There was a bottle of whiskey and a pitcher of ice water on it. Blue lamps rimmed the patio, each dipping a reflection into the water. I ate the steak quickly, a good fillet done medium-rare. I poured two whiskeys, and we drank together.

"I've made a lot of money in my time, Mr. Roberts," Reynard said. "I made most of it before I became blind. I don't want to lose it now. That's why you're here. You won't be underpaid, but it could be dangerous."

Reynard sipped his whiskey. Now his voice was a lower register, more a growl, miles of trudging in mud behind it. The change startled me.

"Suppose you tell me how it is."

"I don't let jakelegs fuck with me," he said. "I don't like it. We are supposed to be businessmen, not thugs." Reynard stopped his voice at a dull roar. He seemed embarrassed at his anger. He fell back in his chair, forming his fingers into a steeple, very businesslike. He went on. "I'm a businessman. I raise cattle here, good quarter horses. I've got some oil on the other side of the section. There's no problem with the money right now. Under these conditions, it makes itself."

"I've never had that happen," I said. It was true. For me love and money were the same. Difficult to get and hold on to.

"It hasn't always been that way," Reynard said in reply. "Suppose we take a walk. We'll talk. I'll show you the place. Pour me a whiskey, will you?" I poured.

Reynard held the leash in his left hand, carried the whiskey in his right. Tiresias led the way along the patio, above the water, then down a slope past the edge of the ranch. We slowly descended a hillock, stone steps cut into the hill, stone walls on either side of the steps. At the bottom was a corral. A few horses grazed at troughs.

"Good-looking, don't you think?"

"Very," I said, leaning an arm on the fence. I hopped the fence and the horses grew alert.

"Get back here," Reynard said. I hopped the fence again. "These quarters aren't broke. None of them are. They'll knock you down as soon as spit." Each horse was sleek and strong-looking.

"When I was in the hospital two of my horses died. Throats torn, slashed." Tiresias led us around the rim of the corral. An open-faced shed held tack and hay.

"I ate a bowl of berries three weeks ago and damn near died. That's when they hit the horses."

"Day or night?" I asked.

"Had to be night. Colby would have been here otherwise."

"Colby?"

"The man who let you in."

"Colby handle the dogs?" I asked.

"Same as me," Reynard answered. He shook the leash, and we sauntered into open prairie, rolling past farm ponds like shiny nickels in a velvet glove.

"Look, Mr. Reynard. I'm not a bodyguard. With your money you could hire plenty of muscle. For that, I don't have the guts or the stamina. I couldn't sucker-punch Little Bo Peep."

Reynard said nothing; we walked.

I said, "I drink too much. I don't do long-haul observation. I get bored too easy." Behind us, the lights of the ranch dove into tunnels of sunset. The Flint Hills grass rustled like woman's hair on a clean sheet. The house had a thick, shingle roof shadowed by the pines. Otherwise, there were no trees on the prairie, just the line of elm and oak toward town.

I went on. "Look, Mr. Reynard. You don't pop into my office and offer me twenty thousand for police work. You never mentioned the police."

"No police," he said.

I followed Reynard along barbed-wire fence. Black Angus strolled dumbly. Tiresias tugged Reynard along a path worn in the pasture, threading the dark and the prairie. Wind whooshed through the Scotch pines. We were in front of the house. I sensed something else tugging at Reynard, something strong and lethal like pride, the inability to come to terms with the contortions of fate.

"Let's go inside," Reynard said. "Maybe I can get through this with a brandy."

I followed him back into the huge living room, then down the carpeted stairs. The room breathed inaudibly. Tiresias curled up on a white shag rug. Between the zebra couches stood the onyx chess set, and a decanter of brandy. Reynard fumbled for the decanter.

"Help me with this," he said. I poured two brandies. A torque of shadow enveloped the room.

"I'm a gambler," Reynard said. "I make money because there are more ways to make seven than to make six. I started out with the Canyon Club."

Cheap detectives don't go to the Canyon Club. At the Canyon a man was expected to fade ten dollars without breaking a sweat.

"I've heard of it," I said.

"Well, that's me. Part of me, anyway. Enough to make a difference. I buy booze at two bucks, break the bottle into twenty shots, and sell the shots for two bucks each. Overhead is protection and good food. I make a tidy profit. I've got a wire service on Douglas Street above a bowling alley. We pay for a few good dance bands." Reynard took out a cigar. I lit it for him.

"Somebody is skimming," he said.

"You want me to find out."

"I want you to find out."

"Suppose it's just bad business."

"You bet," he said. "And my horses are committing suicide."

"I see what you mean."

"Look, Mr. Roberts. The liquor and dice business isn't crowded anymore. We've got some small fry around town running games in the back room. But after the war, the boys in Kansas City consolidated. For the last ten years the name of the game has been business, not muscle. Just a dance band, some green felt, and a few bucks to the widows and orphans. You get it?"

"In spades," I replied.

"Since I've been sick, it's been tough keeping track. I can't involve the boys in Kansas City and I can't involve the police."

"What's your hunch?"

"Gus Canard manages the Canyon. He bags the money, makes a set of books at the club. Colby picks the books up and we go over them every week. We make a second set for the government, then bank the money. A skim could take place anywhere down the line."

"Colby?"

"I don't see how. He's been with me since the war."

"Canard?"

"Anywhere. Gus could be on the take. One of the dealers. Hell, it could be the damn busboy."

"You talk this over with Canard?"

"No."

"How do you propose I get close to the operation?" I hoped this question would end the game. The Canyon was downtown in an uptown world, white napkins and a gold ring. I smoked for a while, watching the night brew a concoction. Tiresias slept, one flank harrumphed by doggie dreams.

"Stickman job open at the club. You're a natural," Reynard said.

"But that puts me out of circulation. Those steady clients, you remember?"

"How much circulation can you get from twenty thousand?"

I lit a wooden match. Sulfur flared.

"You said you had some personal problems, Mr. Reynard. Skimming isn't personal." I touched the match to another cigarette. Reynard sat inside a block of steely emptiness. He blew smoke into the lamplight.

"I've married a young woman. I did it at the time my sight was going, perhaps out of fear of the dark. There are worse things. This is one of them."

I didn't speak.

"Her name is Agnes. She spends her time in town, at the Canyon. Making a fool of both of us. She comes and she goes and she changes clothes. She acts stupid and gay. I want her stopped."

"It's hardly my line, Mr. Reynard. Grown-up people have a way of going off."

"You know what I mean," he snapped. I poured two more brandies. Reynard gathered himself and maneuvered to the chess set. He moved a white king pawn two squares. "Tell me your move when you make it. At times, I'll ask you to describe the position. I may ask a question."

In five moves the game became a King's Gambit. I offered a pawn, mucking the position.

"I told you," Reynard said. "I want my life repaired. It's worth money to me. You tell me about Agnes, and I'll do the rest."

I stood. "We'll finish the game later, Mr. Reynard. For now, it sounds all right to me. Let me sleep on it?"

"Of course," Reynard answered. "But tomorrow."

I went out the big doors into the *whoosh* of pine, the smell of grass and cattle. A wind chime tinkled. Two canoes by a boathouse on the lake clicked sterns. I got into the Fairlane and lit a cigarette and sat smoking. A shadow pressed against the glass in the conservatory. The shadow moved deliberately back into the dark and silence of the palms.

I backed the Fairlane around a purple martin house and into the lane. I drove north on the black macadam to the main highway to town. The shortcut hit bottom alone.

THREE

I drove slowly to the eastern rim of town. A pale moon shed metallic dust on the big houses of the rich, on palaces full of good scotch and hot gossip. Eastborough dozed painlessly in the dim glow; huge lawns rolled away to an organdy maze of maple and pin oak. The sky blinked and grew opaque, roads and streets drew into narrow lanes lined by honeysuckle and spirea; in the soundless evening there came the *plop* of tennis ball and racket, a sound as clear and unmistakable as money changing hands. I never felt cheated driving among the houses of the rich. I always imagined that behind the pearly gleam of wealth there lurked a savage and uncompromising poverty of spirit, a sordid tale or two, the final shaggy skeleton whipping in the closet breeze. I knew it wasn't true, but I never felt cheated thinking it.

At Hillside I cruised along the ups and downs of College Hill, draining myself through the sieve of dwindling traffic, smoking my cigarette, imagining being keelhauled by a wad of dollar bills along an ocean of crap tables. The wind grieved for winter, the shadows ducked along the brick street. Trees swirled. I went south toward the Canyon Club.

Anxiety found a peephole and peeped. I'd done worse than work for bootleggers and gamblers. Kansas had banned the open saloon in 1862. You could get a glass of beer

downtown until midnight, you could buy a half-pint of rye
in a shack across the tracks, or you could make your own.
What you couldn't get was a square drink and a good steak,
maybe a dance with a blonde not your mother. There are
some people who don't mind drinking weak beer in a cold
tavern. And there are some people who don't mind buying
rye from an Okie in bib-overalls. But there are a few who
would just as soon drink French wine and listen to the
accordion with the lamps low. But a nightclub was an open
saloon and against the law. As the man says, Kansas staggers to the poll to vote dry.

I'd known for years that small nightclubs flourished in
the cracks between law and order. Now I knew that Jules
Reynard ran the Canyon with help from Kansas City. I
didn't bother to fault him for it. If the people wanted a
steak bad enough to corrupt the police, then let them corrupt the police. Money had greased the law since time began and it wasn't up to me to hatchet reality. Time would
end before they stopped making dice.

At a roostertail on Hillside I stopped at a shabby hut and
bought a pint of vodka. I put the vodka in the glove box,
then drove farther into the purlieu of south Wichita. South
from College Hill, Wichita levels to a demented straggle
of clapboard and tarpaper, traps slapped together willy-
nilly during the war, and allowed to wind down like cheap
clocks. This part of town was full of Okies, rusted Plymouths, abandoned appliances, dense air smelling of garbage
and rendered guts. Between goat bleats, you could hear
chickens squawk.

The Canyon Club sat on a small knoll at one dead end
of Hillside, overlooking a snipe of brick street. A dirty
creek meandered in the thicket behind the knoll and there
was the sound of water creeping through brush. A gravel
drive circled the knoll. I ascended the gravel and drove
into the parking lot. The lot was big and dark, cut into the
side of the knoll, which rose above the pavement into a

wad of blackjack oak and wild sycamore. Wind rustled in the new green of the oak.

I parked and smoked. Beyond the slender line of broken horizon, a spring storm snapped at the edge of the Flint Hills. Thunder barked far away, and behind the thunder, anarchic flashes bloomed. A seared aroma of ozone emerged. The storm made a molecular progress across the prairie. I thought about hail above the Black Fox Ranch, wind raging through wheat, Reynard blinded to the violent scene. I put the vodka in my back pocket and got out of the car.

The Canyon Club was a block of pink decked out as a Moorish fortress. Behind the block, beneath the shadow of the knoll, the kitchen area was another pink block. Above the kitchen was a limestone office, reached by a stone stair rising from the parking lot to a side door above. The door was dark, stitched with shadows moving with the wind.

Before the war this block of pink had gone by a dozen names. Hades, Flamingo, The Inferno, and The Oasis. Tough guys came and went like Detroit models, worn out before new. In the gloom, I could see enameled scenes of camels, twisted palms, dancing girls. The Canyon was what the boys in Kansas City considered a small club. For Wichita, it was big league all the way. It was decently run and the food was good. There were enough fist fights to make the place entertaining but not too many to scare the girls. There'd been a shooting and a dollop of knifings, but nothing to worry the police. A nice place to go to after church.

I organized for action and walked the gravel path to the kitchen. A shaft of white light pierced the door frame. From inside I heard scrambled voices, the clash of pots and pans. A silly scream escaped. I poked my head around the open jamb to see five or six figures in smocks scurrying about a tomfoolery of aluminum cookery and chopping blocks. I leaned against the door and waited. Beside a row of stoves, a Syrian bent above blue flame, frying enough garlic to choke Mussolini. The Syrian twirled a cleaver with his hefty arm and smacked the blade into the back of a whole chicken. The chicken cracked. Other dark figures in white made salads, washed dishes, bided time, and smoked.

Maye came out of a walk-in freezer. She was small, warped, encased in flour. Her thin body had disappeared nside a cook's apron and gloves. On her feet were black galoshes. With her back toward me she pounded veal. I waited some more. As she turned to wash her mallet, I caught her eye and pushed a finger to my pursed lips. Deliberately, Maye inched to the door with a puzzled look draped on her thin face. Without concern, she leaned against the door, on the other side of the wall from me, hidden for a moment by the wall and the harsh light. I heard her humming softly.

"Mr. Roberts," she sang. A above high C. "What you doing down here with the colored folks?"

"Can I talk to you, Maye?" She turned to the light. "Can you take a break?" I asked.

Maye spread her hands on hips in mock consternation, a wilted look of bewilderment spreading slowly over the sunken features, hollow black eyes, rare cheeks, flat nose. Her eyes glowed with righteous fun. I knew her to be stern as a Mormon tooth fairy, understanding as a whore's midwife.

"You come at the right time," she said. "Dinner is about over. I pound this veal, here. Then I be out."

"Don't say anything, Maye," I said.

"You think I'm a fool?" she said. She grinned all over. "I'll be under the cutbank."

She turned and crossed to the chopping block. I waited by the Fairlane, hidden in shadow.

I'd been hired by Maye after the war to locate her missing husband. I was a kid, hungry for work, and took the job because I liked Maye and because my phone was silent as a sphinx. For ten years, Maye had saved money, and with her four hundred dollars she wanted me to find Sonny, who'd disappeared behind the Blue Light Lounge in St. Louis, Missouri.

I spent one sultry month in St. Louis, searching union halls, poolrooms, rooming houses, and jails. I bribed a dame in the driver's license bureau, and spent time praying in the Salvation Army by the levee. Time and money ran out. But Maye begged me to keep on and sent me fifty dollars. I gave half of it to a pimp in East St. Louis who knew the dives. I spent a hundred dollars of my own turning over rocks in rescue missions. Finally, I tried the pauper lists of a dozen small towns up and down the Mississippi.

They'd buried Sonny in Belleville, Illinois. Sonny shared ground with dogs, murderers, and orphans. I photographed the grave and ordered a copy of the death certificate. I showed them to Maye and she cried quietly in the small parlor of her shack in the north end. Then she promised me vegetables from her garden: okra, beans, squash, and corn. Now I'd drink whiskey in the evenings and help her work the dirt, digging rows for corn, chopping weeds, swatting flies, hoping for a row of shade against the dreadful yellow sun looping in the west. Maye and I were strangely bonded. She didn't complain about the whiskey. I didn't complain about the snuff she took.

Behind me an arc flashed in the blackjack. Maye appeared, black face smeared with flour and sweat, stripping down her work gloves. She took her time with a cigarette.

"Now what is so important, child?" she said. Maye breathed in the night air. She unwrapped her hair from a cloth and shook herself free from work. "And secret, too. My, my."

I extracted the vodka. Maye swiveled her eyes and drew their dark cavities to the club office. She scuttled back a step and grabbed the vodka. Maye shoved the bottle under her apron and motioned me to follow.

We hiked through a clutch of Packards up a slow rise of knoll, along a path worn into sycamore and hackberry. For a minute we scuttled through thicket buried in shaded undergrowth. Rain smell moved on the wind. A small clearing appeared on a promontory above the pink blocks of the club, and Maye spread herself in the shadow of a blackjack. She opened the vodka, taking an ounce of the shining fluid. It looked like liquid moonglow going down. Below, dance music drifted in darkness. There were the sounds of the kitchen, a rumble of thunder far away. Maye passed me the vodka.

"What *have* you done, Mitch Roberts?" she asked.

I relaxed beneath the oak. The air was lazy and thick with storm. In the parking area, a couple staggered against a black car. Angry voices hammered the night, then the couple entered the car and drove away. I lit a cigarette and turned to the vodka.

"Nice place you got here, Maye," I said.

"I'm in the kitchen ten hours. I come up here to sit and think. Right now I'm so tired they'd have to carry me through the Pearly Gates." Maye took the vodka. Her eyes scanned the outline of the Canyon Club. "You didn't come up here to chat, did you, Mitch Roberts?"

"No, Maye. I didn't."

Maye hit the vodka and passed the bottle. "That's good," she said. "Now, what's wrong?"

"Nothing wrong, Maye. I know you've worked here for quite a while. I want you to answer some questions. It could mean a lot to me. I won't tell anyone."

"All right, Mitch Roberts," Maye said. She settled against the rough bark of the blackjack. "You ask," she said.

"What can you tell me about Jules Reynard?"

"We don't see him anymore, Mitch. He gone blind. Not many know that, but I do."

"What's he like?"

"Very quiet man. He seems to me like a mirror in a dark room. You know there's something in the mirror, but it's just something that moves, that's all." Maye was quiet, thinking. "Then, I've seen him hurt people. He's good to the help, but he doesn't say much."

"You ever see him with his wife?"

"Oh, no," Maye said.

"How about Gus Canard. What's he like?"

Thunder twisted south. The moon dangled in the web of leaf and limb like a sorrowful smile. Maye, covered in white smock and flour, glowed mysteriously. A glint escaped from the bottle as she drank vodka. Someone drove a Buick into the parking lot and stopped. The engine hummed evenly.

"He's no good. His temper is mean and he's got a big smile. I don't know anything worse in a man than that."

"Have you heard anything about skimming at the Canyon?"

"No, sir. Rumors don't get to the kitchen."

I crossed my legs, drinking vodka. The smell of rain advanced, faint and languorous as perfume on a beautiful woman.

"Agnes Reynard," I said. "What about her?"

Maye paused midswig. She wiped her chin, spreading flour and vodka.

"You have a favorite bird?" Maye said with a smile. Somewhere between Maye and me the vodka was at work, throwing hard strikes on the outside corner. We were a ways from the knockdown pitch.

"The crow," I said.

"The crow." Maye laughed. "Hmmph. That's no bird. Your crow, he's like a hobo. Ain't no bird. I mean a songbird, Mitch Roberts."

I thought it over. I was in no hurry. "I'm partial to the morning dove. Lie awake hours listening to him."

"Well," said Maye. "I'm partial to the mockingbird."

"But, Maye," I said. "No mockingbirds in Kansas."

"You don't know, but I was raised in Broken Bow, Oklahoma. Mr. Mockingbird lives in Oklahoma. I'd sit out in the evening with my momma and listen to the song. You see, Mitch, Mr. Mockingbird hasn't got any song of his own. He hears a song and he plays with it. Out comes the prettiest music. He has a hundred songs, all different, all pretty. But he don't have one of his own."

I waited. A peony scent trembled up from the deep. Flower beds surrounded the Canyon Club. Florid shadows escaped from small lamps buried in the peonies, each shade playing on the pink stucco. Couples laughed and argued in the parking lot, then disappeared down the gravel drive and into the gathering maze of mist and traffic-signal flash. I felt vodka torpor draining into the cracks and crevices of my weariness.

"And Agnes?" I asked.

"She's a mockingbird, Mitch. Sings so pretty, but no song of her own."

"Does she gamble in the club?"

"I hear she does."

"Does she win?"

"I don't know, Mitch," Maye said. "I just don't know."

"Does she lose?"

"Who doesn't?" Maye said matter-of-factly.

"Does she have regular hours?"

"She's in the club now. You know I work in back, but sometimes I get a peek at the customers. She's here on a Saturday night, you can be sure."

"Does she come and go with someone?"

Maye's eyes shone dense as obsidian, flecks of sandstone and mica. She took a long, slow drink of vodka, working the vodka down in gasps.

"You working for the wrong people," she said. "It's none of my affair."

"I'm not working for anyone yet, Maye."

"I don't know who she comes with. It's not her man, that's for sure."

"Do you know what she drives?"

"She drives a purple Hudson. Big car." I scanned the lot for a Hudson. What I saw was an obscure chord of black.

"I got to go, Mr. Roberts. I've had my break and more," Maye said.

"You won't be in trouble?" I asked.

"No, I won't be in any trouble." Maye handed me the vodka. Then she braced herself against the earth and uncorked two thin legs that struggled to rise. I grabbed her hands and we danced for balance. Maye felt frail and light as an old newspaper.

"We'd best go one at a time," I said. "Can you make it down?"

"Yes," she answered. "You not working for the wrong people?"

"I'll watch it."

Maye struggled down the path. Voices seeped from an inky distance like blues from the county jail. I scrambled after Maye and stopped her, holding her silently. The voices intensified, battles of pitch and modulation muffled by a blanket of thicket and dance music.

"Oh, my," Maye said in a hush. "It's Mr. Canard."

I strained my eyes in the blackness. "Which?" I asked.

Maye cupped her hands over her mouth. "The small, hairy one," she whispered.

A black collar bled onto the pink stucco. In the black collar huddled a small spider of a man. He was the size of a Chinese fireplug, solid and subtle as a punch in the face. His bowed arms were covered with a coarse hair, thick wads of it exploding from the white shirt he wore, the wads webbed and coiled as moss on a cypress knob. He wore his hands in his pockets, rocking slowly heel to toe. At the stump of a barrel neck squatted a thick, mushy face, bulbous nose, and bald head. A swath of slick black swaddled the bald head. I smelled the hair with my imagination, pungent as glue and Brylcream. Canard bobbed his head, showing the red trace of cigar arc. Colby swaggered at Canard's elbow, speaking in low tones.

Colby was wearing the same chinos and vest. He leaned against a black Buick, nodding agreement. Canard turned and ascended the outside stairs to his office and disappeared inside a portal above the kitchen entrance. A third shadow floated by Colby.

"Do you know the other two?" I asked Maye.

"Only one," she said.

"The guy in the vest?"

"No. The other one. His name is Nabil Bunch. They call him Bill. He runs the Little River Club up north."

I'd heard of Bunch. He was tall and cast a dense, muscular shadow. In the reputation line, he'd cut ahead of Genghis Khan, just behind Hitler. He was a westside Syrian, dabbler in gambling, prostitution, and booze. His baliwick was a pillbox near the confluence of the Big and Little rivers, a dank, blue-collar cottage with the splendid, old-world charm of a lanced boil. He was head of a gang known as the Indians, a rough bunch of pencil heads known for crooked poker games and striking matches with a thumbnail and a leer. They were a crowd of seedy hoods who did small-time jobs and aspired to big operations but who didn't have the brains or the connections. Once in a blue moon they hit pay dirt, but their cries and whispers didn't carry to the wall.

A door slammed. Canard sauntered down the stone stairs carrying a satchel. He reached the flagstone path and walked to Colby, then handed Colby the satchel. Colby placed it on the hood of the Buick. The three men stood without speaking, embraced by a spiraling corona of shade. Then they spoke, their voices rising and falling in oceanic regularity. Canard puffed his cigar as he rocked, Colby turned to Bunch, and together they walked swiftly to the kitchen and went inside, leaving Canard by himself with silence and cigar smoke.

Maye and I huddled under another blackjack oak, exchanging nervous glances. Maye brought a towel to her face and wiped perspiration from her forehead. Streaks of sweat and flour laced the bony protrusions of her cheeks. Wind collected in the oak crests, droning a nervous rustle like a roomful of office typewriters. A breath of night surrounded the silhouette of Canard, throwing it against the pink stucco of the Canyon Club. The silhouette quivered like a dreamy apparition. Maye held her breath.

"I don't like this," she said. Her breath then came irregularly, with a stertorous hack.

"I'm sorry," I said. We forgot the vodka.

The Syrian cook came out of the kitchen. He emerged swiftly from the glare and passed into shadow. A new figure followed the cook, a paunchy, hunched figure wearing what looked like a blue suit and a felt hat pulled down. The figure shuffled as he walked, wanting to move slowly but not making it. Then came Colby and Bunch, converging behind him. Colby shoved the blue suit.

He staggered into a ring of stares. I strained again into the night, urging my ears to pick up the ring of talk. What emerged was a jumble and clash of unmelodic noise. Clouds moved, and the moon threw a beam on the black car, and the figures noosed around the car in a tight O. Canard puffed smoke into the face of the blue suit. The figures seemed to drift endlessly, movement trickling in unhurried chains like water in an instantaneously dark cavern. My nerves woke up in a rubber room and played dumb. Maye was a rigid spike jabbed to the center of the earth.

Suddenly, Colby twisted behind the blue suit, grabbing him by the hands, cranking the two hands in an arc down and behind. The suited figure staggered in slow motion, arms pinioned in a V rearward. Canard stepped in and grabbed the figure by the hair, knocking off the felt hat. The hat flew. Canard stood, plainly outlined by moonlight, tugging at the lone figure, one hand curled meanly around the back of Blue Suit's neck. Canard bent Blue Suit down, using his hair as a lever, Colby working the man's hands skyward like a pump handle. Together Canard and Colby moved him forward like a sack of jerk-water shit. Bunch moved to the front fender of the Buick and stood, hands on hips. I thought I saw a Cheshire grin smear his dark features. Bunch put a hand on the blue suit's neck; Canard tugged his hair; Colby levered the hands up and back.

The head smacked the fender of the Buick with a shrill crack. It was the sound of sick, dull emptiness; bone, skin, and metal vectored in the certitude of violence. The guy grunted dully, then Bunch and Canard forced his head powerfully toward the fender. Another smack. The guy's legs bucked. He went limp. Colby circled his arms around the guy's waist. Canard released the hair long enough to puff his cigar and tap the ash. Then together Bunch and Canard threw the unconscious man's head against the metal of the Buick. Maye grabbed my arm. The head hit with a clunk and the guy went down.

Maye was gripped by horror. My own mind went blank against the scene, holding itself up stiff-legged and staggering, punch-drunk like a tired fighter in the eighth. I'd seen cruelty before.

Below, Canard extracted a sheet of paper from his pocket, leaned down, and pinned the paper to the lapel of the guy's suit. The three buzzards then lifted the figure and forced him into the backseat of the Buick. Colby picked up his satchel. Bunch entered the Buick and drove it down the gravel drive. Canard turned and entered the club.

Colby stood alone, watching the steady disappearance of the Buick as it descended the curling drive, heading north on Hillside, rising in a steamy drift of headlight and wind.

Colby ambled to the cream and beige Packard and then drove down the same gravel drive.

Maye looked at me. "Mitch Roberts, I didn't want to see that,"she said. She closed her eyes wearily.

"Go back to work, Maye. Don't worry."

"What are you going to do?"

"Try to catch the Buick."

Maye stood and began to walk. "You want me to call the police? Can I do that?"

"No, Maye, I'll take care of it."

Maye shook her head. "You'd best hurry then."

Maye scuttled down the slope. She turned.

"Don't you end up like Sonny," she said softly.

I followed Maye, descending the path in the thicket, through scrub oak and sycamore. Rain moved like fate in the south. A thin, quicksilver streak shot through the bruised cloud bank. Maye stood engulfed in white light at the kitchen door, watching me hurry to my car. I touched the starter.

My mind became a hayloft with rats. In the loft a thought formed. We all end like Sonny, it whispered.

FOUR

I forced the Fairlane into a decent trot, skidding down
the gravel incline away from the Canyon Club. A wild
plume of gravelly mud flared as the tires cornered and gathered speed. I hurdled the culvert and shot past the iron-
railed bridge at the bottom of the hill. The odors of black
earth and exhaust sailed in. Above the weirdly illumined
dash, tracers of dimly outlined taillights jousted with shadows cast by the shacks hugging the shoulders of Hillside.
At the telescoped end of night a pair of taillights nosed the
steamy embrace of stalled traffic. Another pair floated farther up the hill, fading, reappearing, colliding with the
swell of College Hill, faint beacons in a big sea. I settled
back for a chase, ignoring the dread that broke into sweat
at my brow and seeped out the flannel folds of my collar.
I gunned the motor, running on vodka and gasoline.

From a tangle of trees there appeared a clear glimpse of
brick street rising along an edge of hill. The hill was a dark
thumb, red streaks painted on the nail, traffic extending in
dots and dashes along the route. I was lucky. I could see
clearly the intersections with side streets. At each, I looked
both ways, searching for the black Buick and beige Packard. I ran a stop, screeching around a stumblebum, barely
missing a parked Chevy. The stumblebum gave me an ob-

vious message. I didn't blame him. I kissed the vodka, feeling good and clear and cold.

I flipped on the radio and laughed. Patti Page was half-way into "How Much Is That Doggie." Then Hillside swelled between rows of elms and white houses. I pushed the Fairlane to a steady run making my own wind, my line of sight frozen to the hilltop. The narrow street was bathed in whistling shade, porch lamps streamed together in a gauzy haze. Finally, I saw the beige Packard down a side street, stopped at a light. Colby was slouched at the wheel, smoking, feathering smoke through the window into night. He didn't look back and he had no one in the car with him. The signal changed and he wheeled the big Packard south and disappeared in a hurry for nothing. Colby was on his route back to the Black Fox Ranch. I had it figured that the satchel contained the week's receipts and the books and records of the Canyon. It made sense to start over at midnight on Saturday.

I gunned the Fairlane again, descending the hill, my sight fixed on Arcturus in the sky. There was another red light far away. I hoped it was the taillight of a big, black car edging into Uptown. I hoped the big, black car was in no hurry.

The vodka kissed back. It slid a silver tongue down into my belly and sucked. I wanted a gun.

I sideswiped a stroller and his dog, beating a red light. I contemplated the fate of the guy in the blue suit. A sense of fear joined the vodka in my belly. Maye and I had not witnessed the slow-motion nosedive of a drunk. I'd seen drunks stiffed before, hauled out by beefy guys in vests, kicked in the pants, and left in a ditch. There was nothing elaborate or enjoyable about it, and bouncers took no particular pleasure in their work. I could see guys like Bunch and Canard having fun with a stiff, but I couldn't see the ceremony, the attention to detail, the loving care, being wasted on a drunk on Saturday night in the parking lot behind the club. It didn't make sense. I knew, too, that the westside Indians were mean. They burned puppies and laid odds on the weight of the ashes. There was the story of a drifter who woke with ten fingers nailed to a telephone pole. He'd tried to swipe a case of hootch from the Little River Club. It was the sort of story that created a stir on prayer night at the Baptist church. There had been something else about this scene. Something else, indeed.

There was Colby. If the guy in the blue suit was just another drunk, then Colby didn't make sense. He didn't fit. He was a first sacker with a catcher's mitt. You'd think that the snot-nosed Syrian could have thrown Blue Suit in a ditch all by himself. But the scene had had all the contenders dancing for the title, everybody having fun bouncing the guy's head on metal. It was too much for too little, and it didn't make sense.

Then there was the note. Canard had pinned a note to the guy's chest. Cruising uphill, I lit a cigarette and knew that it was the note I wanted to see. I wanted to see the note before the police.

I caught the Buick in Uptown. Uptown is a slice of the city filled with bars, cinemas, pool halls, and liquor stores. There is a Lutheran church and Catholic church and a place that rents crutches and party supplies. A Rexall Drug sells sodas. The black Buick idled at the corner. A huddle of snooker players hunched in thin light, drinking beer, sucking the last of their whiskey, waiting to go home, crawling downhill into sleep. Beer signs flickered. In the moth-filled glare I saw Bunch behind the wheel and the dark shape of another man in back.

I slowed the Fairlane, politely staying behind. Bunch drove deliberately. The street widened, passing a gloomy hospital, running north into maple and elm. At Ninth Street, Bunch rumbled over the tracks and into the north end. I tossed the vodka. I stayed behind by two blocks, confident that the Buick was an easy target in the dark, deserted streets. Those guys were looking for no one. It's a way to be followed, looking for no one. It came upon me that Bunch wasn't going to kill the guy in the blue suit. There had been too many quick ways into the country, fast exits to dark lanes where they could pike the guy and dump him. If Bunch was going to pike the guy, he would have headed east, into the country.

I lit a cigarette. The smoke clawed a hole to my heart, shredding tissue. Bunch turned north and circled old Maple Grove Cemetery. Maple Grove was a forty-acre necropolis: big mausoleums, stones, monuments, and bric-a-brac shrouded in a thick network of maple and old, red cedar. The place was spooky as a blind date. In fall, I'd walk in the cold and dark, eyeing crows, reading the old tombstones, savoring the violent loneliness, regarding the murky stillness as a private confine. I knew the paths well.

Bunch parked the Buick on a side street. I idled to a stop down the street and clicked the lights. The two men carried Blue Suit into the black mouth of Maple Grove. I shuddered. There had been vodka in the bottle when I tossed it.

I slithered from the Fairlane and opened the trunk. I took off my tweeds and hauled on a denim jacket I kept for fishing. I leaned into the car for a flash, then crossed the street and skirted a stone fence in front of the toolshed. Maple Grove was an earthquake of sound. Night birds whipped. Starlings cackled. The silken maple leaves rustled like crinoline. I peeked, then slipped into the same black mouth.

I rested in the shadow of a stone. A holy couple and one sheep looked down. I waited. In the night, I could see Bunch meander among tombstones and monuments, grunting, the two forms moving like fish in the wreckage of a forlorn galleon. Bunch moved his flash in the maple shade, then stopped. There was no movement then, only the sound of hushed labor, the shuffle of shoes on cedar needles. A few lonely crows flew. The night stayed dark. I wanted a smoke. Acres of darkness away, a few cars cruised on Hillside, their misty headlights dusting the stone flanks of the cemetery.

I moved to the folds of an old cedar. Forty acres of Maple Grove exhaled in the solemn embrace of wind. Bunch and his sidekick carried Blue Suit in a stuttered gait, both stopping to huff and puff. Blue Suit sagged, arms and legs flopping in a rag-mop X. Bunch clicked the flash and again a solid beam exploded onto primitive shapes arranged in ritual symmetry. My flesh folded and crept away. In the instantaneous glare I watched Bunch and his sidekick working, their voices eroded by the dark and the distance. The other man was short and the shape of an oak barrel, his snap brim low. For a while they didn't speak. Then they stopped working and walked quickly to a graveled lane, went along it quietly, and then went back out the dark mouth of the cemetery.

I waited as the black Buick drove away. Moonlight moved in the moving clouds. A silver curtain descended.

Blue Suit was on his back, tied to a stone slab. His suit hung around him like bad news. There was a pure look of cherubic unconsciousness on his fat face. The face was ruddy, two black eyebrows pressing rheumy eyes like up-turned parentheses. He had too much double chin for a guy twenty-five years old. I leaned into his face.

There was a noose around the guy's neck. It was a nice noose tied in a thunderous budweiser, tight as a salesman's daughter. The other end was tied to a brass ring on the ornate end of a concrete flower pot. Another noose bound the guy's legs. The loose end led to grillwork on a mausoleum door.

I took a chance and looked the guy over with the flash. His hands were bound at his sides. With luck, he could get loose in about ten days if the crows didn't get him first. The chubby face cradled a pug nose pushed back into his face. It was an innocent face, smooth as a beach ball. He had a thick mop of brown hair lying in a curly mass around pugnacious ears. I pushed back the mop and eyed the bruise.

It was a beauty. A faint yellow cesspool the size of a half dollar veined by black threads and blue mice. The guy's heart was beating. I took that for a good sign. In the shallows, breath came in twos, weak and steady as a two-diamond bid. He was out and he was hurt. He wasn't going to die. He wouldn't multiply from memory again, but he wasn't going to die.

I jerked the wallet out of his back pocket. The guy was Charlie Allison. There were two hundred dollars in the wallet, a Kansas driver's license, a Social Security card, a pack of cheap condoms, a spare house key, and a few scraps of paper with phone numbers. A card read: Please accept this card as a token of my deepest sympathy. Some jokester. I put back the wallet and didn't take any of the money. I lit a cigarette.

I leaned on the slab. I pushed the round halo of flash on the note pinned to the guy's chest. It was a nice note. Not as nice as the noose, not as nice as the bruise, but a nice note. NEXT TIME THIS YAKKER GOES UNDER-GROUND, it said. I thought that was clear enough.

I figured to drive home and call the police. I'd give them the tip and hang up. I didn't want to waltz around the station house with a fat sergeant who'd probably step on my lovely head. In that time the crows wouldn't eat Charlie Allison. I hustled down the gravel lane and away from the slab. A musty cedar smell floated through the night. I felt uncertain and confused but didn't know exactly why.

I heard the dark car as I approached the front gate. It crunched along a gravel road that entered the cemetery from behind, near the caretaker's cottage and stone warehouse shed. Tires made a muffled hush on the gravel. It drove slowly, splitting a huge dark monument with light, sliding past a cedar copse, two beams outlined there briefly until the lights were extinguished. I ducked. The car stopped and a form emerged. A funnel of light hissed past me when a flashlight popped on. The spotlight darted like a moth. There was a question. I decided it was about me.

I broke. A voice behind me carved a stop sign. I didn't stop. I hopped the stone fence and ran, stooping, crazy with cold vodka boiling my blood. What I heard then, I'd heard before, plenty. If you've never heard it, you don't know. There is almost no use telling about it. The sound is like a metal bee, tumbling and dangerous and fast. It whanged above my head, solid and memorable. My mind and muscles cinched themselves tightly against the rush. I ran. When I reached the Fairlane, I hit the starter. There wasn't another whang. At least I didn't hear one.

Ninth Street disappeared and I was in a neighborhood maze, quiet and respectable. I listened for sirens and heard nothing. I didn't look back. I slowed the car and emerged into the semibrightness of Hillside going south. Black cars and bullets tinkled in my brain like spare change. In Uptown the bars and honky-tonks were quiet. A few guys waltzed lampposts. My fear eased and I began to think.

It wasn't a cop. Maye hadn't called them. No cop could have followed that closely. Besides, the dark car that pulled into the cemetery went right to the spot like it had a map. I knew the guy wasn't a cop because no cop would take a public, wild shot at a shadow. A thug might open fire because he had nothing to lose, though. Thugs didn't mind those things. One thing was certain. Bunch and Canard and Colby had tagged the guy with a note on his blue suit's lapel so that someone would be sure to read it when Charlie Allison surfaced in the morning. The second guy was a little nervous and a lot angry. It explained the wild shot.

I pulled onto Sycamore, hoping that there was muscatel at home. I drove through the dark alley behind my house and parked in the spot beside the rabbits. The big house was dark, cavernous, and creaky. I went up the back steps and into the kitchen, catching the odor of dust and old bacon grease and lilacs in bloom. Big Ben muttered twelve-thirty and I relaxed. It turned out that there was a new gallon of muscatel under the sink.

I walked a tumbler of it to the front porch. The night had cleared. Across Sycamore, a bank of lights glowed in the ballpark. Groundskeepers swept trash from dark ticket booths. One or two cars remained in the parking lot. Otherwise, the darkness held a silence as thick as pitch. I sat in my rocking chair and looked at Christine asleep on the porch rail, one shoulder balanced by a strut, her curly head nuzzled on an ample bosom. She snored softly, a gentle calliope sound. I nudged her awake.

"Oh, hi," she said. She yawned.

Christine was a regular Orphan Annie: big saucer eyes, freckled face, lush lips. She could smile open vaults, melt lead, blackmail nations.

"Hello," I said back. Christine played the organ for the Braves during the baseball season. In the evenings I'd sneak into the park in the late innings and watch the game for free. I'd sit in the darkened grandstand and bring Christine beer between innings. When her loneliness was great, she'd drift over after the game to smoke and to drink muscatel. I knew nothing of Christine except that her brown hair smelled of wild sage and that her skin was soft as a lonely beach. I smiled at her.

"It's ball season," she said with a grin. She pulled her knees under her chin. She had on a bulky wool sweater, jeans, and cowboy boots. She always did.

"So it is," I said. We'd had this conversation before.

"The Braves won. They slaughtered Indianapolis. We had a good crowd. I got a little drunk and came over. Is it all right?"

"Of course," I replied. "But you know. I don't know a thing about you."

"I know about you, though. You live alone and you think too much." Christine reached for the muscatel. I handed her the glass and she drank. She slid from the rail and sat on my knee. "You look tired," she said:

"I am. I've been on the move since morning. There's a problem I haven't worked out yet. Scrambled brain."

"And you want to talk," she said. A ticket taker entered his old Chevy, then lumbered the dead pistons up Sycamore. He twisted the car through a wheel of exhaust fume and went away. Christine nuzzled her hair in my face. She felt warm and sleepy. "So we'll talk about ourselves. You first."

I shook my head and drank muscatel.

"Yes, you first," said Christine. "Mother?"

"All right. Lives on a farm with my grandma. They do fine. I visit the farm and rest."

"Brothers and sisters?"

"None I've been told about."

"Father?"

"Dead as Millard Fillmore."

"Who's Millard Fillmore?" asked Christine. There was a look of genuine dismay crowding her drowsy smile.

"He's just dead. That's all."

"Tell me about him. How'd he die?" I drank some musky. For me the past was a fat teacher in the first grade mapping a solid course of failure and repression; a buddy dead on Omaha Beach, his arms waving in the surf. The past was a kiss in the coat closet; women crying. Gravity, superego, and Freud bowdlerized for the masses. I got schmaltzy thinking about the past. I gulped and started.

"My old man died when I was a kid. Son of a bitch didn't have the decency to hang around to teach me about hitting curve balls. Or anything else. I was three days old when he died. I think that if he had been around I would be playing third base in Double AA ball. I'd have had a good life, riding the bus to Springfield and Joplin, watching guys with talent move up to Triple AAA. In winter, I'd be working in the dusty general store in Altamont, holding on until April when spring training opened.''

"You sure sound sorry for yourself," Christine said. Another thing about Christine. She sometimes scored a bull's-eye on the bullshit.

"Is that what it is?''

"Maybe, Mitch.''

"Then let's say it is. I feel sorry for the whole busload of us. I just want to play third base and leave the thinking to Republicans.''

Christine put an arm around my neck. I smelled sage. "So what about your father," she said.

"To hear tell, my mother was in the hospital in Parsons letting the stitches heal, trying to figure what kind of monster she had just birthed. On the outside, my old man decides to head to Cherryvale to the drive-in movie.

"He took his buddy, Omer Throckmorton, and a couple of girls who were cheerleaders. They took a fifth of bourbon under a blanket in the backseat. It was a hell of a night, drinking whiskey, playing radio, copping feels of the girls. It was late, the cartoon and the news played a second time. Omer and his girlfriend listened to the radio for two hours with the ignition off, so when my old man started the car the battery was dead. Omer poured some whiskey in the carburetor, then the both of them rolled the Chevy from its perch at the drive-in, down the lane, and through the front gate. They pushed the car down a hill, the girls urging them on. The girls were afraid and they had to get home. They probably thought the dead battery was a trick hatched by Omer and my dad. The Chevy finally turned over and off they went down the highway, singing and drinking whiskey.

"It was bright, a moonlit night. You could see down the highway for miles, the highway a glimmering ribbon. Sunflowers danced in the wind. You could smell the oats and the hay. My old man drove, and he decided then and there to drive all the way home with the lights out to save juice.

"Omer tells it yet. My old man was in the middle of a sentence. The two girls were singing. They hit a turnip farmer's truck head-on in the moonlight. Omer says they hit smack. The whole car filled with dust, flying glass, and steam. Sounds roared and died. When it was silent, Omer got out the back door and started running. He was so scared he ran a mile through a field, then stopped and sat in a corn row and smoked a cigarette. Then he went back to the car.

"Everybody was on the road except my old man. The old farmer was sitting in his britches, crying. The girls were covered with dust and blood. The truck had flipped a load of turnips into the Chevy through the busted front window. My old man was inside the car, covered with turnips.

"Omer and the farmer got into the car. My old man had one hand on the wheel. Omer says he didn't finish his last sentence, but he looked like he was ready. Omer remembers my old man saying, 'Jesus Christ, Omer,' he said, 'you know what I got in my right hand?' That was it. The girls cried and screamed. Omer and the farmer dug my old man out of the turnips and took a look.

"My old man sat bolt upright looking pleased and a little drunk, smiling at what he had in his right hand. There was a drop of blood on his lip. It had dripped from his nose. On his temple was a gray-blue bruise. He was dead as a mackerel.

"I went to the funeral on my mother's tit. My old man looked fine in his powder-blue suit, pink tie. His black hair was slicked and wavy. My mother was sixteen then. She raised me with the help of my grandma. I went to war, found out about muscatel, and it's been downhill ever since."

Christine said, "You're funny." Then we went to bed

and started ball season. Later I smoked while she slept, the small calliope notes seeping from her sleep. I thought about graveyards and cops and bullets, but I couldn't sleep.

I left the bed and sat in the gray overstuffed chair, thinking, playing chess, and smoking. In the utter silence of Sunday morning, surrounded by smoke and the lambent swath of lamplight, I studied a game played by Lasker in Berlin. It was a small, desperate game, serpentine, wriggling an idea to the core of unmeaning. In the end, Lasker won as he usually did.

I drank most of the muscatel. Sometime in the night, Christine woke, kissed me, and left the old house. By dawn I was drunk and ready to take Reynard's ten thousand.

FIVE

Woolly worms sparred speed rounds and worked the heavy bags of my eyelids. Ogres marched to college fight songs along the swollen course of my inner ear. Hannibal and his elephants practiced pirouettes in my gullet. What must have been a Moorish caravan dumped campfire ashes down my throat.

It was a bad night. I woke bolt upright in the gray over-stuffed chair, my clothes sweating like a decent lightweight in the fifth round. I wiggled my right hand. It was there, curled delicately around the muscatel jug. Neon festooned my brain, moths soared on brittle wings, and a thin film of diseased dust collapsed against my scalp. I popped another eyelid open and recoiled from the pearly beauty of spring.

A meow tinkled. Francis sat stirring his fuzz noisily on my lap. He ran a pink tongue along a foreleg and allowed the tongue to lick some crusty skin on my right thumb. I sat squashed inside a thread of sunlight, distinctly fiery as it fell on the nuts and bolts of my skeleton. Francis hopped onto the arm of the chair and cast a crooked and sardonic glare onto my face. Through the open front door a thousand sounds clamored, elms rushed in the wind, squirrels darted and dashed in the green embrace of limbs, honks and toots and chugs of people driving by erupted. There was the unmistakable *plop* of baseball bat and horsehide.

51

Some people lived and kicked. I was unlikely to live. The Big Ben on my bedside table said one o'clock. The book of Lasker's games lay open on my lap and the dismembered shreds of Latakia littered my knees. Muscle popped and a thought emerged. I came alive slowly like a mile-long freight moving up Pike's Peak. Forty thousand reasons to die raised their hands. A big, sweaty eunuch smashed a lambswool hammer into a brass plate. I moved upward, feeling my clothes break against me like painted cardboard.

There was too much sun and too much noise and too much animal hoopla for a man who'd drunk the better part of a gallon of muscatel. I hobbled to the shower like a vet from Belleau Wood.

I melted in the hot water. A head appeared like a poached peach. I located a pair of hands and used them to wash the night and the liquor away. I shaved. My face resembled nine miles of chuckholes on a county road. I reached from the shower and flipped on the one-thirty news. There was nothing in five minutes about Charlie Allison and the Maple Grove Cemetery. There were stories about car crashes, plane crashes, and political skullduggery, but nothing about a fat, little man hogtied to a cement slab in a dark cemetery. Nothing about the note, nothing about nothing.

For a time the lack of news didn't bother me. I was more worried about a face smooth as a red ant heap. I felt an indistinct hunger, got out of the shower, and dressed in clean slacks, dark blue dress shirt, and my grandpa's fancy brown vest. When I stepped from the bathroom, I saw Andy Lanham standing beside the oak table, smiling, his head bobbing amid the dead cacti.

Andy was a lieutenant in Homicide at the Wichita P.D. We'd been friends since we'd returned from the war, both of us struggling to collate the pieces of discombobulated lives. So far, he had picked up most of his pieces. He owned a wife, two kids, and a steady job. Our lives mingled in the piecemeal structure of baseball games, chess, and philosophical uncertainty in shades of gray. In the war of nerves against life, we were vaguely on the same team.

Andy was big and red as a beach ball, slate freckles sprinkled randomly on a wide-angle face, hair stealing a lopsided embrace around copper ears. His hands were all knuckles.

He slid around the table. "You look like a hunk of spoiled pork," he said.

"Spoiled pork has a reason to live."

Andy held a teak, Staunton king from my set. In the big room to one side his two kids bounced on my brass bed. They were five-year-old Tinkertoys, towheaded and freckled as a case of measles. They bounced like airy muffins and giggled. Andy tossed the king from hand to hand, eyeing me.

"Game starts in fifteen minutes," he said. Andy looked at the Tinkertoys. They bounced.

"Oh, shit," I replied. I remembered a two o'clock date with Andy to go to the minor league game on Sunday.

"We slaughtered Indianapolis last night," Andy said.

I went to the kitchen and he followed. I made coffee and returned to the alcove. We sat down at the oak table. The twins played with Francis. Andy and I sipped coffee in the sun.

"You ever heard of a guy named Charlie Allison?" I asked Andy.

Andy put down the coffee and cupped his hands under the base of his chin. "For Christ sake," he said. "You're not working again this soon after the trial?"

Andy had shepherded me through the trial. I knew he hoped it was over and that I'd get some decent job pushing aircraft parts along a conveyor belt and find myself a little platinum number with bluebells for a smile. He wanted me in a life of somber necessity.

He sighed. "Never heard of Charlie Allison in my life," he said.

"When you were in Vice, did you ever run into Gus Canard or a guy named Bunch?"

"I'm a cop," Andy answered. "Cops live in the same world as everybody else. Is this interrogation strictly necessary?"

Andy had been a vice cop for four long years. He'd slipped his bonds and found himself in Homicide. I knew he didn't want to remember the bad old days. Since leaving Vice he felt better about himself and his life. These memories were belches in his psyche.

"Just tell me how it works with the Canyon Club and the Little River. That's all I want to know."

Andy stood and hitched his belt.

"The cops in Vice aren't strictly on the take, if that's what you want to know. There are plenty of clubs around town, big and small. They make contributions to the reelection of the D.A. The D.A. makes contributions to the reelection of the governor. The governor has a blind eye and attends church. I don't know where the money goes, but vice cops keep their jobs by being blind. At Christmas they take home a little extra. Sometimes there's a rogue who shakes down the club owner all by himself. It happens."

Blindness trickled like blood in a syringe. I stiffened the question.

"Do you know Bunch and Canard?"

"Creeping crud, Mitch. Out of Kansas City. They've been on the scene so long they think they own the town. It's guys like that who make the payments. When I was in Vice, they left me alone. I think they knew I didn't go along with the deal. As long as Canard and Bunch pay their dues, the D.A. doesn't prosecute." Andy lit a cigar. "They've been working like that since the thirties."

"What about Jules Reynard?"

"Same deal. Higher class than most. Not like Bunch. He's one of the westside Indians. Bunch is a mushy cantelope. Nooody likes that."

"Know a guy named Colby?"

"No," Andy said. "But I'll tell you. This year the shit could hit the fan. There's a hot governor's race and if the Democrats come in, they could come in on a reform ticket. You know there's a new liquor bill before the legislature making a drink easier. You might see six months from now the end of gambling and the beginning of a shot of whiskey in a bar."

The kids developed ominous silence at the window in my front room. Mischief grew like mushrooms in the basement. One of the Tinkertoys had Francis by the tail. Francis persevered.

"Who makes the physical payment of cash?" I asked.

"Reynard and Bunch, I suppose. Nobody else runs gambling with those guys."

"Could you check out Charlie Allison for me? I think some of the boys punched him out last night. There should be a police report. If there isn't, then something is fishy."

"You coming to the game or not?" said Andy.

"I can't."

"Last week you moaned about how we never see each other."

The Tinkertoys built themselves into a pretzel and overturned the jug of musky. Green dribbled to the burnished floor. Andy and I looked at them. They gave back an it-wasn't-our-fault expression.

"Make some calls for me?" Andy shook his head in consternation. "I'll meet you at the pond tonight at six o'clock. We can fish together and talk this over. Just dig up something about Allison. I'd appreciate it."

"Goddamnit," Andy said. "I'm not a vice cop. I can't afford to nose around in their business." Andy stared at his shoes. Finally he said, "All right, goddamnit. I wish

we weren't friends and I wish you'd go back to serving
subpoenas and sneaking into the last three innings of ball
games."

"Vote for Stevenson. Country will shape up."

"My ass," said Andy. He smiled, but it came from a
place far away, from a place Andy had left and didn't want
to see again. Andy's road held family, kids, and apple pie.
Mine was detours and dirt.

Andy spoke. "See you at the pond. Six o'clock. Be there
and bring me a cigar. I'll bring a six-pack from home."

Andy towed the Tinkertoys through the front screen.
They crossed Sycamore and joined the crowd at the ball-
park. I phoned Reynard and told him I'd be out to the
Black Fox in thirty minutes. He said he'd be expecting me.
He didn't say anything about Charlie Allison.

I drove the highway to Black Fox Ranch. A cobalt sky
arched gloriously, dotted by puffy white clouds. Lilac and
honeysuckle seeped, blackbirds, whippoorwills, and mea-
dowlarks played on the prairie. It was a delicious day, nice
enough to make ten thousand dollars out of nothing. I drove
the gravel drive beside the horse pasture. The horses gamboled. I parked in the pine copse and pounded on the big
door. Reynard opened the door, Tiresias at his side.

"It's me," I said. Reynard led me to the flagstone porch.
We sat at an iron table in the sunshine. Below us, the
horseshoe lake dimpled and dappled in a gentle breeze. A
few bass jumped in the reeds.

"I'll take your offer," I said.

Reynard wore seersucker pants and a Banlon shirt. He
poured iced tea and we drank. I belched muscatel on top
of no breakfast.

"I have the cash in the house. I'll get it when you're
ready to leave."

"What about the job at the Canyon?" I asked.

"It's arranged. Gus Canard is expecting you to drop
around sometime tonight. He won't ask too many ques-

tions. I let him think you're out of Kansas City, some punk being put on the payroll.''

"What's my name?''

"Use your own. Canard hasn't read anything but a racing form in fifteen years.''

I sipped some iced tea.

"What about Agnes?'' I asked Reynard.

He was silent. In the windy reeds, red-winged blackbirds dipsydoodled. The air gathered smells: fresh prairie hay, alfalfa, ripening wheat, horses. A string of redbuds were south of the horse pasture, a red gash on green fields.

Agnes hadn't caused a flinch. Reynard's eyes were needle-solid on nothingness. He seemed to me a man adrift on a burning ship, hopeless and far from landfall. If he was right and his wife was with another man, then I could only surmise at his capacity to inflict revenge. I decided I wouldn't think about it.

"You'll run into Agnes at the club,'' Reynard said. "It won't take long and you can't miss her.''

I lit a Lucky, then helped Reynard with one of his black cigars. We smoked.

"The horses that died,'' I said. "How many, how old?''

"Yearlings. There were two. Colby found them one morning on the back section.''

"What was done with them?''

"What do you mean?''

"How did you dispose of them?''

"Colby took care of that. I suppose our vet did the messy work. I don't really know. He's a fellow named Glick, in Augusta.''

"You didn't handle it?''

"I was in the hospital. I could barely hold down the lime Jell-O.''

"You ever heard of a guy named Charlie Allison?'' I asked Reynard.

"Never,'' he answered. "Should I?''

"I'll get back to you," I said, and rose.

"Don't hold out on me," said Reynard. Tiresias gathered himself and stood. I tried to detect the motion from Reynard that controlled the dog, but it was subtle enough to slip by me. I still didn't like the looks of all those sharp white teeth in the dog's face. A pair of swans went by.

"You called Canard about the job. I guess that means you were sure I'd take your money," I said.

Reynard seemed to be studying something with his mind's eye. Tiresias stayed stock-still.

"I'm a gambler," he said at last. "The odds looked pretty good."

We walked toward the house. "What's your relationship to Bunch?" I asked.

"He's a hood. I don't have any relationship to hoods."

"Not now?"

"Ever," said Reynard. He said it loud.

"Anybody else I should look out for?"

"You'll run into my son," he said. I looked for Colby in the house. I saw no one.

"What about your son?"

"I set him up in a little racket over on West Douglas. It's a pony shop; you've probably been there once or twice. Ten folding chairs, a wire window, twenty telephones. You can get down on half a dozen tracks. It's a cracker-and-soda operation. Guy bets two bucks every forty minutes. Some deal. My son is not what you'd call executive material. He drinks too much and he's flashy."

"I suppose I'll run into him?"

"You'll see him at the Canyon. He loses money in my club to impress the ladies. He's twenty-five years old and has the morals of a tomcat. My first wife has been dead a long time, Mr. Roberts. I don't remember how he happened."

The sunshine turned cold. "These horses that were killed," I said. "Were they broke?"

Reynard doused his cigar in a silver ashtray. "I used to break some of the horses. Since my blindness, the horses are sold unbroke. The two that were killed would have been sold this summer."

"Colby doesn't break them?"

"Colby couldn't break toast with a hammer. He's out of Kansas City. He runs errands, does the books. You might say he's more my bodyguard than anything else. He works the dogs."

"You kept the horses on a section?"

"The pasture is a whole section. Six hundred acres." We paused in the sun. "Look," said Reynard. "If you think you can work back from the horses to the people who skim at my club, you're ass backwards. I'm sure there's a connection, but wouldn't it be just as easy to spot the skimming and let the horses take care of themselves?"

"Just curious," I said.

We went into the main room of the ranch. By day the place was not a mysterious sanctum of shadow and shade. There were still two zebra couches, plush chairs, and an onyx chess set. There were still a wicker bar and shiny bottles, still the wet smell of palm from the conservatory. But in sunshine and wind, the big room seemed empty and lifeless. Sounds were sucked away. We sat on the couches.

"I've been studying the game," Reynard said. "With my hands."

Reynard fingered a rook. "I think that last pawn move of yours was a mistake." He moved a bishop, capturing a pawn. We played a few slow moves. I forced a knight to the corner. I still tried to confuse Reynard with wild, ambiguous moves. Later, I hopped a knight into another corner.

"Time out," Reynard said. "Let's take this up again when I've had some time to analyze."

Tiresias led him to a Klee reproduction above a big philodendron. Reynard moved the picture and fiddled with a

combination safe. He returned and handed me a bundle of
bills. My heart thudded.

"Isn't this where I say count it and you say there's no
need for that?" Reynard said. He smiled. It was a salty
smile.

"I'll count it at home," I said.

We walked slowly to the big door. I turned. "Where
does Agnes stay in town?" I asked.

"There's a single-story Tudor across from the golf course
in Sleepy Hollow. Looks like gingerbread and poison ivy.
Are you thinking about staking it out?"

"Just thinking for now," I said. "I'll let you know." I
went through the door into the sunshine. I drove away
looking for Colby, but I didn't see a thing. I had a cold
shiver, brought on by easy money.

At home I changed into jeans and boots. I went into the
backyard and dug five holes and filled the holes with rabbit
shit. I planted tomatoes and built two cucumber hills and
staked a dozen green pepper plants. Mrs. Thompson hobbled down her rickety stairs and joined me. I dug and she
watered with an old coffee can. By July, we'd be sharing
fresh vegetables from the garden. In those hot days I'd sit
on the back porch, drinking muscatel and listening to the
ball game, the summer thick as soup, the fireflies bright
dots. Mrs. Thompson would be by my side and we'd eat
fresh tomatoes and watch the sky turn to gold, mauve, and
black. I put in two hills of squash and then stopped.

I washed, then left for the pond to meet Andy. I drove
north into the countryside. The sky had turned fuzzy pink,
flowing like a woman's scarf. Wind kissed the cottonwoods, and in the creek bottoms cattails jingled. Green
pasture, corn, milo, and endless whirling wheat painted the
land. Cows grazed dells. Along a hedgerow I saw Andy's
car and stopped. From the Fairlane I spotted him beneath
a big cottonwood. He was casting a shiny lure into turquoise water. The water glittered, a necklace of precious

stones. I hefted my tackle from the trunk and hiked across pasture and hopped barbed-wire fences. Andy smiled and casted. There was a can of beer at his feet, propped against a fallen trunk on a mud-and-sand bank. Andy rested one foot on the trunk. The air had cooled, and the hawks, kites, and bats swooped.

"I got a big one before you got here." Andy laughed. "Five-pounder."

"You bet," I said. "Size of a boxcar, no doubt." I shook a spinner free from the tackle box, tied it to the line, and shot the lure into the gloaming. It splashed into a circle of sunbeams. I pulled it home. We fished in silence, circling the pond in opposite directions. I watched Andy pull a small bass to the bank and release it.

"Monster," he mouthed. "Noah should be so lucky."

We fished for an hour, pulling in small bass, releasing them. We met at the cottonwood, popped beers, and drank quietly. I smoked. A dozen Angus gathered at the shallow end of the pond and drank. Evening nested in the gold cottonwoods. The pond was filled by fish circles.

"The lunkers are too smart for us," Andy said.

"Who won the game?"

"Braves, who else? Hot damn, they've got a good team. Hell, those guys could be major leaguers." We finished the beers and stowed the tackle. Stars twinkled in the velvet sky. A few horses joined the cows to drink.

"I have to ask you something, Mitch," Andy said. "It's serious. I need to know."

"I'll try," I said.

"What's between you and Charlie Allison?"

"Just casual sex," I said with a smile.

"I'm serious," Andy said. Nothing in his look made me think otherwise.

"I don't know a damn thing about Charlie Allison. Never spoke to him in my life. Honest."

"Why did you ask about him? What's going down?"

We hiked uphill through the pasture. In places, the blue-stem was knee-deep. A flinty moon wove shadows along a spine of prairie.

"This is square, Andy," I said. "He may have something to do with a case I'm working. I don't know Allison, never met him, and don't know what he's up to. It's just a hunch I'm playing, that's all. I have a reason for asking, but I don't know. I can't tell you about the client, you know that."

Andy lit a cigar. He chewed the end and stared into distances that were dark. Miles away, trucks lumbered down a slice of highway, headlights wavering, sounds of gears and engines like rhino in the bush.

"Look, Mitch," Andy said. "The boys who run clubs have been paying off a long time. This election is going to see a lot of dirty politics. For now, they pay the D.A. and he pays the governor, and everybody stays happy and elected. When I was in Vice, every cop knew and kept quiet and did his job, no questions asked. These days, somebody is rocking the boat."

"What about Allison?" I asked.

"I don't know, Mitch. This Allison is twenty-four years old, just out of law school. He's some kind of runner for the Democratic candidate. They're the outsiders, you know."

Andy slid his rod into the backseat of his Chevy and put the tackle box in the trunk. He relit his dead cigar, stuck it into his mouth, and leaned his big frame against the car roof.

"What the hell is this all about?" I asked.

"Early this morning two guys were fishing off the bridge along the Little River confluence. They found Allison face-down in the mud, hands tied behind his back. He'd been thrown off the bridge. He was unconscious when he hit, and he drowned. He's as dead as you can get."

Cold hands caressed me, purple lips brushed my cheek.

The air was suddenly bone-dry, drained of starshine and moonglow. The flinty moon became a death's head.

"We'll talk about this," Andy said. He got into the Chevy and drove away. I watched the red taillights disappear down the country road, powdery dust rising like mist behind him as he went.

SIX

Storms brooded south and east. Slate-colored shafts dropped onto the prairie. In the liquid distances, waving wheat, milo, sorghum, and corn drew a thatched weave onto the land. Clouds hung like bloody plums above the luminescent shape of a grain elevator, the shape itself a vibrant white hulk. Birds scurried for cover through wind dense with dust and ozone. I drove the Fairlane along a dark bandage of highway and into the pink underbelly of sunset, the highway rising and falling like a heartbeat. My own heart beat rhythmically with fear.

I saw the face of Charlie Allison on a stone slab, fat and pink and cheery, sleep and breath stealing silently through his body. In my mind I saw his face again, this time stone-white against aluminum: a face illumined by the glare of a surgeon's lamp, scalpel peeling scales of skull, hammer crushing bone, inside his head a mushy, gray brain veined with red. I'd seen autopsies and heard the cheerful banter of the doctor as he broke skin, sawed bone. Along the horizon, a powerful rumble broke. I couldn't guess the vortex that had caused Allison's death, couldn't control my feelings of responsibility and guilt for it. I tried to conclude that weariness alone had made me take the ten thousand dollars. I felt like using the money to buy a rowboat, then rowing the boat to Tahiti. And staying there.

Allison had been alive at midnight Saturday. By morning
on Sunday, he was fish bait on the Little River, staring
bug-eyed into six feet of wet mud. I needed to think about
motive and opportunity and all the stuff you read about in
Agatha Christie. Whoever had killed him had known where
to find Charlie Allison in Maple Grove and had done it to
achieve a theatrical effect. It could have been the work of
one of the Indians, but it had to be someone connected
with the mob and the clubs. I lit a smoke and tore the
Fairlane through twilight thick as chowder. My mouth was
dirt dry. The smoke didn't help that. Nothing would help
that.

The killer had been minutes behind me. He drove a big
car and knew Maple Grove. It didn't seem likely that it
could have been Bunch and his buddy in the Buick. I'd
seen Colby leave, but he was a lone driver in a big car.
Canard was unaccounted for, but so were dozens of other
connected punks. The Syrian cook. Anyone.

I whirled into the alley behind my house and drove by
the rabbits and chickens, then parked beside the old carriage house and shed. Mrs. Thompson stood on the upstairs
veranda, her wobbly vision on waves of crows heading to
the rich grain north and west of town. They'd rest and feed
and nest. Mrs. Thompson, like me, couldn't sleep. The
waves of crows drove against the steady south wind and
the storms drove east. You could smell rain that would
strike grass somewhere. I waved to Mrs. Thompson and
went inside the old house. I drank some muscatel.

I began to think. Christine was right; I thought too much.
This time, I conjured a vision of Canard and Colby and
Bunch popping Allison's head hard against metal and felt
the concussion of skin and bone, heard Allison's grunt. I
imagined a form dragging Allison to the bridge rail and
dropping him the fifteen feet. Then Allison was gone,
pressed into the fetid blackness, asleep forever.

I changed clothes in the dark. I wore some clean wool

slacks, a flannel shirt, a pair of tan oxfords, and a tweed sport coat. I combed my locks and washed old shreds of hair from the comb. With luck, I'd last until forty. As it was, I felt my liver and kidneys cringing in the basement of my gut, waiting for more muscatel.

I drove to the Canyon Club. It was a quiet, glowing ark. There were a few cars in the parking lot. Soft music washed the night. One of the Syrian cooks leaned against the kitchen door smoking. He was the same dark man with hairy arms I'd seen the night before. He had the same unemotional stare. I stubbed my smoke and walked the stone steps to the pink portico of the club. Green palms dipped into a Moorish entry. I went inside.

Pale light bubbled. I stopped in the entry and looked back at the parking lot. There was a huge, burgundy Hudson parked in shadow, unlocked, windows down. I took a breath and opened a teak veneer door. I was sucked into the Canyon.

A thick soldier in tuxedo pressed my shoulder. It was not a love pat. The soldier was ugly, but I didn't mention it. Both of us were quiet, making up our minds that I wasn't a cop. I wasn't. The tuxedo would have made a good circus tent.

"I hate to ask," the soldier said, "but I suppose you got a name."

"Mitch Roberts," I answered. I had no problem being respectful. "I'm here to see Mr. Canard about a job."

"You don't say," he said. The soldier sported a black wart on his left ear. A nice spray of hair blurted from the wart. He had wide black eyes, black shadows under the rims, and a brown, splotchy complexion. I couldn't see around his shoulders.

"Mr. Reynard sent me over," I said finally.

"You don't say," he spat.

"You'd be good at Scrabble," I said. The soldier pursed

his eyes into slits, swiveled, and strode across the dance floor. I surveyed the Canyon.

I was in an alcove that featured potted palms. They usually do. Through the half-moon doorway, a bored hatcheck girl supported her elbows and a dramatic yawn. She was blonde with black roots. You could have paved Route 66 with her makeup. She had a Jean Harlow glint, but none of the pizzazz. She clicked her gum. She studied her fingernails. The paint job was chipped.

A bloodred carpet snaked into a big room. The room was low-ceilinged and dark. In one corner a horseshoe bar bumped into the dance floor. The bar was black wood and polished glass. There was a blond man in a white jacket behind the bar. Metal stools with velvet seats studded the horseshoe. At one spot, a man and someone else's wife huddled in forbidden jokery. The blond man loomed at the apex of the horseshoe, his hands flat on the wood. He peered straight ahead, a line you could have hung socks on.

The dance floor was a checkerboard reflecting spackled stars from the off-white ceiling. Round tables covered in white linen waddled around the walls like ducks. Candles flickered on the tables. A few couples danced, a bored waiter with his arms folded stood in one of the empty corner spaces. A red-faced man ate dinner alone. The music roared from a gurgly jukebox. It was a small, glittering jukebox, a brilliant stone lodged at the edge of a bandstand. On the raised stand sat a group of chairs, a piano, and a set of shiny drums. Sunday night—the band must have been home soaking their feet. A brass rail on my right led to another shiny portico and a set of stone stairs descended into a brighter haze.

Glass tinkled. Faint casino sounds drifted from below, from down the stone stairs. Chips and clicks and rolling ivory, barkers and dealers spieling. It was far away and subdued.

I lit a smoke. The hatcheck girl fidgeted with her cross-word. She clacked her gum again. Paul Desmond music was on the jukebox. I smelled a steak. I remembered I was hungry. The soldier returned.

"Follow me," he said. I followed.

The soldier could have walked to Mars in two hours. We strode along the carpet and down the stone stairs. At the bottom of the stairs we were in the casino. It was a square well of luminescence, two crap tables horizontal to the wall on my left. One of the tables was covered. At the other, a bored dealer watched a businessman toss dice aimlessly for quarters and dimes. On my right hunched a chuck-a-luck rig and a roulette wheel. In back, four black-jack tables stood in line. Two ran with seven or eight players drooped above drinks and cigarettes.

A redhead played roulette. She was wrapped in enough curves to make Warren Spahn proud. A white ball hissed in a track and clicked still. She giggled and sipped a high-ball. The soldier stopped at another portico in back of the casino. The portico supported a string of glass beads.

"Through here and up the stairs," he said. "Pound a couple of times." I nodded and went through the beads.

Dark stairs climbed in a narrow hall. It was dark and smelled of garlic and must. A single bulb burned at the head of the stairs, but it didn't do much good. I stood on the landing and pounded. The door was pine and it didn't shatter. I heard a grunt. The door swung open when I pushed.

Canard lay on a black couch. He was covered by a rac-ing form. There was a paunch inside his black slacks. Above the racing form a barrel chest heaved. Above the chest his knockwurst head protruded like a lump. He had moles and a small scar on his chin. Greasy black hair cov-ered big ears. His arms were thick, hairy totems, one bent across his creased forehead. On the floor beside his right hand was a tray with remnants of bread, cheese, and tabouli salad and a glass of beer. He had a cigar in his mouth. It smelled like good fish bait.

He poured his fleshy face into my gaze. His face wore a green pallor pleasant as a dog fight. Black eyes wrestled in the middle of his forehead. At one end of the couch a floor lamp illuminated his bare and callused feet. The office was a shamble of papers, metal baskets, receipt books, and filled ashtrays. Canard's desk was hidden by waves of scrap. A bookcase held black binders and a bottle of whiskey. Beside the desk was an easy chair and a standing ashtray. The place was cramped as an outhouse.

"You're the guy Julie sent over?" Canard asked.

"Yes," I said.

Canard hauled himself to the edge of the couch. He kicked the glass of beer.

"Fuck," he growled. His voice sounded like an overloaded pickup. "I suppose you're the guy from Kansas City. Another one of those."

"You'd be surprised," I said. I said it just for the hell of it. I don't know why.

Canard narrowed his gaze. The green pallor turned chartreuse. The face was broad and oval, fleshy-cheeked, mean as cholera in Calcutta. He was short and probably made up for it with bluster and bad jokes. From the garlic and tabouli, I could tell he was Lebanese. Canard stared at me like I was bonemeal and lime juice. Finally, he shrugged. He stuck his cigar between two fat fingers.

"You ever dealt craps before?"

"I play. Never dealt."

"So, what's your name?"

"Mitch Roberts," I answered.

"You get a hundred bucks a week plus tips. You get dinner once during your shift. Your shift is six to two in the morning. You think you can stay awake?"

"I can stay awake."

"You're on table one with a boy named Tony. He'll

deal for the first couple of weeks. You try stickman. He'll teach you the pitch and the hook. You just learn to spiel and sell all the hard ways on the table. I pay the help on Saturday night. You get Monday off, but hang around tomorrow and learn the ropes from Tony. Don't steal from the joint. I'll break your arms.''

Canard shifted his weight. There was a tabouli stain on his white shirt and he was born with five o'clock shadow. Sweat adorned his lip.

"Sunday we shut at midnight. What'd you say your name was?''

"Mitch Roberts,'' I said.

Canard thought for a moment and came up empty. He swept aside the racing form, wiggled his toes, and stood. He. hitched his belt.

"Taylor's the doorman. He doesn't say much. Tony's been around, so take it from him.'' Canard paused. "You a doper?''

"No.''

"Stay away from booze. Big rumdum like you should stay away from the customer's wives. Now blow.''

I blew. I went down the stairs and through the glass beads. Tony was a small Syrian in a suit and tie. He was sticking for the bored businessman. Tony's mustache slithered along a lip like some starved gartersnake. I walked past the crap tables, up the stairs, and into the alcove. The hatcheck girl was doing a crossword. Tommy Dorsey had replaced Paul Desmond. I shoved a nickel into the pay phone and dialed.

Spud Christian answered after ten rings. He was an ex-G.I. like me. He struggled against the same wake of gray flannel and insurance policies. He lived in a basement apartment, drank ale, and smoked Camels. His chess was good sober and better drunk. He had helped me on a few cases. I slid him part-time jobs to help with the rough patches of unemployment and girlfriends. There were a lot of rough patches. He was a friend.

He helloed with unsteady legs. We talked for a while and I offered him a Jackson to come to the Canyon. I told him to find a burgundy Hudson and gave him some instructions. I told him to wear a sport coat and act tough. I went back into the casino.

Tony the dealer uncoiled his thirty-weight eyelids and tossed me a meaningless look. His peach-smooth face was the color of an olive. Oily eyes looped into a mandolin-shaped face and fuzzy black hair. He held a long white stick in lean hands. The businessman rolled a seven.

"Well, shit," said the businessman.

Tony raked five quarters and pushed a pair of red dice to the edge of the table. The businessman rested his paunch on the table and took the dice.

"Coming out," Tony said. His tone was smooth as raw tenderloin and horseradish. "Get 'em down on the hard ways. Play the field. Any craps."

The businessman was drunk. He rubbed the dice on his shirtfront, brought the dice to his mouth, and blew. He exhaled and tossed quarters onto the green felt.

"Let's see a boxcar," he said.

The quarters fell on Any Craps. Music drifted from the dance floor and mingled with the sound of chips and ivory. Voices droned. Above each gaming table, hooded chandeliers corraled a cozy node of light. A garish cashier booth in one corner was decorated with a painted desert motif. The casino smelled of whiskey and steel.

The dice came up five. The businessman finished his drink and drifted to the roulette wheel. Where the redhead was playing. Her body was inside a red dress. The worms who wove the dress were still inside it, too.

"I'm your new stickman," I said to Tony.

Tony placed the stick on the rail. He grabbed a cigarette

from a chip slot and lit it with a gold lighter. He inhaled through his nose.

"You gone to see Gus?" he asked.

"Been and come back. I'm on six to two, off Monday. I work with you. You're supposed to show me the ropes."

"Ever deal before?" Tony said.

"No. I've played."

"Know the rules?"

"I know the rules."

"Ever do any heavy spiel?"

Tony sipped ice water. His blue suit covered a bony frame, wide shoulders with padding. Through the fuzzy hair, there was a shiny dome. The chandelier was reflected in the dome. "I mean," he said, "you know we're selling short here, don't you?"

"You lead, I'll follow."

I went behind the table. Tony handed me the stick. In my wool slacks and tweed coat I stuck out like a whore at communion.

"I'm Mitch Roberts," I said. "Maybe I should buy a blue suit."

"Tony Steven," he said. "You look like an overdone college boy." Tony picked up the dice and tossed them. The dice split on four and four. "What are the odds?" he asked.

"Six to five against," I said.

"You know them all?"

"Two to one on four and ten," I said. "Six to five on six and eight. Three to two on five and nine. Coming out, the house edge is five percent. It averages down to seven percent on the Don't Come, goes as high as sixteen percent in the center."

Tony swept back the red dice. "Pretty good," he said.

I looked at the table. Pass and Don't Pass lines rimmed the green. Field Bets, Hard Ways, and Any Craps were in an outlined yellow box in the center. Big Six and Big Eight

squared the corners. There are only two ways to beat the
house. The first way is to make smart bets on Pass Lines
and take all the odds the house allows, play slow, don't
drink, don't flirt with the ladies, and go home early if you
win a little. The other way is to never play. I didn't figure
a lot of players in the Canyon Club knew the game or
cared. I figured most of the players drank, flirted, and went
home late. It amounted to a tidy profit for the house from
a simple game.

The tough craps player rolls dice understanding the odds
on every roll. It isn't that hard. When he's losing, he makes
small bets, and when he's winning, he bets the limit with
house money. The tough player never chases bets to catch
up and never plays drunk, tired, hungover, or angry. He
never plays with scared rent money. He knows what he
can afford to lose, but he plays to win the bank. Houses
don't like tough players because they lose small amounts
and win big amounts. But houses don't face that many
tough players.

A soft craps player makes the funny bets, hard ways,
field bets, and any craps, bets that pay off far below the
true odds, bets that look pretty and stink inside. When he's
losing, the soft player chases his money trying to catch up,
and when he's winning, he decreases his bets thinking his
luck can't last. He drinks and smokes and pays no attention. He walks into a casino planning to lose a certain
amount and always loses it. He is never prepared to win
big and loses what he can't afford. He loses the rent money,
the gas money, the baby money; he loses his shirt. He
blames everyone but himself. Craps is a lot like life in that
way.

There is a saying: "In the long run, the house will grind
you down." The saying is true except for the tough player.
The players in the Canyon probably weren't that tough.

Tony said, "The stickman steers cowboys to the center
of the deck. That's your job. Rake the dice and hawk the

bad bets. I pay attention to the players and payoffs. All you do for a couple of weeks is make the spiel and rake the dice. I make all the calls and settle the gripes. Nobody causes trouble here. The big guy on the door is Taylor. He's the bouncer. Tough guy, too.''

The payoff in the center was twenty percent less than the cost of the bet. Anyone playing the field, hard ways, and any craps has bought himself a ticket to oblivion but fast. My job was to stick and talk up the center bets. It wouldn't be hard to do.

"There're not a lot of numbers players here," said Tony. "Some guys start out playing numbers. They drink for an hour and they can't follow. They end up switching to field and hard ways. There ain't a lot of payoffs when it gets down to it.''

The tough craps player allows the dice to run numbers, follows the numbers, and backs his bets by buying correct odds "behind" each bet. The "behind" bet is even money, the best bet any gambler could find, and you only find it in dice games. I didn't think one player in ten even knew it existed. The odds bet is like a kiss from a beautiful girl, but the players never find it. Maybe if they did, the game would change.

"Pass the dice to the right around the table," Tony said. "Treat the ladies nice. They love it and they don't know shit about the game. The drunks out here think ladies are lucky. Let them think it.''

He tugged his tie. The redhead and the businessman were side by side at the roulette wheel.

"Canard okay to work for?" I asked.

"Do the work, pal," he said.

Tony tossed dice. I practiced the stick handle, back and forth with different odds and bets. Tony sipped ice water. In ten minutes no one played craps. Time passed. Tony showed me how to cup dice.

"Look out for this one," he said.

He placed the dice in his right hand, one and one on the top. He pinched his hand and sent the dice tumbling in a uniform roll. The dice stopped short of the back wall and fell out snake eyes.

"Snake eyes. Boxcars," he said. "You see some guy cupping the dice when I'm not looking, you let me know. We let Taylor handle those guys."

Dice cuppers pinch the dice with the ones up and roll the dice uniformly along the table, letting the natural forward tumble bring back the ones or their companion boxcars. Guys in back alleys and street corners use it all the time because they don't have a back wall. When the dice hit a back wall, it breaks the tumble and ruins the cup. Casino tables have a back wall and the player is supposed to hit it. Sometimes a player will try to get away with cupping and missing the back wall. It's always "no dice" when it happens. They still try it.

"We get a loader or two," Tony said. "They'll try to slip in one load. It doesn't happen often, but you can usually pick it up because the dice will flop, roll unevenly." I'd seen loaded dice in the army. I didn't figure such dice were common in a tough joint like the Canyon. You'd have to be desperate to try a stunt like that with a gorilla like Taylor on the door.

An older couple approached the table. They played for fifteen minutes and dropped ten bucks on the field. They didn't gulp. The businessman returned and dropped twenty. He was hitting hard ways and any craps. He muttered and left. From the dance floor came the swishy sound of dancers dragging themselves through dust. Taylor stood still, arms akimbo. The redhead played roulette with worms inside her dress.

"Anybody ever try to pick up bets on the house?" I asked Tony. Some players at a crap table will try to grab off other players' bets or rake in losers before the dealer has a chance to check the table. It is the lowest form of cheating but the hardest to break.

"Drunks," he said. "Nothing serious. It wouldn't pay to get caught cheating the Canyon. They cheat themselves just stepping up to the rail."

"What do you mean?"

"You know," he said. "Hard ways, any craps. They might as well tear up dollar bills and eat them. Anybody on the pass line we just have to wear them down." I began to like Tony. He had a nice, warm voice and soft eyes.

"You watch these guys," he said. "They look at that field bet and their eyes pop. Two, three, four, nine, ten, eleven, and twelve. Double on two and twelve. Guy comes off in his pants when he sees the bet. It's a sucker bet. The gaudier the bet, the cheaper the payoff. Remember that." Tony sipped his water.

At eleven o'clock the redhead moved. She uncurled her too-white legs and hopped off the stool. Her moves would have disabled Charles Atlas. The roulette croupier pushed her a stack of chips. She gobbled them, stuck them in her purse, and lit a cigarette. She laughed with the businessman, then flowed to the cashier and cashed in. I excused myself from Tony's patter and followed the redhead. She went up the stairs and into the dance hall. I followed her along the brass rail and into the alcove. Feverish Kenton rolled in the big room. The blond barman hadn't moved a muscle.

The redhead's dress was a flimsy thing, fingerpaint magenta. For my taste, there wasn't enough hip or leg. The overall effect was congenial if you didn't mind standing in line. I get bored standing in line. She talked to Taylor, then passed me and went out the teak veneer doors.

I smoked in the alcove. The redhead had a nice face, mostly punctuation and very little sentence. Her eyes were thyroid brown, dainty cheeks with dimples, red lips done too sloppy for class. The nose was cute, the chin was cute,

and the shoulders were cute. Cute walked out my door the
first time I saw Ava Gardner in a movie. The redhead's
forehead swept into a flurry of auburn gauze that was probably fashionable. A constellation of brown freckles slid
into her bodice. She wasn't a floosy, but if she tried any
harder she could be. The face was too young to excite my
passion. My passion needed muscatel and an amber moon.
I stuffed my smoke into a bucket of sand behind a palm
and followed the redhead outside.

Spring stars clung to the sky. A strong wind stirred the
oaks and hackberries. The redhead flowed along a river of
cigarette smoke and diaphanous pink. The pink came from
the lights under the peonies. Peonies perfumed the air.

Spud Christian lurked beside the burgundy Hudson. He
held his lank form in a hammer and sickle. The redhead
flowed past Spud. He grabbed her purse. She hissed like a
cat and staggered back. She had her back to a big honeysuckle, a look of surprise rising on her. Spud advanced. I
angled for the Hudson.

"What's the problem, pal," I said to Spud's neck.

He turned. "Don't get tough," he said. "Just toddle
along and fish yourself some pablum."

The redhead jerked her purse. A compact came loose
and she stooped to pick it up. A reasonable flash of bosom
appeared. In the moonglow the redhead was all strawberries and cheesecake. Heavy on the cheesecake.

I googooed the redhead. "Is there a problem, lady?" I
asked.

"This goon made a pass for my purse," she said.

Spud steadied himself. He wore a leather sport coat,
jeans, and a ball cap. He had bottle glasses and a big Adam's apple. He looked like a Dead End Kid.

I curled a short right into his stomach. I pulled the punch.
We snorted in unison and Spud went to one knee. He huffed
and puffed.

"You've got a choice," I said.

Spud glared up. There was a smile inside the glare. He winked. He rose in an attitude of tense expectation. He pretended to gnaw for air.

"Beat it, or I pawn your nuts," I said.

Spud reeled for a while. Then he adjusted his ball cap and walked quickly to his Nash. It was parked in shadow. He started the Nash and drove down the hill. I fired a Lucky and stood in the wind. The redhead pulled herself together. She took out her own smoke. I lit her cigarette.

"Me Jane," she said.

"Mitch Roberts," I said. The redhead threw her hair into the wind. It flowed north.

"I should thank you," she said. "Thanks. How does it happen you're in the parking lot when I need you?"

"I just took the stickman job. Stepped out to have some air. Kind of slow on Sunday night."

"Mitch Roberts. Sounds familiar."

"We've never met. We still haven't." Her dress was some kind of wraparound silk.

"Agnes," she murmured. "Agnes Reynard. You throw a fair right."

"I specialize in sucker punches."

Agnes smiled. "I like a man who specializes. Everything is so ordinary."

She dragged on her cigarette. Her voice oozed a calm and confident insouciance as if she had experience dealing with undereducated stiffs. She was probably used to guys making quick passes under the influence. After a while, she explored her hip with long, pale fingers. Her nails were long and pointy. Behind us, the businessman staggered to his car and started the engine. Spirea and honeysuckle swirled in the exhaust fumes. Agnes Reynard brushed her hair back. She pinched a tick of tobacco from her lip.

"My husband owns the club," she said.

"I know. He hired me."

Agnes Reynard strolled around the Hudson and got inside. An owl hooted on the hillside. She started the engine.

I walked to the window and stood, smoking.

"See you around," she whispered. It was a sulky whisper, soothing as a glass of codeine.

"It looks that way," I answered. She pushed the Hudson into gear. We looked at each other for a long time.

"Don't worry, muscles," she said. "I don't fuck the help." Then the mockingbird flew away.

SEVEN

Spud Christian sagged on the oak portico. It separated the narrow kitchen from an airy sitting room and dining alcove. His left arm drooped in a circle against his body and the door frame. A cold bottle of cheap ale dangled from the crook of his elbow. With his right hand Spud traced lines on the lead interstices of stained glass imbedded in the supporting wall. He sipped ale. The ale dropped down his narrow throat and passed a bulbous Adam's apple.

He smacked his chapped lips. There was a dreamy, tired glaze on Spud's face. Behind the weary grimace was a hint of resignation and fun. He was slightly drunk, hardly enough to make a difference. He traced the lead interstices and watched me fry some bologna.

Outside, the night moved like a mysterious black frock in the elms. Faint caw reverberations hinted that crows were pushing south and east against the wind, seeking lush corn and wheat in a brotherhood of thievery. Two bongs escaped from old Friend's Clock Tower. Four hunks of sliced bologna sizzled and popped in the iron skillet I held above the gas flame. With my free hand I spread mustard and Grandma's picklelilly on two slices of white bread. Gnats of fat leaped from the skillet, staining the stove. I had worked the crap tables until midnight and returned

home to find Spud waiting on the front porch with a bottle
of ale. I turned the bologna and lit a cigarette.

Spud cinched his lank form. "There are a few things
you don't know about women," he said.

"Do tell," I replied.

"Like, for example, I seriously doubt this fight you
staged in the parking lot is going to impress the slinky very
much. I could be wrong, but she looks tougher than a plug
of Red Man. Spending twenty dollars to knock me in the
dust will get you a smile and a handshake. It sure as hell
won't get you clean sheets and some dinky-doo."

Spud grinned and sucked ale.

"Well, you're going to find out, anyway," I said. I
flipped the fried bologna onto a towel. The towel sucked
fat into gray lumps.

"So, spill it," said Spud. He winked wryly. He snagged
a Camel from his leather jacket. He lit the smoke, and we
stood and walked our sandwiches to the alcove. We sat and
ate fried bologna and sucked ale above a chessboard. The
tobacco smells collided with the frothy smell of ale and
night energy. Spud doused the Camel and concentrated on
the food and drink. He studied the chess game. It was an
Alekhine's defense, wiry and tenacious.

"I work for the owner of the casino," I said. "Someone
is skimming from the till. Someone is also pounding his
wife. The guy is blind."

"That's goddamn tough," Spud said. "On both accounts."

"That's what I thought. The owner is a guy named Jules
Reynard. He seems like a jake guy. I don't care to work
for gangsters, but if someone is skimming, then I can do
the work without hitting my conscience with a hatchet.
Besides, I felt for him. He lives in the country in a big
house. His wife is the little number in red. She stays in
town most of the time while Reynard sits in the big house

watching red circles on the inside of his head. It is not a pretty picture.''

We ate bologna. I moved a knight. I had a plan for Spud, so I didn't mind telling the story straight. We'd been friends and I knew he could be trusted with anything of mine. Once, Spud had stood up to a knife in a punk's hand for me and hadn't asked any questions afterwards. When I had the time and the money, I'd hire Spud to do legwork. He had the legs and I had the work. Spud captured the knight.

"I figure the skimming is happening in one of two ways. Either someone inside is dickering the books, shorting Reynard on paper, or the cash disappears on the tables to cheating. If someone is tampering with the books, it must be with the knowledge of the manager, a guy named Canard. If someone is cheating the tables, the rainbow gets bright. Either way, it's an inside job. I think Reynard knows that much and that's why he hired me.''

Spud belched bologna. "What do you mean?'' he asked.

A slab of bologna squirted to the floor from Spud's sandwich. He leaned down to the slab and popped it into his mouth. He moved his own knight and forked a helpless rook on the seventh rank. The rook muttered something under his breath about my incompetence. I'd heard the same complaint before from women and children. I shook it off.

I studied the position and drank ale. I hobbled to the kitchen and poured a tumbler of muscatel. I opened a jar of pickled eggs.

"Last month someone tried to poison Reynard. Or at least tried to put him in the hospital, which they did. While he was in, someone slit some throats of horses he owned. The someone has something to gain from Reynard's business and that could only be someone close to him. He hired me because I'm an outsider and he can't trust his own people. He paid me, and I paid you a Jackson so I could look good meeting his wife. So I could make an impression.''

"So," said Spud. "The red slinky is really Reynard's wife?"

"You got it," I said.

Francis the cat slid through a slit in the front screen. He advanced to Spud's shoes and licked fat and grease from the floor where the bologna had plopped.

"I wondered," said Spud. "It wasn't like you to hang around the Canyon. You're a snooker and skittles man, and you like drinking alone. Unsociable and gnarled. How are you going to make progress on the books?"

"Only one way," I said. "I've got to get a look at the books before they're delivered to Reynard. If I can do that, I can tell if the figures are doctored down. A simple matter of paper embezzlement."

"Those guys are tough. They could pinch your balls."

Spud was right about that. A man treasured his car, his freedom, his tool kit, and his balls. It was wise to draw the line after losing your tools and your car. I looked at Spud and put down the muscatel. He caught my gaze and stopped chewing.

"Mr. Grant wants your company for two days," I said.

"Mr. Grant? For Christ sake, who do I have to kill?"

"Supply me with that camera you borrowed on the divorce job last year. Have the guy ready to develop pictures whenever I need him. I'll give you two Grants, one for you and one for the photographer. I need the camera as soon as possible."

Spud nodded. "I can do that," he said.

"Then I want you to visit a veterinarian in Augusta. He's a guy named Glick. He must have an office somewhere over there. Reynard's horses were killed in April. Find out where he disposed of the remains, get any photos he took and copies of reports or records he made, quiz him on any opinions he may have formed."

"I take it the police weren't called?"

"The police weren't called. These guys handle their own problems," I said.

I moved the hapless rook. Spud hopped a knight and captured the other rook. He waved good-bye. My king and queen simpered, sulked, and wrote me a nasty letter. Spud devoured an egg, then another. He wiped an arm across the gooey remains on his lip. I ate an egg and resigned the game.

We rose and I walked Spud to the front screen. A scented night drifted in the doorway. Under a canopy of star and cloud, the sleeping city wheezed.

"Another thing," I said. "See if you can pick up anything about Reynard when he operated out of Kansas City. Tidbits or doodles, it's all helpful."

"Be the hell careful," Spud said.

I peeled two fifties from a roll. I handed them to Spud. After a thoughtful pause, he folded them into his shirt.

"Just be the hell careful," he said. "Guys like you and me we come back from the war without a scratch on the outside and the first Sunday we fall down a manhole after church."

Spud walked to his old Nash and drove south on Sycamore, disappearing gracefully in a forest of Victorian wrecks and storefronts. I stripped and entered the crawl-space of my bed amid rafters of sleep and attic struts of dementia.

I woke from whatever-you'd-call-it. Francis the cat sat practicing scales on my chest. Millions of postmen and plumbers banged around the block, talking to housewives. I showered, ate some toast, and read about Mantle's afternoon in New York. For an hour, I wrestled with the idea of buying a blue suit and a white shirt. I found the suit at the Salvation Army downtown and parted with a ten-spot. I shot some snooker and then pointed the Fairlane toward Black Fox Ranch.

The highway wound through quarter-horse country,

wheat fields, and rangeland. Hills rolled to meet a cobalt sky dotted white with fuzzy cumulus wads. Cala lilies waved in the wet creek bottoms. Yellow sun streamed through the delicate redbud trees; herds of black Angus strolled in grass alive with bees. I wheeled into the gravel drive.

Something was out of phase. I slowed and flipped my Lucky into the roadside ditch. Two cars were parked in the pines, a blue Plymouth and a larger, dun-colored Mercury. I parked beside the Plymouth and walked to the big doors and pounded. Something inside me looked forward to seeing Reynard and to playing our chess game. He seemed like a regular guy, and I appreciated his trouble. The door swung open.

Reynard wore a pale pink dress shirt, deep blue wool slacks, and a white sweater draped loosely around his waist. Black hair swept back cleanly, and he smelled of soap and leather. Tiresias heeled beside him, thirty thousand white teeth glittering.

"It's Mitch Roberts," I said.

Behind Reynard, other figures moved in the big room, one big lump in the recessed area, another smoking a cigarette, his body draped against the wicker bar. Reynard went stiff as an Eskimo Pie.

"Let me handle this," he said quietly. We walked into the big room.

The lump was a size-seventeen neck dressed like a cop. He wore a felt hat inside the house and his brown shoes didn't match his black suit. He was holding a spiral notebook. The middle of his blocky face held a nose that had been broken, reset, broken, and reset.

"Gentlemen," Reynard said. "This is one of my men."

He nodded in my direction. I slid to the bannister that led upstairs and leaned against it, looking bored and annoyed by the delay.

"We'll be through here in a minute," Reynard said in

my direction. I said nothing. The wind and sun entered the big room and emptied into a cloying silence. The cop by the bar snorted.

The blockhead spoke. "You were here all Saturday," he said.

"I don't go out often," Reynard said. "Certainly not Saturday night without any help."

"This Colby," said the cop. "Where is he right now?"

"In town for groceries, fuel, and feed."

The cop made some notes. "I suppose we can have access to him?"

Reynard nodded.

The front door swung open. A small towheaded ferret slid into the room and held his palms open and down. "Nothing doing," he said. He stood there in the open doorway.

"Close the damn door," said Blockhead.

The small cop shoved the door. He grimaced as the wind sucked it into a loud bang. Blockhead mounted the stairs and stood by Reynard. They whispered. Blockhead gestured to his buddy beside the bar. They huddled and whispered some more while the small cop twiddled his thumbs. I noticed Creon poised noiselessly on the outside flagstones. The lake dozed in a limpid atmosphere. I didn't know these cops and I knew my share. The meeting broke.

"We've got to have someone," Blockhead said. "I'm telling you."

Reynard tugged Tiresias alive. He led the cops to the big door and they left. We stood quietly as the two cars roared downhill. I watched the cars curl around the lake and wade into wheat and bluestem. They were gone, finally.

Reynard unfastened Tiresias's leash. He wound it in his hands and wadded the leather cord into the pocket of the white sweater. He descended the carpeted stairs and sat on a zebra couch. Creon slinked through one of the glass doors, made his way across the carpet, and sat erect beside Tiresias.

"Make me a whiskey?" Reynard said.

I walked behind the bar and mixed a Bushmills and water. I coughed when I got to the couch and Reynard took the drink.

"Who are those guys?" I asked.

"Vice cops. Tenderhearted fellows, too. The big guy with the notebook was Dunce Murphy. Only he doesn't like the name Dunce."

I didn't know Murphy. Since Andy Lanham had left Vice, I'd steered away from vice cops. Reynard leaned into the chessboard and moved a knight pawn two spaces. His action surprised me. I studied the move.

"My guess is you've heard about Charlie Allison," I said.

Reynard sipped the Bushmills. I shoved a bishop. Reynard felt the move and smiled. We exchanged a few moves in silence, air and shadow playing in the windows. Reynard lit a black cigar.

"I make payoffs to those guys," he said. "It comes as no surprise they'd be interested in the murder of a reform investigator. Seems Allison was murdered and dumped into the Little River. It happened Sunday morning. Anyone would think I had something to do with it because Allison works for the Democratic candidate. He was making inquiries at the Canyon, probably gathering dirt on my operation to use in the next campaign. Hell, it happens every four years. The outside party always runs to clean up the liquor and the gambling. It would be nice to think that they can be beaten in the election. Right now the D.A. and the governor need to tag someone for this murder. If they don't tag someone soon, then Allison is a martyr. Hell of a ticket."

"May I have a drink?" I asked.

"Sorry," Reynard said. "Help yourself."

Reynard studied the board with his hands, moving them slowly, carefully over the pieces. While I mixed a brandy and ginger ale, he questioned me about the positions. He jumped a knight into the center. I captured a pawn and Reynard moved a rook. He relaxed.

"They've offered to tag you?" I asked.

"Gently so, but yes. The guys in Vice want their payments to continue, but they can't let the Allison case go unsolved. It seems Allison was beaten unconscious by goons and dumped off the bridge. Naturally, I'd be stupid enough to murder him or hire it done. Murphy wants a suspect in a week or so. If I don't give them one, they turn the heat up under me. They apologized and left."

Reynard snapped his fingers. Creon and Tiresias rose simultaneously and trotted through a side door that led to the back of the ranch house. I stubbed my smoke in a crystal ashtray and ascended the carpeted stairs. I stared at the big lake and the hillside that swelled into prairie grass and a fat sun. Reynard sat still, his hands on his blue slacks, his eyes void.

Finally he said, "How did it go at the Canyon last night?"

"Fine. I'm officially the stickman. In fact, I'm on duty in about an hour."

"All right. What about Allison?"

I skirted the sunken area and stood beneath the Klee. On a gray matte field, stick figures balanced geometric items, pink fluff and lyric nonsense. The philodendron was green, the carpet white. I felt dark inside.

"I watched Canard, Colby, and Bunch bounce Allison off the hood of a Buick Saturday night. He was out cold and they drove him away. He wasn't dead then. I know he wasn't dead."

"That's fine," Reynard snapped. "I don't mind them bouncing the clown around, but who killed him?"

"I don't know," I said. Misgivings danced in my conscience. I sipped the brandy slowly. It wouldn't do to show up at the Canyon wearing a buzz.

Reynard stood and stretched. He shrugged, untied the white sweater, and draped it around his shoulders.

"I knew the reform candidate would snoop around the club. It's nothing new, happens every four years. Every time around there's a reform candidate, and when he gets elected, things quiet down and the reform candidate goes on the take. It's a joke. But the snooper is not supposed to get killed. That is not part of the game."

"I don't suppose it was."

"Did you meet Agnes?" Reynard said offhandedly.

"Yes," I answered.

"How did it happen you saw Allison bounced?"

"I was in the parking lot having a smoke. Fly-on-the-wall sort of thing."

I decided to omit the tale of Maple Grove. Reynard had paid me ten thousand to break the skimming routine and to follow his wife. I liked Reynard but didn't fully trust his motives or reactions. It seemed best to keep the secret. It would do no one any good to spill it right now.

Reynard inhaled cigar smoke.

"You realize, don't you," he said, "that this fits in with the poison, the horses, and the skimming?" He pushed his face into an oval of sun. "In a couple of weeks I'll be out of business, sitting downtown in a cold cell. These fools in Vice can't think of any other solution." Reynard drained the Bushmills. "Ten years ago these guys weren't fit to lick my boots." The anger subsided.

"Your position on the board is interesting, I think," Reynard said.

"It stinks," I said. "I've got to go to work."

Reynard ascended the stairs, his movements without Tiresias stuttered.

"What did you think of Agnes?" he said.

"I don't think about her." It was not convincing.

"Very diplomatic." Reynard walked me to the big door. "She was a receptionist with the last expert who attended me. She was the last woman I ever saw clearly. The last woman I'll ever see. It was easy to be astonished under those conditions. Think about it."

"Will you be all right for now?" I asked.

"Hell, yes. But I don't have much time."

I walked to the Fairlane. I watched Reynard standing alone, wind stirring the pink shirt, and behind him the big room open and shining. Reynard's eyes were fixed on a point far away, beyond the grazing horses and Angus, beyond the broad prairie choked by bluestem and wildflowers. I drove down the gravel driveway toward the city and the Canyon, thoughtful.

There were only a few cars in the Canyon lot. A red sun sank behind oaks and hackberrys, long shadows dragged through sand. Traffic swept along Hillside: aircraft workers, soldiers, and salesmen heading home to the wife and kids, a dose of television, and a game of pitch. Inside my blue suit I felt like a loaf of bread. The lapels were an inch too wide, the sleeves an inch too long, the neck an inch too big. Other than that, it fit fine. The shoulders were borrowed from Knute Rockne. No one could complain about the scuffed shoes. I planned to hide them under a crap table.

The Canyon was hushed. The hatcheck girl slid me a come-hither smile oozing rancid honey. Her name was Micki "with an i." She had two little girls at home. The ex came by every two weeks and beat her up once in a while for fun. I winked at Micki and walked to the bar. I ordered ginger ale and drank it.

The dance floor was empty. One of the waiters sat studying his books, counting change. The juke was dead. At the end of the bar, an Air Force tech sergeant nursed a beer. It was five-thirty and in the dusty sunlight the Canyon looked slightly shabby. In the casino, ice and small change tinkled. A slot clanged once. The blond bartender didn't speak. He stood rooted by his hands to the shiny bar.

I thought about Jules Reynard. Following my talk with Maye, I'd followed Bunch and the Syrian to Maple Grove. They had hogtied Allison to the slab. A few minutes later, someone had aimed a busy bullet at my body. The same guy who'd taken the shot had sailed Allison into the river. It was all a deadly setup: the poison, the horses, the murder. I needed to look at the books and I knew my time was limited by vice cops. It made an ironic, brutal sense.

The ten thousand was more money than I ever hoped to have in one place, a chance to head for Montana and buy land, to fish, plant vegetables, grow apples and cherries in the valley of the Bitterroot. A vague awareness rattled inside my skull. Any action impelled by money was likely to subvert rectitude and honor, to make a man lose his senses. I kept telling myself that Reynard was playing it square and that this job was just another case of employee theft, a cheating wife. I'd heard it before. I sipped the ginger ale. The explanation slipped like a ghost into the closet of my heart.

At six o'clock I ambled to table one. Tony the dealer leaned against the back wall, a bored expression impaled on his olive face. No one played craps. There were only a few blackjack customers. The cashier, a small mouse with gray hair and mustache, paced in his booth.

"Bueños tardes, kimo sabe," Tony said.

"Kind of a mixed metaphor," I replied.

"Where the hell did you dig up that suit?"

"I made it myself."

"I believe it," he said.

Tony poured dice onto the green felt. "You'll see why Canard gave you Monday off. It will be slow all night."

In one hour three players strolled to the table and lost money. I sticked and called the hard ways and any craps. It was underwater craps, played in slow motion, silently as guppies in an aquarium. The blackjack tables had more action. Taylor the doorman strode through the casino and disappeared up the back stairs. I didn't spot Canard until eight o'clock.

He waddled through the glass beads and approached the tables. He spoke to a croupier, then stopped beside the crap layout.

"How's he working out?" he asked Tony.

"Swell," Tony said.

Canard eyed me. He wore a blue blazer open over a white shirt, gray slacks, shoes with black tassels. They were rich clothes, but dirty and wrinkled. He smelled of garlic.

"Take a break, Roberts," he said. He looked at Tony. "Close the table. I want to talk with you."

I walked away and watched as Tony covered the felt with blue quilting. Canard walked Tony to the back stairs and they disappeared into darkness. I wandered to the dance floor and pushed open the swinging kitchen doors. There was a rush of steam, fried grease, and garlic. The kitchen looked like a Syrian cruise ship bound for Alexandria. Maye stood in one bright corner beside a cookstove. She chopped scallions. I walked over and touched her shoulder.

She turned and her eyes widened.

"What are you doing back here, Mr. Roberts?" she asked. She was wearing a white smock. Her face glistened.

"I took a stickman job here. Keep it to yourself about us." I put my finger over my lips. Maye said nothing. She turned and resumed her chopping.

"This sure isn't turning out right," she said.

"I'm on break. How about dinner?"

"Rule is," Maye said, "you all eat in the kitchen when we got a crowd. Otherwise, I can serve you at one of the corner tables. We got fried shrimp and garlic salad. That will have to do."

I walked to the bar and ordered beer. I went into the

corner beside the bandstand, sat down at one of the round
tables, and lit a smoke. A few couples walzed to Rosemary
Clooney. Some bored cowboys rode the bar. The waiters
weren't quite busy. I smoked and wondered what Canard
and Tony were discussing. I hoped it wasn't me.

I waited. Finally, Maye slid along a back wall of the
dance floor carrying a tray of shrimp, french fries, and
salad. She placed the tray on the table and looked at me.
She shook her head and walked away.

I ate quickly, savoring the garlic salad. Between bites, I
saw Agnes Reynard enter the Canyon. She stood in the
palmy portico. This time she had on a pair of jeans, sandals, and a lace blouse with rhinestones. Her shoulders
seemed thin, densely freckled. In the frosty light, she
looked like a little girl. She hustled to the bar and ordered
something that wound up red and full of shaved ice. It was
not a Wallace Beery drink.

Agnes sipped her drink. I thought about photographing
the books. I needed time to slip into Canard's office. I
needed to know Canard's schedule, the kind of car he
drove, when he took his breaks. Maye might know the
details. So would Tony and Agnes. I decided to try to piece
together a picture by talking to all of them. It seemed worth
the chance, but my hemline went sweaty at the idea. For
ten thousand dollars, it seemed necessary. I finished the
drink and walked past the bar. Agnes eyed me. I winked.

"Where did you get that suit?" she said.

I stalled for effect. "Made it myself," I answered. I noticed a smile, but it was far away, like a coal-mine fire.

I sticked for three hours. The hushed casino filled with
breathless tension. Blackjack players grazed cards and
drinks like sheep; slot players fed nickels to their shiny
friends. Agnes slipped between the casino and dance floor
like a pendulum. A tough would ask her to dance, she'd
flirt, dance, then return to the roulette wheel. Her drink
turned out to be gin and grenadine.

At eleven o'clock, Johnny Reynard descended the casino steps. He was a scale model of his father, sleek as a palomino, dark as hazelwood. He wore a salt-and-pepper sport coat fitted smartly above a silk shirt. His eyes sat deeply above burnished bone, his hair rolled in waves from a smooth forehead. Three gold rings adorned his right hand. He smelled of whiskey. Agnes Reynard held him around the waist.

"Coming out," I said.

Three players dropped bad bets onto the felt. A platinum number held the dice. She grinned furtively at a bald dope across the table. She threw six.

"The point is six," I crooned. I raked the dice to the blonde.

Johnny Reynard dropped a five-spot onto Any Craps. My stomach growled at the bet. The blonde threw a nine. I raked two bets and scooped the dice back to the blonde. She giggled and the bald dope strolled around the table and pinched her. Taylor walked down the stairs and stood beside Reynard. Agnes ran her hands through Johnny's hair. I noticed. Reynard swayed and dropped another five-spot onto the Hard Way Eight. It was a short, drunk bet.

The blonde threw a seven. I raked in the bets. Tony clapped a dice cup over the bones and covered them.

"New shooter," he said.

He tossed a pair of red dice to Johnny Reynard. Agnes caught my eye. She ran her hand along Reynard's shirtfront. She fed him some gin. He gulped it greedily.

Reynard covered Any Craps and Hard Way Eight with fives. He rolled a seven and Tony paid him.

"This boy is hot," Reynard said. Agnes left the table and returned with what looked like a whiskey and water. She handed the drink to Johnny. He drained it.

"Down and dirty," Reynard slurred. He dropped fives on Any Craps. A cowboy in the corner followed suit. The bald dope dropped some quarters onto the Big Eight. Reynard whirled the dice to the wall. They tumbled into snake eyes.

The blonde clapped. The table was generally pleased. Tony paid.

"Come to Papa," Reynard said.

I raked the dice to him. His face glowed with booze and excitement. He was smaller than his father, but built from the same sleek model. The blonde edged to Reynard and smiled. A few couples tumbled from the dance floor and gathered to watch the hot shooter.

Reynard stayed that way. He held the dice for twenty minutes, rolling craps, hard-way boxcars, and sevens. He lost the dice to a six, and the table groaned. I figured Reynard to be up about three hundred dollars.

"Get your bets down," I said. "Yes sir, hard ways, any craps, bet the field."

Tony smiled. The platinum number covered a hard way. Tony scooped some dice to her and she threw a nine. Then she crapped.

In the next hour, Reynard held the dice four times. He bet the center of the table, folding bills above Hard Ways and Any Craps. Agnes plied him with whiskey. He tossed deuces, trays, and boxcars. He stuffed the winnings into his coat pockets. At midnight he drifted to the bar. Agnes drifted along.

"Pretty lucky stiff," Tony said.

"I'll say," I replied.

My shift stayed awake for two more hours. Couples finished dinner and drifted to the tables. They lost money and went home. Nobody was hot, everybody lost. Reynard circulated through a few young women who dealt blackjack, Agnes not far behind. He swayed from the whiskey. I helped Tony brush the table and stack chips. Tony emptied the money box. We covered the table with quilting.

"See you tomorrow," he said. "You did just fine."

I washed my face in the washroom and stepped to the

bar. The dance floor was dark; waiters stacked chairs. A black man mopped the floor. He was big, with a fire-scarred face. The blond barman wiped the bar with a towel. I ordered a double manhattan and sat, drinking in the reflected glow of the jukebox. The manhattan was strong and sour. It matched my mood.

Reynard flirted with the hatcheck girl. He stood with Agnes in the pink alcove, then he opened the teak veneer door and waded into the night. Agnes put on a blue jacket and waded after him.

I smoked two cigarettes. Then I finished the manhattan. Anxiety drew inside me like stitches in a wound. I tipped the barman and left the Canyon, heading for a gingerbread and poison-ivy house in Sleepy Hollow. On the way, the stitches snapped and bad blood seeped like a black river into basalt caverns.

EIGHT

Demonic silence fell in the city like erupted ash. It sagged in the elms and hung in the new mimosas like a cloak. I followed my headlamps along the deserted streets, passing rows of residential houses, clinging to expanses of bluegrass and cedar hedge, empty and dark, to whiskered visions of family life, wives sleeping in curlers, children tucked away.

The way to Sleepy Hollow lay past Uptown and along the sedgy shoulder of College Hill, past silent bars and honky-tonks, nearside drugstores, hardwares, and cinemas, and finally into the shrouded bottoms of creeky hollowland. Sleepy Hollow was sleepy and hollow, a fantastical, curvy panorama of brooks and dales and warrens, tangled in the confines of the city golf course. On Yale I parked in the shadow of a thick spirea.

I lit a cigarette. My smoke hung in a glaze of radio glare, and in the glare Gogi Grant sang "The Wayward Wind," her cool tones rising in the smoke, too. On the eastern horizon, through a tangle of cottonwood and maple, Arcturus spiked itself on a black cloth. Preternatural clouds swung in the trees. In the murky distance, a huge expanse of golf course rose and fell in the darkness. I looked at the Tudor.

It was a handsome, squat house covering a corner lot.

A single story of gray mortar wound in a rough L along
two sides of the lot. There were two doughnut-shaped panes
in each heavy door and a single row of medieval leaded
windows at each corner. Ivy climbed the walls up to a
walnut panel nestled beneath a thatch roof. Elms covered
the square corners. One chalk walkway snaked around an
ornate birdbath and disappeared into a concrete driveway.
There was a big, white garage in back and a tangle of
spirea, chokecherry, and mulberry. It was the kind of place
where the Wolf Man would have built an aviary.

Agnes Reynard's burgundy Hudson was nosed up to the
white garage. Behind the Hudson someone had parked an
MG-A. It was a convertible, sporty enough for the Prince
of Wales. From the leaded line of windows in the Tudor,
lamplight seeped and wavered. Through the windows I saw
nothing save a few solid shapes, bookshelves, a Boston
fern, shimmers that passed for gas flames.

I pulled a flash from the glovebox and stuck it in my
pocket. Then I hopped from the Fairlane and hiked to a
concrete bridge above a quiet, snaking creek. The creek
flowed through the heart of Sleepy Hollow and ultimately
wound through the golf course. I poked in the thicket beside the creek until a clearing opened beside the Reynard
driveway. I leaned through honeysuckle. I could smell the
heat of the MG. From my hidden perch, I shot a ray of
light into the MG and followed the ray to the front seat.
On the steering column was a registration banded to a plastic envelope. The MG belonged to Johnny Reynard. Fifty
or sixty heartbeats later, the ice melted from my veins and
I went back to my car.

For an hour I camped in the Fairlane while one radio
station after another faded to silence. The night air and
summer stars burned around me. I tried not to think about
the son and the stepmother, or about the blind man alone
in his empty house. My own trouble seemed monumental
at times; the dreary dishes in the sink, the empty winter

nights with the wind alive in the frosty windows, and the inevitable morose ponderings with chess and muscatel as allies. I had, in my own life, confronted the contradictions of hope and despair, wound and repair, and enough boundless buffoonery to last a lifetime. But blindness was a spider in the soul.

The gaslight flickered and the leaded windows gleamed. No one came or went and the lights stayed on. Finally, full of cold fear, I drove home.

At the Canyon, Johnny Reynard had played the wrong bets. Yet he'd come from the table with seven or eight hundred dollars. Some players could toss dice all winter without luck like that, luck that fell on Johnny Reynard like a monarch butterfly falls on a child sleeping in a garden of petunias, luck like a luscious kiss from a fairy princess. I wanted to believe in Johnny Reynard's luck; I wanted to believe in fairy princesses and curly towheads asleep in flowery fields. But in a world of warts and viruses, there weren't fairy princesses. Children went hungry. And eight hundred dollars didn't drop on people like butterflys in a summer field of hay.

I knew it would take time to decide what I believed about the crap game at the Canyon and skimming from Jules Reynard. But there was no mistake about the MG parked behind a burgundy Hudson. Johnny Reynard had won eight hundred dollars at the Canyon Club. He'd pasted himself to Agnes Reynard and left the club at three o'clock in the morning. A million singing butterflies couldn't tell me that he wasn't still there.

I drove slowly through downtown and then across the river bridge under the hulk of the Broadview Hotel, a brown mantis with winking eyes. Near my old house, a vision of the ballpark loomed with gray outfield walls, towers banked against a starry sky. I had only one thought: a simpler life, an easier way to make a living, digging the dirt, tending animals, watching for forest fires from the spicy confines of a watchtower. There was too much trouble with war and childhood, trouble from love, trouble private detecting. Even if I had ten thousand dollars stashed safely in my steamer trunk at home, nothing could make it easy to tell a blind man that his son had spent the night with his wife. I'd give the ten thousand to make it go away.

I whirled the Fairlane behind the row of old Victorians, rumbled down the alleyway, and parked beside the rabbit hutch. The rabbits nibbled thin air. I checked the newly planted garden and went inside the house.

A round head poked above the broken back of my gray chair. Disparate rays from the brass lamp fell on the head. Some snores escaped from it in easy, ponderous notes, risible in the symmetry of sleep. I opened the refrigerator and poured a glass of muscatel. The head jerked.

"Is that you, Mitch?" a voice said.

"Directly," I answered.

The head bobbed. Andy Lanham, homicide detective, looked around the chair. He wiped sleep from his eyes. A blustery, worn-down expression crowned his look.

"Jimmied the door and came in," he said. "I thought you'd be home early. I don't suppose it's early."

"You want a beer?" I asked.

I stood in the kitchen. The sagging walls smelled of fried bologna and bacon grease. Andy rose and shuffled inside his baggy brown suit, easing himself into the creases that grew on cop clothes. He strode to the kitchen and huddled inside the pale refrigerator light. Wind danced curlicues in the bay windows of the alcove. Thunder moved somewhere. The spring smell of dust and rain swam beneath the windy surface.

"I'm here to find out about Allison," Andy said.

I sipped muscatel. The sweet juice scoured an inch of memory from my mouth. I looked past Andy into the alcove. Lamplight and stars mingled in the remains of a chess game, shiny black and tan Staunton pieces flecked by deep haloes.

I'd expected to meet Andy soon enough somewhere in the cracks between friendship and work. Andy had the same problem. We'd faced the difficulty before on some big cases and both friendship and work had suffered, coiled in the uncertainty of morality and necessity. Andy was a good cop, troubled by his responsibilities. Responsibility troubled me as well. Still, we knew each other well enough to pay close attention. It was the kind of atmosphere in which confusion had a chance. We were good friends who needed a fence.

"So how about the beer?" I asked again.

Andy hunched around me. He reached into the refrigerator for a bottle of Pabst. He uncapped it and drank deeply.

"I had a nice conversation with my chief today," Andy said. "It was about the Allison case. Medical finished the autopsy and Allison is on ice in the basement of the station. You recall I told you he was unconscious when he drowned. That's part of the story."

Andy drank again. He stretched his big frame and shoved red hair from his face. His brown suit hung around him like bear skin.

"Let's go into the other room," I said.

Andy followed me. I sat in the overstuffed chair. Andy pushed his rear onto the windowsill and balanced, staring at me. Wind flounced the elms outside. Elm limbs rattled the eaves. Some muscatel fingered a place deep inside me and rested there like a whipped mongrel. Andy began to speak in slow, unmodulated tones. It was the funereal sound of a somber canon.

"Doc found deep bruises on Allison's forehead. He looked closer and found slivers of metal and paint in the hair and in the folds of some lacerations. You don't get metal and paint slivers from falling down in the mud."

"I thought you said the guy was tossed from the bridge?"

"He was tossed from the bridge. When I talked to you, I assumed he was knocked unconscious by the fall. The way it looks now someone bashed his head against a car."

"You assume?"

"Don't be an ass," Andy said. He stepped from the sill and turned his back. He stared for a long time at the dark form of the ballpark across the street. Elms waved wildly. "The doc analyzed the paint," Andy said. "You'd be surprised how much you can learn from a paint job. Black paint, high quality enamel, the kind they dab on expensive cars. It was new factory paint."

"Go on," I said. Andy wanted this out in one blow. I'd let him blow and then it would be my turn. I hadn't decided yet how to explain the situation to him, my involvement with Reynard, my presence in the parking lot that dark night. I didn't think I'd tell him about the cemetery. I didn't know exactly why, but it was the way I felt.

"Anyway," Andy said. "Allison was unconscious when he hit."

He turned and sat again on the sill. "Another thing," he said. "We don't believe he was banged on the bridge. We think he came from somewhere else."

"How do you figure it?"

"Doc found stains on Allison's clothes. There was a little oil and some grease on his suit. Maybe like someone had hauled him on the floor of a car or in a trunk."

"Why couldn't he have been banged, then shoved over the bridge rail at the same time?"

"Why would someone do that? The fall from the bridge would surely knock him out. He'd be easier to haul if he were unconscious. Like I said, it's only a theory."

"So the doc thinks he was knocked out somewhere besides the bridge, hauled to the bridge, and dumped?"

"That's it."

"I saw Allison get banged," I said.

Andy stared at the floor, then walked slowly to the old kitchen. I stayed in my chair and watched the elms dart in the night wind. I heard Andy pouring muscatel into a tumbler. When he returned, he extracted a new cigar from his bearskin and lit it with a wooden match. He exhaled a puff of smoke. The smoke hovered in a wad and ascended to the ceiling. I leaned to the nightstand and flipped on the radio. Soft music played. Elms creaked as the wind rushed in their embrace.

"Of course," Andy said. "You want to tell me about it?"

I fumbled for my pipe. I put some Latakia in the bowl and spent time lighting the mixture. The Latakia smell was like black earth and peat. As I inhaled, the first raindrops tumbled to the rotting porch and kissed the bay windows. Smoke seeped into the walls; the wind rose and swelled and faded.

"I took a job at the Canyon," I said. "I'm supposed to be finding out who's skimming from Jules Reynard. As a sidelight, I'm looking to find what Agnes Reynard does with her evenings, and who she does it with."

"You're working for Jules Reynard?" Andy asked. The disappointment soaked through like sweat.

"Yes," I said.

"He's bad," Andy said. "I didn't figure you to hire on for the bad guys."

"I made up a reason."

"The reason wouldn't be money?" Andy was right and he knew it. There wasn't much to say that God and Aristotle wouldn't see straight through.

I thought for a while. Finally I said, "I had it all worked out in my conscience. At the time there wasn't any problem helping the guy with his wife. I saw him sitting in his big house all alone and I felt for him. Knowing nothing about him, still I felt for him. It doesn't take much to feel for a guy who's blind and whose life is going sour. I made up a reason for working in the casino, too, telling myself that it was just business and that if someone like me didn't do it, then somebody else would. Everybody gambles and drinks, so I figured that finding out about the skimming was just like any other job. Helping the guy spot an embezzler. I told myself that the Canyon could be a bank, or a gas station for that matter.''

"Suppose I go that far with you," Andy said. "I was a vice cop. I took home eighty-seven bucks a week. Still, there were plenty of times when I looked the other way to keep my job. There's some dirt under everybody's fingernails.''

"You could say that. Anyway, I took the job. Maybe there was nothing good about it then. Maybe not now. But I took Reynard's money and I owe him. Something, I don't quite know what. Loyalty, maybe. I won't kill anyone for the guy and I won't hide his dirty laundry if there is any. For now, I'm playing it straight down the line with Reynard until he shows me different.''

Andy sucked some cigar smoke and finally smiled. "This is funny," he said. "Now tell me about Allison. He's one guy who doesn't have any theories and doesn't find this much fun.''

I went for more muscatel. Andy followed. I cut some bologna and spread mustard on four slices of bread. Then I handed a sandwich to Andy. He stuck the cigar in his mouth and handled the sandwich.

"I was having a smoke," I said. "The first night at the Canyon I took a break and saw Canard and Bunch come out of the back door with Allison. A guy named Colby came along. Then they took Allison and pounded his head against a black Buick. Allison was out cold. Bunch and a Syrian drove Allison away. They loaded him in the backseat and disappeared.''

"Doc was right," Andy said.

"As far as it goes."

"You know," Andy said, "this guy Allison worked for the Democrats in the reform candidacy. He spied on the clubs, collecting dirt to use in the campaign if they had to."

"I heard."

"Well, let me tell you something else."

I waited. Andy walked his sandwich into the big room. The brief rain had stopped, leaving the elms steamy. A morning dove cooed low notes, resonant and looped.

Andy said, "I'm off the case."

I unlaced my shoes. Andy's face paled and he put on his felt hat. He didn't eat the sandwich. It stayed in his hand like a softball.

"What's going on?" I asked.

Andy drained the muscatel from his glass and puffed on the cigar. His face reflected weeks of sleepless activity, his blue eyes rimmed red, lines and creases riveted at the mouth and brow.

"The D.A. took Homicide off the case. The office is working it as a vice case because of the connection to gambling, liquor, and the election. In reality, the boss wants the whole case put on hold for a week. He's trying to let the boys at the state capitol decide what to do. In short, they've got to find a patsy for Allison's murder or the Democratic ticket will ride into office on the corpse. They'll ride the corpse hard and put it away wet."

"How does that mean they take Homicide off the case?"

"Guy named Murphy is head of Vice now. He knows Reynard, Bunch, and the rest of the boys who run gambling and liquor in this town. If Murphy can give the D.A. a suspect with enough clout, then they can take the heat off the election in the newspapers long enough to put the case to sleep. Vice finds a suspect and the payoff scam stays the same. If they can't find a patsy, then the Democrats will play hardball reform and probably win the election. If that happens, then the D.A. is out of a job, and so is the whole vice squad and half the Republicans in town. They need a murder suspect, Mitch, and they need one bad. They need a suspect bad enough to tag Reynard.''

"I follow," I said.

"Another thing. Reynard looks real good for it now. They think they can set him up as the guy who hired it done. I know he's blind, but if Vice pinches him, the heat will be off for a while. Even if he's not convicted, the heat will be off, and your boy Reynard can find another career. He'd be through here.''

I thought that over. "Unless someone finds the killer,'' I said.

"You mean Mitch Roberts, boy detective?''

"It might be both of us.''

"You forget I'm off the case," Andy replied. Then he frowned and took off his hat. "You've got my interest.''

"I told you I watched while Bunch and Canard bounced Allison's head on the Buick?''

"Yeah, so?''

"I followed Bunch and a Syrian when they took Allison for a ride. Allison was alive then.''

Andy spoke. "He drowned. So he wasn't dead during the drive.''

"Those guys drove Allison to Maple Grove. I hid out and watched while they tied him to a cemetery slab. Bunch and the Syrian drove away in their Buick.''

"Do you figure Bunch and the Syrian returned and took him away?''

"I don't know," I said.

"Tell me more," said Andy. "Remember, I'm off the case.''

He smiled, put down the sandwich, and took off his suit coat. He threw the coat onto the brass bed, undid his suspenders, and let them drop to his sides. In the kitchen, he retrieved a green gallon jug of muscatel and brought it back to the big room. We filled our tumblers.

Outside, gray strokes painted the east. Pink creases broke above the outfield wall of the ballpark and twitters erupted. Jays and finches yawned. Andy walked to the alcove and slid an oak chair beside my big gray outfit. He twirled the chair and draped himself over the back, his arms dangling on its lattice supports.

"I love this shit," he said.

"I saw Allison on the slab for a few minutes. Then another car pulled into the cemetery and drove straight to Allison. I ran away like a good boy. Whoever was in the car took a shot at me."

"Jesus Christ," Andy said. "He missed?"

"This time," I answered. "I drove away and didn't know anything about Allison until the next day when you told me he'd been found dead."

Andy drank some muscatel. His face flushed pink like the sky. "How do you figure it?" he asked.

"How about Bunch and the Syrian? They could have had a change of mind and come back. Dumped Allison in the river."

"It doesn't make sense that way," Andy said. "Too much wasted motion and time. We apply Newton's principle of parsimony to explain things in the simplest way possible. Why would they run the guy to the cemetery and then come back?"

"Right," I said. "And they didn't have time to get a change of orders from someone else, either."

"So you rule them out?"

"Absolutely. For now." I sipped muscatel. Sparrows wrecked their lungs, cheeping.

"So who do you figure?"

"Anybody else," I said. "In the dark I couldn't recognize the car or the guy. Come to think of it, I don't know that it was a guy. It could have been a woman."

"Give me a hint."

"Well, my first thought was of Colby, guy who works for Reynard. If it was Colby, he could have had the time. It could have been Canard, guy who manages the Canyon for Reynard. Canard knew where Allison was headed. The motive would have been to get Reynard pinched and take over the business."

I turned off the brass lamp. The big room was bathed in a formless light. I surveyed the burnished floor, the olive drab blanket on the bed, oak chairs, and antique oak table. There was fishing gear, books, and cartons of pipe tobacco scattered in counterpoint to dead cacti and my prints of Hopper and Schlecter. The room seemed comfortably tired. It held the faint rain smells of tea roses, mimosa, and honeysuckle. The neighbor's rooster crowed twice and stopped.

"Any other ideas?" asked Andy.

"Agnes Reynard," I said.

"Reynard's wife. Sleek number who sleeps late?"

"You know her?"

"Met her when I worked Vice. She gets around, but then again so does syphilis. What makes you think of her?"

"Just thinking. I still think too much."

"Let's back up," Andy said. He poured another muscatel. I took the jug and poured one myself. Andy's face grew red. He looked medium rare. "Why kill Allison in the first place?"

"What I said before was just guesswork. Really, I don't know. Andy, I found a note pinned to Allison at the cemetery. The note said that if he came around the Canyon again, he'd be underground. Did the cops find the note?"

"No note," Andy responded. "Whoever killed Allison did away with the note. Didn't care about giving him another chance at the Canyon. It would seem to make it one of Reynard's boys, not his wife."

"Could Johnny Reynard have done it?"

"You mean the kid Johnny?"

"Yeah, his son."

"I'd say yes if Jules had told him to do it. Ordinarily, I'd say Johnny Reynard isn't ripe enough to pick for a job like that. He's small-time. Maybe, though, he's stupid enough to try to break into the big time with a scheme like this."

I thought it over. "If Reynard wanted to double-cross his pals, then he could have had his son waiting at the cemetery. Slick as hell, he could have come into Maple Grove and done the job."

"That doesn't work, either," Andy said. "Reynard would have known the finger would point at him."

"Maybe Reynard actually wants to give Vice his son as the patsy. Think about it."

Andy doused his cigar. One junker lumbered up Sycamore and stopped at the corner. Gears clanked. It chugged away.

"What's Reynard's motive in giving Vice his son?"

"All right," I said. "I don't have much. Just a lot of idle theories splashing around a big, black ocean. We need a kiddie pool fast." I was trying on ideas like old suits. Nothing fit unless you knew about Agnes and Johnny. There was a reason for Jules to frame his son.

Andy stood. He weaved the suspenders around his shoulders, dove for his hat, and found it on the bed. Striped sunlight lay on the brass bedstead.

"Shit," he said. "I'm off the case. If you come up with something, give it to me. I'll keep my ears open. This whole case could be connected to the skimming at the Canyon. All I know is, I need a bath." Andy donned his hat.

I followed him to the porch. He leaned against the rotted railing, one hand on the balustrade. Pure cobalt morning poured through the elms.

"What are you going to do?" he asked.

"I'll try to check the books at the Canyon," I said.

"Keep my eye on the tables for skimming. It should say something about why Allison was killed. What, I don't know."

Andy said, "Those guys are all rough. Keep your eyes open." Andy turned and pushed his hulk from the rail. "I guess that didn't come out right, Jules Reynard and all," he said.

A milk truck stopped down the street. The milkman hopped out and towed a rack of milk and cheese to one of the old Victorians. Beside Andy, a green garden spider rested in the vortex of a silk web. Dew rested there as well. Air moved in the web like fingers on violin strings.

"You know," Andy said. "A spider spins a perfect web. Then he eats the damn thing and starts again the next night. Spider is perfect, not like us."

Andy and I stood quietly. The milkman ascended the rickety old stairs and handed me two bottles of milk. He smiled and went away.

"You be careful," Andy said. It was the second time my friends had said the same words to me. I watched Andy drive his blue Plymouth down Sycamore and stop at Maple. Then he drove east across the bridge toward his home, his wife, and his children.

Robins clowned in a peony patch. Early morning chimed a clear, soft note. Half cockeyed, I slept in my blue suit, with neither dream nor movement.

NINE

In the morning, Rita slipped into my consciousness. She wore lizard green. It flowed down her body like a river in pinyon pine country. Xavier Cugat played a one-note samba and the samba shivered in Rita's hair like sunbeams. I rolled over and looked at her.

She had cool mica eyes, articulated bones, and a long, mannered neck. Her skin was the color of a Sandusky peach, fuzz and all. Long fingers and pale hands hinted sensuality and sensitive indifference. It was the kind of question a man always wonders if he can answer. Her legs were shapely as palms on the beach. Rita wet her lips with a red tongue.

I smiled as Rita danced to my side and looked down. She placed her body on the bed and held a soothing conversation with my soul. Then she touched my temples; my own gaze was on the temple of her stomach that rose and fell like an angel wing. It was a flat stomach with the hint of womanly bulge. I heard a samba inside. Rita ran a finger through her hair. It smelled of straw and apples. I reached for her thigh and Rita slipped a tongue into my ear.

I woke as Francis the cat snored purrs into my face. He stretched, yawned, and licked my ear. Francis in the morning sun was the color of a Sandusky peach, fuzz and all. He smelled of backyard straw, not at all of apples. His

111

furry stomach bulged, probably from mice. I rubbed sunlight and sleep from my eyes. Francis meandered across the blankets and yanked his body down off the bed.

I looked at my blue suit. It had all the homespun charm of a two-car crash, all the wrinkles of very old money. I raised myself from bed, took a long shower, and walked the suit up the back stairs to Mrs. Thompson's three rooms. I gave her three dozen eggs and a stack of bananas. Mrs. Thompson ironed the suit. Then I weeded and watered the garden, fed the rabbits, and tried to clean the clutter from my rooms. Then I sat in the alcove and made some calls.

Spud Christian didn't answer. I knew time was short for Jules Reynard, and what I'd seen parked in the driveway at Agnes Reynard's gingerbread house last night didn't make me think that the answers I would provide Jules would make him happy. I was willing to be patient with Johnny and Agnes, but I couldn't afford to let my knowledge cool its heels while Jules cooled in a cell downtown. If Jules was going down for the count, then I wanted him in the ring with his corner men, including me. Misgivings and concerns rambled around my conscience looking for appropriate loopholes and dodges, but nothing could convince me I didn't owe Reynard some loyalty after taking his money. Even Andy Lanham hadn't questioned that judgment. It was one I'd have to live with. I hoped I could. Working for a thug was not my idea of Sunday school.

I gagged on the thought of Johnny and Agnes alone in the house on Sleepy Hollow. Johnny was full of himself, loaded with charm and flair. In most situations, I figured he could be harmless enough, as most charming men are. Agnes was like sulfur matches. You needed to close her cover before striking. I didn't think Johnny had sense enough to close covers anywhere. Agnes looked tough, a dental receptionist with an enamel heart. She was a gold-digger with claws. It seemed likely to me she would try to destroy her husband if she stood to gain. She stood to gain.

I supposed that Johnny stood to gain, too. Everybody stood
to gain except Jules, who stood to lose. Just a blind thug
whose time had come and gone. The crudity of the situation chilled me.

I put on some dungarees and drove to a game and nov-
elty shop built into the recesses of an old saloon on West
Douglas. This part of town had been where Wyatt Earp
and his friends held forth, and the streets were old and
brick and packed with facades. From the joke store I chose
a couple of pairs of red gambling dice and a chapbook on
dice: loading, palming, and cheating. At a mom-and-pop
on Maple I bought a big T-Bone, tomatoes, lettuce, and a
gallon of orange juice. I stocked up on smokes, muscatel,
bologna, swiss cheese, and pipe tobacco.

I puttered and broiled the steak, made salad, and drank
some orange juice. In early afternoon, I rocked on the front
porch and read the chapbook. The steak was juicy, and
early spring was everywhere with lilacs, tulips, peonies,
and red tea roses. The sky was soft as milkbreath, the air
pure blue as Miss Muffet's corset. From the ground there
escaped a mushy aroma of roots, tubes, and stems. Robins
stuck beaks into black loam and hopped like popping corn.

The sun swept south and east, and Mrs. Thompson joined
me on the porch. I fed her some tomatoes, romaine, and
lemon iced tea. She nibbled the salad like a rabbit, and we
watched the sun dance in elms, showering the yard with
warm shadows. I phoned Spud again, but got no answer.
I was anxious to get the camera and take a look at the
Canyon's books. I knew there should be two sets, one for
Jules and another for Canard. Gus Canard had to be in on
the skimming, otherwise it was an inside cheat job from
the tables. What I'd seen of Johnny had made the second
possibility possible.

Mrs. Thompson watched as I used my Staunton chessboard as a table. I put the chessboard on my knees and for
an hour practiced palming dice. I scattered four dice on the

chessboard at random. Crooking my thumb and index finger, I held an extra die in the hollow space made by two fingers. Then I swept my hand above the four dice on the table, finally settling a palm above one. Pretending to take one of the die with my fingers, I picked it up with my palm and released the hidden die, sending it spinning along the chessboard, at the same time holding the new die in my palm. I practiced fast and slow, sweaty and calm, then practiced with two dice in my palm, tossing a third.

After the first hour, I switched hands and practiced with my left. I discovered I was right-handed with a vengeance. Mrs. Thompson thought I was touched.

The three-thirty factory whistles blew south of town. It was a long groan and a worker's lament, the solid major chord of wage slavery and family life. Mrs. Thompson shuffled away and returned with my blue suit neatly pressed on a wooden hanger. She had added a white handkerchief. On the lapel was a pale red tulip.

I phoned Andy Lanham at the station and left a message, then drove to the office and scouted around. There were three messages slipped under the door. One was from an insurance agent, one was from a typewriter repair shop, and the third was from World Book Encyclopedia. The World Book suggested that each of my children would be dunces without their product. I went into the office and paid some bills and wrote notes to some steady clients explaining the situation. Jake the barber stuck his head around the corner with a hello. We made a fishing and baseball date, then I drove home.

I took a hot bath and sat on the brass bed with orange juice and Rita dreams. The five o'clock news foretold storms from Nebraska, high winds, rain, and hail. There was nothing about Charlie Allison. Mantle had a good day in New York. The Thumper popped two in Chicago. In general it was a fine day for everyone except Charlie Allison and Jules Reynard.

In the flat evening sun, the Canyon appeared like an aged flamingo. Pink paint chips lay scattered in the peony beds. The desert scenes were all faded. There were languid tones in the amber sun and rising dust. I sat in the deserted parking lot and smoked a Lucky and thought of the Canyon as a fat madam, not retired, but on her way out. Too much paint and too many miles. I went inside.

The bottle blonde stiffed me with a frown. I didn't flirt enough to make it worth her while to smile. I went to the bar for my ginger ale. I took the glass into the kitchen. In one corner a Syrian was beating a naked chicken. The chicken didn't fight back. Maye held her feet on a metal stool. She was smoking a small cheroot. Fluorescence smothered the room with woolly glare. Dishwater, grease, and MSG soaked from white walls. Maye stared at me.

"Good evening," she said. There was a look of mild disappointment in her expression.

"Maye," I said. "Do you know what kind of car Canard drives?"

"You just won't quit," she replied.

She sucked her cheroot. An incandescent dot appeared at the tip and a spool of smoke escaped. Behind me, another chicken split with a crack.

"He drives a big Cadillac like you and me never going to own."

"What color?"

"It looks like a gun."

"How about some dinner about seven-thirty?"

"You come back here to the kitchen. We're going to have more customers tonight than last."

"What's on the menu?" I asked.

Maye rolled the cheroot in her hands. They were cracked and burnished as horsehide by linseed oil. From the dance floor marched some dispassionate Harry James, one trumpet and a short stack of trombones.

"I'll have you some veal and peppercorns. There's some

kibbe, too, if you want it. But I don't know what you're doing working for Mr. Reynard, a man like that. I don't do nothing but cook, but I don't know what you're doing. I just look around and see things. You know what I'm saying, Mr. Roberts?''

"Trust me, Maye," I said. "I'm trying to do right."

"I sure hope so," she said. "You're a nice boy."

That's right, I thought. I'm a nice boy. I touched Maye and told her I'd be along at seven-thirty. She nodded and managed a small smile, more hopeful than meant.

Maye looked at my suit. "That tulip does look nice, Mr. Roberts," she said.

I finished the ginger ale and went to table one. Tony leaned drowsily against the back wall.

"The tulip is nice," Tony said.

"I made it myself," I answered.

In my suit pocket, two red dice burned cool holes. I helped brush the table, stack chips, and count money. Those dice grew heavy and complained about lack of oxygen. It started me thinking about religion and justification by faith. My heart raced.

Tuesday evening at the Canyon oozed like gray clay. Shortly past seven o'clock twenty square dancers plunged to the floor in a rondo of hay-nonny-nonnies and dosey-does. The women cantered around the dance floor in white crinoline and lace piled above fifty yards of fluffy slip. All were portly and toothy, raised on fried bacon and rhubarb pie.

Their partners were scrawny bucks wearing black string ties, dark wrinkled trousers, and white cowboy shirts. The square dance droned in the casino like an earache. They wouldn't gamble, but they drank a little whiskey and ate beef.

At the table, a tired factory hand lost five dollars and ambled his body out the door. There was no sign of Agnes or Johnny, or of Colby. The hatcheck girl picked her teeth with a fingernail file. I sticked and talked baseball to Tony. He didn't seem interested in sports, chess, or politics. He wanted a new Mercury and a path to the hatcheck girl's thighs. At last we settled on bored silence.

At seven-thirty I went to the kitchen. I ate veal piccata, garlic salad, some kibbe, and a slab of apple pie with cheese. I drank some mineral water and listened to my liver yodel. My kidneys doffed a hat. Then I went into the parking lot with a cigarette and found Canard's gunmetal Cadillac parked beside the back stairs that wound to his second-story office.

I walked back inside and through the kitchen to survey the back approach. A steep bank rose from the edge of the parking lot into hackberry and oak. Two windows peered bleakly from the office onto the wilderness. The windows were shuttered and grim. Dirty yellow rays escaped the shutters and tinkled on the cutbank like lost pennies. The door at the top looked like plywood and tenpenny nails, a simple Yale lock above a handle. I'd been in Canard's office and hadn't noticed a safe or strongbox, and the office didn't look burglarproof. Perhaps I could jimmy the door, take some pictures, and scamper down the back stairs. It could be done and it had to be tried.

During the next two hours a couple of sump-handle brothers from Haysville lost money. They complained and groaned and breathed fire. They rolled sevens and twos and bet foolishly. A mousy waitress delivered shots of whiskey to the brothers. Three hundred down, they staggered away, openly surmising that the dice were crooked, the table crooked, the stickman crooked, the dealer crooked, and God Himself a miserable NO-GOOD. One lady in mink watched her starchy husband lose thirty dollars. They argued and left. Gus Canard came down his stairs and wandered into the casino. The square dancers went home after dinner.

Johnny came in at eleven-thirty. He handed the hatcheck

girl a new borsalino. She giggled and flirted with stunted eyelashes. Johnny shook Taylor's hand and staggered down the casino stairs. He wore a powder-blue oxford shirt open above a cashmere cardigan sweater. Two stiff legs balanced drunkenly inside his pleated trousers. Johnny smelled of Canoe and whiskey.

Across the room, Canard snapped his fingers. The mousy waitress appeared with a shot of whiskey and handed it to Johnny. He smiled and slugged the whiskey. His gills pumped alcohol and hot carbon. I saw Agnes Reynard amble down the stairs and sit at a roulette table. Canard clapped Johnny on his cashmere back. Agnes crossed her legs inside an orange sun dress. Her knees were bony, not like Rita's at all.

Couples played slots. The casino shimmered from the sound of bells, clangs, gongs, mutterings, comings-and-goings, glass, and ivory. Johnny and Agnes played roulette and seemed to be winning. The blackjack tables hummed. One tall gent in a black tux attracted a crowd with a string of drunken wagers. He lost. The crowd murmured. Winning seemed more exciting to me, but I wasn't a crowd.

Past midnight, Agnes and Johnny walked in a smoky filigree to the crap table. They joined an Air Force captain and an anniversary couple. The captain played right, tough craps, betting numbers, taking the odds. In an hour, he had managed to eke out twenty-five dollars and was satisfied with his showing. The anniversary couple spatted and lost. Johnny leaned above the table, glee on his smooth features. Agnes clung to his waist like an inner tube.

"Coming out," I said.

Tony hopped some red dice to Johnny. He cupped them and gave them to Agnes. She blew on the dice and smiled. Johnny tossed a ten-spot onto Any Craps and rolled a twelve. Tony paid and returned the dice to Johnny. Johnny snapped his fingers for the waitress.

"Fish in a barrel," Johnny said. He stared at my red tulip. "Man here rolls nothing but heaven."

His Canoe evaporated into whiskey and he shoved another ten onto the center bets. He shot the dice, hitting the wall hard to an eleven.

"A winner again," Tony said. Tony slid a pile of chips to Johnny. I sticked the dice to Johnny and Agnes picked up the red cubes and held them to her breasts. With her cheeks flushed rust color, black eyeliner, red lipstick, she was cute as a box of spoiled Red-Hots. She belonged in the lost and found at the bus station.

Johnny held the shoot for fifteen minutes, horsing field bets, any craps, and hard ways. The Air Force captain lost his twenty-five on right bets, grunted, drained his vodka, and went home. The anniversary wife got sick and was carried to the car.

"Some dice," the captain said as he left.

"Some shooter," Tony said.

I waited for a chance. At the end of the night, it came. Johnny left the table for whiskey. When he returned, he stood against the far wall, tossing dice my way. Agnes found his side and they kept shooting wrong dice, craps, field bets, and hard ways. Johnny was up three hundred dollars. Then the dice hit the back wall and rested on a seven.

"A winner," Tony said. He reached for the dice.

I palmed one of the twins in my pocket and scooped the shooters from the table. I hooked a thumb behind one of the pair and slipped the substitute and its mate across the table. Tony halted and glared. He studied the dice and returned them to Johnny. Johnny lost two bets and left the table with Agnes on his arm like a hound. I stuffed the shooter in my pocket. Bill Halley's drummer smashed my heart with a stick.

The casino emptied. The tall gent in black left and his crowd followed. The mousy waitress gathered drink glasses

as the croupiers brushed their layouts. I covered the crap
table and said good night to Tony. In the main room, waiters stacked chairs and the fire-scarred man swept the floor.
Small houselights buried in the spackled ceiling revealed
dust, disuse, and food stains. The nameless barman feigned
an expression of bored unconcern. Behind the feign was a
mask and behind that a mirror. I walked outside.

Night drained through the elms. Peonies and black earth
joined the wind. I smoked a Lucky and strolled to the side
stairs. There was a gunmetal Cadillac parked at the base
of the stairs. The burgundy Hudson and the MG were gone.
I tossed the Lucky into a chuckhole and drove toward
Sleepy Hollow. The streets were deserted and no one followed me.

I put the shooter into the pocket liner of my suit. Johnny
Reynard had used the cube to collect another three hundred
of what table one owed him. Either he was blessed as a
swaddled babe or the dice were lumpy. I cruised down a
dark Central Street and wound into Sleepy Hollow feeling
sour as old tennis shoes. I knew what I'd find at the gingerbread house and it wouldn't be Hansel and Gretel.

I drove slowly past the house. The Hudson and the MG
were parked in the driveway. I drove away.

Spud's Nash sagged in front of my old Victorian. I rolled
into the alley and rumbled into my slot beside the rabbits.
Wind rose in the elms and the rabbits twitched nervously.
Thunder shook in unknown places. Across the fence,
chickens clucked under their breath. I walked to the side
of the dark house and mounted the front steps. Spud tossed
his Camel and rose.

"How's the stickman?" he asked. Spud wore paint-
stained dungarees and a ball cap. His work shirt was mis-
buttoned.

"Come in. I've been trying to call you."

We went inside the old house. I flipped on the brass floor

lamp and went into the kitchen for orange juice. Spud searched the refrigerator for muscatel and poured a glass.

"What's the story?" I asked.

Spud reached into his back pocket and extracted a small camera. He handed it to me.

"The guy was out of town. That's why it took me two days. I had to call his wife and she let me into the shop. I talked to the guy on the phone and he'll do the developing. The fifty dollars was fine."

I changed clothes and Spud made bologna sandwiches. Then he smoked a Camel on the porch and watched the wind. I pulled the brass lamp into the alcove and turned on the overhead lamp. I dropped the shooter onto the oak table. It shimmered like a ruby.

"What the hell is this?" Spud said. He munched the sandwich.

"Johnny Reynard has been shooting the lights out of table one at the Canyon. He's been doing it with this."

Spud fondled the cube. He held it up into the brass lamp.

"Let's roll some craps," I said.

With the chessboard, I made a wall. Spud clacked the die against the board and it rebounded onto the oak surface. It showed six. He tried again. He threw one, then six, one, one, six, and one again. Spud whistled and threw a lonesome three. In fifteen tries, he tossed six and one twelve times.

"I'd like to own a pair of these," he said.

I rummaged in the kitchen and found a pocketknife. When I returned to the alcove, wind banged the windows. Spud studied the cube.

"You say Johnny Reynard won money with these clangers?"

"Around fifteen hundred in the last few nights."

"You think he's cheating?"

I looked at the cube in the brass halo. I rubbed the knife blade across one side of the die. Red paint chipped away and I sensed a rough spot in one corner. I picked at the spot with the knife point. A chip fell away from the corner.

"What the hell?" Spud said.

"Tungsten," I said. "Commonly used to load dice. This particular beauty probably has half a dozen loads. It obviously comes up one and six. Makes a nice way to roll boxcars, any craps, and hard ways. Snake eyes. For a guy who bets the center of a crap table, it would be money in the bank."

"I see what you mean," Spud said. He thought. "You think Johnny Reynard is stealing from his old man?"

"I think so. But he's getting help from the club manager. It's a slick way to skim club profits until Canard and Johnny can get rid of Jules. Simple and unbeatable."

"How did you get the cube?"

"Palmed it from the table tonight."

Spud finished his sandwich. Francis the cat strolled into the alcove and hopped onto the table. He purred and picked at a cockleburr buried in his neck. I flipped on the old Philco radio and found some Nat Cole. Black bushy clouds rumbled low in the north and west. Spud adjusted his glasses.

"I talked to the veterinarian in Augusta," he said.

"What's the story?"

"He didn't mind talking, but he didn't have much to say. The doc used to work for Reynard at the Black Fox on a regular basis. Seems the ranch ran a pretty-good-size herd until four or five years ago. Since Reynard went blind, they only keep three or four horses around. Your friend Colby feeds the horses and there was a Mexican who cleaned the stalls and hauled alfalfa.

"Doc Glick remembered the Mexican fellow called during the night some months back and said a couple of horses had been killed. Glick drove to the ranch to take a look. He says that he saw Colby and that the horses looked pretty badly torn up. Colby doused the mess with gasoline and set the horses on fire. Glick drove back to town an didn't think much about it. Says Colby told him he should mind his own business. Glick says he knew Reynard was a gambler or had a shady reputation, so he figured it was some kind of vendetta. Glick hasn't been back to the ranch and has no intention of going. Seems Colby let the Mexican go."

"Glick didn't have any records, photos, or notes," I said.

"Didn't need any."

"How old were the horses?"

"Says they weren't even broke yet."

"Thanks, Spud," I said. "I appreciate the information."

Spud stood. "You look tired," he said. "If you're going to use the camera, I hope you've got a way out."

"I've got a plan," I said.

"I'll tell you something else. I talked to some of the guys down at the White Way snooker hall. These guys were old stiffs and gamblers themselves. They'd heard stories about Jules Reynard. There was this one guy named Sammy said he'd heard a story about Reynard when he was still in Kansas City. Seems he heard about Reynard's first wife and how she ran around town with a young hood on Reynard's time. Reynard found out about his wife and the hood. Well, a couple of butchers found the young hood heels-up in a meat locker at the Armour plant. Someone found Reynard's wife, too, only they found her in the Missouri River under a railroad trestle."

Lightning creased the sky. Nacreous slashes appeared like stars in the bay windows. Thunder followed.

"I'm glad to hear it," I said.

Spud walked to the front screen. Francis tagged along, rubbing his back on Spud's leg. Rain whispered in the trees, thin sheets struck the black pavement. It fell in a brief, blue cascade.

"This guy Sammy said the wife was murdered in nineteen thirty-eight. I don't think your Jules Reynard is a simple fellow. Sammy thought he was a hard case."

"Thanks, Spud. I'll consider it."

"See you tomorrow?" asked Spud. I nodded.

Spud sloshed into the rain and drove his Nash into the night.

I stripped and lay down in the dark. The rain stopped and the wind died.

TEN

Humans are weeds converged in furious war. Their perpetual assault exterminates beauty and denies cultivation its due. I began to think of my involvement in the Reynard case as an example of weedy growth masquerading as work. In three days, I'd learned about Jules, Johnny, Agnes, and Gus Canard, and there wasn't a decent trait among the lot. I'd done it for money. There wasn't any excuse about that, and what I needed was a decent, honest way out, a way allowing me to keep some self-respect and a batch of honesty. I hoped the answer was a trip to Black Fox Ranch, a report on skimming, cheating, and a graceful exit, stage left. Weeds are sticky, unlovely things. I felt them growing in my garden.

I entertained these Hobbesian musings while rocking on the front porch in a diminishing patch of sun. I had a quart of orange juice and a volume of end games by Rubenstein before me. At the office I'd chased down a Hudson for the First National Bank, served two subpoenas for my lawyer pal Graybul, and stuffed some ad envelopes. The back garden was watered, the cat fed, the rabbit hutch cleaned. My new blue suit was well-pressed, and I'd picked a fresh tulip for the lapel. Finally, I showered, fluffed my physique, and prepared to leave for the Black Fox.

I sealed Johnny Reynard's die in an envelope, loaded

the small camera, and put the camera in a leather reel bag.
'I put the reel bag under the front seat of the Fairlane. As
I drove across the fields to the Black Fox, I used the time
to think. Late afternoon ambled on the prairie, cloud
shadow and hushed willow playing on bluestem. Horses
gamboled, paints and Arabians and good quarter stock.
Angus cattle grazed dumbly on green hillsides. The sun
poised amid white cloud, lazy creeks rippled, and the wind
stirred clumps of delicate redbud. It was the kind of day to
lie down on a blanket with Rita and run your hands along
her flanks, open a bottle of new Beaujolais, and convert
the loneliness and despair to money and love.

I emerged from bottomland and cattail country and found
the blacktop that led south into the Flint Hills. I listened
to some Nat Cole, Julie London, and Rosemary Clooney.
I didn't smoke. The air smelled of new hay and winter
wheat. I even decided to teach Rita to spincast for bass.

I parked in the Scotch pines. Tiresias sat by the front
door, his ears perked, his motionless body shiny and alert.
Colby answered my knock.

"Mr. Roberts," he said. He wore some chinos, boots.
He stepped aside.

Colby walked to the recessed stairs and spoke to Reynard. Then he disappeared into the back of the house, followed by Creon. Tiresias trotted through the door behind
me. Reynard was on the zebra couch listening to a radio
concert broadcast. Symphonic music stirred in the shadow
patches of carpet. Stacks of paper and documents littered
the glass coffee table. Reynard wore slacks and a white
shirt.

"You've found something?" he said.

I walked down the stairs. Reynard lit one of his black
cigars. Our game spread along one side of the table. Wind
rattled the patio doors. Sun poured through.

Reynard said, "Colby and I were going over the books.
I'm still trying to figure the skimming. I know revenue is

constantly down, sometimes in small amounts, but steady. Our costs aren't up that much."

I sat on the zebra couch. Tiresias lurched down the stairs and heeled by Reynard's elbow. I lit a cigarette and riffled smoke into the silence. It was Mahler on the radio. I tossed the envelope onto the glass. Reynard heard it hit.

"What's this?" he asked.

"There's an envelope in front of you. Open it."

Reynard drew a fingernail along the seal. It opened, dropping the die to the glass. Reynard studied the die with his hands, rolling it in his palm, testing the contour with the fingertips. A curious expression crossed his face, amusement, consternation, comprehension, all at cross-purposes.

"I'll make a guess," he said. "Loaded dice."

"I took it from table one during my shift last night. Last night I cracked it with a knife. I dug one tungsten spot from the upper right corner of the 'one.' I scraped some paint from the other sides. There are half a dozen imprints. Tungsten, I suppose. The rolls are ones and sixes."

"Losers," Reynard said.

"Losers to you and me. If a guy gambled on the center of the table, making his bets on any craps and field, he would win money. I played with the die last night and when you miss a craps, you make a field bet easy. There's enough play in the dice to miss once in a while. That's just normal. If you didn't overdo it, the other players wouldn't notice for an hour. The dealer wouldn't take as long."

"You noticed?"

"I've been at the club for three days. In that time, someone has won consistently at table one. He plays for a couple of hours, then staggers home. He takes three or four hundred and packs it in. Streaks like that could cause revenue to drop. Don't you agree?"

Reynard rose. Tiresias rose. "Would you like a drink, Mr. Roberts?" Reynard extracted a leather leash from the side table and snapped it to the choke collar around the dog's neck. Together the blind man and his dog walked to the bar.

"Make mine orange juice or ginger ale," I said.

"You've taken the pledge?"

"Taking my work seriously. Drinking interferes."

Reynard mixed a Bushmills and water. He poured ice in a tumbler and covered the ice with orange juice. His movements displayed mystical dexterity in the sea of bottles and glass. He returned to the zebra couch.

"Who is the big winner?" Reynard asked. His voice formed ice, cold, violent, and spare. I felt he'd made up his mind to something.

"Look, Mr. Reynard," I said. "I suppose the winner might be accidental."

"That doesn't seem likely. Spill it."

"Three nights your son is the winner. He comes in around eleven, gambles for an hour, then leaves. He bets stupid, holds the dice for fifteen minutes, then hits a number and loses. He doesn't pay much attention and he's usually drunk."

Reynard struck glass with his fist. Spidery cracks erupted in the tabletop.

"I'll kill him," he said.

Reynard sipped some Bushmills. Mahler loosed a crecendo. Some of the chessman had toppled and I spent time rearranging the game. The shatter had brought Tiresias to his feet. He stood, eyes riveted on Reynard. Reynard shook the leash and Tiresias heeled.

"Is he working alone?" Reynard asked.

"I've paid attention to the action. I can't spot Johnny palming or cupping dice. He grabs the bones and rolls. When he walks to the table, I eye his movement and haven't spotted a dice switch. Besides, Mr. Reynard, I frankly don't think he's smart or sober enough to cheat."

"So he has inside help."

"What do you think?"

"My son isn't brave enough to cheat me alone."

"It would seem so," I said. Lucky smoke streamed into my poor lungs like flame.

"What kind of help would he need?"

"Gus Canard. Probably the dealer. I've talked to Tony enough to believe he's following orders. Probably doesn't have a stake in the outcome. It makes for good skimming."

"Make me another Bushmills, would you?" Reynard said.

I mixed the drink. Reynard unleashed Tiresias and snapped his fingers. The dog trotted through a side door and disappeared. Mahler drooped a notch, quiet, moody strings. My own musical taste ran to Louis Armstrong and Bach. I didn't understand lush, romantic stuff. I handed the drink to Reynard.

"How did you get the die?" he asked.

"I palmed it from the table."

"Do you think Tony noticed?"

"I doubt it. He glanced over as I picked it up, but I scooted in a substitute and it passed. I'll find out tonight, anyway. If they know, then the skimming will let up for a while. It will stop until I go away or until you are arrested."

Tiresias loped into the room, followed by Colby. Colby walked to the stairs and leaned on a rail.

"I'm here, Mr. Reynard," he said.

"Don't leave for town yet," Reynard said. "I want to talk to you for a minute. Roberts will be here for twenty minutes yet."

Colby said, "I'll be in back." He left.

Reynard shifted his attention. He sipped the Bushmills. "I want you to work a few more days," he said. "Keep your eyes open and report to me. Are you planning any more moves?"

"I'll look at the books tonight. I'll try to get photos. If

Canard is doctoring yours and keeping two sets, then you should be able to compare your books with the real ones he keeps for himself. If there's no difference, then your losses are strictly cheating from Johnny. In that case, I'd suspect Tony the dealer and your son are operating freelance. It's been known to happen in casinos before.''

"I still don't think Johnny has the brains or the guts for it."

Reynard placed his hands on the glass and explored the spidery cracks. He shifted some papers and pulled the chessboard to the center. He ran his fingers across the board, drawing the tips in an arc above the pieces. Outside, the sky revealed a frieze of clotted pink, sun and redbud and purple shade. A meadowlark tweeted.

"There's something else," I said.

Reynard hopped a knight. "You've got trouble on the board," he said.

I studied the position, then moved a bishop. Reynard was right. I sipped orange juice. I'd been sober two days. My perceptions were aberrant.

"I followed Johnny after he left the club for the last two nights. He leaves at closing time. I shut down the table and I'm right behind him."

"Why would you do that?"

I paused. The wind broke through the winter wheat in a fluid current. "Agnes hangs on him when he plays." Silence crawled in the big room.

"Does he enjoy that?" asked Reynard.

"I wouldn't know."

"What do you know?"

"I know his car is parked at the house in Sleepy Hollow when I drive by. I don't stay all night, just two hours the first night. Agnes is there and Johnny is there and it's three o'clock in the morning. You make what you want out of it."

Reynard stroked Tiresias. "I told you I'd kill him."

"Give it up," I said.

Reynard laughed. It was a sneer like a knife slicing skin, long and ragged. His hands and face turned white and his eyes tightened into a painful, wasted stare. "I've been on top too long," he said. "I don't give it up like that."

"It's time now."

"You don't know what the hell you're saying. Being small is your way. Being big is my way. I'll handle the trouble now that I know what it is."

"Your trouble won't stop just like that. No trouble does. You can't beat your way out and you can't buy your way out. Not ultimately."

"Get me the photos and we'll go from there."

"Then I'm through," I said. "My obligation to you ends at that point."

"Not until then."

"I made the deal, Mr. Reynard. I wish to hell I hadn't, but I did. I'll get the photos, then we're through. For myself, I've got a score to settle for Charlie Allison. That one is on the house. Then it's paid in full. I've been your eyes and I'll be through."

"You're washing your hands?"

"If you want to put it like that."

"Get the photos," Reynard said.

"You hurt Johnny and I'll come after you," I said.

Reynard paused. He puffed the cigar and sipped some Bushmills. The Mahler finished.

"You fucking punk," he growled.

"I wondered about you," I said after a while. "I felt sorry for you. But you bought me like you buy everybody else. Well, you've got your money's worth. But it's just about over. I won't look back. You do anything to Johnny and you're my business."

"Get the photos," Reynard said.

"If I can."

I stubbed my cigarette in a crystal ashtray and rose. Ti-

resias popped to attention and Reynard walked me to the
stairs. Colby entered the room.

"Trouble, boss?" he said.

"No trouble," Reynard said.

I went outside into blue shadow. The pines whispered in
a mild wind. Three brown squirrels cavorted in the pines,
hopping and twirling acrobatically. I studied the perfect
confirmation of a colt. He nibbled prairie grass and ambled
to the brow of a hill, roan highlights glancing at sun.
Through the window of the big house, I watched Colby
and Reynard huddle. Reynard swung an arm violently. I
drove down the gravel drive and away from Black Fox
Ranch.

The highway was an empty, narrow finger. Suspicion
clanked around my brain. It seemed likely to me that Canard had enlisted Johnny to run Jules out of the casino business, that the poison and horse killing and skimming were
all a scheme to convince Jules that the gambling business
wasn't healthy for him anymore. It seemed a rough way to
deliver a message, but these guys weren't ballerinas and
gambling wasn't dancing.

I wasn't close to discovering the killer of Charlie Allison, but the motive made sense. Whoever killed Charlie
Allison probably wanted to frame Jules. That made it Gus
Canard and Johnny. The only problem with that theory was
the premise and the facts. Gus Canard didn't have time to
close up and get to Maple Grove on the night of the murder. Perhaps he could have hired the job done, maybe one
of the Syrian goons in the Canyon. I didn't think Johnny
had the brains to kill Allison, but I'd been wrong on sure
bets before.

Then there was Agnes. She gained if Jules took a fall.
Maybe she wanted Johnny and the big house. Maybe Johnny would look better if he owned the Canyon and not just
some crummy horse parlor in West Wichita. Maybe Johnny thought so, too, and planned this whole scam. Maybe

Truman shouldn't have dropped the A-bomb, maybe Plato was right and Aristotle wrong. Maybe I should learn to sew and get married. Maybe I could bake a cake.

The Canyon relaxed in a shaded cocoon. A gunmetal Cadillac was parked by the outside stairs. I parked and went inside.

Micki the hatcheck girl eyed me without interest. She clacked her gum and rubbed a stoic eyeball against her crossword. Black roots surfaced from a platinum swirl. I hiked past Taylor and headed for the kitchen.

Maye leaned in a back doorway, smoking a thin cheroot. She smiled as I approached.

"What's for dinner, Maye?"

"That all you think about? Food?"

"When you cook it," I said.

She laughed. "I could find you a steak, a small one."

"I'm through with it tonight, Maye. I thought you'd like to know. I haven't killed anyone and I haven't sold all of my soul. I think I can buy it back."

"I'm glad, Mr. Roberts," Maye said.

"We gardening together this summer?" I asked.

"Sure thing," she said. "You be here at seven for that fillet. I've got peach ice cream, too."

I winked at Maye and went through the swinging kitchen doors. Cowboys rode the bar. One couple nodded over spaghetti in a corner. The dance floor was lonesome as Quasimodo on Sunday afternoon. I strolled to table one and said hello to Tony. It was six o'clock.

I sticked for an enlisted man who felt hot. He dropped fifty dollars on field bets. The Air Force captain returned to the table and rode numbers, plowing the table steadily against rocky odds until he won a few dollars. He drank steadily and well. The enlisted man stayed away from the captain. He kept losing foolishly. The captain left the table.

I took my break and ate the fillet, garlic salad, and a

bowl of peach ice cream. By seven-thirty I was back on the table. The enlisted man had gone, replaced by a herd of Moose clubbers. The Moose club had slots, but no crap games. These guys were warming up for their meeting and some hot bingo.

Gus Canard sauntered through the casino twice, looking the place over like a raptor on a thermal. The blackjack tables filled. The casino developed a tense rush of energy. Two or three dolls in satin lined the roulette wheel, giggling as they lost their husbands' money, shouting when they won a small bet. There were more giggles than shouts, but they had fun. The mousy waitress brought me orange juice. I drank the juice and talked to Tony and sticked the table. The evening wore away like old shoes.

Johnny and Agnes arrived at midnight. As I watched them cross the busy dance floor, Agnes seemed flushed. They sat at the bar and ordered drinks and drank them. Agnes wore something diaphanous. Her bony legs were too bony, but she showed enough thin thigh to attract attention. Jukebox noise tore through the place like small-town gossip. Agnes dropped from her stool and led Johnny to the roulette table. They played and laughed like kids. The satin dolls left the wheel and discovered their husbands at the bar. The husbands looked like doctors.

Johnny Reynard strolled to a blackjack table and sat, slumped as a beaver coat. Agnes followed him on unsteady high heels. Some brown ribbon bound her auburn hair. The blackjack tables were sloppy and noisy with the drunken sound of people losing money and laughing over it. Soon enough, Johnny developed a small crowd. It surrounded him in an arc of humdrum motion. I couldn't tell if he was winning or losing, but money always draws a crowd. It's like a guy poised on a fifth-story ledge.

The gambling waned. Slowly, tables emptied of the sound of money and people. Johnny sat on his stool, hitting, staying, drinking whiskey. Agnes buzzed around him

like a bad cross-examination. I watched the waiters stack
chairs and busboys bus tables. The blond barman wiped
the bar and stacked his glasses, then unloaded the cash
register and rolled quarters. The cashier totaled figures.
Tony and I wiped the crap table and quilted it. Tony stuffed
some cash in a strongbox and stacked the chips. We hadn't
spoken for two hours.

Gus Canard pushed through the glass beads and stood
beside Johnny and Agnes. The fire-scarred black man swept
the dance floor. He was a big man with roseate scars on
his face, webbed fingers, and no thumb. Canard leaned
against the blackjack table, taking up time and talking to
Johnny. Agnes nodded and laughed. It was a thin, undis-
tinguished laugh. Canard clapped Johnny on his back, then
mounted the casino steps, shook hands with Taylor, and
went outside. I walked to the bar and ordered a ginger ale
for the road. The barman grimaced and poured the ginger
ale. I downed some and left.

The night was cool silk and warm cotton. Summer stars
burned through oak and hackberry shadow. Canard's Cadillac was gone and the windows of the office were dark. I
felt for the camera under the front seat and put it in my
pocket. Sweaty fear and determination gurgled in my stomach. I drove the Fairlane down the hill and went south on
Hillside to a dead-end copse of mulberry. A clapboard
shack hunkered down a dirt road. It was dark. I parked the
car and walked up the crest of hill, then down the other
side. From the brow of hill, I was directly above the Canyon, near Maye's hideout. I overlooked the stairs and the
parking lot.

I opened the reel bag and examined the camera. I also
had two jimmies, a small flash, pocketknife, and a screw-
driver. Sweat drained into my shoes. Adrenaline whizzed
in my brain. An owl hooted encouragement. Below, I could
see a Syrian scrubbing dishes in the kitchen, his face bob-

bing in yellow steam. The burgundy Hudson and red MG were in the parking lot. Time froze.

I sucked air and moved. The office stairs rose before me. I stumbled up them, reached the top, and slid a jimmy into the lock. The lock wasn't complicated. Sweat and nervous energy shook my hands. That was complicated. The jimmy slipped and fell inside the tumbler. It clicked and the door opened.

Garlic and bad air rushed past. The office was dark as a coal shack. I pulled the door closed and stood sweating in black infinity. My eyes sought the details in the blackness. I flicked on the tiny flash and looked around.

I was beside the couch, awash in racing forms. I walked to the desk and rifled each drawer in turn. I unfolded the black ledgers on the bookshelves and found receipts for supplies, food, payroll records, and utilities payments. I found tax records, roast beef sandwiches, and a rubber. There was the detritus of a gambling history and nothing very neat. Canard wouldn't keep sloppy books for Jules Reynard.

The books were squirreled in a sideboard beneath a stack of racing forms and receipts. They were two hardback ledgers, blue ink, red lines, neat printing, dates, tables, and entries, all parallel and unequal. I studied the ledgers beneath a floor lamp, taking the chance that no one would see the glow. I spread the ledgers on the desk and snapped twenty photos. I folded the books and put them back in the sideboard. Then I snapped off the lamp and the flash and stood in darkness.

A scream spiraled in the night. My blood flowed north. Another low, terrified scream mounted and broke, followed by scuffles and a tangle of bleak, unsure cries. I stood in the dark as seconds flowed underground. I strained to hear and feel reality. I stuffed the camera and the jimmy into the reel bag. Thunder rumbled far away and then there was silence. I crossed the dark room and opened the outer door.

Wild night roared in the oaks. An empty parking lot spread before me, shimmering in the moonlight. I descended the stairs and stood in the dark, listening and watching. Movement spread in one corner of the lot like a stain. A figure huddled in the burst of lightning. Blood slammed in my heart. I moved for shadows and the movement itself.

As I moved in the darkness, I remembered Charlie Allison and the spidery crack of glass on Reynard's table. A black car loomed. My hands were drawn quickly into a V behind my back and I felt my head go down. There was the thick, sucking sound of bone and skin and metal together. I staggered in fields of pain, roaring bursts of it welling inside. I was part of the night and the metallic fear, bathed in nebulae, washed to a far shore of dreamless sleep. My head smashed into metal again.

I kissed earth. There was the struggle to breathe, a conversation, and a pair of shoes. I smelled Canoe and whiskey.

Then I was alone.

ELEVEN

"You've a concussion."

A cold shoehorn slid its way into my mouth. Gritty fog pounded my eyes above a glittering swath of broken glass. I felt hands lift my head and I drank water from a glass tube.

"There. You rest now."

I mumbled incomprehensibly from bandages.

"My name is Lucy, and Dr. Fiske says you'll be just fine. Rest, and you'll be up and around in no time."

Images sparred in a smoky ring, brown idols in raingear and mukluks. Mush dribbled in midair.

"Where am I?" I managed.

"Don't you worry. You're in the hospital, and I won't leave you tonight."

I groped after a face. I found an overfried bratwurst. I imagined myself sleeping in a leafy dell, water slipping from rocky ledges to deeply opalescent pools. A galaxy whirled into focus and became an isolated patch against inky darkness.

"What happened?" I said. My jaw throbbed. I raised my head. I lay in a white room, my tortured view directly on a white sink. Hollow white sheets hovered above me and something white spoke delirious sentences that made no sense. My tongue was a slab of gorgonzola.

"Help me sit up," I said.

"Don't be stubborn."

"I feel sick." I did, too.

"That's quite normal."

"More water."

Lucy was a nurse. She stuffed a pillow behind my head and allowed me water in small sips. The glass straw was cold and my head ached as the water fell into my throat.

"How long have I been here?"

"All day," the nurse said. She was nothing to me but a murky harbor full of rocking ships. Movement invaded my eye. Then there was strong shadow and solid form.

"How you doing, Mitch?" Another voice.

I recognized Andy Lanham. He was in a rumpled trench coat and drowsy felt hat. His face was an exhausted mask.

"Please don't try to talk," Lucy said.

"Turn on a light," I said.

"Don't be ridiculous," said the nurse.

"You look like shit," Andy said. "I told you to be careful."

Lucy felt my wrist. While she watched my pulse, I fought nausea to a draw. We each took our corner seats, waiting for the final bell. Cigar smoke corroded my view of the beautiful dames in the front row. They were there, I knew they were there.

"I'd like to talk for a while," Andy said. "I need to know what the hell happened."

"Will you be quiet," Lucy said.

"It's all right," I said.

"Don't be ridiculous," Lucy said.

Andy leaned above me. He was a pair of red eyes and a blob of mustard tie.

"What happened?" he asked.

"Will you two be silent?" Lucy said.

I thought it over. "Like I told you, I was making some photos of the ledger books at the Canyon. I got the pictures and came out of the office and went down the stairs. I heard someone scream, then a struggle. I walked into the parking lot and the next thing I know someone bangs me against a car.''

Lucy snorted and fluffed my pillows. ''This is ridiculous,'' she said. Then she sauntered across the room and read a *Life* magazine.

''You're a lucky boy,'' Andy said.

''I don't feel lucky.''

''Do you know who did it?''

''No idea. It was dark. Someone got me from behind, levered my arms into a V above my head, and slapped me against the hood. I don't remember a thing after that until your ugly mug.'' I sucked some tired water from a glass tube.

''You've got some deep bruises on your head.'' Andy sat on the bed. He took off his hat and wiped a hand across his face.

''I hate hospitals,'' I said.

''You're still a lucky boy. Any other impressions?''

''Well, there was someone else down there with me. A big pair of shoes. I can't be sure.''

''You say someone banged your head on a car hood?''

''That's it. Nice job, too.''

''Sounds familiar to me,'' Andy said. He took out a cigar and fiddled with it.

I wiggled my hands. They worked. I used them to hoist myself against the bedstead and look around. The nurse sat hunkered in a circle of fluorescence. Venetian blinded windows peered onto a redbrick wall, rising somber into a starry night. There were two chairs in one corner, and on a swivel tray at my arm there were utensils, thermometers, needles, and dials. The walls were white except for a putrid green stripe at shoulder height. Gray curtains hung wadded on a metal tube above me. The white toilet reminded me of my nausea.

I stretched and tried to concentrate. Pain knotted along my neck, arched in my back and shoulders. In place of my left jaw, there was a geegaw of wiry resistance. Hangovers and lost love were nothing compared to concussion. Andy dropped his felt hat onto my knee.

"Take it easy, boy. I do mean you are lucky," he said. "How do you feel?"

"I hurt bad. My head mostly."

"Doctor says you'll have to stand it for a while. They can't use painkiller on a concussion."

Andy licked his cigar and snuck a glance at the nurse. He needed a glass of beer and a smoke. Nothing but a long cruise with Rita on a small yacht sounded good to me.

Andy spoke. "Doctor says you shouldn't barrel race or do underwater photography for two weeks. No sex for ten years."

"That will make twenty altogether," I said.

Lucy dropped her magazine. She walked to the bed, took my pulse, and forced some water down my throat. She asked me how I felt and I told her. She mocked disgust and sat down with her magazine. I decided I would flirt in the morning.

"So, what the hell happened?" I asked Andy.

"You were meant to die," he said. He licked his cigar and looked at the nurse again. "I don't know why you're not dead, but you were meant to be. You should be with Charlie Allison right now. I don't know why you aren't."

"I don't understand."

"I don't, either," Andy said. There was conversation in the hallway outside. It drifted through a pine door.

"Why don't you tell me," I said.

"At three o'clock this morning the dispatcher at headquarters got a call from a woman. High-pitched, cracked voice, very excited. The woman said there were two seriously injured men under the Little River bridge. Asked for an ambulance and for the police. One of our guys got there a few minutes later and found you laid out on the bank. He could see that you'd taken a fall from the bridge, landed in the river like a bellyflop. Flat on your snoot in the mud. Broke your jaw and gave you a bad concussion. Ambulance brought you to the hospital and you've been here all day. Here we are.''

Andy snapped his fingers and fiddled some more with the cigar. "You explain that shit to me," he said.

I struggled against the nausea. "Whoever pounded me against the car hood dropped me from the Little River bridge. They expected me to die.''

"Ain't it a coincidence?''

"It sure is," I said. Sweat and fear drilled holes in my heart. Hot and cold shakes found my hands. "The same thing happened to Charlie Allison.''

"You catch on quick," Andy said.

I tried to think. Nothing happened but pain. "You said there were two men under the bridge.''

"Two," Andy said.

"Well, who was the other guy?''

"Johnny Reynard," Andy said.

Andy's words wormed inside and laid eggs. The eggs made glassine splotches in a bloody sack. There was a picture of me in the Ardennes forest, the dead-cold winter night like a dream around me, brutal, frozen, irrational. The dead men in my squad seethed with maggots, even in the cold. Then I saw worms everywhere, gnawing the bodies of Johnny Reynard and Charlie Allison.

"What about Johnny Reynard?'' I asked.

"He's down the hall. He's in bad shape. Someone tore him to bits. His face is a pulp. Parts of it are gone—ears, nose. He's lost a lot of blood.''

"Will he make it?''

"He was dumped into the river along with you. Whoever did it planned for both of you to die.''

"But will he make it?''

"He will," Andy said slowly. "He's going to lose his sight."

A dreadful sickness overcame me. "He's blind," I muttered.

"His face and arms are shredded. Poor bastard."

Then Andy stood and wrapped the trench coat around his brown suit. He put on his hat and stuffed the dead cigar into the side of his mouth. Andy doubled and trebled in my vision. I raised my hands and examined the bandages on my head.

The nurse stood. "You should go," she said to Andy. She flipped off her reading lamp. A full moon drove blue shafts into the room, bars of it falling to the floor. The brick wall outside was like a block of ice. Andy and the nurse stood bound by striped moonlight.

"Who the hell made the call?" I asked.

Andy shook his head. "There's a hell of a thing," he said. "Both you and Johnny Reynard were laid on the riverbank like neat corpses. There was a towel under your head. Your damn clothes were wet and covered by mud, so we know you were in the river. Whoever called the cops took the time to wade into the river channel, drag both of you out, then put a towel under your head and look you over. Dragging you two through the mud and the driftwood was hard work, Mitch. Someone saved your ass."

"But why didn't they stick around?"

"I don't know. But you would have drowned." Andy walked to the pine door and turned. "Your pal Spud was here," he said. "So was Christine. Your mother and grandma are coming in this morning. I don't think they know the whole story, so make one up. I'll be down at the station house, but I'm going home now to get some sleep. I'll be by to see you later today."

"Who called the cops, Andy?" I asked. The nurse body-blocked the question.

Andy walked out through the pine door. Iodine and cold

steel slithered in. Lucy washed my face and gave me a pat. She cooed and I slept.

I woke buried in darkness. A shining moon bathed the brick wall. My feet were cold and my jaw throbbed. There was jungle noise in my head. There was also a shadowed mass submerged in yellow.

"Mr. Roberts?" a voice said. "Is that you?"

"Who is it?" I managed to whisper. Pain and powerless fear echoed inside my hollow skull.

"Are you all right? This here is Maye."

She moved into a puddle of moonlight. Her frail hands were clasped in front of a print dress. Thin shoulders huddled in a shawl. Behind her was movement.

"Maye," I said. "What are you doing here?"

Maye hovered above me like a sapphire.

"We saw the nurse leave and came in. We shouldn't be here now and we've got to go pretty quick. We don't want nobody to see us here."

Maye touched my face. She pushed aside some sweat and looked me over.

"My," she said. "You do look like something. I guess you're going to be all right, though."

"Maye, you can come to the hospital tomorrow. I'd like that."

"You don't know," she said.

"I don't understand."

"We done saw what they did to you," she said.

I waited. "Tell me," I said.

"You know how I go up on the hill and take a smoke and something to drink when my work is done? Last night I was up on that hill with some vodka and cigars. I saw what they done to Mr. Johnny Reynard and then I saw what they done to you. It was a terrible thing, but I saw what they done. It happened so fast, Mr. Roberts. I saw it when they took you away and I followed as fast as I could. I remembered you followed that other fellow, and that's what I done for you. I saw how they took you to that river bridge and how they bundled you out and threw you over the rail. I almost screamed out loud, Mr. Roberts, because I didn't think they was going to do that.''

Tears welled in Maye's eyes and fell, sparkling, down the ebony edge of her cheek. She stood in fiery moonshine.

"How did you get me out of the river?''

Maye reached into the darkness. Slowly, some bulky shadows inched forward. From the black emerged the huge form of the fire-scarred man led into moonlight by Maye. He held himself slightly bowed inside work clothes. He twirled a cap in his big hands. Viscous scars knotted his face. There was no thumb on one hand. His oval face expressed gentle confusion.

"This here is Mr. Flowers,'' Maye said.

I choked.

"Mr. Flowers was on that hill with me. He went down the bank of the river and pulled you out and laid you on the sand. I called the police, and when we saw they came, we left. Mr. Flowers here done that.''

The fire-scarred man stared at the floor. His cap made flannel circles.

"Maye,'' I said.

"Mr. Flowers and me, we're in the kitchen together.''

"Maye,'' I said again.

"I know,'' she answered.

I looked at Mr. Flowers. "Thank you,'' I said quietly.

"He don't talk,'' Maye said.

I squeezed his big hand and it squeezed back. Mr. Flowers stared some more holes into the floor.

Maye spoke. "They put a dog on Johnny Reynard. It was an awful thing, Mr. Roberts.''

Pale dawn anchored the brick wall. Opalescence rose like well water.

"You go home, Maye,'' I said. "I'll be fine now.''

Maye and Mr. Flowers pushed open the pine door. My

room was silent then, filled by rose shafts. Pink tendrils ascended the brick wall. All around me in the morning, breath abandoned the dying.

TWELVE

Gray afternoon dangled in a bowl of daffodils. Grandma cried, Mother lamented; now, I was alone with pain and a gorilla in my head. A big nurse named Clara flowed into the room like Roumanian cement. She wore two or three chins tucked beneath a wad of Westphalian ham. One chin had warts. Translucent fat dripped from her arms. For twenty minutes she stuffed orange Jell-O and shaved carrots into my mouth, then followed them with buttermilk. The buttermilk hit like a sledge. Clara grinned and cooed, but the coo came out like a stertorous snore. She stuck my arm and drew blood, wrote on my chart, flipped on the radio. Then she raised two steam shovels and pounded out the door into the smelly hall.

I called Andy Lanham at headquarters and asked him to hurry to the hospital. He was interrogating a suspect and told me he would finish and come by. I asked Clara to check on the condition of Johnny Reynard and she told me he was in intensive care, blind and mauled. Clara said he wasn't talking and probably wouldn't for weeks. It made little difference. I knew what I was going to do and how.

I forced myself out of bed and paced the cold floor. I took fifteen minutes to cross the room, but I made it back in under five. I took off my cute nightshirt, found my clothes, and put on my white shirt. It was stiff with river water and caked as a week-old doughnut.

Furious dizziness struck and I sat down hard on the bed. Stars and nebulae and galaxies loop-de-looped in my funhouse brain. A pair of knives and forks tangoed along a puke-green beach. I lay down and the knives and forks stopped dancing. The dizziness passed and things started to make sense. I spent the afternoon thinking, dredging up logic and deduction. I knew who had mauled Johnny Reynard and who had used my head as a mallet. I knew who was skimming and I knew who was after Reynard and why. I had earned my fee, but it had cost Johnny Reynard his vision. There had been murder and enough brutality to put a Quaker off his feed for a month. It was time for the violence to end for good.

I phoned Jules Reynard. His voice cracked clear and cool across the miles.

"Where are you?" he asked.

"Never mind that," I said. "I'll be out to the ranch tonight at seven o'clock."

"There's nothing to discuss. You've told me what I need to know. My son is skimming and screwing my wife. I'll handle it."

"I'll make it hard on you if you're not at the ranch. I want Canard and Colby there, too."

"This better be good," Reynard said. Silence like atomic war descended over the miles. I heard Reynard breathe and then puff on his cigar. I imagined him reclining on the zebra couch, sibilant wind whispering from the lake, Tiresias and Creon erect like spikes.

"It will be fun," I said finally.

"If it's the ten thousand bonus you want, I'll have it delivered to your office."

"Keep the money. I've earned my fee. I want something else and it isn't money."

Reynard waited. Music joined the sibilant wind in my

mind. Separated by twenty miles of wheat and horse pasture, I saw Reynard clearly, vision rarefied by his own blindness, my own double sight by the acres of pain and money that divided our souls and views of life. Reynard calculated people as he calculated things, using them as means to an end, to humble, humiliate, and goad. He used people and used them up. Now I was used up and I was supposed to go away like garbage.

My own vision was nowhere as coherent as that. I hadn't the ability or the nerve to hover above people like a hawk, and I hadn't decided on any alternatives. My own hope lay in the land, taking nothing from the earth and staying quiet. People troubled me and I stayed away from them, becoming a hermit. It was killing me slowly, but I wouldn't be taking anyone with me. Reynard was taking everybody. I decided not to let it happen anymore. I'd give some of the money to Maye and Mr. Flowers, some to Spud, and then try to find ten acres along the Clark Fork River in Montana.

"Colby and Canard will be here," Reynard said. "After tonight we're finished."

"I'll be there," I said. I hung up.

Andy arrived twenty minutes later. He looked at the orange Jell-O scraps and stuffed a pudgy finger into the mess. He laughed.

"Next thing you'll be sucking milk toast," he said. Andy dragged an easy chair from the corner. He smelled the daffodils, looked at my chart, and took off his trench coat. He sat down and stared at me with big, liquid eyes.

"Did you get some sleep?"

"A whole six hours. Best for days. I still haven't touched my wife in a week," Andy said. "That's a hell of a note."

"It's going to be over tonight," I said.

"How'd your mom and grandma take it?"

"Lousy," I answered.

Andy said, "The D.A. is busting a gut. He can't play games anymore after what happened to you and Johnny. He has to make a real arrest or it's his ass with the voters and the governor. It looks like we've got a goddamn gang war, for Christ sake."

"I'm going to lay everybody out for you tonight," I said. "I want you to make the arrests."

Andy drew his face into a puzzle. There were deep, tired lines around his eyes and some fresh creases along his forehead. Age and strain were gaining on both of us.

"What the hell are you doing in that shirt?" he asked.

"You're taking me out of here."

"I am not."

"You are, too."

"I am not."

"We could do the Katzenjammer Kids all day, but I'm leaving this dump today."

"Suppose you tell me what this is all about. Maybe I'll play along."

"I'm going to Jules Reynard's ranch tonight at seven. I want you to come along about thirty minutes later."

"You can't do it, Mitch," Andy said. His voice lowered and he looked at me hard. "You're busted up bad and the doc says you need rest."

"And Charlie Allison is dead. He was twenty-five years old and never had a chance. Johnny Reynard is blind. At worst, he was a slob who didn't do any real harm."

"Tell me about it and I'll handle it," Andy said.

I got to my feet. The floor was cold as barroom love. Nausea cruised in a Cadillac with the top down.

"I can't do it that way," I said. "This is something I have to do myself before someone else gets killed."

"Who else could get killed?"

"Agnes Reynard," I answered.

Andy whistled. "The tootsie who married Jules," he mused. "Who would kill her?"

"Jules Reynard had a wife in Kansas City a long time ago. She crossed him and wound up bobbing for snails under a railroad trestle along the Missouri River."

Andy thought it over. He closed his eyes and relaxed into the chair. Frank Sinatra started to sing on the radio. He was pretty good.

I grinned. "Hell, you'll make captain out of this arrest."

"You're going no matter what I do?"

"Yes," I said. "Just like that."

Andy rose and buttoned my shirt for me. He pulled on my blue suit. It stank of turtle shit and catfish and had the strut and camaraderie of a life on its own. Clara came in the room and squawked like a two-hundred-pound rooster. She retrieved a doctor who lectured me on responsibility and health, my concussion, the Lord Jesus, and finally told me to go to bed and avoid aspirin. We left the hospital under a barrage of warnings, especially about booze. From the street, I heard Clara bellow.

We drove across town in Andy's blue police Plymouth. A gray sky frothed, purple-edged from the prairie north and west. Wind drew through the elms. On skid row the bums huddled in groups, sharing wine and silly talk; clots of bums parked outside pool halls, beaneries, and cheap cinemas. Women held down their skirts and men pinched their hats. Andy steered through the brick downtown and across the Douglas bridge. We drove above the river, murky with whitecaps and waves. We skirted right field of the ballpark and passed a row of boxcars. I heard the *plock* of fungos on horsehide and watched baseballs rise in arcs above the field, then disappear. Clouds thickened in the north and the wind steadied.

Andy rumbled through the alley and stopped beside the rabbit hutch.

"I had the Fairlane brought here," he said.

Mrs. Thompson hobbled down the stairs and stood holding Faith and Hope by the ears. Faith and Hope peeped and twitched their noses. Andy helped me into the house.

He sat me down on the bed and said, "I suppose I have to dress you."

"It would help," I answered.

Andy rummaged in the bathroom closet and found some pleated gray trousers, a red flannel shirt, wool socks, and Red Wing boots. He knocked around the oak dresser and extracted polka-dot shorts and a white T-shirt. We struggled for ten minutes with the ensemble. My head felt like a drive-in fight.

"How's your vision?" asked Andy.

"Double."

"Why do you want me at the ranch thirty minutes after you get there?"

"I want you to arrest Agnes Reynard for murder. Bring her with you. It will add considerable drama."

Andy sat in the gray overstuffed chair. I arranged myself on the bed. The sky turned yellow and the wind howled. Crows and starlings streamed north.

"Just what evidence do I have?"

"I'm telling you. Arrest her for murder and bring her to the ranch. While you're on your way, you might tell her about the gallows at Lansing. I want her to crack when we are out there."

"If this doesn't work, it's my ass with the D.A. And probably my badge. I can spare the ass, but I've got a wife and kids."

"Trust me," I said.

"With this trust shit and a dime I can get a Charles Atlas pamphlet."

Andy stared at my portrait of Carl Schlecter, a great chess artist dead of starvation in the second year of World

War I. Andy and I fought the second war and since then there'd been another. Experience bound us and I knew what he was thinking. He was thinking how complicated existence was and how impossible to understand, and finally, on a stormy spring night, that he was going to act solely from friendship and belief. It summed up our lives.

"Agnes lives in Sleepy Hollow?" asked Andy.

"Cater-cornered from the golf course."

"All right, goddamn it," he said. "I'll drag her out at seven-thirty."

"Take the highway east to Rose Hill Road and then south. Black Fox is a rambling ranch perched above a horseshoe lake. There's a red barn and some outbuildings. Gravel road into Scotch pines. Park there and come in. I'll unlock the front door. Just blast in like Buster Crabbe."

Andy threw me a windbreaker. "It's going to storm," he said. He walked to the kitchen and went onto the back porch whistling. From the back stairs he said, "I'll bring my ray gun."

I hobbled to the kitchen. A black sky boiled like mud coffee. I made some oatmeal and drank orange juice. I set the alarm for six o'clock and took a nap. When I woke, lightning creased the sky and there was sudden thunder. The heavens shimmered with ghostly orange light. My head was dull as a cinder block, but the double vision had cleared.

I washed my face and stared at the scarecrow in the mirror. He looked something like me except that he had bandages on his head and his eyes were ringed by blue-black bruises. He was a smiley helpful sort of guy, but he had a mean streak and no ambition. I brushed his teeth and told him to be polite and not drink so much. He followed me to the front porch and sat rocking.

I read Heidegger's *Being and Time*. Heidegger thought that being alive was like being "thrown" and constantly falling. It had the same physical unease and uncertainty as falling toward the unknown called death. We get used to the sensation and don't talk about it, but it's always there and always dark. The bottom is something that happens to other people, and when it happens, they are alone and nobody can help. *Splat*, you're dead and everybody says they're sorry and sends flowers and in two weeks you're a hole in the ground. Heidegger answered this with love, but he didn't think it was easy. I shut the book and hobbled down the back steps and got into the Fairlane.

Black storms north of the city advanced. The wind died to whispers, and along the creek bottoms small birds dug themselves into the grass. Streams of crows, starlings, and hawks sought refuge in cedar hedges and stands of scrub oak. The blacktop road struck south into electric distances, the sky everywhere a black cauldron of forces. The sun sliced through some clouds and broad rays of gold and mauve speared the earth. Then the wind died again, and there was the smell of ozone and hail. In the rearview mirror, I watched rain advance across the prairie like silver curtains above green wheat. Turgid yellow curled under the cloud and the rain smelled of iron. The temperature plunged suddenly, and there was an eerie silence.

I hauled the car into the gravel drive just as plops of rain struck the windshield. Canard's big Cadillac was parked in the pine lee. It gleamed like a weapon. Three quarter horses huddled against the red barn, tail to head. The Black Fox burned in the mist like a torch.

I walked to the front door and knocked for the last time. The door opened and Colby stood in front of me. His face was white and gray as sandpaper, the blue eyes sunken. He wore a white shirt and jeans, cowboy boots, and a dark leather vest. He looked smaller now, somehow violated.

He said nothing. I flicked the lock on the door and followed Colby into the room.

Two lamps burned brilliantly. Jules Reynard sat on the zebra couch captured by lamplight, our chess game in front of his face, the black and white pieces outlined by haloes. The big room was inert against the storm, the white carpet, the Klee, the philodendron, and the beige walls pressed by the black storm. Glass trembled in the wind.

Canard faced the storm, gazing at the boiling clouds. He had on the same black pants and rumpled white shirt. A bald spot on his head shone like grease, the hair a mess. He turned.

"Mitch Roberts," Canard said. "Some fucking guy."

"Shut up, Gus," Reynard said. Canard turned back to the storm. Colby walked to the stairs and stood silently. I went down the recessed stairs and sat on a couch facing Reynard.

Reynard ran his hands above the white pieces and moved a piece. I checked him and he moved his king. He smiled when I moved and took a rook.

"You're in for it," he growled. Reynard shoved a bishop across the board and sat gloating. The end was near and I knew it. He played brilliantly.

"You're not very damn good," Reynard said.

I lit a Lucky. "I told you to leave Johnny alone."

"What is this shit?"

Reynard couldn't see my bandages and black eyes. Our chess game was over and we were playing with real lives. The rules were the same, but the stakes were higher.

"The game is over," I said. "It's not over the way you think. I told you not to move on Johnny until I had a chance to check the books. I told you there was a chance he wasn't skimming and I wanted to make sure. You couldn't wait. You had to make a move and prove you weren't helpless."

"Keep talking," Reynard said. "I love to hear shit dribble."

"You had it all figured out. So you put a dog on Johnny because you believed he was skimming and sleeping with your wife. I told you the evidence wasn't in and I wanted you to wait for me to learn the truth. You thought you knew the truth. Maybe you wanted to believe Johnny did it. You're more than blind, Reynard."

"You're talking junk," Reynard said. "You can't prove I did shit to Johnny and neither can anyone else."

"I can prove everything."

Canard walked into shadow and stood looking at me over a crystal lamp. "Hey, Julie," Canard said. "I don't know anything about Johnny skimming, I swear. I didn't do Allison."

Reynard lit a cigar. His face was pure Kabuki, shrill and mysterious.

"It's something I'll take up with the boys in Kansas City," Reynard said to Canard. "You know what happens to guys who cheat me."

Canard wiped sour sweat from his face. He stank of garlic and kibbe.

"Johnny is blind," I said. "Torn to shreds."

Reynard's face sought Colby. "I heard he was dead," Reynard said. Colby moved against the stairs. Thunder crashed to earth. "I said, I heard he was dead," Reynard said.

Colby said, "I guess not." Reynard raised his head to me.

"He'll be blind a long time. But he's alive," I said.

Thunder pealed again. Lightning snaked like fingers across a black, boiling sky. Rain increased in gusts.

"It's your move," Reynard said.

"Pay attention," I said. "My first night at the Canyon I watched Colby, Canard, and Bunch beat up Charlie Allison, throw his body in the backseat of Bunch's Buick, and drive him away. I told you that, but I didn't tell you I followed the Buick into Maple Grove. Bunch and his goon tied Allison to a slab with a note on his lapel and then they drove away. I looked at Allison and he was alive. I know he was working for the reform candidate and this game has been played before. You run the guy out of the casino and everybody goes about their business. But something happened this time.

"You see, what I didn't tell you was that I was in the cemetery when someone in a big car pulled in and drove right to Allison. That someone shot at me. I didn't know who it was, but it had to be someone who knew where Charlie Allison would be. I worried about it, but the next day Charlie Allison was dead. I could have stopped it, but I thought it was going to be all right."

Canard walked to the stairs and stood beside Colby. I watched them but didn't see a gun. Tiresias and Creon trotted into the big room. Reynard sensed the dogs and snapped his fingers. Each reacted and took up positions beside Reynard like sentries. They flinched when thunder struck.

I continued. "My suspect for the Allison killer was someone connected with you, obviously. That made it Bunch, Colby, or Canard, or one of their goons. After the poison and the horses, it was obvious someone was trying to run you out of the business at the Canyon. Colby and Bunch and Canard may have had a motive to bump you. You own the clubs and take the profits. Maybe those guys were tired of stooging for you, so they figured to force you out. It looked open and shut.

"Bunch didn't do it. I knew that right away because he had his chance and instead he tied Allison down and drove away. I didn't think Canard had time to leave the club and follow, but he could have had a goon follow. Colby could have done it, but I didn't figure he stood in line to inherit the Canyon. Maybe he was working for Canard."

Colby shouted, "Don't listen to this punk."

"Be quiet," Reynard said. He puffed the cigar. I waited for the thunder to cease. "It's still your move," he said.

"Like I said, I couldn't figure Colby for the Allison murder because he had no interest in the club. If something happened to you, the club belonged to Canard and Bunch. In fact, with you out of the way, Colby would have nothing. That seemed to let him out."

The storm progressed. Tense silence grew like a spider web, a strange, magnetic calm.

"Then Johnny came on the scene. He had motives, all right. I watched him cheat the Canyon three nights running. I watched him drive to your wife's house and stay. It seemed to put him on the hot seat.

"But last night something strange happened. I snuck into Canard's office and found a set of books. They were duplicates, except for the figures. Canard was skimming on paper, taking the profit and leaving you with a set of fake books. It proved Johnny wasn't skimming by table cheating. If there had been table cheating, then Canard wouldn't have needed two sets of books. When I left Canard's office, I wasn't sure what Johnny was doing, but I knew he wasn't skimming. I couldn't decide where the crooked dice came from because I didn't think Johnny had the guts to cheat. He'd never won before, and that seemed to confirm that he wasn't a cheat. But the crooked dice came from somewhere. I took some pictures of the ledgers, but I don't have the film because I took an unscheduled bath. But the skimmer wasn't Johnny."

Reynard controlled his disbelief. He ran his hand along a dog's flank. Hair bristled on its spine. Low growls erupted like magma.

"I don't believe it," Reynard said. "Gus."

Canard was silent. He lit a cigar, and we all listened to the wind rage. Waves on the lake rolled. "The guy is full of shit," Canard said. "He can't prove it."

"What's my motive for lying?" I said to Reynard.

"All right," he said. "Go on."

"A few days ago I started thinking. Someone killed two of your horses. You may remember my first day here when I hopped the rail. I had to hustle back because those yearlings were wild as hell. It started me thinking. Then I talked to a veterinarian in Augusta named Glick. He told me the dead horses were unbroke yearlings. He said the horses were torn up and Colby was burning the carcasses when he arrived. You assumed the horses had their throats cut and I took it for granted you knew. It sounded right at the time. But, Mr. Reynard, they didn't have their throats cut."

"What are you saying?" Reynard asked. Now the wind tore through the prairie, howling. Rain stretched and drove in fists.

"Those horses were on six hundred acres. Nobody could have gotten close to those yearlings. Certainly not two of them. Even if you had experienced cowboys down here, it would have taken two or three jeeps and a lot of time. I don't think it happened that way."

Reynard bowed his head. "Dogs," he said.

"Dogs," I said quietly

"Let me do this guy," Colby said. Reynard stroked the dogs.

"I don't get any of this," Canard said. He wiped his face.

Three sets of headlights broke the storm and weaved up the gravel drive. Chunks of time broke away like icebergs. The big door opened and Andy stood in the doorway, wind and water flowing around him. He held Agnes Reynard by her arm and her eyes were wide and alarmed.

"What the hell," Reynard said. Canard and Colby stared at Andy. Colby moved.

"Take it easy, boys," Andy said. He dragged Agnes

into the room. The door banged in the wind. "Some of my police pals are outside." Andy smiled.

Agnes wore Andy's trench coat. She looked like a wet cat, small and scared. Her auburn hair struggled on her head like cake batter. Rain swept into the room.

"Who is it?" asked Reynard. His voice rattled in the storm.

"My name is Lanham. I'm a lieutenant in Homicide. Mr. Reynard, I've just arrested your wife on a murder charge. She's taking it for Charlie Allison." Agnes sobbed then, big welts of fear in her chest.

Agnes looked at Colby. "Tell them," she begged.

"Shut up, you whore," Colby said. He edged for the bar. Andy watched him. Canard hung on to the stairs, surprise and fear on his face. Lightning illuminated the prairie.

"Let's everybody relax," Andy said. He stared at Colby with malice.

"Back to last night," I said. "I'm in the parking lot and someone knocks me out. But first someone puts the dogs on Johnny. Then someone dumps both of us in the river and leaves us for dead. Only there were two witnesses in the parking lot who saw everything. They can identify the people who tried to kill us."

"Who are these witnesses?" asked Reynard.

"Forget it," I said. "I'm here and Johnny is alive. You asked Colby to put the dogs on Johnny. I know he can handle them. Since I showed up in the parking lot, Colby decided to kill me, too. He probably realized I had seen the double ledgers and could clear Johnny."

"I'm not saying anything," Reynard said.

"All right," I said. "But you know Colby can handle the dogs. You have to figure he killed the horses, too." I paused to smoke. "Why do you suppose Colby would poison you and kill the horses? Why do you suppose he would kill Allison, if he did, and hope the blame comes to you?"

"You tell me," Reynard said. "Like you said, he won't get my business."

"He wanted your house, your oil, and your money. He wanted your wife, or maybe he was just using Agnes as a way to get everything you owned. It was Colby."

Agnes slumped and wailed. Sobs racked her and rain swept into the room. Thunder crashed. Andy put his hand into his suit pocket.

"Colby set up Johnny," I said. "Johnny wasn't cheating the Canyon and he wasn't skimming. He didn't know shit about skimming. The guy skimming was Canard. He made a duplicate set of books and took you for a percentage. Johnny was set up, and I figure Colby knew Canard was skimming and took advantage of the situation to blame Johnny."

Canard waddled back to the crystal lamp. "Look, Julie," he said. "You been around a long time. I wanted my fair cut, that's all. But I didn't do nothing else and I didn't do Allison."

"He's telling the truth," I said. "Canard was cutting you down with the books, nothing else. He didn't kill Allison and he didn't set up Johnny."

"Tell them." Agnes sobbed. "I didn't kill anybody," she said.

"Shut the hell up, will you?" Colby said.

I went on. "You hired me and Colby started to worry. He saw an opportunity to kill Allison and he knew you'd be blamed. He didn't scare you away by killing the horses, so he thought he'd pin a murder on you. Colby doubled back to the cemetery and killed Allison by throwing him into the river. He wanted the D.A. to come down on you. With you out of the way, he could have Agnes and your money."

Andy watched Colby. Agnes slumped like old luggage. She was finished crying and her eyes were vacuums. Colby leaned on the bar and stared into the storm.

"Like you said," Reynard replied. "He can't get the club. So what's his motive?"

"Agnes," I said.

Reynard lowered his face. The blood was gone from him.

"Colby is the man," he said.

"Yes," I said. "You blinded your son for nothing."

Agnes broke away from Andy and stood pleading with Reynard. Rain and tears streamed down her face. Her voice became shrill and hysterical.

"I didn't kill Allison," she screamed. "I tell you I didn't. I helped Cole because he said we could have it all. But I didn't kill anybody."

Colby sprang on Agnes. He struck her with his fist and she went down like a sack of magnets. She screamed. Colby kicked her with his boot. Andy drew a revolver and trained it on Colby. For a time, the scene was static.

Finally I started talking again. "I don't know how they got Johnny over to Sleepy Hollow those nights. I do know Agnes substituted dice so I'd believe that Johnny was table skimming by cheating. They wanted me to report to you that Johnny was cheating and sleeping with Agnes. That's what happened, Mr. Reynard. Colby and Agnes knew if you found out that Johnny was doing that to you, you'd have him killed. They knew you. Then the cops were supposed to arrest you and then they'd have your house, your money, and your oil. They didn't give a damn about the Canyon."

Agnes raised herself. She sobbed. "I had benzedrine. Johnny came over for that. He was crazy for benzedrine. Colby found some and Johnny would pass out from benzedrine and liquor. We knew Roberts would see his car."

Colby kicked Agnes again and I heard his boot drive in with a dull, sick thud. Andy crouched and moved, driving Colby back with the revolver

"This scene is over, folks. You're under arrest, Colby," Andy said.

Reynard struck the dogs and they rose instantly. Snarling, they sprang on Colby. He screamed and staggered back to the bar. The dogs tore into him as he screamed. There was a sickening sound of teeth and a furious fight, wild with broken glass and tangled furniture. Blood and broken flesh appeared as the dogs found Colby's neck. I whirled as Andy fired his first shot.

"No," screamed Reynard.

I dragged Agnes aside and watched the dogs tear Colby. Andy maneuvered above the man and dog. Two uniformed cops ran into the room. Andy fired twice and the dogs fell.

"Get the sheriff and an ambulance," Andy said. One cop ran back into the storm. The room was quiet except for Agnes and the rain.

Andy and I knelt above Colby. Reynard stayed still, his head buried. Black blood pumped from a gash in Colby's neck. Two pale eyes stared ahead, unseeing. His face was burned hamburger.

"I don't know," I said to Andy.

"Wrap him up," he said.

I found some towels behind the bar, then wrapped them around his neck and pressed. The uniformed cop returned with a first-aid kit and began to work.

The second cop came in. "They're on their way," he said.

"It might not be soon enough for Colby," Andy said.

"I don't know," I answered.

Colby twitched, but the black blood pumped into the towel.

The uniformed cop took over for me. Andy and I rose together and walked past Agnes to the front door. Reynard's face was blank. Canard huddled on the stairs. Andy and I stood outside in the night. I lit a cigarette and Andy sucked on a cigar. The wind died and a pale moon rode the clouds.

Then across the black, wind-tossed prairie we heard a siren.

JULES REYNARD–MITCH ROBERTS, played at
Black Fox Ranch near Wichita, Kansas, during the first
week in May 1956.

KING'S GAMBIT

White (Reynard)	Black (Roberts)
1. P-K4	P-K4
2. P-KB4	PxP
3. B-B4	Q-R5 check
4. K-B1	P-QN4
5. BxNP	N-KB3
6. N-KB3	Q-R3
7. P-Q3	N-R4
8. N-R4	Q-N4
9. N-B5	P-QB3
10. P-KN4	N-B3
11. R-N1	PxB
12. P-KR4	Q-N3
13. P-R5	Q-N4
14. Q-B3	N-N1
15. BxP	Q-B3
16. N-B3	B-B4
17. N-Q5	QxP
18. B-Q6	QxR check
19. K-K2	BxR
20. P-K5	N-QR3
21. NxP check	K-Q1
22. Q-B6 check	NxQ
23. B-K7 checkmate	

COLD CASH

ONE

From my perch halfway up the briar-choked cliffs I looked back to the beach and the sea. A sodden sky drained into a choked confusion of ships and men, and in the folds of black smoke drifting seaward a line of 88s thumped menacingly along the beach, hurling sand and flame in its wake. Machine gun fire popped. I cradled the head of my buddy Smitty and concentrated on the cool, blue hole in his forehead, then on the blood and pus that oozed from the hole. I extended my hand to caress the wound, and my hand floated down an inky corridor full of wheelchairs and portraits. Somewhere in that undefinable space a telephone rang, and I woke up.

I levered myself from bed and sat inside a gray March day fumbling for cigarettes and consciousness. Black shadows hung in my three rooms like portraits. Outside, a cold rain clattered through the elms like machine gun fire. One tattered awning thumped in the wind. I'd dreamed Omaha Beach for ten years, and the dream had become as much a part of me as private detection and baseball. I shoved aside an ashtray and a copy of Tal's chess games and answered the phone.

"Hello," I managed. My voice clunked like a broken-bat grounder to first.

1

"Is this Mitch Roberts? The detective?" A rusty nail embedded itself in my ear. At the end of the rusty nail was a hammer, and at the end of the hammer was some dame being drop-kicked to Krakatoa. The scratchy noise of morning television came from the receiver.

"What time is it?" I offered.

"I beg your pardon?" said the other voice. One-two-three-four-five. Syllables sudden as lashes from a cat-o'-nine-tails.

"I said, what time is it?"

"It's after noon. Is this Mitch Roberts?"

I dangled my feet into a pool of winter. My three rooms were one-half of an old Victorian on Sycamore Street, across from a minor league ballpark. There were enough objects in the three rooms to sustain a sort of life: one great room with a brass bed and olive drab blankets, gray overstuffed chair, brass reading lamp, bookshelves, footlockers, and fishing gear; a kitchen set off by oak panels and stained glass; a dining alcove, antique table, and bay window, shelves crammed with dead cactus and chess books. A portrait of Carl Schlechter, the chess champ, stared across the room at Hopper's *Early Sunday Morning*.

I got a cigarette lit and inhaled.

Smoke snorkeled into my lungs. The lungs were astonished and began to breathe.

"I'm sorry, ma'am," I said. "I'm Mitch Roberts."

"I'm sorry, too. Sign on your door said all day Saturday."

"All day starts around noon," I wisecracked.

"Are you going there? Our granddaughter's been taken."

I sat up straight. "What do you mean, 'taken'? Kidnapped?"

"Well."

"Have you tried the police?"

"They won't do any good. It's a family matter." Well,
I thought, at least we agree. Cops are great after the fact.
Lawyers do nothing but take a cut off the top of trouble.

"Get some lunch, and I'll be down as soon as I can
pull myself together."

"We'll be there." The voice hung up, taking with it the
nail and the hammer and the television noise.

A hot shower kicked on the Briggs and Stratton in my
chest. I'd been a detective for eight years, but I was beginning to feel like an etching submerged in mild acid;
strong, but fading slowly. I dressed and sipped coffee and
hurried, going into the wind and rain of early March.

Lincoln Street was the color of sweaty beef liver, and
as I drove the Fairlane through the gathering gloom of
spitting snow and sleet and felt the wind tug and tear at
the cloth top of the aging car, I felt hungry and ready. I
had a small hangover that would have kept King Kong
moaning until eleven, and the soggy front seat stuck to
the back of my cords like a leech. At the corner of Broadway and Lincoln I hit my first red light and sat smoking
a cigarette, drawing the smoke into my lungs and puffing
it out in a gray, wafting cloud that hovered against the
windshield and gradually disappeared, leaving me with a
perfect view of Wichita in late winter.

While I waited for the light, I peered through the frozen
clam juice rain and down a muddy alley that ran behind a
row of small businesses, disheveled single houses, dry
cleaners, and beauty shops. The alley slumbered under a
cover of deep gray mud, blue slush, and dirt. Piles of
brush, discarded TV sets, oily transmissions, and layers
of rusted pipe made a counterpoint to tipped garbage cans.
The houses on one side were all dirty white, single story,
and square, the backyards of mud and fallow vegetable
gardens and broken birdbaths surrounded by ugly wire
fence. In the backyard nearest Lincoln Street a dingy mon-

grel on a tether held his paws up to the wire fence and barked at nothing in particular.

Wichita, without its layer of elm leaves, lilac blooms, swaying mimosa, and yellow forsythia, without its Easter shawl of pink and white spirea and the drifting scent of honeysuckle, lay naked and abused and gray. It was like living inside an oyster, and looking up that alley was like stumbling into the bedroom at a party, looking for your coat, and surprising the host's wife and his best friend in a fiendish embrace. Nobody looks any good that way, and it's damn embarassing. Then the light turned green, and I drove through slushy Lincoln Street heading for my office.

I pulled the car into the gravel parking lot that fronted a row of tiny offices. I bounced through chuck holes full of ice and mud and stopped in front of Jake's barbershop. Jake stood inside an explosion of incandescent white light, cutting the wild red hair of a kid perched on a piece of pasteboard balanced between the arms of Jake's old black leather barber's chair. The kid squawked and squirmed, and Jake snipped hair and jawboned with a crippled geezer in overalls while the kid's old man dried tears and did a jig to amuse and distract his son. When I turned off the headlights, Jake looked up and saluted with his clippers and buzzed into a crooked red cowlick. Jake burred the cowlick down half an inch, then broke into a malignant, demented grin, swept the hairy white sheet from the kid's shoulders, and handed him a wad of bubble gum. The kid stopped crying, got down from the pasteboard perch, and stood between his father's legs while two grease monkeys in stained worksuits from a local car dealer escorted the old crippled geezer to the barber's chair for his weekly shave.

I rolled the window down on the car and flipped the butt of my dead smoke into a mud puddle, then got out and walked to the door of the barbershop and leaned beside the whirling red-and-white barber pole. The kid and his father came out the door, the kid bouncing on his old man's shoulders and chewing a mound of sweet, pink gum. His hair looked like a haystack the cows got into, and he wore a blue-and-red Wichita Braves warm-up jacket. My own father was dead before I said my first word, and this was a Saturday ritual I had missed. Just for a second it made me feel bad and wonder what kind of father I might be. Somewhere in my past there had been the thought of it, and the woman to go along, but it was all a memory now.

A bell over the door rang when I went inside the shop.

"Ten nicks for a dollar and a quarter," Jake said. The barbershop laughed in unison.

"How about a special?" I asked. "Since we're just past Lincoln's birthday."

"And what might that be?" Jake asked.

"After the haircut I get a set of free tickets to the theater and a derringer ball in the back of the head. Deal?"

"With a haircut like I give, who needs the derringer ball?" Jake said. The old geezer in the barber's chair guffawed, then quieted when Jake held the gleaming straight razor flush against his cheek. The barbershop was full, and it was Saturday, and in the background KFH played Vaughn Monroe.

"Say, Jake, how long has that old black Chevy been parked in front of my office?"

"Trouble?" Jake asked. He lathered the geezer's rough silver stubble. Then he reached in a hot, antiseptic cabinet and poked his hand into a rack of steaming, white towels. He got out a towel and covered the geezer's neck. "I wondered about the black Chevy." Jake wiped his nose with the back of his white sleeve. "The old dame inside there has a face like a C-clamp."

"Fine, but how long?"

"Oh," said Jake. "Thirty minutes."

"What's the chance of a shave this afternoon?"

"Good," said Jake. "What's it about?"

"I'll let you know," I said as I walked out the door into the sleety downpour.

I ambled through the slush to the glass door of MITCH ROBERTS INVESTIGATIONS and stood staring at myself reflected back through the *o* of ROBERTS. My old gray felt hat with the black band covered a receding forehead and fading, ash-brown hair. Two furrows above, blond eyebrows tunneled east and west like back roads out of Stromsburg, Nebraska. I wore brown ribbed corduroys, a green-and-pearl-checked Pendleton shirt, and a light brown wool sport coat, complete with patches at the elbows. Drops of cold rain tumbled from the brim of my hat. I wore clean underwear. My tan oxfords were buffed and polished. For a time I stood in a reverie, and when I looked up and through the *o* in ROBERTS, I saw the woman with the C-clamp face staring in reflection through my own reflection. I pushed open the door and went into the dark and the damp.

"Are you Mitch Roberts?" Her voice creaked like a door to the haunted house at some magical amusement park. I turned and doffed my felt hat and sat down behind the old oak desk that housed half a dozen skip-chase files, a carton of cigarettes, and two twenty-dollar bills folded and taped to the bottom file drawer.

"Please sit down," I told her politely. We looked each other up and down like Dempséy and Tunney in the center of the ring. She wore a black polka-dot dress that fell around her ankles and tickled black nursing home shoes. Her gray winter coat frayed at the cuff, and a cheap, glittery rhinestone butterfly flapped on her lapel. Her hair was stiff and flat, and her broad nose stuck out below mean black eyes. The rain plocked at the windows outside.

"You're late," she croaked. "I'm Maud Cobb."

"Mitch Roberts."

"Yes, and you're late. This is our second time here!"

"I'm truly sorry, ma'am. I had a big night last night, and I didn't get home from work until very late. In my profession you can't always pick your hours, and you certainly can't pick the hours of the people you tail. I've always loved sleeping on Saturday, and I picked this particular Saturday over all others because the weather was good for sleeping. You have my apologies. If you've got trouble, I'd certainly like to hear about it." I hadn't been lectured like this since second grade when I'd broken four windows fouling off pitches by Skinny Wade.

My speech seemed to float out to sea. Then through the door slid a small man in tweed pants and a blue work shirt with "Robert" in script over his heart. The small man went about five-six and looked like a ferret.

"I locked the car, Mother," he said.

"Sit down," the old woman said. The small man sat down. He stared at his work shoes.

The old dame looked at me. "My husband, Robert," she said. "He works Saturday morning, and that's why we couldn't be here until noon. Of course, it's well after that now."

"Madam, I sincerely and most honestly apologize for the inconvenience I have caused you and your husband." She frowned.

"What do you charge? We don't have a lot."

"It depends on the job. Not more than twenty-five dollars a day, and expenses. I work on Saturday and Sunday and evenings. I don't lie to clients, and I don't pad expenses. You get what you pay for, which is more than I can say for most."

"Twenty-five," she murmured. "That's a lot."

"Suppose you tell me what's on your mind. Then we can talk money if you like."

"It's about our daughter, Bonnie," she said. "It is hard to talk about. Very hard. She isn't what we wanted her to be, and she hasn't behaved very well. It's not our fault.

Not one bit. We did everything we could, but she isn't any good. We did everything the Lord commanded, but she isn't what she should be.'' The small guy fidgeted.

"Now, Mother," he said.

"You want me to talk to the Lord about your daughter?" I joked.

"You are a very sharp young man," Maud said stonily.

"I'm sorry, Mrs. Cobb. Sometimes the use of humor is called for to loosen social situations. Perhaps this wasn't the time. Sorry."

The small man spoke. His voice was calm and came from years of speaking between the cracks. "Please, Mr. Roberts. We do need your help."

"Suppose you tell me about it. Skip the editorials."

Maud glowered at the small man. "Suppose I do. Our daughter is not out of high school. She has had a child. She isn't worthy. We paid the bills at the hospital. Or, at least, we are trying to pay the bills. But the father does nothing. He won't. He doesn't deserve the child."

"Let's back up a little, Mrs. Cobb."

"Yes?"

"Your daughter doesn't have the baby now?"

"No. That's what we want. We want the child back. Her name is Elizabeth."

"So where is the baby?"

"With the father." Maud Cobb puckered her lips. She looked as if she had just swallowed a green persimmon.

"You tried the police?"

"They won't do anything. They told us this was a domestic problem. They said the father had as much legal right as anyone. They don't know. The father is a godless, soulless beast."

"Maybe what you need is a lawyer. What about that?"

"A lawyer named Graybul said the same thing as the police. He told us that there was no more legal right on one side than on another. He said that this issue, as he called it, would go to court, and the fight would be long and expensive. He also said the father might leave at any time, and there wouldn't be a thing to be done. He could just disappear and take Elizabeth. Mr. Roberts, Elizabeth needs a home with us. She can't be raised in a godless home by that beast. She needs the guidance I can give her.''

"I see. What does Bonnie think about all this?''

"Bonnie?'' Maud said.

"You remember. Your daughter, Elizabeth's mother.''

"She agrees with me. She wants us to have Elizabeth and raise her in a Christian home. She is too young to make these decisions herself.''

"What did Graybul say about snatching the baby?''

"He said it would be quick, cheap, and legal. He advised that course. But, we can't accomplish it ourselves.''

"You want me to find the baby and snatch it home?''

"Yes.''

"And the father? Who is he?''

The small man raised his eyes. "His name is Richard. Ritchie Polkis. He works at an auto parts store on Washington Street, down near Waterman.''

"You mean the Greek Polkis?''

"Well, yes,'' the small man squeaked. Ritchie Polkis I'd never heard of. But Ritchie had an older brother or two who grew up in Wichita pulling the wings off flies for fun. As grown-ups, the brothers broke legs, stole cars and motel TV sets, and burned the occasional warehouse. They were a fun-loving and devout crew. I sometimes saw Georgie Polkis, leader of the clan, shooting snooker for fifties down at Scotty's Club Billiards on West Douglas. His knuckles were the size of softballs.

"So, I'm to look up this kid Ritchie and, without getting myself slaughtered, get the baby and bring her home?''

"Are you afraid?'' Maud asked slyly. She adjusted her rhinestone butterfly.

"Of course. You would be, too."

"Please, Mr. Roberts," the small man said.

"How old is Elizabeth?" I asked him.

"She will be four months," Maud interrupted. The small man deflated and stuck his eyes back on his shoes.

"The littlest missing person," I said.

"Not missing," said Maud. "Stolen wantonly."

"Yes, well, stolen then," I said. "Look. It's not the usual stuff. Just so you know, I can do it, but it goes against my nature. Let me check into it and see if I can get a line on this Ritchie Polkis without causing too much ruckus. I'll see if I can't figure a way to get Elizabeth back without doing any damage, either to her, to you, or to myself. We can't afford a lot of violence. Danger and shooting and fighting aren't good for babies or private detectives or grandmothers. So, if I think I can find a way to snatch the baby without hurting anybody, then I'll do it. I'll charge you twenty-five dollars a day for a few days and then check in with you. I'll do it as soon as I can. But, it's cash-and-carry."

Maud frowned. She reached in her purse and hauled out two twenties and a ten and handed them over the desk. "A receipt," she snapped.

I wrote a receipt. She smoothed her polka-dots and left her chair and walked stiffly through the door and out into the sleet. Robert rose and walked to the desk. He rubbed his hands together as his eyes darted like rabbits.

"If there's anything I can do," he began. "I mean, you can call me at Sears's appliance repair during the day. I could help. I wouldn't be afraid. I was in the war, you know. But you'd better call me at work." He paused and fidgeted in a funny, despairing way. "You know, I think Ritchie lives in Plainview or Oaklawn in one of those shacks. You know?"

"Fine, thanks, Mr. Cobb. I'll let you know. Don't worry."

Robert Cobb took his tiny self through the door and entered the old black Chevy on the passenger side. Through the blinds and the snow I saw Maud exercising her C-clamp mouth. They backed up and drove away, splashing mud.

I flipped off the ceiling lamp and sat for a long while in the dark and the damp thinking about a woman I knew years before. There had been some talk about a baby and a house and stuffed animals. I slipped open some cigarettes and then went next door to the white light of Jake's barbershop. I hopped into a chair and talked about fishing and spring training and tried to stop thinking about the woman I knew long ago and about babies and stuffed animals. Jake covered my face with a hot towel.

TWO

I came to in the barber's chair. I saw Miss March with her blue dress billowed around luscious hips. There was a smudge of cotton panty peeking out from the blue dress, and Miss March looked happy and embarrassed. Jake leaned on his broom with his chin spiked to the end of the handle and his hands folded on the point. The shop was dim and cold. Jake looked out the front window and listened to a melancholy tune on the radio. It was still, save for the tune on the radio and the plop of cold rain in the cement gutter outside. The sky was magenta-toned and dark, and the cars that loped by on Lincoln Street cut the drifting fog with yellow and red lights. Fog hovered in the barren elms, and the cars lumbered like chained ghosts in their steamy exhaust. I fished for a cigarette and hooked a stale one. My match flared, and Jake swiveled on his broom pillory.

"March, and look at it," he said.

"I've been asleep. How could that happen?"

"You've been down a couple of hours. You looked tired and started to snore like a chain saw."

"What time is it?"

"After three."

"My God," I muttered. "I've got to get going."

12

Jake sat down in a chrome-and-leather chair next to the cash register. The register stood open, with the bills and change gone from their trays. A pile of colored hair was swept into the corner of the shop, streaked like Joseph's robe. Above Jake's bald head, Miss March flashed her orange blushing cheeks and swung her platinum hair in the brisk calendar wind. Her behind was a juicy apple.

"Dreaming, I guess," I said.

"Well, it sounded like some doggerel straight out of rack and ruin."

My gut burned from no food, and when I took in cigarette smoke, two gremlins scraped my lungs with a number-two wood rasp. "Jake," I said, "you ever have a dream that keeps coming back? A dream that's not so good, but you can't shake it?"

"Yeah," Jake said. "I dream I'm a two-bit barber in Wichita, Kansas. I dream I own a grubby barbershop on Lincoln Street, and I dream I got two lummox kids who wrassle for East High and want to go to college. Then I dream I got a wife and a mortgage, and I dream I'm getting fat. There's only one thing worse than being a barber."

"Yeah," I said. "What's that?"

"Dentist," he said. "Looking in mouths all day. I see moles and crust and dandruff. There's some guys come in with splotches, but mouths . . . Jesus."

"My dream's different. I dream I'm in this house, and the house has two stories. It's dark, and I've got this feeling I'm separated from people I ought to be protecting. Private Eye as metaphorical Seeker. I go from room to room in the dark looking for people. I can hear them talking and looking for me, too, but we can't find each other. I get locked outside the house. I hear them inside that big dark house. Echoes then and smothered talk. It's like something is going to happen and I don't know what it is,

and there's nothing I can do about it. The people are inside
the house, and I'm outside."

Jake took out a cigar. He sat down in the dark and put
a flaming match to the end of the cigar and sat back.
"Well, it could be worse," Jake mused. "You could be a
dentist."

"I've got to get out of here. What do I owe you?"

"Forget it. Take me to opening day down at the stadium
and buy me a hot dog. I'm looking forward to ball season
and fishing."

"We'll fish next month, for sure," I said.

"Sure thing," Jake said.

The late-afternoon streets were empty. Snow fog swirled
around the red neon coffeepot sign on Betty's. The coffeepot flashed and faded, and faded and flashed, and with
the streetlights turning red and green and amber dipsy-
doodles in the fog, and the red airplane guide tower haloes
dotting westward to the airport, slowly disappearing in
misty rings, I half expected Orson Welles to pop out of a
manhole cover and slink along the wet brick with a load
of poison penicillin.

"Client?" asked Jake.

"I've got to get a move on. There's some work to do."

Jake heaved on his overcoat, and I got out of the barber's chair. I felt stiff and hungry. Jake flipped open the
front door. A cold wet wind hit. In the blue-red glow of
his cigar, Jake was smiling.

"See ya," he said.

I got in the Ford and drove down Lincoln Street to have
a talk with Bonnie. I figured she was really my client, not
old Mrs. Cobb and her polka-dot shift. When I reached
Lorraine Street, I turned left into a quiet section of brick-
and-frame houses. Most of the yards contained one rickety
garage and a silver ball for the birds to stare at themselves
in. This neighborhood hid all the third-grade teachers, shoe
repairmen, Dodge mechanics, and repressed, sentimental

housewives. I stopped at the corner of Orme and looked across at a square, white box. The front porch was a cement slab with a crack in the middle of the slab. Each half of the slab tilted slightly in the opposite direction. Above the matchbox garage someone had jerry-built a bedroom. The bedroom teetered in the sinister dark like a tree house in a Bo tree. There were rips in the rusted front screen, and where there were rips in the screen, wind and rain and snow had cracked the cheap veneer on the plywood door. The tin mailbox bore the legend: COBB. Faint light seeped from behind blinded picture windows on either side of the front door. I shut down the motor, lit a cigarette, and slithered through the slush. It was a dull, cheerless, airtight death's-head of a house. I knocked on its nose.

I straddled the crack in the porch and waited. Moonlight filtered through snow fog. Dark rows of wood-and-brick boxes slumbered behind creaking cedars and a thick evergreen hedge. Two lizard eyes stared at me from behind a wall of hazy darkness.

"It's you. Have you got her?"

"Uh, Mrs. Cobb?"

The door opened. "Have you got her?"

"No, I don't have her. What I need is some more information. I started thinking this over. There were some questions I didn't ask. I need to know the answers before I really get started on this thing."

"You want to come in?"

"Yes, ma'am," I said. What else? I thought.

There was plenty of silence and the sound of creaking elms.

"All right," Maud said. "Come in."

I fell into a room that stank of stale sweat, BABO, and boiled potatoes. A blond television in one corner burned purple and blue images around the square room, lighting up a fuzzy red couch with white doilies on the arms, a matching red recliner, and black walnut end tables. There were no books or magazines or records. Waves of thick, putrid heat rose from a floor register buried in the pine-wood floor, and one small room became another small room. The other small room held a round oak table with a bowl of fake fruit on top. I looked at a picture of a little girl in Mary Janes. Hair tonic evaporated from my head.

"Now, you were saying," said Maud Cobb.

"Oh, no thanks. I'll stand. You don't happen to have a pitcher of Gibsons with lots of ice and some little round cocktail onions?"

Maud stared at me. There were storms in her Atlantic.

"Some more humor, Mrs. Cobb. Sorry." I fiddled with my thoughts. "How did you get my name, Mrs. Cobb?" I asked at last.

"Mr. Graybul." She folded her hands into a nugget. "He said you were reliable."

"Yes, I know Mr. Graybul, of course."

"Mr. Graybul said you were honest."

"Well, I am honest. Except, that is, with the women I love and the guys I fish with." Icebergs joined the Atlantic storms. My humor sank away, glugging.

"Please," she said with finality.

"I want to talk to your daughter, Mrs. Cobb. There are some questions I need to ask, some angles I need to fig-ure, things that might help me get the baby back and keep everybody out of trouble."

"I can tell you what you want to know."

"No, Mrs. Cobb, you can't. And I wouldn't ask any-way. Let's not argue this to the Supreme Court. As the great Kierkegaard said, 'Either Or.' "

The old woman looked over my shoulder, all the way to the Repressed Christian Hall of Fame. She turned and motioned for me to follow. We went up a narrow flight of carpeted stairs and into the Bo tree bedroom. Heat from the floor register rose up the narrow incline in a fetid rush. I followed Maud Cobb. After a short climb, we were in the hot tree house. Maud turned and waited for me to straighten.

She was curled like a pretzel on a white hospital-style bed. A Winnie the Pooh lamp shed a pale concentric shroud on a white enameled nightstand and an orange pinewood toy box. A blue bunny rabbit skipped on the pinewood box. Some dirty venetian blinds shuttered two small windows. The walls were bare. A wastrel wicker rocking chair whimpered in one corner. The room was cheery as suite 1313 at Bedlam State Hospital.

"Thank you," I said to the old woman.

She folded her arms and leaned against the door frame; her black eyes speared through my words.

"We'll be just fine alone, Mrs. Cobb," I said loudly. She turned and threaded her way down the narrow carpeted stairs, holding the sides of the papered walls for support, pausing to look back with a frown every step. She stood in shadow and heat at the bottom and then walked around the corner into TV noise and BABO.

I pulled the wicker chair across to the bed and sat down. Bands of pale yellow light and black shadow striped Bonnie. The bedspread was white with blue and pink and green yarn balls in neat rows. It was Beelzebub's idea of a bedroom.

"My name is Mitch Roberts," I said to the girl. "You don't have to be afraid or anything. I was hired by your folks to get your baby back home. Okay?"

Bonnie's arms were wire thin and her goldfish-colored hair was pulled tight from her forehead into a ponytail. Her pale green eyes crossed slightly. Cute freckles powdered her wan face. She wore blue jeans, sneakers, and a faded gray sweatshirt over a red blouse. She was part cherub and part Medusa, a regular *fleur-du-mal* of a kid.

"You know where my dad is now?" she said.

I took out a cigarette. Bonnie held out her hand and I shook out a second cigarette and she took it in one of her freckled fingers. I lit her cigarette, then lit mine, and we sat there smoking. She inhaled like Bette Davis. She'd probably never heard of Bette Davis.

A thin whine erupted from downstairs. "You're smoking! Don't get ashes everywhere." Then there was quiet except for television buzz. I flicked ashes down a heat vent near the door. Bonnie covered her mouth with her hand and snickered.

"Don't tell on me," I whispered. Bonnie giggled.

"Daddy's downstairs," she said. "You know what? He's in the basement like some worm underground."

"Yeah," I said brilliantly.

"That's where he stays. He hides down there from my mother. He's got stacks of radios, and he talks to people he doesn't know. That way he doesn't have to say anything real. He's got jokes taped to the walls, and he tells them to strangers. He gets jokes out of the newspapers or off TV, then he writes them down and sticks them on the wall. And he hides downstairs from the world."

"Okay, your father is a ham. He never told me that."

"My father is a bug."

"Yeah, and maybe he makes more contact than most of us. He arranges for blood donors, and helps people who have accidents, and reports to folks when their kids get hurt. During the war, ham operators ferried messages for men who were wounded or dying. And maybe he hides downstairs and you hide upstairs. So what?"

Bonnie was quiet. She smoked her cigarette like a pro and put the ashes on the windowsill behind the blinds.

"Look," I said. "It's beside the point, so let's start over and be friends. I want to help you, and I need to know about Ritchie. What's he like?"

"Hell with him," Bonnie said. She said it to the window, and her voice was far away.

"Where'd you meet him?"

"At school."

"He went to East High?" It was nearby.

"Oh, come on, you got to be kidding. Ritchie go to school. No way, ever. I'd cut out from the lunch line, and sometimes Ritchie'd be across the street. He'd drive us around to the park and we'd drink beer. It was pretty cool, really."

"You and who?"

"Ritchie and me and Lurleen Curtis. Lurleen is a friend of mine. Sometimes he'd have his big brother George along, and then sometimes there'd be some other girls from school."

"Other girls?"

"Yeah, you know. The whole gang."

"When did this start?"

"You know. When I got to high school."

"You got pregnant a year ago about now, didn't you Bonnie?" She pushed her ponytail against the wall. "Was it sometime in March or April your sophomore year?"

"Yeah, so?"

"How old is Ritchie?"

"He's maybe twenty. He knows his way around, and he's real cute."

"Does he live in Plainview?"

"Maybe. So?"

"Is that where he took you? "

"So?"

"Does Ritchie hang out anywhere?"

'He might hang out at the Big Bun," Bonnie said. "You know, we'd go up there and put mustard in the salt and order hamburgers and drive away. He goes to Eddie's Bar on Maple, and he got me in there once, too. They let me in because I was with Ritchie and George was there. I think I look eighteen, don't you?" Bonnie stopped and stubbed her smoke out on the sill. She leaned close to me and batted her eyes as if she were some kind of teenage knockout. Then she got onto one arm on the hospital bed, which raised her gray sweatshirt. There were six good inches of skinny belly.

"Come on, Bonnie," I said. "You know any good reason why Ritchie would want to take Elizabeth? This is important, so let's stop fooling around. I need to know."

"Gimme another smoke," she said. I took out my Zippo and lit her a smoke and lit one for myself. We were quiet. Finally, Bonnie said, "I don't know why Ritchie would want my baby. He told me for a long time while I carried her that he didn't want nothing to do with me and that I shouldn't keep the baby. He didn't damn care. Then one day he came with his brother George and they busted in, and my mom wasn't here and they both took Elizabeth. I was sick then and couldn't stop them. He scared me and then they left. Ritchie told me he'd kill me if I said anything."

"Does the Polkis family have a grandma or grandpa?"

"I don't know about his folks," she said.

"What hospital did you have the baby delivered in, Bonnie?" I asked.

"County," she answered, and looked away sadly. A tear kissed her eye and furrowed and rolled down a field of freckles.

"Who was the doctor?"

"Saunders," she said. "Cleveland Saunders. He's a nigger."

I flinched. "Okay, okay," Bonnie said. "So what, anyway?"

"Does Ritchie have a job?"

"He works the parts store on Washington Street. I don't know if he still does, but he did once. He had lots of jobs. His brothers give him money, too."

"You want Elizabeth back, don't you, Bonnie?" I asked. "You'd want to take care of her yourself, wouldn't you?"

"You know what she does?" Bonnie said abstractly.

"You know what she does?" I shook my head, deciding to let her go and see where it went. "She puts down newspaper on the kitchen floor when I go downstairs for a sandwich. I'm making a sandwich, and she's there spreading newspaper around the floor so I don't mess the floor with crumbs or mustard or something. I hate it."

I stood and pushed the wicker chair back to its corner. Then I walked to the bed and put my hand on the back of Bonnie's head and squeezed. I set a pack of cigarettes on the sill and slid a book of matches into the cellophane wrap. Bonnie held my arm in her thin hand for a moment. She examined the mangled little finger on my left hand.

"Your finger," she said looking up.

"Caught it in the turnstile on ten-cent beer night at the ballpark."

"Sure." She smiled.

I went slowly downstairs into the television haze and the boiled potatoes and the BABO, and said good night to Mrs. Cobb, who sat still in her fuzzy red chair staring at the gray images on the TV screen. The images drifted through the haze to her glasses and drooped there in electric puddles. She didn't move a muscle. Then I walked through the nose of the death's-head and into the black-and-white snow fog of Saturday night.

THREE

On certain ragged bloody nights no man should be alone. I sat silently in my gray overstuffed chair, fingering the tufts of white cotton spitting from its worn arms, listening to the cold dark gather inside an infinite hush, feeling sorry and responsible for all the bad things that happen. I was in that time of life where aching shins and nearsightedness and cuts that don't heal become facts. As Martin Heidegger wrote: Death is something that happens only to other people, never to you. *Das Tot ist ganz Anders.*

Outside, beyond the fly-specked window, over the rotted and peeling front porch, a street lamp flickered and tossed three nacreous dots on the floor. Francis the cat lay curled and snoring on one of the nacreous dots. I blew cigarette smoke into the fixed gaze of my portrait of Carl Schlechter and felt my own tired consciousness meld with that poor, starving face. The path through the universe occludes, the stars shudder, the ringed and spiral nebulae falter.

I wrapped myself in a dark navy peacoat and yellow scarf and walked down Sycamore Street to Maple. The snow fog swirled and eddied. There were no cars and no human beings in sight. The mist drifted. I reached Andy Lanham by pay phone and told him how it was with me.

22

He quickly told me to come to his home and cook dinner and allow the world to drain pus. He didn't ask twice.

I stopped at a good grocery on Harry Street and bought six boned chicken breasts, a pound of early asparagus, some heavy cream, and butter. The Lanhams lived on Minnesota with two sons, one and a half bathrooms, and a dog named Spot. For a guy with existential angst and a problem with babies and neurotic old women, the prospect of a night with a regular, all-American family seemed cheerful. Besides, Andy was a friend and a member of police Homicide, and I figured to get some useful information from him about Georgie and Ritchie Polkis as well. I could earn a fee and dine splendidly.

I parked in the drive and walked up the flagstone path. Andy answered my knock. "Mitch Roberts, well, all right."

"Hi, Andy."

Andy's wife, Elaine, came to his elbow in the doorway. She was dark haired and beautiful. We called her Frosty because of the white streak in her roan hair.

"Hi, Frosty," I said, going in.

My own three rooms on Sycamore housed the leather-and-brass darkness of funeral parlors. A vase of dead daffodils sat on my round oak table in the dining alcove. For weeks I had read Poe and Heidegger, smoked a borrowed calabash, and failed to wash the dishes. My place reeked of latakia and Ivory soap and reel oil.

But Andy's two-bedroom frame was bright and blond as a high school cheerleader. Red and pink geraniums, Christmas ferns, and spotted begonias flourished in big windows, bright rugs covered the burnished wood floors, and pictures of children with braces mushroomed everywhere. I gave Frosty my hat and coat, and she took them to a closet in the hall. Small wool coats and tiny rain hats and red galoshes tumbled out of the closet as she opened it.

"You guys hungry, I hope?" I asked. We all walked to the *Better Homes and Gardens* kitchen.

"You bet." Andy laughed. He leaned against a white tile counter and handed me a glass of red wine.

"I propose chicken Kiev with flourishes and ruffles, asparagus in lemon and butter with cream, and a Caesar salad." Andy smiled and held his glass against mine. Frosty shut the refrigerator and walked to us and held her own glass out. We toasted each other silently. Andy and I had become close friends and had both handled some tough cases in the past. There had been a time when Andy thought of quitting the force, but now he seemed more satisfied and content with his fate.

"I'm feeling better, Mitch. The force is working but after all the shit." He hugged Frosty, and they smiled. Andy was a good cop and a good father and a good man. My own fate should be so kind.

"You two are responsible for the Caesar salad. You should have the fresh Parmesan, some eggs, a pinch of Romano, romaine lettuce, garlic, and lemon. That's little enough to ask. I'll cook the Kiev and the asparagus. If we work this right, we'll be soused and eating in an hour."

I sprinkled flour and pepper on the chicken breasts and pounded them flat with a rolling pin on waxed paper. Frosty fashioned lemon-and-butter sticks and put them in the freezer. Then she tore loose romaine leaves and washed them in cold water and patted the leaves with towels. I wrapped the breasts around butter wedges, then rolled the breasts in egg and breadcrumbs and put them in the refrigerator. We sipped wine and smoked.

"I'm working something, Andy," I said.

Andy sat at the kitchen table. Frosty sipped wine and watched the eggs boil.

"You want to talk about it?" Andy asked.

"It's not why I'm here, but I would like to kick it around. The trouble is, I can't tell you about the client. I will say that if there's any trouble, you'll be the first to know.''

Andy was a big rawboned man with red hair and emerald-green eyes. He scratched a kitchen match on his fly and flamed a chewed cheroot.

"God, I wish you wouldn't smoke cigars," Frosty said.

"I'm quitting tomorrow," Andy replied. She poked his arm. "I'm listening," Andy said to me. Frosty put peanut oil in a deep-fat fryer. It sizzled.

"In general," I began, "how tough is Georgie Polkis?''

"Tough."

"Come on. How tough?"

"He gargles ammonia."

"Very funny. And I read Ambrose Bierce in the dark. We're all tough in our own way. What's his?"

"I know his reputation. He's on contract with the big boys out of Kansas City. He crushes bones for them when some guy is a little late with the interest payments. He calls wives and kids when the poor slob is on the road. He shows up late at night. I'm told that he buys and sells and delivers stolen property. He has something on the ball, too; otherwise the boys in Kansas City wouldn't let him handle their collections. He takes chances and he doesn't squeal. That's his reputation, anyway.''

Frosty worked over the Caesar salad. "Anchovies?" she called. We filled our glasses. The wine was Spanish and tasted like oranges and dust.

"We think he burns, too," Andy said. "He may do arson on contract for the Kansas City mob, but there's a small chance he's in business for himself. It's hard to tell. The boys at Arson have some theories, but they don't have anything definite.''

"All right to turn on the radio?" Frosty said. We drank wine and heard Gale Storm sing "Dark Moon."

"Then he strong-arms interest payments, runs dope and money maybe, and commits arson," I said.

"Right."

"How are the chances that he free-lances?"

"He may have his own interests. As he grows big, the chances of that grow bigger. You may have heard about the single-engine Cessna that burned at the airport about two months ago. If you park a plane out in the weather and tie it down, there's very little chance that it will just burst into flame. This one did. The guy who owns the plane had a few big debts he couldn't quite pay off. The theory was that this guy would like to turn some of his tangible assets into cash. You can understand how a guy like that would want to burn his airplane, especially if he could turn the nuts and bolts into cold cash."

"I can see the business sense in that."

"Well, two months ago, the Cessna burns. Arson guys are sure it was torched and pretty sure it was a job done by an amateur, or maybe a pro new to the job. It was just gasoline and a match late at night. They're trying to touch Polkis for the burn, though there isn't much evidence yet. They're trying to break the owner and make him talk. So far, it's no soap, and Polkis is free. I guess the insurance company is shitting dollar bills."

"I don't suppose Kansas City would have been interested in burning the plane."

"Not enough cash involved. Those guys burn restaurants and warehouses, not airplanes. The crate was worth five thousand dollars, tops. The mob wouldn't be interested."

"So it looks local, and your boys finger Polkis because he does that kind of stuff."

"That's it."

"Not much," I said.

"Not much at all." Andy sighed. He frowned and gulped Spanish wine. I washed the asparagus and put the stalks in half an inch of water with salt and butter, then slowly added cream as the asparagus simmered. Peanut oil bubbled in the fryer. I grinned at Frosty.

"We ready?" I asked.

"Fire, Gridley," she said.

Frosty got the breasts from the refrigerator and handed me the cold plate. I dropped chicken in the hot oil and each piece sizzled. Frosty sprinkled Parmesan on the romaine. She poked a fork into the asparagus.

"Getting there," she said.

I took two golden Kievs from the oil and dropped in two more. Andy laid knives and forks on the walnut dining table. He fired two candles and turned out the lights. We drank wine as the radio played Guy Mitchell singing about how he never felt more like singing blues because he never thought he'd ever lose her love.

"Damn," Andy said. "The boys are working out in Florida now. Two months more and Eisenhower fires out the first ball at Crosley Field and life makes sense again." Frosty served the asparagus as I ladled the Kievs onto each plate. In the candle glow we clicked glasses again, then settled to eat Kiev, Caesar salad, and vegetables. The world erupted to a healthy glow.

I finished a Kiev and some wine. "You have any reason to think that Georgie could handle more personal things like kidnapping and extortion?"

Andy munched some salad. "I'll tell you a story," he said. "Then you make up your own mind." Andy finished the salad and gulped some wine. He put down his fork and began. "Last year a bingo parlor burned down. The fellow who did it was an Indian named Garfield Little Bear. He had a flat face and a pigtail, and he was fat. Well, one night he goes out to the bingo parlor in the country on Sixty-ninth Street with a can of gasoline, some rags, and a box of matches. He breaks into the parlor with a crowbar, then goes back to his truck for the gasoline.

According to the fire department, they can pretty well reconstruct his movements.

"The parlor was one big room with rows of fold-up tables and chairs. In front there was a stage where they have the popcorn-ball machine. It was all very business-like, only the parlor wasn't paid for and they weren't making any profit and the building was mortgaged to the hilt.

"So, Garfield Little Bear poured five gallons of gasoline around the big room. He soaked the curtains and the floor and the stage. Then he went back out to get another five-gallon can from his truck. He walked back into the place and opened the swinging doors to the little kitchen side room. The kitchen had an industrial stove, sinks, and a stand-up refrigerator. I can imagine him now, standing there in the dark, swinging his five-gallon can. It was dark in the kitchen, and Little Bear begins to dump gasoline on the floor. The next thing, he was shaking hands with Saint Peter. The parlor exploded like a Roman candle. The fire department boys found his crowbar, two five-gallon cans, and the truck registered to his wife. He was a Dresden firestorm. I think they found a turquoise ring. Isn't that a cute story?"

"Very cute," I said. Frosty gathered dishes. She kissed Andy as she passed by his chair.

"How does that happen?" Andy said. "You wouldn't think Little Bear would pour ten gallons of gasoline around a bingo parlor and then light a match inside, would you?"

"No, I wouldn't. So what happened?"

"The fire department came to me after the fire. They asked if I'd be interested to know that they thought it likely that the institutional stove was going full blast when Little Bear dumped his five gallons of gasoline under it. I told them I'd be interested. They showed me evidence of residue and explosion source and blast force. They believed that the explosion originated with the stove and that when

Little Bear poured gasoline under it, it was lighted already.''

"He dumped gasoline on a burning fire."

"Yeah, and that's not all. We found rags and string and matches in his truck outside. He was not stupid. It was obvious that he was going to dump the gasoline, go back outside and light the rags wrapped with string, then throw the rags inside the parlor. The parlor burns, but not Garfield."

"Some parlor trick," I said. "But what about a pilot light? "

"The only pilot in the place was in the water heater in the basement. There was no blast there."

"So, you think it was murder?"

Frosty bustled in the kitchen. She came back with Camembert and French sauternes. There were cheers all around. I lit a cigarette.

"We checked around," Andy said. "It turns out that Little Bear liked to drink and shoot snooker. He played with Georgie down at Scotty's Club Billiards. George is good, and Little Bear lost three or four hundred dollars in one night. Unfortunately, Little Bear didn't have the money. You just don't lose money to George that you don't have. The story was that Little Bear felt heat for a while."

"What's the theory?"

"The theory is that Little Bear agreed to torch the bingo parlor to pay George. The theory is also that it would be good business to kill two birds with one stone, so George set up Little Bear. It was a setup. We can't prove it, though."

"So George is capable?"

"Yes, he's capable. He's also unpredictable. The guys at the department who know him say he can be a regular guy. Then, he gets mean, and you've got to be careful. He can be totally ruthless and totally charming. He's a snake."

The candles flickered in winy ambience. Frosty pushed

her chair against Andy's chair and circled her arms around
his chest. I got connubial shakes.

"How about his brother Ritchie?"

"A punk," Andy said. "Don't know anything about
him, really."

"Where does he live?"

Andy walked to the living room and came back with a
phone book. He thumbed some pages. "At 3228 Acres
Lane in Plainview. Some detective," he said.

I kissed Frosty on the forehead and put on my felt hat
and my peacoat. "Take care of yourself, okay?" Andy
said. I smiled and went outside and left them to kiss and
hug.

It was still a damp and dreary Saturday night. I drove
south on Oliver Street, heading toward the part of town
you lived in if you worked the assembly line and worried
about baby colic and pay envelopes. South of Pawnee I
turned east and sailed into a Sargasso Sea of clapboard
huts built during the war. Plainview had sprouted in days,
and it looked that way. The shacks were squared and
fenced by wire, and there were no trees. Junked cars stood
in shadow, with their oily transmissions spilled willy-nilly.
I found Acres Lane and cruised by Ritchie's dark hut and
stopped at the end of a sandy lane. There were no streetlights, and the dark and the fog fell on Plainview like an
executioner's hood. I sat quietly smoking a cigarette while
my eyes cruised the neighborhood.

I found a crowbar and glass cutter in the trunk toolbox
and walked across the sandy lane toward Ritchie's house.
Some dogs barked far away, and an invisible moon burned
in fog. My hands began to sweat, and I walked into deep
shadow at the corner of a ticky-tacky garage. The garage
hugged the edge of the shack. A mulberry tree spread
withered arms in the fog and dragged some scary shadows
around, too. The roots had bucked the cement driveway.
I edged over to the house and peeked into a small window

into what looked like a bathroom. There were no movements, but silence pounded like high surf. I backed up and grabbed the garage door rope and yanked the door open quickly. Then I hustled inside the garage. It was musty and dirty. I pulled the door closed and stood heaving.

Inside the garage there was a door to the house. I slid my ear to the plywood door and listened. I heard a faint refrigerator buzz and a leaky faucet. A clock ticked faintly. I grabbed a sliver of wire from my coat pocket and eased it into the lock. After a minute or two the door gave, and I fell into a black, foul cubbyhole.

Beer cans overflowed a rancid sink, spilling onto a soggy, curled linoleum floor. The three-burner stove was covered with thick dead grease and cigarette butts. I checked the cabinets and the refrigerator and found a box of Cream of Wheat and a bottle of cheap wine. I walked into the tiny living room and stared at a ruined couch missing one leg. Dirty clothes spiderwebbed a lawn chair, and a set of homemade shelving held some cigarettes and an oily carburetor.

The bedroom was an improvement. The cheap mattress lay on a floor littered with cigarette butts, wine bottles, and newspapers. A high school portrait sat on the dresser. It was a young girl, not Bonnie Cobb. I picked up the photograph and held it to the feeble window light that crept through venetian blinds. A skinny dark-headed girl stared out at me. The inscription said: All my love, Lurleen. I tossed the chest of drawers and found a small .22 pistol and some ammunition.

I left the bedroom and wiped down the kitchen doorknob. I went out through the garage and walked across the sandy lane to the Ford. I put the crowbar and glass cutter in the trunk and placed the wire jimmy in the glove box. I drove out of Plainview and into civilization. At Kellogg and Oliver I found a pay phone and called Andy.

"Hello," he muttered. "This better be good."

"Sorry, Andy," I said. "I know it's late. I hope I'm not interrupting anything."

"Just coitus," he growled through his teeth.

"Oh." I laughed. "Nothing major, I hope. Listen, I have some more questions. It won't take a minute."

"All right," he said. "Make it snappy."

"Does Georgie have a wife?"

"No. He did once, I think, but she got off the bus a long time ago. As far as I know, he doesn't have any girls. He's a man's man, you know."

"I presume Ritchie isn't married?"

"How should I know?"

"Now, how about the matriarch? Does George have a mother? Is there some kind of Greek Polkis family in town with a grandma lurking around? Is there a maternal instinct?"

"George's mother in black?"

"Yeah."

"Hell, I don't think so. I think the old lady is dead. George lives by himself on Wellington Place at Thirteenth. He doesn't pal, not even with his brothers. I guess he's mostly business." I was quiet for a minute, thinking. "Say," Andy yawned. "What do you want to know all this for anyway?"

"I'm still just working it out. I promise to keep you informed if I run onto anything."

"Be careful, Mitch. This guy is murder."

"Thanks," I said. Andy hung up.

I put the phone on its cradle and studied the grafitti. Then I lit a cigarette and stepped into the fog and black of Kellogg Street. There was no baby at Ritchie's and no likelihood that either George or Ritchie would have snatched the baby because of their unbounded love for babies in swaddling clothes. I saw nothing in Ritchie's place to suggest that the baby had ever been there. Only a few connections offered hope for making sense out of a baby snatching that seemed to have no real point. There was a black doctor at the County Hospital named Cleveland Saunders, and there was a swell-looking bimbo named Lurleen who loved Ritchie. Then, there was Ritchie himself. I knew that as soon as I punched Ritchie's ticket, George himself would get on the train. It wasn't much, but it was a way to earn twenty-five dollars.

I drove north to Savute's spaghetti house and bar on Broadway and sat in the schmaltzy pine barroom for an hour, drinking tap beer and smoking cigarettes. A cheeky blonde with buck teeth and baseball earrings sat next to me on a stool and asked me to guess her age. She looked good, but beyond the third beer and fifth smoke, she stopped looking that way. I tossed away some nickels in the pinball machine and listened to trucks pound north to Nebraska. Then I drove home to bed in the cold and damp. I tossed and turned and worried and finally dreamed about babies and stuffed animals of a long time ago. It passed for sleep.

FOUR

I woke from a car-wreck dream. Sunday afternoon bled to death in the west windows of my kitchen and dining alcove, smearing red-and-orange smudges in stained glass, splashing oak- and ash-colored pools onto the dark wood floor. The air quivered with dusty motes and shafts of sunshine. My rooms pulsed and darkened as the clouds rolled south across the thin sun. From my brass bed I looked out at the gray concrete walls of the ballpark across the empty parking lot. A red box kite floated in the motionless air, buffeted then by a breeze. It dropped and looped and recovered. At four o'clock in the afternoon I lit my first cigarette and met March.

I padded to the kitchen and made coffee and stood in the dusty gloom and silence as the percolator popped and bubbled. I smelled the coffee aroma as it rose into the folds of my crusty green bathrobe. In the backyard, my muddy Ford nosed the brown, rickety garage, and above the garage exactly seventeen black crows preened themselves on telephone wire that crisscrossed the back alleys and the weathered Victorian houses along Sycamore and Maple. The rabbits in the backyard twitched their noses and poked their faces into the wire hutch confines. The neighbor's chickens cackled.

I walked the coffee to bed and wrapped myself with Grandma's pink namesake quilt and studied some games from Tal's Soviet championship performance in Moscow. Then I fell into a studious daydream, imagining myself on a cold metal chair in the Soviet Hall of Sport, Russian winter swirling dead white and infinite outside. Tal himself had been a Georgian outsider in Moscow, a fiery misfit, which I guessed in Russia was the moral equivalent of Stepin Fetchit at Paramount. There had been a cunning vigor in his games, a maniacal sense of mission and justice, of élan and valor, qualities missing in the stolid, implacable games played by European Russians. I imagined a fellow like Bronstein, wrapped in bearskin and mukluks, clutching his tepid end-game studies and confronting the turgid Tal and trembling at the approach of the southern tidal wave. It was Tal who had made ten straight pawn moves against the world champion Botvinnik and had managed to confuse and crush that collectivized oracle under a glowing stream of brilliant moves. Maybe Tal wasn't Stepin Fetchit. Maybe Tal was Jackie Robinson opening at third base to racial taunts, and maybe baseball and chess were two of the few places where justice had a chance to win.

I woke a second time. Smoky blue light hovered in my rooms, and from somewhere the smell of meat loaf and green beans seeped through the walls. As the shower ran steamy water, I thought about the baby and tried to organize some loose ends about the case in my mind. I had no doubt that Ritchie Polkis was the father and that he had been at the Cobb house with brother George. They had snatched the baby, but there seemed no altruistic or paternal reason. My foray at Plainview convinced me that the baby was long gone. George posed some questions in my mind: Why had he gone to the Cobb house? Why was the baby important to him, but why was the baby no longer important to Ritchie? George was tough as nails, so how could I avoid violence? On the other hand, Maud Cobb frightened me with the violence of her own dispassion. She was as motherly as broken glass, and I'd noticed no crib, no clean diapers, no rattles. The baby had been swept away like particles of sand in a windstorm.

I had a good feeling for Bonnie. I sensed that under that tough exterior, chain-smoking, and bitterness, there was a sensitive human being writhing to be set free. Her come-on was an act, and her hard-case attitude covered a lost girl looking for kindness. Maybe even her involvement with Ritchie was a search for love, a cry in the wilderness, a prayer to heaven. You can't blame people for seeking affection. Most of all, the case didn't make sense as a regular baby snatching by an anxious father. The outlines of the players and the facts made me nervous for the baby and for Bonnie.

In my time, I'd looked for purebred dogs, mongrels, stolen coins, concealed jalopies, and wives who'd gone over the hill, but I had never looked for a baby. Wives leave a trail of motel registration slips. Jalopies tend to draw attention. But, as far as I knew, babies didn't do much of anything to leave a trail. By the time my shower was over, I had decided to begin the chase with Ritchie himself, then have a chat with Dr. Cleveland Saunders, and let the chips fall. After that, it was anybody's guess. But my first move was going to require some teamwork. I dressed and left the house, looking for an old friend and fellow vet named Spud Christian.

Spud hibernated in the basement of a worn orange-and-green tenement on Oakland Street. Oakland curled down-hill behind Shoemate's Liquor Store and the Uptown Theater, a part of town where the poor and the very poor exist on short rations and beans. I labored the car to a stop in the snow-slick street. Sooty snow lay piled on the porch stoop of the tenement, and green paint flecks littered the dirt yard. Inside the screen a central stair wound and disappeared into mush-brown wallpaper, soaked and rotted. Wallpaper hung in gunks from broken laths. I climbed down some dark stairs and pounded on a door.

"Spud," I yelled.

Somewhere water dripped. Somewhere a radio buzzed. Piranesi could have lived somewhere on the premises. Finally, I pushed open the door and walked inside. There was a sloppy mountain of ale cans on the floor. A black Naugahyde couch slouched against one blank wall, and foam gushed from a tear in its plastic arm. Two basement windows gathered pale, wispy light and bathed it on the wet beige walls. The dining table was piled with newspapers, books, notepads, and chess sets. On a rickety metal chair there was a pot of mush growing green moss.

"Spud," I yelled again.

A pig's snort erupted from behind a cloth partition. I saw Spud lying facedown on a mattress, his head wedged into a dark corner and his white feet poked from beneath a comforter.

"Wake up, buddy," I said.

Spud lifted his head from the mattress. His hair was snarled from sleep. He rubbed his eyes.

"What day is it?" he asked.

"Sunday," I said. Spud grabbed his glasses from a table and studied me with a puzzled look on his sleep-wrecked face.

"I've always hated Sunday," he said. "All it ever meant to me was church and the day before Monday."

"What have you been doing?"

"I was up all night over some equations for school." Spud was going to college on the GI Bill and was studying abstruse mathematics, the kinds of things that are squiggles and squirms on chalkboards. Spud's chess game was first-class, and his politics one step behind Stevenson. He was a good, tough, loyal friend.

"Can you function in polite society during your exams?"

"Sure, why?"

"I need you for a job. Tomorrow." Whenever I could, I used Spud in my work. He needed the money and was very purposeful.

"I've got an electrical engineering exam," he said.

"I need somebody, and you're it. It's only going to take a few hours at most."

Spud dragged a hand across his face, waking up. "So what's the play?" he asked.

"Twenty-five dollars for an hour's work. I'm going to expense it to my client."

"That's fine," Spud said. "Who do I have to kill?"

I laughed. "Nobody."

"Well, I sort of hoped it was Eisenhower."

"How about getting dressed? I'll buy you some dinner and tell you all about it."

In ten minutes Spud had pulled himself together and manhandled his way through the calculus books. He put on a pair of paint-splotched dungarees, tennis shoes, and a clean flannel shirt. He pulled on a gray windbreaker, and we hunched through his hole-in-the-wall to the outside world. I drove through the neighborhoods of the near East Side as Spud soliloquized:

"Troglodytes of the world unite. You have nothing to lose but your brains. What we have in this country is class struggle. Roaches, annalids, microbes, viruses, all clamoring after the two-car garage and a big blue lawn with no crabgrass."

"Don't be bitter," I said.

"Do you know what color the troglodyte flag is?" Spud asked.

"No," I said suspiciously.

"Black," Spud said. "Black flag." He laughed.

We drove across Kellogg to Market, then north into the

dark emptiness of downtown. In the winnowing sunshine, snow fog boiled and glistened in lamplight. I smoked and listened to Tommy Dorsey on radio and then pulled the car to a halt in front of the Fairland Cafe. A steamy plate-glass window sign flashed in bold red: CHINESE AND AMERICAN FOOD. Yellow light flooded the sidewalk, and I heard the funky, clanking sound of a pinball against glass. There was a Chinaman squatting in the alley smoking a cigarette. The Fairland was the only cafe downtown open all night. It catered to the old and the broken-down and men who sat over coffee for hours. One block south was the bus station. I followed Spud into smoky brightness and a smell of pork buns, fried rice, and MSG.

We sat in a wooden booth along one side of the cafe. Five or six bums bent over coffee at the counter, and one old man who looked like Kropotkin held forth at a For-mica table in the center of the partitioned back room. A pimpled kid on crutches danced with the pinball machine near the cash register. The kitchen was far in back, and I watched a Chinaman in a white cook's hat washing dishes.

The waitress hobbled to our booth. She was tiny and no more than two thousand years old. Her lips were painted fire-engine red, like waxy Halloween lips. Her dentures were red stained. She smiled, and we ordered coffee and menus.

"So, tell me about the case," Spud said.

"I want you to talk to a fellow who may have kidnapped a baby. I want you to talk to him because I don't want it known that there's a case. I've come up with an idea."

The waitress delivered our coffee in porcelain mugs. Spud slurped some coffee, then dumped some sugar into the steamy stuff. I ordered chop suey, mashed potatoes, and blueberry pie. Spud had chicken-fried steak, Texas toast, and refried beans. We ate and I explained to Spud about the baby and about Bonnie and her parents. I told

Spud about Ritchie and George and cautioned him about the reputation George had acquired.

"What did they do with the baby?" Spud asked. He lit a cigarette and wiped some refried beans on his dungarees.

"I don't know, but I've got a bad feeling about it. Here's what I want you to do. You've surely got a suit in your trousseau."

"Somewhere," Spud said.

"Tomorrow I want you to look real pretty in a suit and tie. Put some tonic on your hair. I want you to look like something semiofficial on a low level, something that works for the county government maybe, a bureaucrat or social worker. I want you bright eyed and concerned. Then I want you to go to the auto parts store on Washington near Waterman and talk to Ritchie Polkis's boss. I want you to tell his boss that you're from the County Department of Health and that one of his workers is causing a serious health problem by refusing to vaccinate his child. Maybe you could take some notepads and impress the boss that way. Tell the boss that county records show him as the father of Elizabeth, and that no record of vaccination has been made or filed. Tell him that this matter is quite serious and ask him to report it to Ritchie. You can even add that if something isn't done soon, the law will step in. Then demand to be given notice of the whereabouts of the baby. Then I think you should ask to speak privately with the father. If that doesn't shake up the boss, then nothing will."

"Pretty tricky," Spud said. "You think maybe Ritchie will get rattled and give something away."

"That's right. Press Ritchie, demand to see the baby. Demand to be given her whereabouts. Say you'll go to the district attorney about child neglect and raise a fuss."

"All of this is fine, but what about my identification?"

"Leave that to me," I said.

"Where will you be all this while?"

"I'll be in the car across the street. When you leave, I'll tail Ritchie. I want to see him break and run if he does. You can find out a lot about a man when he's running. I doubt that he'll go to the baby, but he may go somewhere for help. He may talk over the problem with someone. You're going inside because I don't want my face to be seen quite yet. Besides, I don't want to be stuck with representing myself falsely as a government worker."

"This guy is a punk?"

"True-blue, from what I hear."

"What if he swings on me?"

"Beat him up, like in high school."

Spud laughed. "Me, an electrical engineer," he said. "What are you going to do after that?"

'I'll go see some people. I'd like to see a man named Cleveland Saunders, who delivered the baby."

I dug a bent fork into blueberry pie and smiled at Spud.

"Poor baby," Spud muttered. "We'll see if we can't take care of Ritchie tomorrow. It will be a pleasure."

"Thanks," I said.

"I have to go to the john," Spud said. He rose and walked into the MSG haze at the back of the cafe. In hardly a minute he returned and sat down.

"Damn," he said. "The privy door wouldn't open. I pushed and heaved against it. Then the old Chinaman comes out of the kitchen and says 'Fat man faw down inside. Door no open till fat man get up.' " I asked the waitress and she said Dolley, who sells newspapers on the corner, walked into the bathroom, drunk as usual, and fell down, passed out. He's wedged between the door and the toilet, and nobody goes inside until he wakes up." Spud laughed and finished his coffee.

I paid and we put on our coats. The old man in back lay facedown on the cafe table, snoring. Some of his gray hair lay in mashed potatoes. We stepped outside into fog and a starless black night.

"Fat man faw down inside," I said.

"Where's my twenty-five dollars?" Spud answered.

FIVE

Eight-fifteen A.M. appeared like the inside of a garbage pail. Low gray clouds bumped against a stiff north wind. The cloud tide tumbled newspapers, paper cups, and empty grocery sacks through the slushy streets. Mounds of blackened snow stood in the gutters where city crews had piled them. I leaned in the doorway of my place, looking out the screen door and over the left field wall of the ballpark, beyond the line of boxcars strung along the river, and onto the brown and beige buildings downtown, looming like tombstones in a frosty field. Crows and starlings bounced in the gutters, pecking at stray garbage and hamburger buns, seeking food and a friendly face.

Man harbors sudden hope for March, hope that the gray mantle of winter will precipitously drop, that the Tokay grapes and field roses in the arbor will bloom overnight, that the honeybees and red cardinals and fireflies will suddenly dance in dreamy, warm air. He hopes that soon grubby-faced kids in schoolyards will trade yellow galoshes and footballs for sweet pink bubble gum and bats. But what there always is and always will be is the factory whistle at 8:30 and starlings hammering at the cement like nails into a coffin.

Mrs. Thompson, upstairs, scuttled like a crab. I drank

my coffee and listened to Don McNeill talk in soothing
tones to a young actress about her career. I thought about
baby Elizabeth, then dressed in some baggy blue corduroys and a pink button-down dress shirt, gray tweed sport
coat and a gray snap-brim. I fired the car and drove across
town on Murdock and stopped at the City-County Health
Clinic. The receptionist was a thin, yellow-haired waif in
a white cotton smock. I told her that I needed to speak to
a doctor about a very private problem. She eyed me like
Harold Stassen perusing *Les Demoiselles d'Avignon* and
handed me an information sheet the size of Rhode Island.
Then she gestured to a row of metal chairs surrounded by
squashed cigarette butts. I sat down on the chair I found
and studied a pamphlet about head lice. Finally, I strutted
out my best late-for-work look and convinced the receptionist to let me speak to a social worker because my job
was on hold.

Soon a tall, muscular black man in white-and-green
hospital togs led me to a makeshift office at the end of a
long, antiseptic hallway. He sat in a wood chair behind a
metal desk and lit a bulldog pipe. Fluorescent light
x-rayed our souls.

"There's something wrong down there," I said som-
berly. "I'm worried. I've got to get to work."

"Symptoms," he said.

"It hurts. Burns."

"You'll have to see a doctor. The law requires us to
report every matter like this to the proper authority on the
county level. It's kept confidential, and we need the name
of your, well, partner. It's not the kind of thing where we
send letters to your friends and relatives."

"I've got to go to work." I glanced at the clock on the
wall, a pained look on my face. "I'd like to come back
and take care of this. Do you have a card?"

He leaned across the desk with the card.. Dewayne
Small. County Department of Health.

"I'll call you," I said.

"Your name," he said quickly.

"Townsend," I said. I walked down the antiseptic hallway and drove the car south on Hillside until I reached Oakland street. I descended into Spud's cave and pounded on the door. He opened it quickly.

"Good God," I said mockingly.

Spud wore a blue serge suit, a pink English-cuff shirt with a pointed collar, a red tie, and brown polished brogues. His hair was combed and clean. I handed him the business card.

"You like it?" he said.

"The red tie is too much," I said.

"I'll change it."

"Have you had breakfast?" I asked.

"No, and I'm hungry." Spud changed his tie for a conservative blue one and tailed me to the car. We drove on Kellogg to the small diner called King's X. We sat in a booth surrounded by misty plate glass. Some mechanics and deputy sheriffs and third-shifters shared the L-shaped fountain. The floor was black-and-white-checked linoleum, and the waitress was sleepy eyed and slow. We ordered waffles, sausage, and coffee. I handed Spud a pad and pencil taken from his worktable. We gobbled some sausages and waffles.

"Any final ideas?" he asked.

"You're now Dewayne Small from the County Department of Health. The point of this excursion is to get Ritchie worried. I want him broken out in the open so I can get a shot at him or whomever he's dealing with. Maybe this is innocent, but I don't think so. I'll park in the lot across from the parts store. You go in and contact the manager and have your talk with Ritchie. Pump him good, but realize he'll probably stonewall you. The real payoff is that you have to see that baby and that you'll be back in touch. You might tell him that regulations require him to allow you to visit the home and examine the baby, or that a doctor do it and certify the vaccinations. That should thrill him. When you've pushed him enough, come out the door and I'll be watching."

"Then what?"

"Then we wait for Ritchie and follow him. It would be a miracle, but he might lead us to the baby. Your twenty-five dollars includes riding around with me today."

"Throw in lunch at the Fairland, and it's a deal."

"You drive a hard bargain." I tipped the sleepy waitress a dollar. Then we drove through morning fog to Washington street, an area of warehouses, machine shops, and wholesale dealers. I passed the parts store and parked in a post office lot. I aimed the rear end of the car north so that I could look in the side mirror and see a clear view down Washington Street to the front door where Spud would go inside.

"Come out after your chat and go to the front of the post office, then inside the building, then come out this side door and get in the car. Push Ritchie very hard."

Spud stubbed his cigarette. "Check," he said. "But I don't know why this can't be a rainy spring day in Los Angeles, and why I can't be Bogie carrying a bottle of rye into a bookstore and making love to Dorothy Malone."

"Look at yourself in the mirror sometime."

"Sayonara," Spud said, slipping out of the door.

I watched as Spud plowed the wet snow, crossed the busy street, and disappeared inside the parts store. Trucks sped by loaded with pipe and cattle. Spud became a watery shadow with the parts manager behind lettered glass. I settled back to smoke for thirty minutes. Then Spud appeared and walked deliberately across Washington Street. He turned the corner and went inside the post office and then slipped back out and into the car and lit a cigarette.

"Well?" I asked.

"Ritchie Polkis is not smart, but he's not stupid, either."

"What happened?"

"The manager took it hard, like you thought. He yanked Ritchie out of the back room and made him go into an office alone with me. It was a glassed-in room with a coffee machine and a water cooler and a dirty sink in one corner. I told Ritchie who I was and gave him my card and made like some officious bastard in a Kafka story. I told him about Cleveland Saunders blowing the whistle and about the failure to prove vaccination. He was nervous as a steer. He lied right away, telling me that the baby was with its mother. I called him a liar, or as much as one when I told him that we'd already checked with the mother. I pressed him on that. Then he told me that his grandmother had the baby."

"That's a lie, too."

"Then I took a chance. I wasn't sure about his grandmother, but I told him we'd checked that, too, and that it was a criminal offense to lie to an officer of the Department of Health. I thought he was going to wet his pants. Then I changed to the nice-guy routine and told him I didn't want to make trouble, that I just wanted to make sure the baby was vaccinated. I told him I'd come out to his place and check on the baby. He nearly croaked telling me not to bother. He tried the grandmother lie again, but I let him know with my smirk that I knew he was lying. Then I took another chance. I don't know if you'll like this."

"You know I trust you. What?"

"I told him I'd be back tomorrow and expected the baby to be here. He said no, and I said I'd be back."

I tried the side mirror and didn't find Ritchie. "It sounds good to me," I said. "There's a good chance, though, that Ritchie will check out Dewayne Small and find out he's a tall, muscular black man."

"We chance it," Spud said. "Do I get another twenty-five for tomorrow?"

"I might have known." I laughed.

"Add it to the bill," Spud said, grinning. He spit tobacco tics to the snowy ground. We sat quietly then, listening to radio music and watching the parts store. I heard some spring training news and finally five minutes of Jo Stafford. When the noon whistle blew, Ritchie came out of the parts store and got into a maroon sedan.

"Here we go," I said.

The maroon sedan headed north on Washington Street into a tractless jungle of used car lots, body shops, refineries, and warehouses called the North End. At Thirteenth Street the sedan bumped across a set of railroad tracks, past a smoky chemical plant, and into the Victorian odyssey of midtown. I followed Ritchie easily, changing lanes, slowing and speeding. It was always easy to follow a man whose mind was distracted and worried. Following an errant husband was also easy because of his guilt and excitement. Ritchie went north on Broadway in heavy traffic.

"I know where he's going," I said.

"Yeah?" Spud said.

"He's headed to his brother's house on Wellington Place."

"The tough guy?"

"There isn't any tougher."

"Leave me at the next corner and I'll walk home."

"This is twenty-five dollar a day stuff?"

"Be careful, now. I want to live to make fifty years old."

Ritchie turned the sedan from Thirteenth onto Wellington and pulled into the driveway of a green two-story Victorian. I drove by on Wellington and watched Ritchie park and climb the porch steps and go inside. I drove one block and turned the corner and parked.

"I think we're onto something," I said.

"I'm frightened," Spud said.

"Join the club."

We smoked and watched gray clouds swirl low. Some geese honked overhead. Two gray squirrels played tag on telephone wires, and in ten minutes Ritchie and George opened the front door of the old house and came down the steps quickly.

"George is built like a mausoleum," Spud said.

I got some field glasses from the glove box and spied the two figures standing in the yard talking. George was shaped like a robot, square and solid. He had a broad, pockmarked face and a flat nose. His black pin-striped suit was square shouldered, and the legs were cut loosely over shiny patent leather loafers with tassels. A pink shirt was open at his neck beneath a shiny silk scarf, and a gold chain hung on his left wrist. Gray tinged the edges of his slick black hair. The brothers walked to the maroon sedan. Ritchie backed the car from the driveway and drove south past us and into the slushy distance. I followed as he zig-zagged Main Street heading into downtown. The noon traffic had dwindled, and following was easy. Ritchie found First Street and went into the ventricle of the city. He crossed Douglas Avenue and parked in a truck zone.

"No respect for the law," Spud said.

I found a vacant yellow zone in front of the Allison Hotel and watched as the brothers jaywalked on Broadway and disappeared into the marble face of an office building.

"Stay here," I told Spud. "I'm going to try to catch them if I can. Move the car if you have to, but keep your eyes open. Spud nodded.

I bounded into traffic and dodged a truck. A bald man in a plumber's van yelled something about my mother and father. I ran north on Broadway, then hurried through two brass-and-glass revolving doors. The office building inside was sandstone, walnut, and dark glass with flute-worked sunflowers and buffalo. Brass chandeliers swung from a vaulted ceiling and reflected in pools on the black marble floor. Twin elevator shafts divided a marble staircase that wound to the mezzanine. The lobby reverberated the hushed musing of business and commerce. A blind man sold candy from a counter in one corner of the lobby. Suddenly I saw the split tail of George's striped suit swish around an elevator door. Two secretaries and a janitor shared the cabin. The door hushed shut.

I leaned against a marble wall and lit a cigarette. There was a brass arrow above the elevator door, and I watched the arrow creep along a half-moon of brass numbers. The arrow halted on three, seven, eight, and eleven. The other elevator came back down, and the door whooshed open and a voice said, "Up, please." The voice belonged to an old chicken in a glossy green dress. Her gray hair ringed her head like frosting on a doughnut, and a thick pair of bifocals twirled from her neck on a rhinestone chain. I smiled, and she clicked a wad of gum between her dentures.

"What's on eleven?" I asked.

"No," she clucked. "What's on first. Who's on eleven."

"Not bad," I said. She smiled.

"Do operators wait on eleven for calls down?"

"Sure they do," she answered. "You take your rides up to eleven and wait there until the other car hits bottom. When the other car starts up, you start down. It really takes brains."

Two businessmen shook wet snow from topcoats and cleared their throats, going inside the cabin. "You coming?" the chicken asked. I shook my head, and the doors closed silently. I watched then as the first elevator descended to the lobby. The doors opened and a crowd got out. The operator was a young hen with blond hair and black roots. "Up, please," she said.

"You remember the big guy with the black suit?"

"Who's asking?" she said. The hen was the size of a thermos bottle. Her pink sweater was cheap, but she filled all of it. She wore a blue-and-gold man's high school ring on her middle finger, the ring layered with dirty adhesive tape so it would fit.

"I'm a cop," I said.

"In a pig's eye," she answered shortly. The hen had a blue suitcase under each eye. Her fingernails were chewed stubs.

"It's that clear?"

"Hey," she said. "Blue cords and a pink shirt. I've seen a lot of cops, and my janitor boyfriend works with cops. Cops hit on me like carp to cheese. They all wear white shirts with frayed cuffs, and shiny black pants."

"Okay," I said. "The big goon snatched a baby. If I find the kid, it goes back to its mother." She eyed me hard. "Honest," I said.

"Eight," she said quickly. The door closed and the young hen whooshed up a dark shaft.

I walked the stairs to the eighth floor and went through a creaky fire door. Typewriters clacked in the hushed, carpeted hallway. Somewhere a teletype reported the news from Wall Street. I flipped a mental coin and walked left down the hallway past doors of frosted glass and gilt lettering, through the thick smell of furniture wax, leather, and soiled money. The hallway squared the building, offices on one side, stairwells and elevator shafts on the other. I saw twenty-five or thirty names of individuals and firms. I finally reached the central corridor and started back around again, smoking a cigarette. I loitered in the quiet hallway and gave up and went down the stairs and through the revolving doors and outside. I hopped across the street and slid into the car with Spud. He was smoking.

"What happened? Where have you been?" he asked. "Those guys came out and left."

"Damn it," I muttered.

"It's been thirty minutes," Spud said.

"I followed them to the eighth floor and waited. I thought I'd spot them, but they never came out to the lobby. For some reason they must have taken the back stairs outside. I sure thought we'd follow them when they left."

"What now?" Spud asked. He flipped his cigarette into a slush mount.

"Take your pad and pencil," I said. "Go into the lobby and make a list of all the offices on the eighth floor by name and number. Then go upstairs to the eighth floor and walk into each office in turn and ask for Mr. Polkis. Tell the receptionist you have some documents for him. There's got to be one receptionist who will acknowledge the question. The rest will look blankly."

"Good idea," Spud said. "What about lunch?"

"I'll park the car and wait for you in the Fairland down the block."

"Goody, goody," Spud said. "Can I have milk toast?"

"Fat man faw down inside," I said.

"Where's my twenty-five?" Spud asked, going away.

SIX

Spud leaned back in the dark booth, his pale head swathed in waxy neon patches. He pinched his eyes from fatigue. We had eaten a big lunch, and the cafe clattered and clanked as dishes and utensils were stacked and washed by the Chinese help. One old Chinaman, grinning over black teeth, pushed a wet mop under our feet, nodding his bald head like a crazed woodpecker. "Solly, solly," he cackled. Then he smiled again and swept his wet mop in swift, plopping arcs. The mop's soapy tentacles smacked against the work boots of a heating mechanic at the next booth. "Solly, solly," the Chinaman said.

As we drank our coffee, the cafe slowly filled with the desolation of greasy spoons everywhere. Two weary waitresses hunched on four elbows, smoking, allowing the thick smoke to collect in brown wads above the shiny black surface of the cold grill. The nameless pimpled kid danced the pinball machine, and a tiny Chinese girl in a slinky cheap dress and long earrings read *Screen Magazine* behind the register counter. The Chinese girl might have been forty-five or she might have been fifteen. In the glare and steam it was hard to tell.

Spud shuffled to the fountain and back. He chewed a wood toothpick, sucking it back and around his mouth, then worked it with his right hand like a spade, digging for blueberry seeds. Spud had spent forty-five minutes tramping around the eighth floor of the office building while I drank and smoked. He had returned to order the special: spring roll, ham and beans, coffee. While Spud sat with a smug, diffident look on his face, I ordered chow mein and milk, waiting for him to speak. Then we ate lunch and talked about the cold war, civil defense, and beatniks. We were in favor of beatniks, but against the cold war. Spud played "Heartbreak Hotel" on the juke-box.

"There are eight separate offices on the floor," Spud said. "I suppose there are maybe fifty or sixty people employed in them. There are a law office, a travel agency, an insurance company, and a stockbroker down on his luck. There was also a financial planner and a consulting engineer. No, there weren't any carnival barkers or palm readers."

Spud handed me his written list. Five red check marks caught my attention.

"What are the checks?"

"Offices there were closed for lunch. That narrowed the field, unless our boys went in and then locked up after they left. Take a look at the last one on the list."

The last item read: Kirkland, O'Malley and Reid. Room 830. "Yes, " I said.

"They're lawyers, of course. The office has double glass doors, names written in gold script. I walked into the place, and there were two receptionists, one on each side of the doorway. They looked up, and I clutched my note-pad and walked over to the one receptionist who was young and had a pretty smile. 'Mr. Polkis,' I said. She cocked her head and looked at me like I was a swizzle stick. She looked surprised and nervous and called her partner, Mil-lie. Millie sat across the way, an older, heavyset woman with gray hair, and thin bifocals on her nose. This Millie

turned blue and asked me what I wanted. I told her I was
looking for Mr. Polkis because I had some documents to
give him, and then I asked if I was too late to catch him
in the office. Millie picked up the phone and made a call.
Then she left the room for a couple of minutes and tells
me they have no Mr. Polkis in the office. I said, 'Well,
they just came in,' and she said, 'Well, I wouldn't know
about that.' ''

I studied the list again. ''And the other two offices?''

''Geologist and engineer. Both looked like one-man operations, and the men were busy and annoyed by my questions.''

''It looks like our boys went to a lawyer.''

''That's the bet, all right.''

''Who are those guys?''

''William G. Kirkland, B. Robert O'Malley, and Louis
Reid. An associate named Wilson Kunkle was also listed
at the bottom on the glass. It looks like a four-man operation with at least two secretaries.''

''What are those two hotshots doing, running to slick
lawyers anyway?''

''It could be they wanted legal advice about the visit of
the health inspector. They might have wanted to check and
see if the county could really make trouble about the
baby?''

''Maybe,'' I agreed. I drank my coffee and watched the
dregs form dunes in the bottom of the porcelain mug.
Chow mein dropped into my duodenum and went five
rounds with a cross intestine. When I thought about it, I
knew that George Polkis was not a man to run to rich
lawyers when he found a splinter in his finger. George was
a man who killed for revenge and burned for profit, and a
man who played tough snooker for fifty dollars a game.
He also didn't seem the type to take the back stairs running from a county health inspector. Besides, I knew
enough about lawyers to know that you don't walk into an

office and sit down with the boss. You have to have a retainer and a regular relationship, and neither George nor Ritchie were the retainer types. The thought crossed my mind that their back-stairs escape had been made to protect the lawyers, not the clients, and that maybe this visit was more than a routine legal checkup.

"And maybe not," I went on. "I want you to hang around in case I need some more help. I think now it's not a bad idea to return to the parts store one more time. I'll back you up. Be at your place tomorrow morning, and we'll flush Ritchie from his hole again. It should be fun."

We left the cramped booth and paid the Chinese girl at the register. She made our change without looking up. Outside, the sky was white and thin as cake icing. A gruff north wind rushed into the crevices and valleys downtown, rattling plate glass and kicking pellets of snow. The dull gray of March cracked, parting slightly to reveal roiling thunder fists, rain-headed clouds streaked by velvet sunshine. The fancy women held down dresses and hats, and the men tripped on topcoats. Behind the pastel cloud images, sun and brownstone reflected in the department store windows, and I saw a young girl on one knee dressing a headless mannequin in a flowery, spring dress. I caught her eye and winked and tipped my felt hat. She blushed and waved one of the mannequin's arms. Spud and I walked to the car.

"Where are you going now?" Spud asked.

"High school," I said.

Spud laughed. "Are you serious?" He lit a cigarette, and with his own he lit mine. I drove across town on Lewis Street, through acres of redbrick warehouses, produce outlets, and truck depots. Wind creaked in the broken elms, and the sky cleared to watery silver. Beneath the shadow of a rotted rooming house porch on Ida Street a single purple crocus swayed in mud. A brown tabby poised on a porch swing arm, watching two squirrels hootchie-koo in a catalpa fork.

I drove Hydraulic Street into a tightly bunched residential section of duplexes and white frame homes. Spud was quiet, then said, "All right, what gives?"

"I made an appointment with the school counselor. I thought she could give me some information on Bonnie or Lurleen, and maybe on Ritchie, if she knows such things. It's a long shot, but information helps."

"What do you think she might know?"

"I'll feel my way around. It's like doodling for water. You doodle and doodle, and maybe the stick turns down and you've found some water."

"What kind of tale will you give her about the baby?"

"I'll check the old bag out. If she's sympathetic, I might try the truth. If she's the old geezer I think she is, then I'll turn on the false charm. I just hope she doesn't hit me with a ruler. That's been my experience with high school counselors."

"We go to the parts store early tomorrow?"

"Check."

I dropped Spud off at his apartment on Oakland Street, then drove to Douglas and headed for East High School. The wind howled like a cranky nickelodeon and the sky cleared. Sun shafts struck ground as heavy clouds parted.

East Douglas was lined with ornate two-story homes, back streets webbed by small offices where the middle class did business surrounded by lilac, forsythia, and bluegrass. The houses there were thick and square, and in the middle of it all sat East High like a spider in a shiny sinister web, balanced and waiting patiently, dutifully sending its tender young from a sack, loosing them upon the world in bunches. Some of those young spiders spun their own webs, then sat in the shiny center devouring innocent insects; some of the young were themselves devoured, food for other insects, but most went their own way to watch the wind tear their imperfect webs, to spin endlessly and respin their sheenless webs from silk.

I parked on Douglas across from the school. East High was one square of magenta brick, broad stairs leading from an open field up to three sets of double doors. The school was crowned by a brick bell tower and four black spires. Above the doors, carved in marble, were the words: KNOWLEDGE TRUTH AND BEAUTY. I lit a cigarette and sat in the swirling gray light. Then I threw my smoke into a dirty puddle, jaywalked, and highstepped the wide stairs and threw myself into the gaping mouth of KNOWLEDGE.

KNOWLEDGE smelled of sawdust and paste. A single broad hall rose and trembled on both sides of me and disappeared between two piles of metal lockers. Leaded windows allowed icy light rivulets to scatter on the waxed floors. In the slit of a door I saw a jowled man with a pointer at the blackboard, probably teaching the intricate message of Manifest Destiny and civil obedience. The hall vibrated with the hushed mumble common to lunatic asylums and high schools. It was the mumble of human life flushed into the toilet of existence. In its way, the mumble was more articulate than the most delicate philosophy.

I skirted the trophy case and walked into the harsh light of the administrative offices. A thin-faced matron squinted from wire-rim spectacles and leaned her bony head over a slate counter. Six or seven secretaries bent above clacking typewriters, and I saw a big clock on the wall pounding out minutes. There was a red fire drill horn and a picture of Abe Lincoln. I told the matron I had an appointment with Miss Wunderland, and she pointed to a door in the corner of the big room. I went through a swinging gate and knocked on the wall beside the open door. It was odd being back in high school after all these years.

"Yes," a voice said. I fell into the room and was lost in her cool green eyes.

"Mr. Roberts," she said. "Cynthia Wunderland."

My breath circled nebulae, and I stood silently stunned.
"Sit down, won't you?"

"Thank you," I muttered and sat in a straight oak chair.
The office was big and airy, two tall windows rattling in
steady wind. Behind the counselor, on a white wall, watercolors reflected the silver light and the waving elm arms
outside. Cynthia Wunderland sat very straight behind her
desk. The desk was piled with file folders, notebooks, and
reports, and in one corner a green vase held flowers. "I
called you this morning."

"Yes, of course you did."

"I'm sorry, I'm a little taken back."

Behind her small shapely ear there was a yellow pencil
drawn back through auburn hair. "Mr. Roberts," she said,
"You look exactly like a private detective. It's actually
rather thrilling."

"Do I?" I asked stupidly. Cynthia Wunderland looked
like anything but a high school counselor. A dark woolen
sweater wrapped her like a cocoon, and discrete gold
chains entwined her smooth neck. Her hair was held in a
disheveled sunny pile on the back of her head with a bar-
rette. Wispy hairs transversed her fine ears.

"Yes, you do," she said. "I'm thinking primarily of
the look of a rather tired predator. An old lion lying in
brown grass." I noticed a degree from Mankato State University on the wall with the watercolors.

"You're from Minnesota," I said. "And I'm not that
old. Tired, maybe, but it's the weariness of the world and
nothing you can put your finger on."

"I'm Norwegian," she said. Her lean face balanced between high cheekbones and a sharp arc of jaw. Pale lipstick kissed a full, soft mouth. It was a beautiful face,
strong and intelligent, and her eyes twinkled from a play-
ful mischief. Under moonglow her skin would have been
the color of old bronze. "What I mean," she said, "is

that there is an independent look about you. You probably realize that it's a bit tough.''

I gazed outside to the swirling elms. In the distance a redbrick-factory furnace belched smoke from a stack. I watched the ocean of middle-class roofs and the March sky toiling above them.

"It's funny," I said. "It's funny being back in a high school. I don't think I've been inside one since before the war. I can remember all the smells and the way light bounces from the floors, and the feel of the place. I suppose the boys still throw butter pats onto the ceiling of the cafeteria. Maybe if you work here, all those sights and smells and memories recede.'' Cynthia Wunderland smiled. "Actually," I went on, "I could never figure out what those beveled windows were for, the ones with angled glass intersecting the bottoms of the tall windows. Every high school I ever saw had those extra panes at the bottom of the big windows.''

"The wind," she said. "The glass is made so that the windows can be opened and so that the wind will funnel to the ceiling and not blow papers around. And the sights and sounds never stop being memorable.''

Her neck plunged to a sharply defined collarbone and wide, perfect shoulders. She held her hands in a bouquet on her desk, tidy but not stuffy. Her fingers were narrow and womanly, the nails cleanly buffed. She looked pagan and calm as the bottom of the North Sea.

A bell clanged, and students rushed in the hallways. "Miss Wunderland," I said, "I called you because there is a serious problem with one of the students here.''

"Bonnie Cobb," she said.

"Yes, Bonnie Cobb. I didn't tell you much over the phone, so I'll tell you now. Bonnie has a baby, and you probably know about that. The child is named Elizabeth, and from what I understand, she went home to live with

Bonnie and her parents on Lorraine Street behind Sunnyside School.''

"I'm aware of the entire situation.''

"Then you may be aware that the baby was stolen from
them last week.'' Cynthia Wunderland touched her throat
with one slim hand. "I've been hired to find the baby and
bring her back home. This is a very unusual case, and I
need all the help and information I can get. This is confidential, of course.''

"That's terrible. I don't know. I'd like to help, of course,
but what can I do?''

"You can give me some information.'' She brushed
wisps from her ear, then tucked the wisps away. Her
movement was concise and pure, like piano music. Her
appearance was both mannered and angular.

"My information can help Bonnie?''

"Yes, and it goes further. We both have the same eth-
ical obligation to Bonnie, and that is to help her all we
can. It's that simple.''

"All right, Mr. Roberts,'' she said. "I'll trust you if it
will help Bonnie. I don't mind telling you that this makes
me very nervous.''

"Tough guys don't lie,'' I said. She smiled and nodded
and then walked to a gray file and came back with a manila folder. She sat down and opened the folder, shuffling
papers. "Go ahead,'' she said, "I'll help as much as I
can.''

"I liked Bonnie when I spoke with her. Am I wrong?''

"No, you're not wrong. Bonnie is insecure and unhappy. I know little of her home life or of her parents. I
gather she has resentment directed to her folks, but I've
never actually met the father. Resentment toward parents
isn't all that unusual, either, for that matter. Her mother
counseled with me several times before the baby was born.
I found her cold and demanding. She wanted the baby
adopted at birth, and she seemed overweening in that de-

mand. Bonnie could hardly get a word in edgewise, but I feel that if she could assert herself, she might shake herself free and blossom in some way through resistance. Bonnie has real potential, and she is intelligent.''

"You mean she's tough.''

"Well''—Cynthia Wunderland laughed—"if that's how you put it.''

"When did Bonnie get pregnant?''

"It was at the beginning of the school year.''

"What did she do?''

"I talked with the family at length. Bonnie seemed ambivalent at first, but the more we discussed the baby and her plans, the more her ambivalence dissipated. It isn't my task to make her decisions, just to discuss the options and help. Finally, she decided she might want to keep the baby. Then in October she went to the Booth Home for girls, where she stayed until she had the baby. She continued her studies through the pregnancy. Then she went home and started classes here during this semester.''

"What do you know about Ritchie Polkis?''

"The grounds keeper runs him off twice a week. He hangs around the school parking lot, with not much to do but bother the girls and pick fights with younger boys.''

"Is he the father of Bonnie's baby?''

"Oh, yes.''

"Did you ever counsel with Ritchie? Did he ever become a factor in its birth?''

"No, there was no mention of his responsibility in this. He's probably not the kind who cares much either way.''

"What about Lurleen Curtis?''

Cynthia Wunderland looked surprised. "Lurleen,'' she said. "What on earth does she have to do with this?''

"I'm not sure. You were going to trust me.''

"All right. But I don't understand why you would ask me such a question. Lurleen is in the Booth Home right

now. Like so many teenagers, like Bonnie, she fell in with
a boy and is pregnant. I don't know who the father of the
child is, but Lurleen is very angry and unhappy. She won't
talk to anyone about it, and she won't seek help. She is a
fierce type, very independent and rough."

"Who cared for Bonnie at the Booth Home?"

"She was treated by Dr. Rolfe there. I think her delivery and hospital care was done by Dr. Saunders at County
Hospital. He is a fine doctor and a fine man. Rolfe just
makes rounds on contract for the County. He visits and
prescribes aspirin. You see, the Booth Home is like a dor-
mitory where the girls can go until their babies are born.
Not many girls get real love and acceptance from their
parents, and certainly they get none from the other students. At the Booth Home they get shelter, and they get
support from each other. It's the best we can do under the
circumstances. It's really rather medieval."

"How many girls keep their children?"

"You'd be surprised. Most decide to keep them."

"The others?"

"Adopted. The arrangements are made through social
service agencies months in advance, and the babies are
gone in days."

"Who makes the arrangements?"

"The doctor and the personal lawyers for the families.
It is all done under the auspices of the Probate Court."

"How much interest is shown by fathers?"

"None. If they're interested, the two usually marry and
muddle along. Sometimes that works out amazingly well."

"Is there anything in your file that might give us a lead
on the baby? I'm grasping at straws now. All I know is
that Ritchie came to the house and took the baby. The
family is frightened, and Ritchie threatened Bonnie."

"I'm sorry," Cynthia said. "If the baby goes home, I
lose track. If there's an adoption, I certainly lose track.
There is a school nurse who sometimes helps with child-

care ideas, but in Bonnie's case that hasn't happened.''
Cynthia slid the pencil away from her ear and tapped it on
her desk. "Perhaps you should ask Ritchie Polkis?" A
sympathetic smile licked her lips. I pulled out a cigarette
and then pushed it back in my pocket. Cynthia laughed.
"You could go down to the boys' room. You'll probably
find some smokers there.''

"Nix, teach," I said. "I'd probably fall in with the East
Side kids and end up in reform school." I paused, listen-
ing to the wind and student mumblings. "Do you know
Ibsen, Miss Wunderland?" I asked.

"Oh, yes. I was born in Norway before the war. My
father was a diplomat. When the war came, my father and
mother brought me to Canada, then Minnesota. We read
Ibsen at home.''

"Then you know there is a corpse in every cargo."

"Yes, I know," she said quietly.

"I hope there isn't one here," I said. "I really do."

Cynthia Wunderland frowned and looked at her folder,
then gazed out the window. The grounds of the school
were alive with milling students. They gathered in homely
knots at street corners and huddled under naked elms.
They stood around flower beds, where white iris struggled
against the cold wind. I rose and we shook hands. Her
palm was cool.

"Thanks, Miss Wunderland," I said. "I'll keep in
touch.''

"I wish you would. Please, if there's anything I can
do . . ." Her voice trailed away. I stood staring at her stupidly.

"Do you like baseball?" I said suddenly.

"I loathe it.''

"Next Saturday the Braves and the Dodgers are playing
an exhibition game at the park. Major league teams tour
the country playing for the people in minor league towns.
Guys like Snider and Furillo and Campanella and Ma-

thews and Spahnnie and Joe Adcock. It's an afternoon game, and with any luck it should be warm and clear. I wonder if you'd go with me?''

"I don't know," she said.

"I'll buy you hot dogs with relish and mustard. They have good hot chocolate.''

Cynthia smiled. "In that case, I suppose I must. I live on Green Street.''

I turned and tumbled happily through the bright hall, feeling considerably younger and less hostile. A janitor ran a waxy red mop down the center of the floor. I descended the wide steps and sat in the car smoking a cigarette. I thought for a while about Bonnie and Lurleen and the Booth Home. A kid with greased hair and black ducks stuck his head in the car window. He wore a button-up blue sweater, white shirt. There was cracked paste on his pimples. "How about a spin, pops?" he asked. Pops, I thought, then started the car and drove away.

As I reached the downtown buildings, a limpid sun dropped below a cloud bank. Purple and red rays pierced the river bridge, burning in the amber-meshed cottonwoods and maples. I breathed deep and placed my lips on Miss Wunderland's cheek. The kiss was like a strawberry phosphate. I saw a corpse in the cargo, and then I reached my old Victorian. That night I smoked my calabash and read *Ghosts* and finally, when night came, I slept.

SEVEN

A cold, fractured moon rode the sullen morning sky. Mist rose in elm limbs, and above the tangled limbs the blue sea of tranquility raced gray clouds. There seemed no dawn, only a gray mantle suspended like darned wool in melting snow. The rabbits paced nervously in their hutch. The neighbor's chickens clucked, and as if from the bottom of a dreadful ocean, the massively trunked catalpa trees and elms surfaced like empty ships. There was no human sound in the early morning, just the underground water seeping.

I showered in darkness and put on some brown cords, a wool shirt, and Red Wing boots. The thought of Cynthia Wunderland drifted in my rooms, and I conjured a tactile vision of the soft white swale of her neck, the sweet place where her fine ear curved to meet the swale, and the lovely strong bones of her shoulders. I shaved in blue light and imagined her leaning into me, her breath sweet on my face, her strong hands around my waist and inching along the river of my backbone. I flicked on the bathroom light and patched myself with a styptic pencil to repair the self-inflicted gash in my throat. I walked to the kitchen. I poured some coffee and put on a blue windbreaker and lit the cold calabash and went onto the front porch in the

cold. Mrs. Thompson and her cat, Francis, were in the
front yard. Mrs. Thompson was draped in a tattered
housecoat, and she wore black, unbuttoned galoshes. Her
frizzy hair fluttered in ragged gray tufts in the wind. She
scuttled, oblivious as a crab, and when Francis caught her
meanderings, he rubbed his fluffy back on her legs. She
was old and deaf, and she preferred the utter silence of
early morning, fearing the bric-a-brac social daytime with
its mishmash of cars, bicycles, and trash trucks. She feared
most people, and she feared the gossip of our neighbors
like Mrs. Aley to the south, who believed irrationally that
Mrs. Thompson was a witch. Fearing as she did the ram-
paging daytime and the idle talk of neighbors, the old
woman washed herself clean in early morning silence.

She plucked paper and twigs and weeds from the scruffy
yard and pushed the refuse into the pocket of her gown.
She pecked at the ground like some hungry and forlorn
bird who has not flown south. I finished my coffee, then
went to the yard and swept my hands along the brown
flank of Francis's side and helped Mrs. Thompson pick
weeds. Then I walked in silence to the river and along the
riverbank in fog and mist, shrouded by my thoughts.

At first my thoughts were spoors beneath a dank forest
floor, buried in fibers from ancient plants. I walked the
riverbank under the Douglas Street Bridge, past the brooding bulk of a hotel, watching as yellow light flicked on in
the hotel windows, where salesmen inspected their brushes
and where maids and cooks stood smoking morning cigarettes. Then the spoor thoughts became small ferns, growing and spreading branches. I sat on a board dock of the
old boat house, its great silent timbers looming like some
old southern plantation above me, reflecting dully in the
swirling river water, the creaking of wooden hulls beside
me on the pylons. Birds burst into symphonic harmony,
and I circled west around the river and through the dirt
streets and narrow alleys of the old Wichita cowtown where

cafe signs winked and blinked until I came to the Quaker university. Finally, I reached full circle to my rooms and went inside, knowing that from beneath the forest floor of uncertainty, my thoughts had produced life.

Later, in the sharp glare of a small cafe on North Broadway, I ate two eggs with ham and hash browns and catsup. Then I drove to Oakland Street and picked up Spud Christian. He wore his suit and white shirt and a skinny black tie. Spud and I drove in silence, smoking cigarettes, past the gleaming East High School and to our vantage point in the post office parking lot opposite the parts store where Ritchie Polkis worked. Spud was pensive, and he smoked his cigarette without speech.

"Be careful," I said finally. He smiled and nodded at me knowingly and crushed his cigarette in the ashtray.

"If something goes wrong, I'll just bail out," he said.

Spud left the car and crossed Washington Street, dodging trucks and cars. He disappeared into the shadows and reflections of plate glass, and as I watched the minutes passed. Soon Spud appeared at the door and walked quickly to the curb and stood sniffing the cool March air as trucks geared by. Then an oil tanker sped past. Spud stood still, allowing the traffic to ebb.

Then I saw Ritchie Polkis standing in a gravel alley peering at Spud from behind a telephone pole. He had on a gray work shirt and blue pants, pointy black shoes, and a ball cap pulled low on his forehead. He looked slick and honed, and as he stood behind the pole, he rubbed his hands and watched Spud from his dark, piercing eyes. Another tanker sped by on the street and threw slush onto Spud's shoes. Spud stepped away from the curb.

Ritchie tugged the bill of his cap and inched from behind the pole toward Spud. The scene began to unfold with a maniacal density, as if I were looking at Picasso's *Guernica* through binoculars, each detail blown to gigantic, unearthly proportion. Then Ritchie lunged at Spud as

I screamed, and Spud slipped into the ice-clogged gutter, balancing and teetering, then gaining his balance by grabbing a wad of Ritchie's shirt collar. Spud swung a right at the kid's ear, and the kid spun back and sat down hard on a bus bench. I ran across the street and stood in an alley, watching Spud and the kid.

Spud righted himself and stood above the bench. Ritchie stood and swung wildly with his right hand. Then Spud backed the kid into a small parking lot, and while I watched, the kid whipped out a shiny knife and flipped the blade open. Spud jumped back and crouched, then backed against the red brick wall of the parts store. The kid spun the knife hand to hand and growled something I couldn't hear. Above Spud, The Rainbow Bread Girl smiled her benign, commercial smile.

I ran across the lot and stood behind the kid. The knife was a black switchblade, and the kid continued whipping it hand to hand. I grabbed his right wrist and held on like a junk-yard dog. Ritchie was surprised and froze stiff and turned his head. Spud stepped straight from the wall and drove a left like Joey Giardello's to Ritchie's ear. There was a sharp crack, and Ritchie went down like a wet tent in a windstorm, lying on the concrete with one arm bent under his chest and his legs crossed, twitching slightly. Blood the color of pimiento juice seeped from his ear.

"Pretty good shot," I said, puffing.

"He scared the hell out of me," Spud said. His breath starred the cold air. "He must be crazy."

Ritchie twitched like a hula dancer. "What happened inside?" I asked. The traffic rumbled on the street, and we stood in the cold, our frozen breath leaking in the thin, March air. A cab driver stopped his checker cab and stared at the confusion, then put a microphone to his mouth. "Let's get out of here," I said.

"You don't think he's dead?" Spud asked.

"You'll be out of jail in ten years. Come on."

We walked quickly to the car, and I drove into Linwood
Park and through the trees. Spud rubbed the knuckles of
his hand. "They told me the kid quit," he said.

"I'm not surprised. What did he say in the parking lot?"

"I don't think he knew I wasn't Dewayne Small. He
warned me that I should lay off and said he was going to
cut me just a little to make sure the message stuck. I'm
not sure he meant it, but the look in his eye was pure
lunatic. But, I don't think he knew I wasn't with County
Health."

"Good," I said. "But if I make a move on Ritchie now,
I think they'll go to the Cobbs and cause trouble. It's too
great a risk, now that we know Ritchie could explode.
Anybody that would pull a knife like that is dangerous as
hell."

"He scared me, all right."

I curled through the shaded park and emerged on Lincoln Street, then wound into trees again, dappled sun and
patches of snow gleaming in the Scotch pine arbors.

"What now?" Spud asked.

"I'll go see the doctor who delivered the baby. Maybe
he can help. The high school counselor gave me some
good ideas about doctors and lawyers." I pulled to a stop
on Oakland Street, and Spud got out of the car and stood
in slush. "Stay out of the way for a bit," I said. "Ritchie
is sure to go to George and tell him your play. Don't go
to the Club Billiards, and stay out of Eddie's Bar on Maple. I don't want to come after you with a putty knife and
a paper sack."

"Don't worry. But if you get a line on Ritchie, I'd like
to help. His play with the knife angers me a little." Spud
grinned and pounded on the hood as I drove away.

I killed an hour at a drugstore on Hillside, drinking two
strawberry sodas and eyeing a young blond waitress. I sat
on a shiny chrome stool, thinking about Ritchie and his
tango with Spud. Ritchie had tried to push Spud into

traffic. That kind of chance would only be taken by a kid who was naturally crazy, a kid raised on violence.

I stuck my straw into pink foam at the bottom of the soda glass. There was a suck and a clatter, and at the end of the white marble counter, the blond waitress frowned at me. Her dips and doodles fit tightly into a neat uniform, and while I sat still, she peeled and sliced a banana. While she worked, a pink tongue appeared at the corner of her lips. Her eyes were blue lagoons and white white sand. I tipped her and left to keep my appointment with Cleveland Saunders.

EIGHT

"A county hospital," said Cleveland Saunders, "is one part state penitentiary and one part local jail. It is a serious mental institution, a living hospital, soup kitchen, looney bin, and old folks' home. Nothing here is pretty. Every six weeks the County Commission fires one of the staff— an orderly, a cook, or night nurse—for taking sexual advantage of one of the patients. Usually, the victims are mental patients. There are two doctors on call, tired as hell, and three or four volunteers from the local Medical Society. Much of the practice here involves sewing the heads of patients who hurt themselves while already hospitalized for some other illness. The patients are on hold, Mr. Roberts, and being on hold means that they have no future. For these poor people, the horizon is a vast, limitless blank. Do you know how hard it is to get well when there is nothing in your future save pain and deprivation?"

Cleveland Saunders spread his massive hands on a metal desk. The doctor was a huge man with deep brown eyes and a weary expression on his flat face. His hair was frizzled gray and his forehead deeply lined.

"I imagine," I said. "But Bonnie Cobb. You delivered her baby here sometime around four months ago. Elizabeth."

"Mr. Roberts," he said slowly. "I have been at County for fourteen years now, and I have delivered more than five hundred infants into this world. I haven't got the vaguest idea who Bonnie Cobb is, or if I delivered her baby. Perhaps you could refresh my memory."

"Bonnie is a skinny thing with red hair and freckles. At the time she probably weighed all of a hundred pounds, baby and everything. She spent some time at the Booth Home, then came here to have her baby."

"Nope."

Sunlight strained into the tiny office. We sat in the corner of the third floor of the Sedgwick County Hospital. Through the dirty venetian blinds I saw downtown rising meekly into the powder-blue sky. Before me spread the Ghetto, a collection of tar-paper shacks and dirty brick duplexes into which Wichita poured all its black men and women. In one corner of the office there was a medicine cabinet with the usual collection of instruments, syringes, and vials. Along another wall sat an examination table. Behind the doctor, hanging on a puke-green wall, were both the diploma and the certificate. They were from institutes in Alabama.

"Perhaps you have her records," I said.

Cleveland Saunders looked down at his desk as cafeteria sounds reverberated dully. There was muffled laughter.

"Is this important?"

"Very."

"Perhaps you would comment on the propriety of my releasing confidential medical information to someone I don't know, about a patient I can't remember?"

"Bonnie Cobb had her baby here four months ago. The father is a man named Ritchie Polkis. He is both a bad citizen and a bad father. Bonnie was at the Booth Home, looked after there by a Dr. Rolfe. You delivered the baby and cared for her here; then she went home with her baby. Her parents took care of Elizabeth until a week ago. Then the baby was taken from the home by force, perhaps with threats involved. I was hired to find her and bring her home. My only interest is in Bonnie and the baby. My own duty involves confidentiality and trust as well. This story can be confirmed by a phone call to Maud Cobb, or to Bonnie herself, for that matter. What else do you need to know?''

Cleveland Saunders locked my eyes. "I don't understand how talking to me can help.''

"Doctor, I'm going to tell you something. I have what you would call a hunch, and nothing more. Based on my observation and my instinct, but still a hunch. If I'm right, then a crime has been committed, but either way it's a dangerous situation for Bonnie. I'm hoping that you can give me some inside information about the operation of the Booth Home and about certain personnel there, in hope that information like that will prove useful. Right now its nothing but a hope and a hunch backed by some theory.''

"Go on," he said.

"Ritchie is a punk. His brother is worse. His brother is a dangerous man with a criminal record. He is small-time, but in Wichita he's what you might call small-time-big-time. Ritchie took the baby on a quiet afternoon in the middle of last week. Since that time there has been literally no trace of the child. I know that because I've checked. So I have to ask myself what would two guys like that want with a baby?''

Saunders opened a desk drawer. He took out a small-bowled English briar and filled it with twist. "Go on," he said again.

"Doctor, I think they sold the baby.''

Dr. Saunders's face went blank. "Sold the baby?'' He groaned. "My God, what can you mean, sold it?''

"Look," I said. "It figures. They didn't take the kid out of paternal instincts. There isn't any other motive that fits their behavior. I guess my question is how you would go about moving a baby into the stream of commerce?''

Cleveland Saunders rose from his chair and walked to the window that looked over Ninth Street. Below him stretched the Ghetto, the grain elevators, and shoe shine parlors. He stood staring out the window, puffing his pipe. "Just a minute," he said and walked into the hallway. When he came back he said, "I've had a nurse go to the basement for the records on Bonnie Cobb. I've been thinking that there may be something I can help you with. I'm not sure." We were silent. Then he turned and stared at me over his pipe. "Do you know how many Negroes practice medicine in this city, Mr. Roberts?''

"No," I said.

"One." Cleveland Saunders turned back to the window. An ambulance siren rose and fell through the emergency entrance. "Last week," he said to the window, "there was a middle-aged man brought to the hospital by the police. His name is Wayne Washington. The police found him knee-deep in the Arkansas River. He had a penny whistle around his neck, and he wore boxer shorts and a T-shirt. There was ice in the river. He was piping tunes to the sky, and the police picked him up and the Probate Court held a hearing on his sanity. The hearing was to determine whether Wayne was a danger to himself or others. That's the legal standard, you know. Do you know what I found when I examined him?''

I said "No."

"His blood pressure was two hundred and ten over one hundred and thirty. He was malnourished. He was not undernourished precisely, but malnourished. He had a respiratory infection, and his teeth were rotten. I was stunned when I looked at his teeth during the standard inspection of his throat. Most of his back teeth were hollow and black. They were like termite-infested wood. He had gone through the sixth grade and then left school. Then, I saw something I rarely encounter. Wayne had chilblains on his fingers. His right hand was inflamed and swollen from the constant cold in his room. Here was a human being in our midst, suffering from cold and malnutrition." Cleveland Saunders walked back to his desk and sat. He puffed his briar patiently. Two orderlies spoke Spanish outside the door, then moved on.

"Anyway," he went on, "there was an official hearing held on the fifth floor here. The fifth is a psychiatric ward. The Probate judge conducts those hearings on Wednesday afternoon. On the average, there are four or five hearings, and each lasts about fifteen minutes. Can you imagine deciding a man's fate, deciding the course of his life and future in fifteen minutes? The Court in this case had appointed a lawyer for Wayne. The lawyer, of course, had never spoken to Wayne, and was introduced to Wayne and his mother and sister on the spot. One police officer testified, and the psychiatrist testified. The psychiatrist was nervous and hurried and was paid twenty dollars for his examination and was, thus, understandably anxious to return to his office. The lawyer made jokes with the judge. Ten minutes later, Wayne was on his way to Larned State Hospital for the Mentally and Criminally Insane. There, he will receive shock therapy and powerful depressants. His teeth will continue to rot, and nobody will think to treat his high blood pressure."

A nurse came into the room and handed Saunders a manila folder. He thanked her and she went away.

"Hell of it is, Mr. Roberts, Wayne claimed he was making rain. That's all, just making rain." Saunders laughed ironically. "You know," he said, "it rained during the sanity hearing and rained for two days thereafter." Cleveland Saunders studied the manila folder.

"Not much unusual in here," he said. "Just my usual medical notes and a photocopy of the birth certificate I must have signed. But I do remember the girl now. I also remember her mother and the father of the baby. What a mess."

"How so?"

"The father, Ritchie Polkis, was adamant that the baby be given up for adoption. There was a disturbance on the wing one night when Bonnie was staying here just prior to the delivery. As I remember now, he threatened her and had to be removed. There was no violence, mind you, but some very rough talk. One of our big orderlies took care of it. I remember that I had calls from the Booth Home about Bonnie, too."

"What do you mean?"

"The home was under the impression that arrangements were being made for the baby to be adopted. I simply told them that I didn't know of any arrangements like that. It's not really something I have anything to do with anyway."

"How is it arranged? "

"Most of our young women are not married. Lawyers arrange for court documents to be drawn, then the mother signs her consent. If there is a father, then he signs a consent as well. The Probate Court legalizes the final arrangement. I know very little about the actual process."

"But who finds the adoptive parents?"

"Various social agencies. Lutheran Social Service. The Catholic League."

"The Booth Home?"

"Rarely, but I believe they do that as well." Cleveland Saunders examined a square document. "Well," he said, "here's the birth certificate." He handed the photocopy to me.

"Doctor, who called you from the Booth Home?"

Dr. Saunders examined his notes. "I think it was Dr. Rolfe. Yes, I remember. We had quite a discussion at the time."

"What was said?"

"As I recall, Rolfe wanted me to make a recommendation about adoption."

"You made one?"

'Of course not. It's not my function. I would never make a recommendation one way or another."

"But Rolfe did?"

"Yes, I believe he did."

"That's unusual?"

"Very."

"Doctor, let me ask you something. What sort of person is this fellow Rolfe? I mean, what can you tell me about him personally and professionally?"

"I'd really rather not discuss another doctor in that fashion. I believe you can understand the delicacy of that sort of business."

I studied the certificate. It was a standard form signed by Cleveland Saunders, listing the date of birth of the baby and her vital statistics. The line above "Father" was empty.

"Doctor, I can appreciate the ethics of discussing another doctor. But ethics has nothing to do with selling babies. It has nothing to do with making threats. If Rolfe is involved, I've got to get a line on him. There is nothing to make me think he is involved, but I have to make sure. That means asking questions. You can think of it as another sort of treatment for one of your patients." Saunders sat smoked his pipe, thinking. "Please, doctor, it's very important. You must know that."

"All right," he said. "Rolfe I don't like. In the first place, he is a lousy doctor. In the second place, he cuts corners. I wouldn't trust him with an infected splinter. He has an office in Kechi, but he exists mostly through appointments to visit the juvenile detention centers, the Booth Home, and the jail prisoners. Treating the poor is thought of as low, demeaning work. It takes no concentration and no dedication. Or that's the theory that Rolfe works on anyway."

"Doctor, if I were going to sell babies for profit, how would I do it?"

The doctor drummed his fingers on the desk. "I don't have much experience in the field, Mr. Roberts."

"A guess," I said.

"A guess would be that you need someone to fake documents, file them with the proper court, then make delivery. But it's very dangerous, and you would likely be found out. On the other hand, it would not be hard to accomplish. Only the natural mother could stand in your way initially."

"Did Bonnie Cobb want her baby?"

"That's what the arguments were about. She wanted to keep the child after her initial depression wore off. She was adamant about that. And the more they kept after her, the more adamant she became."

"They?" I asked.

"Yes, of course," Saunders said. "Her mother, too."

I stood and shook hands with Cleveland Saunders. I handed him the documents and asked him to get in touch with me if there was anything he could remember about Rolfe or Ritchie Polkis that might help. I handed him my card and he walked me to the rickety elevator. I stood at the end of the long green hallway, listening to a racket like a monkey house at the zoo. I smelled lime soap, iodine, and urine, then rode to ground level and went out the glass doors. I stood sniffing the March wind, thinking. The wind carried a dead odor of rendering plants and stockyards and the refineries north of town. I got inside the car and turned on the radio and drove across town as Patti Page sang a song.

I parked in a loading zone across the street from an office building downtown. Late afternoon sun cut shadows on the sidewalks. Each window held cloud reflections as I jaywalked, and rode the elevator to the fifth floor. The little hen steered the elevator and recognized me from the day before. I tipped my hat and walked down a stuffy hall and walked inside the disheveled office of Jack Graybul, an attorney who often engaged me in skip-chases and repossessions. His secretary, Laverne, sat behind a typewriter and a pile of documents.

"Oh, it's you," she said. Laverne had been Jack's secretary since the early Pleistocene. She was a cross between Emma Goldman and Lucretia Borgia. An Old Gold dangled from her lips; ashes dotted the front of her woolen shawl. She was shaped like the scoreboard at Yankee Stadium.

"You mean it's *only* me, don't you?"

"Now that you mention it," she said.

"Laverne, is the boss in?"

"You're speaking to the boss," she growled.

"Well, then, is Jack in?"

"His body is in his chair," Laverne said.

Jack's office was cramped and cold. On his walnut desk sat a plaster judge with the legend: SUE THE BASTARDS. Jack sat in a leather chair with his feet on a windowsill. The windows led out to a dead brick wall.

"Don't bother to sit," Jack said. "You won't be here that long."

I sat. "Thanks, I don't mind if I do."

Jack dropped his feet from the sill and swiveled his chair. "Mitch, you know I'm only kidding. You're my favorite nonpaying client. There are others, but you are my favorite."

"Jack," I said, "I need some advice."

Jack opened his desk drawer and took out a tiny sand clock. He sat the clock on a date book, then turned it over. Sand fell down.

"I would ordinarily require a hefty retainer. But in your case, I believe I will simply refuse to answer. Unless, of course, you would care to write out a check. On second thought, make that cash, cold hard cash."

"What would you do, Jack if you were put in charge of an adoption?"

"Are you serious?" he asked. "You know someone who wants that done?"

I saw dollar signs in his eyes. "Maybe," I said.

"Why didn't you say so?" Jack grinned. "It's simple. We file a petition with the Probate Court, we publish notice in the local newspaper for a week, then we file the requisite consent forms. There is a short hearing in front of the judge. Have these people got money?"

"This has to do with the couple you steered to me this week. Their problem is confidential, so I can't tell you their story. You'll have to trust my judgment on this. But I know they don't have much money."

Jack's crest fell. He leaned back then, the savage and hopeful look gone from his face. Jack was a thin man with an aquiline nose and close-set eyes. His hair was gray, and cigarette ash and dandruff peppered his black suit. I would have bet that there were brown shoes and mismatched socks under the desk. He was the kind of man who gets knocked down in the streets by cars. He had made little money over the years, probably because he was reasonably honest.

"Suppose someone with a baby wanted to make some money on the adoption. Maybe a payment from the people who finally adopt the baby," I said.

Jack stuck a finger in his ear and jiggled. "My advice, Mitch, is don't get involved. Something like that is in a gray area between legal and illegal. For a lawyer, it is definitely unethical. Risky. You're talking about selling a baby."

"Yeah, I guess so."

"It's been done. Usually the payment is covered by a contract that calls for the adoptive parents to meet the mother's expenses of birth and provides something for lawyers' fees. But it stinks, Mitch. Lawyers don't touch such a deal if they are really smart. Mothers don't, either, you know?''

"What do you know about Kirkland, O'Malley and Reid?''

"Upstairs," Jack said. "This is in confidence?''

"Yes, and very important.''

"You're not selling babies, are you?''

"No chance," I said.

"Right," Jack said. "The three guys used to be good, but they're getting old now. They made good money in oil and gas. The old guy, Kirkland, went to Virginia Law School, I remember. He was driving across the country to San Francisco when his Model A broke down and he stayed in Wichita, opened an office, and made a go of it. Hell of a story.''

"What about their honesty?''

"You could ask that about any lawyer." Jack puffed a cigarette and allowed ash to drift onto his suit. "The old men of the firm used to be straight as an arrow. But they hardly practice anymore. O'Malley is still there, but there are some new boys who handle the show.''

"Kunkle?''

"Yeah, a guy named Kunkle.''

"What's his story?''

"If I say something, you can keep it under your hat?''
I nodded. "Kunkle is a sleazeball like something you find under the refrigerator.''

"How's that?''

"He practices junk-ball law, taking out default judgments on poor people, then executing on their sons and daughters. He does bankruptcy for shady business. He would sooner cut your throat than play fair.''

"How hard would it be to start a racket selling babies? Would it be hard to get the documents together and make all the arrangements?''

"It could happen,'' Jack mused. "But it would never

be a big racket because the Probate judge would smell a rat.''

"Why?''

"The judge would see a flood of consented adoptions from the same lawyer or firm. He would sense that it's unethical, and no judge would allow it for long.''

I stood. "Your sand clock is empty,'' I said. Jack turned the clock over.

"It's funny that you came in asking about Kunkle.''

"It's not that funny,'' I said.

"Yeah, it is.'' Jack rose and looked out the window at the brick wall. "Kunkle, upstairs, is a very politically connected sort of fellow. That makes it funny. He runs his brother's campaign every four years. His brother is a lawyer, too.''

"Yeah,'' I said, waiting. Jack stood in the dim window rubbing his chin. Then he turned.

"His brother is Randolf Kunkle, judge of the Probate Court for the county of Sedgwick.''

"You don't say.''

"Now,'' Jack said, "you want to tell me about this?''

"I can't right now, Jack. I haven't got anything. When I do, I'll let you know. I may need some more advice if I get any further with this thing.''

"I'll give you some advice right now. These boys are Democrats with a capital D. They run the Sheriff's Department and the County Commission. They build the roads and bridges, and they give the old ladies jobs behind desks. We haven't got a machine in this county because we don't need one. We have a good-old-boy network, and that's better than a machine any day of the week. What I'm saying is—watch your ass.''

I smiled and left the office. I tipped my hat to Laverne and the little hen who ran the elevator, then got into my car and drove on Maple Street across the bridge and down Sycamore to my house. It was suppertime, and long shadows filled the yards. Someone fried bacon. I pulled in the front driveway and stopped.

The maroon Ford sped by, going fast. I saw it in the rearview mirror, then watched out the passenger window as it disappeared on Sycamore and Douglas. The wind kicked some hot dog wrappers through the streets and slush puddles. The driver of the sedan was a big mausoleum with a black coat. A broad-brim hat was pulled low over his face. Then I remembered what I had learned about following men who are preoccupied and nervous.

It was a long time before the taste of iron left me.

NINE

Perhaps curiosity sent me to visit the Indian woman. Perhaps it was a nagging idea half-hidden in my unconscious, and maybe it was simple stubborn need to know. But that night I made three phone calls and left for El Dorado. Because the Cobbs didn't answer their phone, I dropped a note into the mail slot of their house on the way out of town. I warned them that George Polkis had spotted me, followed me across town to my house, and would probably know my game. I warned them to take care. The second call went to Cynthia Wunderland, who answered with a violet purr, sweet as honeyed cherries. I told her I wanted to talk about the Booth Home, and she told me to come to her house when I was finished with business in El Dorado. My third call was to Andy Lanham, who told me where to find Althea Little Bear, widow of the man murdered by arson in a bingo parlor.

The crystal evening drifted westward, leaving the horizon a patina of pink and gold strands. Old Highway 54 became a pure black chain dropped onto the rolling hills, hedge apple rows, and stark, distant cottonwood groves. I drove with the windows open, feathering smoke from my cigarette into the thin, cool wind, watching the lovely spring Virgin rise slowly from the nether world into the

shimmering, inky sky above me. Spica glimmered at her
waist like a sapphire. I ran the car out of town quickly,
gaining the wheat and milo stubbles east of town, the shiny
mirrored farm ponds and the muddy rivers that surround
Wichita, the night both cool and sweet from early spring.
Burma Shave signs rose and descended a hillock. Hand-
painted cardboard slogans advertised eggs, milk, and
homemade pickles for sale. The yellow, marbled eyes of
a possum glittered in milkweed beside a dark red barn.

I felt as if I'd known all of this disarray since before my
own birth. I felt something infinitely sad about the weathered farmhouses engulfed in a swollen ocean of prairie,
kerosene lamps burning beneath a canopy of fiery stars,
and something deeply abiding about the arthritic men and
women, knuckles at the windowpane, waiting and watching and toiling with the soil and the animals of the earth.
I understood the profound loneliness and the shameless
sentimentality of it. I thought about my own grandmother,
a tireless woman of the earth. I flipped on the radio and
went down a slope into thick shadow listening to Gogi
Grant singing "The Wayward Wind."

Now I was detecting the only way I knew, working
partly for revenge, and partly inspired by the clear liquid
of fear. I began to hate George Polkis for the connections
he had to all the important, dirty people who had risen
through swamps of power and greed, achieving a vile re-
spectability that grafted itself to decency like a cancer.
The case smelled of money drifting like ash into all the
right places, cold cash that stinks and rots the soul. It
smelled, too, of little people in terror, giving up before
they ever got started. I thought about the connection between Wilson Kunkle and George Polkis, and the more I
thought about it, the more I believed the connection led
straight to the Sedgwick County Courthouse and Probate
judge, Randolf Kunkle. About Bonnie Cobb I knew very
little, but she seemed decent to me, frightened, alone,

uncertain. She seemed like the kind of vulnerable meat that buzzards like George Polkis and Wilson Kunkle would tear and devour. I wanted revenge for her then, and for the other wretched inmates who are sentenced for life, their crime being poverty and loss, the execution taking place by guilt.

But I was frightened, too. I remembered the black mass of George Polkis as he stood in his black suit, arms akimbo, and his gray hair and silk tie wisping in the wind. His ears were as big as country flapjacks. You could slip a railroad tie under the shoulders of his coat. And George had one advantage over the rest of us: He would not hesitate to commit the vilest act with pride, without emotion. So, I drove on to El Dorado in the gathering dark, beneath the swirling spring stars, hoping to drive a stake through George's heart before he prowled the night again with his baby-selling scheme, if that's what it was. But to drive a stake into the vampire's heart, you have to catch him in his coffin, asleep at midday.

El Dorado is a deep-root weed in Wichita's backyard. Years before, oil and gas had made it prosperous, along with the few men who owned all that black stuff beneath the earth. The downtown was boardwalk surrounded by shacks and frame houses. The Walnut River drowned the shantytown once a year in spring, then sank back to its muddy course. On the town's western edge, refineries towered like cruise ships in an ocean of grass, light and flame and steam billowing skyward from flare stacks. To the east, the Flint Hills swayed like a treeless sea, the last of the great tall-grass prairie that once grew wild bluestem higher than a man's head, one hundred square miles of wilderness and wind. El Dorado was a pool hall and a drugstore and a dirty cowhand, toothpick dangling from his toothless mouth. I drove by the ornate County Courthouse and headed into the poorest part of town, down by the river beneath a welter of rotten catalpa and stunted elm.

I parked beside a tar-paper liquor store. I could hear the river gurgle in the distance. Gypsy moths pounded against the dirty glass of the liquor store window as a neon sign clicked and buzzed hideously. Hugging the side of the liquor store, a set of board stairs wound to the second story of a dilapidated storefront and disappeared onto a dark landing. Althea Little Bear lived upstairs. I stubbed my cigarette and bounded up the board stairs. I heard no sound save the rush of the river and the click of neon and my own thudding fist on wood. The door opened like a sepia wedge.

The woman had the broad, flat face of a Plains Indian. She wore a simple gray dress and black shawl, and her lineless face expressed nothing but the expectation of pain. Black pigtails framed her face, which was handsome, sad, and dignified, the pigtails disappearing into the shawl. Past her shoulder, inside the high-ceilinged hollow room, one light bulb revolved on its cord. Its swinging halo made her features mysteriously beatific. She said nothing, but regarded me with unspoken despair.

"I'm not a cop," I said.

She stared at me. "That's something anyway," she said.

"My name is Mitch Roberts, and I'm from Wichita. I want to talk to you for a minute about your late husband and a guy named George Polkis. This may not make much sense to you now, but it will if you'll give me five minutes. No trouble for you."

"I already talked to the police. I don't care anymore." She glanced over her shoulder and to the cold room. I took out a cigarette and offered her one. She took the smoke and placed it in the pocket of her dress.

"I want to get Polkis. I want to get him once and for all. I know that won't bring back your husband, but it might help other people who need it like you do."

"What other people?" she asked. In the belly of the room, born of the sepia shadow and the swinging halo of light, a nasal moan erupted, a kind of grim, mincing howl. "You gotta go now," she said. She turned and then shooed me with her hands. "Go on. You're going to make him mad."

"Look." I said. "There's a baby missing, and I think Polkis stole her. I'm a private detective looking for some information, and what you tell me might let me get something on Polkis I can use to get back the baby. If I can get a line on his dealings with Little Bear, then maybe I can make a deal for the baby. I want to get the baby back to her mother. She's just a kid herself, and it would mean a lot. You can help me if you will. Right now I'm working against thugs and lawyers and judges. I want the baby back with its mother, and I want these people punished. That's it."

Fear and resignation collected in the flat moon face. Her dark black eyes studied me for a time, and I heard the growl commence again. She turned and walked into the darkness, leaving me to face the open door. I walked inside after her.

Four steps into the room I saw an Indian slumped over a bare wooden table in the dining room. Althea Little Bear backed herself into shadow, then huddled on a single bed with her arms around a skinny Indian boy about eight years old. There was a bruise on the boy's cheek.

An alternated bump of neon illumined the two shabby rooms, revealing in that weak, harsh glare bare floors and wet, peeling wallpaper, the single bed in the bedroom; in the kitchen, the wooden table and three wooden chairs, and a rusted water basin. The Indian slumped over the table held his head in his hands, a fifth of whiskey at his elbow. I looked at the woman.

"He's my man now," she said softly. The boy sucked

his finger and said nothing. "I told the police everything I knew."

"What did you tell them?" I asked. I moved to the woman and sat on the bed. I lit a cigarette and the smoke disappeared in cold silence.

"Little Bear told me he owed money to George Polkis. He told me he had to pay it back. When he got drunk, he gambled and lost his money, and this time he *had* to pay it back. He told me that night where he was going, and I knew I couldn't stop him, so I didn't try. He never came back."

"Is there anybody who knows where he went that night other than you and George?" The woman looked sadly at her man.

"It was never any good here in Kansas," she said. "We came from Dakota to work on the railroad in Nebraska, and Little Bear began to drink. He drank and he beat me. It was nothing then to be beaten when he came home from work tired and drunk. On the railroad job he made some money, but he spent most of it on whiskey and gambling, and there wasn't any left at the last, and we lived like animals. We were away from the people, away from our lives with the people, and I don't blame him. He withered here, so far away from home."

"Where did he get the gasoline, the rope?"

"I don't know. I told this already."

"Did Polkis ever come here?"

"He came here once for money. He hit Little Bear and threatened him."

"Did you tell that to the police?"

"No, I was ashamed of my man then." The Indian stirred in the next room. I watched his Halloween eyes rise and focus, the black liquid glazed red. He put the bottle to his mouth and gulped, then hacked.

"If I can nail Polkis, I can get this baby back. It's my

only chance. Is there anything else?'' I put my hand on her shawl. She stayed rigid, tense as ice.

"This baby," she said. "George Polkis stole it. You're not lying to me?"

"No, I'm not lying." I looked at her hard then. The boy stirred and placed his hands on his mother's arm.

"I'll tell you," she said. "But I'm afraid. It only matters for my son. This man in that room is not better or worse than Little Bear. I want my son to be back with the people, back in Dakota on the Rosebud. If I tell you something, maybe you can help with this."

"Yes," I said. "But you may have to speak with the police again. I'll surely try to help you, though."

"No, I can't talk to the police."

"Look, I'll try. I'll try it without the police."

The woman carressed her son's head. His eyes were bleary from sleep and fear. "I want to go to the people."

"Do you have family there?"

"Yes, many." She placed her hands in a pile on her lap. "This Polkis brought the gasoline and rope and some whiskey here one night. I saw it. He sat in the next room and talked to Little Bear. I told no one because of pride, and I thought it didn't matter much then. I was afraid Mr. Polkis would hurt my boy if I told. Do you understand? Then, there is something else, too. This man here worked with Little Bear. I know Little Bear told him about what he was going to do. That man at the table knew, but I never told the police he did. He would beat me for that."

"He remembers?"

"Yes, he remembers."

"This could be important." I stood and gazed on the cold bare room, so sad and empty and bleak. "I think this may help get the baby back, and I'll do what I can to get you home to Dakota." The woman showed no hope in her face. I started for the door.

"Neah, hey!" The Indian stood and weaved wildly.

"Drink, hey, drink," he shouted angrily. His face was red and pocked. His black hair hung loose. He stuck his head into the naked bulb and pushed shadows crazily around the room. Then he growled and held out the bottle. I walked to him and took the bottle and drank. The whiskey was cheap and hot, and I choked it back and cleared my throat, hacking. The Indian sat down and grabbed the bottle and smacked it on the wooden surface of the table. He motioned me down into one of the chairs, then made his arm into an L and leaned forward.

"Takehole," he slurred. "Comeon. . . ." His vowels slid into silly infinity.

"Let's just drink," I said sharply.

"Noooooooo. Takehole." His eyes loomed red as an ape's asshole, his neck rubbery as a chicken's. I leaned into his face and grabbed his hand and squeezed his wet fingers. He flexed a scabrous arm and pulled. The woman and boy stood in half shadow, the child wrapped in the gray shawl, the shawl covering his narrow shoulders as he huddled at her hip. The Indian strained against my grip, and bared yellow teeth. His face was smooth and unlined as soap, his expression wracked and heaving. I smashed his arm to the table, then panted expectantly.

He grinned at me insanely. "Drink," he said happily. I hit the whiskey again, then rose and walked past the woman and boy who seemed frozen to the floor. I reached the door and turned.

"Come with me now, if you want," I said.

She herded the boy to the door and stood in front of me, unwavering and calm. The Indian slumped.

"He'll beat you," I said.

"I know. I been beat before." She looked back at the man slumped over his table and whiskey. "That's true, now, what you told me. George Polkis stole a baby?"

"Yes, it's true."

"What is the baby's name?"

"Elizabeth," I said. "What's the man's name behind you?"

"He says he's Little Wolf, come to take the people back to the Powder River lands. You ask the railroad, they'll tell you he's Alex Taylor, called Dog. He can't help what he is. It is not his doing. His soul has left him. Now, you go on."

I walked slowly down the stairs, my heart filled by a raging, angry pity. I looked back at the landing and the darkened door. The night stank of the dirty river and stale beer, and in the eerie neon glow, gypsy moths banked in irrational curves. I leaned on the warm car hood and stared up at the second floor and the blasted crater of light that seeped from the dirty windows. The light reeled in moving glare.

Then I drove west through El Dorado and out on the old blacktop highway that wound through Towanda and connected with Wichita's dirty North End. I had a witness that tied George Polkis to cans of gasoline and rope, and tied him to an Indian that had burned like a roasted wienie. The problem was how to use the witness and not push Little Bear's wife into her own kind of bonfire. On the other hand, tagging Polkis for the arson murder didn't solve the problem of Baby Elizabeth; it only provided some leverage on the situation. There was only one way to get her back, and to succeed I had to find something or somebody to trade or sell to Polkis in return for the kid, or to tie Polkis up so tight that he had no choice but to deal with Mitch Roberts. The thought occurred to me that I might double-cross Polkis. But vampires had terrified me as a kid.

I crossed some tracks and watched the refinery flares and red warning flashers on grain elevators lying over the North End like signals. I caught myself staring at the broken stubble fields, the worn stands of corn and milo, and the far-off twinkle of farmhouses. In my own dream, I did not notice the black-and-white sheriff's Plymouth.

The red-button top plopped and plopped in my rear view mirror, throbbing in circles. There were two bulky shadows in the front seat, wrapped around a strapped shotgun and a radio. I slowed and pulled onto the gravel parking area of a tiny roadhouse bar. From the open door of the bar a filmy ribbon of Hank Williams flowed like wine. A Hamm's sign swung in the wind, its glare dimmed by an electrical short, which kept the neon flickering. I stopped and the Plymouth crunched to a halt on gravel behind me. I took off my gray felt hat and sat waiting for the blue haze.

The deputy who got out of the driver's seat wore his beer gut like some guys wear muscles. He smiled a Cheshire grin, wide white teeth flashing from beneath a cowboy hat with a star pinned to its crown. The other deputy stayed in the Plymouth, talking on the radio. I recognized the first deputy then, the bloated face blotched by red veins, the wide Dumbo ears, the pig's nose and the whiny, know-it-all voice. His suit was brown, with a gray coat; he carried a loaded weapon and a billy club. He grinned and pounded the club in his meaty palm.

He leaned down to the window. "See yoh license theah, bo?"

"What's the trouble, officer?" I said politely.

"We gonna get theah, bo." The Plymouth door slammed, and I watched as the other deputy waddled to the rear of my car and leaned against the trunk. He was thin and tall, but had the same simple look of superiority, the same loaded gun and billy club. I handed Fatso my license. He looked at the license and tossed it back.

"It's Mitchell Roberts, then," he slurred. "Come on out here, bo."

I got out and closed the car door. I felt like a dime in a quarter slot.

"Turn around and spread 'em," he said.

"I don't think so," I said. There was an awful silence and some lovely Hank Williams, sad and far away.

"What's that?" he said meanly.

Finally I said, "You got something to say, then say it."

The thin deputy circled the Ford and stood with one foot on the fender. He unlooped the club and tapped it in imitation of his partner.

"Who are you boys?" I asked. They gave no answer, just smiling and tapping their clubs in the cool night air, the moths circling wildly. "Never mind," I said, "I got it. Marx and Engels, right? Or Amos and Andy?"

The thin deputy rubbed his lantern jaw. His skin was metallic in the glow. Suddenly he whirled his club at the radio antenna, and it snapped off cleanly and clattered on the hood, then fell to the gravel.

"You animals wear me out," I said slowly.

"What are you?" the fat man said. "Private investigator. I been told your snooping is annoying in every which way."

"It could be worse," I said.

"Oh, yes?" he questioned.

"Yeah," I said. "I could be a pea-brain deputy sheriff on four grand a year." I said it fast and swiveled to the thin deputy with my left hand coming up hard from my waist. It struck his cheekbone with a crack. I didn't hear Fatso move as I moved, but I heard a whoosh from behind and heard his club smack hard into my arm. The wild sound was enough to make a butcher sick, and then knotted cords of pain exploded above my elbow, sizzled then to my fingers. I fell to one knee, hanging on to consciousness like a drowning man to a life vest. My arm numbed, and nausea come to me as the world swirled darkly.

The thin deputy scrambled to his feet. "Goddamn you," he said. He grabbed my hair and hurled me face down to the gravel. Constellations darted in my head. Fatso stuck his boot to the back of my neck. The thin deputy leaned to my ear. "So you'll know we ain't fucking around, there is a message for you to stop sticking your nose where it don't belong. Next time, you could be fish bait. I don't know what you think you're doing, but for you it ain't nothing but a dead-end street. I do mean dead. I know you can hear me, so I'll tell you once more. You been seen coming out of that nigger doctor's place at County. You might go back to that hospital, but you'll be in a cold box. You wouldn't like that." Fatso pushed his boot deeper into my neck. I saw real stars burning in the night and a stubbled cornfield and sunflowers waving arms in darkness. The gravel seemed a boulder field.

Fatso said, "We can have your ass whenever."

Fatso kicked my neck and I felt the billy club strike my back and kidneys, but I felt it only as an abstract thing, simple roar and flash. I whirled then in firelight flicker at the bottom of a deep cave.

TEN

A fine English summer passed, and then another. The horse chestnuts were unusually fair and green, their white blossoms shimmering against a pale sky. Puffy clouds rolled in from Ireland. Then a dirt farmer threw his skinny face into mine.

"You hurt there, sonny?" he hollered.

I opened my eyes to find the farmer's face in a gray whirligig; then it settled, my own consciousness spinning furiously. The skin below the farmer's cheekbones were drawn to a sunken fist where some country dentist had extracted his back teeth. Lichen-colored stubble covered his jaw. I groaned, and the night twirled like a baton in a majorette's artful hands.

"Here," the farmer said. He rolled me over and I saw the blessed Twins, the two brothers Castor and Pollux, blinking in the night sky, Regulus rising, dressed in bright red, and the Milky Way scattered like gems on the zodiac. Pain twisted my stomach to tight clumps. "Them boys must have not liked something you said, son. You feel like you want me to call a doctor or something like that?"

"No," I groaned. "Help me up against the car."

The old man steadied me as I leaned against the hood. He clawed his filthy jeans pocket and extracted a pint of

I. W. Harper whiskey. He handed it to me, and I sipped the hot liquor, feeling cyclic heat beat into my body. I choked and felt as if someone had driven dowels into my right forearm. Pain racked my hands and arms and I felt broken inside.

"I am sorry, boy," the farmer said when I stopped choking. "We all watched from the door, but them boys was going to do what they did, and they was nothing we could have done to stop it. You ought to get yourself a doctor. We watched down here one night when they pulled some farm kid out of his truck by the feet and then bounced him around on the gravel. Don't think it was them there boys, but they all do it just for fun, so it don't make no difference anyhow. What you done anyway?"

I felt as if I had dragged a rickshaw around Shanghai for twenty-five long years. I held up my arm and gained a brief grip on the farmer's bony shoulder. "I asserted that all ideas, even those of space and time are subsequent to experience. Those guys were Kantians; they disagreed."

The farmer rubbed his jaw. "Say what?" he said. He handed me the whiskey.

"Never mind," I said. "It was a personal thing. I asked for it, you might say. Would you help me to the door?"

The farmer grinned. "Girls?"

I nodded, and the farmer pulled me around the car, holding me about the waist as he opened the car door, then carefully placed me behind the wheel. A Patsy Cline tune floated in the cool air. Several bulky shadows watched us from the blue darkness around the door to the old road-house tavern. The farmer leaned into the Ford, turned on the ignition, and placed my trembling hands on the steering wheel.

"How far you going?" he asked.

"Wichita," I answered. "I'll be okay."

"Steer clear of them deputies. Next time they'll make you hurt worse." He paused and touched my shoulder. "I did enjoy the way you knocked that one old boy down, though.''

I drove very slowly, the farmer watching me through the cold blue light of the parking lot, rubbing his jaw as I tumbled onto the black highway.

I bumped and jarred my way from Towanda to Wichita on the old highway. The world seemed filled by pain, and when I finally pulled to the curb in front of Cynthia Wunderland's frame house on Green Street, the pain had become nothing but a dull ache, echoes no longer attended to by brain or body. I switched off the ignition and sat in the dark. I saw Cynthia sitting on her porch swing, slowly rocking in the evening. She rose and came to the car.

"Mr. Roberts?'' she said quietly. She wore a Shetland sweater of gray wool. Her auburn hair was down, falling around her shoulders like waves on a rocky beach. She smelled like a ski slope in winter. I felt sick and put my head on the steering wheel. She opened the door and placed her arms around my shoulders as I fell outside.

"Come on,'' she said. "We'll get you inside.''

We hobbled across the lawn like two gimps in a sack race, fell up the porch stairs into the yellow light, and paused. Inside the warm, calm house, I could hear the strains of Mozart's *Jupiter* Symphony. Cynthia eased me inside and placed me on a brown couch. I looked at the room. Two Navaho rugs covered the wood floor, bathed in brassy light. Turner prints decorated the beige butterfly walls and reflected a blazing fire. There were bookshelves along one wall, a small writing desk, and a walnut dining table. The kitchen was a bright slice leading into the distance. A deco swan held five purple iris. To one side, through a dark passage, I saw the foot of a canopy bed, and farther into the dark there was a cello and a music stand.

"Iris won't be in the shops until April,'' I said.

Cynthia sat at the foot of the couch, her hands folded

into wads of concern. "They're sold now in California," she said. She looked at me. "You're a mess," she said. "But other than some bruises on your head, there's nothing I can see directly. Do you need a doctor?"

"I'm smiling on the outside, crying on the inside. No doctor, though." The pain was impossible to judge.

She rubbed her long fingers across my forehead. "My God," she said. "You're burning up."

"I'm reminded of my grandma," I managed. The smile fell from me then, and I felt real worlds collide inside my body.

She said, "Tell me what happened and what you need."

I leaned my head onto a couch arm. The fire cracked in a soothing way. "Two deputies cornered me outside of town. They were obviously sent by someone to scare me off this case, to make me think twice before I considered tracking down Bonnie's child. They turned me over on the ground and hit me on the kidneys with sticks. They were very good. There's not much fat on a man's back, and you can hurt him inside and leave no bruises. It's an old cop's trick."

"Let me look," she said.

Her eyes glinted green as the maharaja's emeralds. She wore jeans and brown deck shoes. She took off my jacket and wool shirt and looked at my arm.

"I'd better call a doctor or ambulance," she said. I took her hand and held her back as she tried to rise. I motioned with my head for her to sit.

"All right," she said. She lifted my undershirt and studied my back. "You're wrong," she said. "There are plenty of bruises. We'll talk later."

Cynthia disappeared into the kitchen and came back with alcohol, torn sheets, and a snifter of cognac. While she rubbed my back, I sipped brandy and talked about the detective business, my years in the war, my love of baseball and philosophy. She washed my face and arms, then swabbed my cuts with iodine. She told me about her family, about her diplomatic life and the end of it when the war came. We talked about music, disagreeing about the baroque and the romantic.

The fire burned low, and Cynthia placed a small log on the flames. She handed me some brandy.

"I can't believe this is happening," she said.

"Evil is all around. Even in a place like Wichita, you'd be surprised at the evil. Most of the people only imagine what it's like from books or movies. The reality is shabby, and all the more surprising because it is so common and vulgar. I shouldn't say it, but you lead a sheltered life."

"Probably so," she said. "What are you going to do?"

"I want you to get me into the Booth Home for a visit. I want to see Lurleen Curtis and talk with her, and I think your help in arranging a visit would come in handy. I don't want you to be involved beyond that. These guys mean business."

"These guys?" she asked.

"Polkis, his brother Ritchie. Others, perhaps."

"Oh," she said. "Are you able to eat some soup?"

Cynthia left, and returned with some broth. She sat on the couch and spoon-fed me.

"Why are you doing this? You can't be paid much."

"It's what I do," I said.

"Does it make you happy?"

"I have a hard time with that."

"Well, what is your definition of happy?"

"My definition of happiness is playing third base anywhere on a spring day, with the grass smell everywhere, and a well-oiled mitt."

Cynthia smiled a slow, patient smile. "So, tell me. Is it for happiness and satisfaction that you became a private detective in a small prairie town?"

I sipped some brandy, smelling the snowy, soapy smell of Cynthia as she sat at the foot of the couch, her auburn head aflame with reflected light, her hair flowing down her strong shoulders. The pain had gone away, and I was a numb image staring at her beauty.

"There isn't any reason, or none that I can make out. Perhaps we exist only to struggle toward knowledge, doomed to fail, but doomed to try. I want to know the reason for my struggle, even if it makes me unhappy trying to learn."

"Happiness is the reason," Cynthia said. "Satisfaction, achievement, creation, and success are reasons themselves. There isn't anything to know beyond ourselves. The struggle is to become content, not to know. You've set yourself an impossible goal."

"I set it myself."

"And so you became a detective."

"I don't know, Cynthia. I became a detective in this town because I was tired of drifting. I'd come home from the war to a world of crew cuts, big cars, and good jobs. I didn't fit in, and so I tried college. I walked around the campus watching these kids nuzzle one another, knowing that I'd killed a German captain with my bare hands in the mud and watched his eyes burn closed when he died. Everything seemed disorganized and cheap and false. I couldn't think of money and achievement and success in quite the same way anymore. There is nothing romantic or melodramatic about it. I saw the world as cheap and money-grubbing. Cold cash makes the world run, and the Republicans dominate the process. Besides, the rent needed paying, and I couldn't think of anything else to do. Being a detective is mostly snooping and selling information to banks, car lots, and finance companies. I investigate the odd burglary when an insurance company wants me to testify that their client should have kept his money in a safe instead of in a mason jar. I drag wives back home who aren't ready to come. I have no excuses for myself. My life is built on ruins, like some jungle huts erected above Mayan temples. It's like everything else; I struggle and I desire, and when that stops, I'll know I'm dead."

"You sound proud of being unhappy. Do you wear it as a badge of courage?"

"I'm not unhappy. I mirror nothing. I survive and I move on. I fight complacency."

"And the good years, when are they?" Cynthia walked to the kitchen and returned with her own snifter. Oblong freckles dotted her cheeks, and in the firelight she looked like a mink, soft and sleek.

"The good years," I murmured, the slow wine of remembrance seeping inside my thoughts. "They were the four years between my first kiss and my first love. They were terrific. After that, I've been undersliding the bag."

"Undersliding the bag?" Cynthia said.

"It's baseball slang for almost coming in safe. A guy hits a low inside fastball to the wall in deep left center field, then he takes off around the bases in a cloud of dust. He rounds first, hits the bag at second, and over by third he sees the coach waving his arms like crazy. In the corner of his eye, he sees the fielder grab the ball and heave it home. So he takes off for third base and the left fielder has thrown it to the shortstop, who relays it to the third baseman. So, the guy goes into a slide, and he's way ahead of the throw, safe by a mile you'd think. Only he slides too early and he doesn't make it all the way to the base. So, he sits there in the dust with the crowd screaming and yelling. The third baseman catches the ball and bends over and tags the guy out. The guy should've been on third base, standing up, shaking the dust from his trousers, getting cheered by the crowd, seeing his girl in the stands waving and smiling, letting the coach and the boys pat him on the butt and shake his hand. Instead, the guy is sitting there in the dust, and the crowd quiets, and when he looks into the dugout, his teammates look away in shame. Undersliding the bag—so close, yet so far away. It seems the way of life to me.''

Cynthia smiled. "I hope not," she said.

"Say, that reminds me. Are you still going to the baseball game with me Saturday?''

"If you can stand up," she said. We laughed. I felt her snuggle to me just a bit. "Who was your first kiss?" she asked.

"Little girl named Ellen in the fourth-grade coat closet. You remember the dangers of the coat closet, don't you?''

"I'm afraid I do. The fourth grade in Canmore, Alberta, was stocked with fingerlings like yourself.'' Her face opened with an expression of delight.

"Anyway, after that peck came my first real kiss on the mouth of a little girl named Carol. She was blond and blue-eyed, and for the life of me, she was wonderful. I used to go to her house for dinner, and her mother would pray over the meals. Now, I'd heard prayers before, real quick ones with talk about vegetables and being thankful. But this prayer her mother said was spoken solemnly and slowly and took the breath from my body. It scared the hell out of me, all that holy gobbledygook. It turned out they were Catholic, but I thought I'd fallen into a coven of witches. Every little boy in the sixth grade wanted to take that little girl to the picture show on Saturday night, but she was so fine and so lovely that nobody had the guts. I guess everybody was afraid she'd say no. Still, in my innocence and passion, I loved that little girl with a burning, fiery love.''

"She had become an object of your affection. The operative word there is 'object.' ''

"Oh, my, yes. But it was pure and selfless love for all that. I was paralyzed with it. I sat at my desk and scribbled notes and mooned and daydreamed about her silky skin and shiny hair. She was an angel. And then one day on the way home from school I walked past the local library on the square, and there she sat. She trapped me between a police car and a culvert. It was early spring, and the honeysuckle smelled like perfume and the birds were singing, and then she asked me who I liked. I shook all over with a trembling born of pure dread and then wrung my hands and then shook my head no. Then, she told me she'd tell me who she liked if I told her who I liked. My God, the mind of a woman. I told her I wouldn't go first, no, sir, thank you, ma'am. Then she trapped me. Exchange the names on a piece of paper, she said, and what could I say to that? Besides, my heart was brimming full with the news of my love for her. So, I said yes, and simultaneously we wrote the names on a paper. I wrote: "You." And when I took her paper from her white hands and saw the "You" she'd written, my heart burst from my skinny chest, and it was the happiest day of my life. I'll never feel that way again, never ever if I live to be two hundred years old."

Cynthia Wunderland looked at the fire and smiled and sipped her brandy. There were crinkles in the corners of her wide, bright eyes. "You were the envy of the sixth grade."

"Yes," I said.

"How long did the liaison last?" she asked.

"Nearly two and a half months," I said. "Practically an entire lifetime."

"And so you gave her a real kiss on the mouth?"

"Well, sort of a real kiss on the mouth. I had to lead up to it, but, yes, I gave her a real kiss. Several in fact."

"You'll always remember the first?"

"Always. I took her to the movie that Saturday night. My grandma was opposed, but she gave me the extra dime anyway. I met Carol there and we sat near the back. Even so, there were fifteen kids sitting behind us, watching our every move. We settled in and the movie started, it got dark, and those kids leaned forward in their seats. With grand fear I put my arm around Carol and began to sweat. I looked at her in the dark and sensed fifteen pairs of eyeballs on my neck. Carol watched the movie, waiting. Roy Rogers galloped across the screen, and the girl in the seat next to me was waiting to be kissed. Tension was thick as the ankle of an elephant, and then, halfway through the movie, my arm went to sleep. I tried to move it secretly, but I felt only pins and needles and a deep, burning shame. I felt like running away because I still hadn't kissed her. There was action on the screen, but I couldn't make myself kiss her. Carol looked at me and batted her eyelashes, but I couldn't do it. I was a failure.''

"Well," Cynthia said. "You must have done it somehow later.''

"Yes, I did it. The movie ended and the credits flashed on the screen, and I felt than a pure sense of failure and regret and despair, all in the sixth grade.''

"Perhaps you're being melodramatic.''

"Well, I was stuck anyway. I stood and Carol stayed seated and the kids behind us snickered. I felt like a complete pinhead. Then, I screwed up my courage and leaned over, aiming for her lovely, smooth forehead. I'd decided to kiss her forehead and be done with it, but just then she stood up from her seat quickly and cracked me on the nose with her head. I saw stars, stuck my lips to her head and kissed her. She looked at me like I was goofy and put her small hand to her mouth. The kids behind us rose and filed into the lobby. Then she took my hand and I felt the blood running from my nose and I saw drops of it fall onto the white of my T-shirt. I tasted the rusty, dense salt of my blood and sweat mixed. I tilted my head back as she led me out of the dark into the yellow light of the lobby, blood smeared on my shirt and my face, all over my hands. Then, she did the most beautiful and noble thing.''

"All right, silly," said Cynthia. "I'll bite.''

"In front of all those kids," I said, "in that crowded, milling theater lobby, popcorn bags on the floor, the old manager pushing children out the swinging doors, she grabbed me around the neck and placed her sweet lips against my mouth and kissed me for two minutes and more. There was blood all over her white pinafore and on her rosy mouth, too. Blood smeared that innocent, adolescent tongue. She grabbed me, and we kissed again and I kissed back. The blood flowed, and I didn't care, and the kids clapped and giggled, and I walked Carol home in the twilight with the fireflies zigging and zagging in the soft evening."

"Made your reputation, didn't it?"

"It gave me the courage to kiss."

"Even when you're afraid?"

I nodded yes.

Then Cynthia Wunderland moved to my face and placed her fingers on my cheek. "Doing it when you're afraid. Now, that's the definition of courage, isn't it?"

"I suppose," I said.

Then she kissed me. Her lips were soft and full and landed on my mouth like autumn leaves, smelling of smoke and apples. I kissed back as Cynthia leaned into the velvet couch. "You haven't forgotten how to kiss?" she asked.

"Practice," I said.

"Devil," she said. We were both quiet, sipping brandy. Then she said, "What's changed since those years?"

"Nothing, really," I answered. "I'm older now, and I've spent time in a foxhole waiting to die. I met some rich people who made their money from the sweat of the poor or from the labor of others. I met some poor people desperate enough to rob."

"And childhood? " she asked.

"It's idealized. I was a poor kid, cold at night, hot in the day. I grew up in a small Kansas town where half the boys and girls in my school had ringworm; their parents fought or drank or beat them up. They were lonely, scared, troubled, frightened, uncertain, crazy, hungry for love. You name it and kids somewhere have it, just like adults. You can look backward all you want, but the world never changes.''

"You're disillusioned," Cynthia said.

"Disillusioned is one thing. I'm tired now, too.''

"Afraid," she said.

"Afraid, too," I answered.

"And that's where your theory comes in. You struggle, and I've defined courage as struggle in the face of fear. You do it even though you're tired and disillusioned and crazy and troubled and hurt. You go on, and you don't give up on people, and maybe when you come to the end of the line, you find a certain kind of knowledge. Maybe you don't call it happiness then, but when you come to the end, you can use judgment and call it satisfaction or wisdom. I suppose until then your operations are based on luck and principle and the hope that between luck and principle there are people with understanding who'll meet you halfway. That's what I call happiness.''

"And what do you do when the investigation reveals that there isn't any point, that there's nothing behind any of the doors you've opened?''

"What do you do when some hick sheriffs beat you up?''

"That's different," I said.

"How?" she asked.

"That's personal," I said.

"It's all personal in your sense of the word. All of it.'' Then, leaning above me in the fire flicker, she kissed me lightly, her lips a mere whisper on my cheek.

"You know," I said, "Mozart spent every waking day of his last ten years worried in some way about money. He died lonely and rejected by his city.''

"Pointless, wasn't it?" Cynthia said.

"Well, I see what you mean. But happiness can't be the point."

"Mozart makes me happy," she said. Then she rose from the couch and walked to the phonograph. She plopped a record on the changer and came back and leaned against my legs.

"Schubert's lieder," I said. "Can you get me into the Booth Home?"

"I'll try. It's a place that is very protective of its girls." The Schubert drifted dreamily in the firelit room. "The war was the end?" she asked.

"When you've danced in the dark with a girl and felt her soft skin and her velvet dress, and smelled her like lavender against your shoulder, then tanks and guns and death make little sense. Perhaps I should learn to grow older more gracefully."

The rain began then as drops plopped slowly on the banked roof above us, then increased and gained rhythm until the air outside drummed steadily. Cynthia rose and walked to a brass basket and placed a log on the dying fire. Some sparks rose and hissed in the flue. She returned and snuggled against me on the couch.

"It's easy to be hard-boiled in the day. But it's another thing at night," I said.

"The Sun Also Rises," she said, and smiled.

"I've noticed your beauty," I said.

"You're sweet. You know, I haven't been with a man for a very long time."

"I can't use my arm," I said.

"It's all right."

I remember her hair and her small cries and my own deep longing, and then the crepuscular night twined us in fire shadow and we slept, covered by an afghan, curved and wet as vines.

ELEVEN

For a long time after, I sat in the car, smelling Cynthia and the rain and the black fecund earth. Then the rain ceased and the sky twisted to a black misty frond, and in the east one bright star glistened. One by one the lights in Cynthia's old house on Green Street went out; first, the small lamp above the kitchen sink, then each brass lamp, and finally the small lamp on her nightstand.

Before I had left her, I had explained my concocted web of connections between lawyers, doctors, and judges, and about the old Indian and his midnight whiskey in El Dorado. I said I believed George ran a game that involved selling babies, but that I didn't know how it was done or who was doing the most important parts of the work. I also told her my hunch about Lurleen Curtis. Cynthia had become silent when I finished my tale, and she lay for a long while with her soft hair tangled in my fingers, breathing with the regularity of the rain. I had not told her that I'd seen a maroon sedan rush past my place on Sycamore with George at the wheel, stern and grim as a mausoleum. I don't know why I left that part out, but it frightened me, and I thought that that was reason enough. I started the engine and drove through the rain-slick streets to my home.

I wheeled past a burger stand on Maple and turned into the alley that runs between Maple, Sycamore, and Elm. Mud clogged the narrow lane, and I bounced and slid though ruts, garbage, and dank weeds. Then, in the swampy mist a flashlight beam cut the murk and fell on my face. A bulky shadow stood behind the beam.

"Far enough," a voice said. I slowed the car and stopped behind my house. The beam wobbled my way through an utterly silent night broken by frogs croaking in the river coves. I saw the unmistakable shape of a cop in my headlights.

"Kill those lights," he said. The voice belonged to a peach-fuzz corporal in uniform. He aimed a service revolver at my forehead. "Who are you?" he demanded. "What's your business here, buddy?" Peach fuzz loaded his voice with authority, but I could tell he was scared. I knew scared cops pulled triggers.

"I live back here," I said. "No problem." The gun steadied in my face as he looked me over. "You don't want that gun to go off, and neither do I."

"Let's see some ID," the cop said. I moved slowly, pulling the wallet from my pocket with the precision of a Swiss clockmaker. I handed him the wallet, and he studied my driver's license in its plastic window.

"You live around here," he said stoically.

"No shit," I said. "What's this all about?"

"Take it easy, buddy," he said. He handed me the license and stepped back into fog and mist. "Take it home and take it easy. Park and walk around front."

"What is this?"

"Just move, pal," he said.

"I get it," I said. "You took tough lessons from Ward Bond, right?" I bumped the accelerator, and the Ford jumped into a puddle. The cop grunted as a bucket of muddy water splashed his uniform, and then I gunned the car and threw slime in a spray. I drove around the ramshackle garage and nosed the car in between the chicken coop and rabbit hutch. Light streamed in waves from my house, a house I had left dark and locked. One cop stood on my back porch, his hands on his hips. I got out of the car and walked around the side of the house.

"You the guy lives here?" the porch cop yelled.

"Yes."

"Get on to the front," he said.

I pushed through a lilac bush and saw the ambulance standing in my driveway. Two white doors yawned into darkness, and the red lamp on top flopped in the mist. Two attendants in white stood smoking on the driver's side. There were three black-and-white's parked in front of the house, their radios crackling. From somewhere a flashbulb popped and went black. Two cops paced the sidewalk as an elm dripped rain.

"Hello, Mitch," someone said. Andy Lanham looked down at me from the front porch. He was smoking a black cigar, rocking in my rocker, his feet on the porch rail, his face shiny and expressionless. I walked up the steps and stood on the porch watching his cigar ash glow red and fade. I saw shapes moving in my rooms, bulky shadows talking and opening drawers and cabinets. I lit a cigarette and waited in the dark.

"I have no choice in this, Mitch," Andy said.

"In what?" I asked.

"We'll get to that."

"Let's get to it right now."

"Look. There are three cops on nights now. When the call came in, I knew the address and decided it was better for me to handle it than some stranger in a bad mood. Those guys can sit and read the ball scores, and you and I can go through our dance together. But the guys at the department know you and I are friends, so they'll expect me to dot my *i*'s on this. I can't cut corners on this case, or they'll nail my balls to the wall downtown."

"So, your boys are trashing my house."

"The boys are searching your house. I'm sorry."

"I'm a suspect in something?"

"Not exactly."

"Spill it, then."

"Where were you at ten or eleven tonight?" Andy asked.

"In my laboratory transplanting a brain." A big plain-clothesman appeared in the lighted screen door. He wore a rumpled suit and felt hat. I recognized him from Homicide.

"I'll crack this joker," he said.

"Beat it," Andy said. The cop frowned and disappeared inside my house. "Like I said, I'd like to do this right. You came to my house and asked a lot of questions about our friend George Polkis. So, I know you're working on a case. Next night, this happens, and now my job is to match the questions with the answers and make sense out of this. Your job is to answer my questions and be glad I don't let Davis there out of his cage."

"Suppose we split the difference. Give me a hint?"

Andy sucked his cigar. "Christ," he said. "I never could get anywhere with a nihilist like you."

A uniformed cop walked up the porch steps. "Doc's through," he said. Then he went down the steps and stood in the wet grass beside a black-and-white.

"All right," Andy said standing. "Come on." I followed Andy down the steps and through the yard. We reached a forsythia hedge that divided my front yard from the neighbor's patch. I saw a white sheet and a pair of shoes under the sheet. A bald-headed little man with spectacles and a black bag stood by the sheet, wiping his forehead with a hankie.

"He's all yours," the little man said. He walked away as Andy went to one knee and pulled back the sheet. The wet elms and hedge had dripped rain into black, slick puddles on the sidewalk. Radios cracked in the squad cars, and when Andy lifted the sheet, I saw the brown, wooden face of Cleveland Saunders, his features molded to a mask, dead eyes open and staring.

"Shit," I muttered.

I went to one knee beside Andy and put a fist on my chin. "I know him," I said.

"This is the hint," Andy said.

A uniformed cop approached through the rain. "They're ready for him," he said. Andy nodded and we stood. The two ambulance attendants walked a stretcher to the sheet and stretched it beside the corpse. Andy pulled up the sheet, and the two ambulance boys hoisted the pulpy load of human waste onto the stretcher and carried it away. I watched the bearers place the stretcher in the doorway and shove it inside, then start the ambulance and drive north along Sycamore toward police headquarters downtown. Red lights whirled in the misty silence. I walked behind Andy to the porch and he sat back down in the rocker. I stood with one foot on the rail, looking at the forbidding outline downtown made in the night. The plainclothesman came to the screen. "It's clean," he said. He came out the door and sashayed to the black-and-white in front and got inside it. Andy sucked his cigar thoughtfully.

"You're not a suspect, Mitch," he said at last. "I have a certain faith in your rectitide, but still there is a form book. I flow with the form book, and you flow with the form book, and we come out right in the end. The form book says I have to ask you where you were tonight, and the form book says you have to fight me. The form book says I have to have some answers in the end."

"Does the form book say that guys like Cleveland Saunders have to get killed?"

"I'm just a cop," Andy said. "You want metaphysics, take it to college or church."

"I feel like hell," I said.

"You look like hell. What happened? Your cheek is all puffy and you're walking like a gimp."

"Why go in my house? Why toss my place?"

Andy turned his head to the screen door. A matted swatch of blood lay pasted on the wire. "There's another patch on the porch," he said.

I said, "Oh." I lit a cigarette as another uniformed cop climbed the steps.

"Anything else?" he asked.

"Take off," Andy said. The cop hopped down the stairs and got in a cruiser and sped south to Maple and disappeared. Rain fell into the empty streets, thick and demoralizing as medieval philosophy. "Now, its between you and me," Andy said. "This guy Saunders was shot around ten or eleven tonight. I got a call about an hour later from the old dame who lives next door. We found the body by the hedge, just where you saw it. He'd been dead around an hour when I got here, flat on his back with his arms out like a cross."

"Mrs. Thompson upstairs is deaf," I said.

"I know her," Andy said. "A couple of the boys did three rounds with her tonight, and she won by a knockout. She was obviously scared, so we left her alone."

"Good," I said, "thanks."

"The old dame next door heard a shot and spent an hour thinking it over before she came outside and saw the body. It looks to me like the guy got it on the porch and staggered into the yard and died right there. I tossed your house on the off chance that it was a burglary in progress and there might be a sign of the entry. The boys didn't find a thing. Well, they did find your gun, but I told them to leave it alone. I'm sorry to say this, but I need to take you downtown for a formal identification." Andy rocked and stared through the rain at the dark ballpark. "I'm sorry for the guy," he said.

"Why does this shit happen?" I asked nobody in particular. I looked at the rain, feeling miserable and tired. "You try to live quietly, and you wind up being killed for it. You try to hide, and people talk behind your back. You come out in the open, and they take potshots out of jealousy or envy or greed. You operate on love, and that turns to mush, and when you operate as if you don't care, your heart goes cold and you die anyway. Now, here's a man like Cleveland Saunders who does good to the world, and somebody kills him like a dog in the street."

"Get out, then. Go live in a cave."

"Maybe I will."

"You can't, Mitch," Andy said. "Nobody can get out. You couldn't get out of it if you went blue in the face, kicking and screaming. You and me, we see the worst the world has to offer. When guys like you and me try to hide, it just doesn't work. Having a conscience doesn't make you responsible for all the evil in the world."

"I don't know, Andy," I said. "I feel as if we're all responsible, and as if the responsibility were a tornado raging over a brown field, tearing through shacks and farmhouses. Every time an innocent man dies, the weight of our responsibility increases."

"You think too much," Andy said. "I want you to tell me about Cleveland Saunders and what you're working on. Let's make it enough that we find the killer. The doc is doing an autopsy on Saunders now, and we can go downtown, have a cup of coffee, and make a beginning. Philosophy isn't worth shit when somebody dies. Now, let's go."

I hobbled through the rain behind Andy. I felt like talking and singing and drinking and walking to Montana and riding the rails to the Columbia River Valley and going gray into death as a hobo.

TWELVE

As we rode in silence, Andy smoked his black cigar, and the wind blew smoke in swirls. A big, tough detective drove, and the big, tough detective wrapped his kid-gloved hands around the steering wheel, sticking his jaw in the air like a flag. I gazed past the glowing cigar at the blue murmurous river, bruised images of buildings downtown floating on the surface of the water like so much garbage. Mist rose in the bank reeds and hung in the cottonwoods like wet wash, rising farther, mingling there with smoke and exhaust, then gradually lifting above the city lights until the vague shimmering miasma became a sloppy slice of milk toast, obscuring everything but a sliver of yellow moon above the ballpark pressbox.

I had been sick many times, beaten and jilted by women and rousted by cops, sat on by pugs of every description and size. There had been times on Omaha Beach, in the gray dawn, with the rumble of 88s shaking the beach, when the smoke and ash of gunfire and the smell of death billowed above the horizon like solid steel—like the morning my buddy, Smitty, lay dead and cold beside me—when I thought I had lived and died and gone to hell without a grieving tear or shudder for my loss. And there had been a time later when I lay in the cold snow of an Ardenne

117

winter, seeing my own breath freeze in my face, panzers clanking through the hard cold, when I believed truly that hell was here on earth. And the ride to the morgue with Andy and Cleveland Saunders was the same way. I felt angry and sick unto death.

I looked across the seat at Andy. He cranked his big head around as if it were robotic and stiff. He took the cigar from his mouth.

"Spill it now," he said coldly. The words whizzed at me like bullets.

"George Polkis," I said.

"I'm all ears," he answered. Andy crammed the cigar into his mouth and pulled at the collar of his greatcoat.

"I think Polkis and his little brother have a line on high school girls and their families. It sounds ridiculous, I know. They shake down scared girls and their families, then get the families to agree to an adoption. I think they strong-arm their way inside, but I haven't even begun to figure it all out. I took this case a couple of days ago, and since then I've made some progress. The little brother is probably a flunky of some sort, but he fits into the picture like nuts on a sundae."

"So, what about Cleveland Saunders? I've got a dead man in the backseat. How does it figure that he shows up cold as a fish on your front porch?"

"I talked to him at County Hospital. I asked him for help and information on the birth of a little girl and for some information on adoption and the Booth Home. The little girl I'm working for had a kid at County Hospital and he delivered the baby. The baby is gone now, stolen from her. Saunders didn't say much, really, but he did look interested when I mentioned a Dr. Rolfe over at the Booth Home."

"You think he was ripped for something he knew?"

"Yes. There is no other way."

"That's tough," Andy said quietly.

The tough cop wheeled over the Douglas Street Bridge and into the crusty bowels of downtown. The streets were slick from fog and rain, and when I moved, I felt numb along my back and side. Lower down, my body burned. I didn't bother to think about my left arm, an arm black-and-ugly-blue from the billy blow it had taken. The car pierced a tunnel of glossy orange and red street lights. The big cop slid the Plymouth down an asphalt gangway and into the city police garage. A black cop in uniform swung a meaty arm, and we stopped.

Andy looked my way. "Suppose we go upstairs and wait until the doctor calls us down. There's a pint in my desk."

We piled out of the Plymouth and walked to an elevator in the corner of the garage. An old man stood beside the doors, propped on a homemade cane, picking his nose and wearing a strange, tired grin. One bored sergeant stood beside the old man, his arms crossed, a look of studied boredom on his cruel face. The old man popped his head in nervous circles, and from somewhere catcalls and jeers seeped from the city jail. We climbed on the elevator and rode to the third floor. When the door whisked open, I followed Andy into his tiny cubicle office, sat in a wooden chair, and stared through a grimy, flyspecked window at the steamy visage of downtown, forsaken and cold as an iceberg.

"Here," Andy said. He handed me a bottle of rye, and as I pulled at the rich liquid, I felt a burning in my stomach. "You know," Andy said, "I believe George kills certain people in order to leave messages around town. You take that Indian fellow, for instance. There was some humor in that, if you think about it. It was like setting a trap for some fellow in the Queen's Gambit. You sit behind the board and smile, and for five or six moves nothing in particular happens. Then on the seventh move you make a quiet pawn move and look up from the board. You watch your opponent study the move and then watch his face slacken when he realizes he's just lost a pawn, and probably the game. It's mean and gives great simple pleasure. The point I'm making here, Mitch, is that gunning Cleveland Saunders on your front porch, when the motive would be so obvious, doesn't seem to fit George's style. He's smarter than that."

"I've been on this case for two days," I said. "Yesterday George cruised past my house. He had been following me."

"Tell me exactly what you have, and I'll take care of it. You have to level with me right now."

"I have to make a call. Let me make one phone call, and when I come back, I'll tell you what I know."

"Okay," Andy said. He poured a paper cup of rye and leaned back from his desk. His face was flushed red and pinched from fatigue. "You still look terrible," he said as I walked away.

I telephoned Spud Christian. He answered sleepily after ten long rings, his voice across the line swollen and rough. He was quiet as I asked him to drive quickly to my house and dig in the footlocker for two thousand dollars I had hidden in a collection of chess games by Keres. He sighed when I told him to take the two thousand dollars and drive to El Dorado and deliver the money to an upstairs shack and put the cash in the hands of an Indian woman with a child and then to take her quickly to the bus station and put her on the road to Rosebud. I wanted the Indian woman and her boy back with the people, away from the awful cold rooms and swinging lights and angry nothingness. Spud said little, and in the utter silence I could hear studied concentration take hold of him once he understood my complete seriousness. When he hung up, I stood for a time in the pea-green hallway smoking a tasteless cigarette, listening to the catcalls and the jeers and the cries whirling in my ears like the memory of some vicious, snarling animal. I went back to the office and sat in my chair.

I spent five minutes twisting a tale for Andy to unravel, a tale of a motherless child, a murderous young tough, and some fancy lawyers behind an oak door.

Finally I said, "I went home yesterday, wondering why a couple of tough guys like George and Ritchie would break for a fancy lawyer, when you'd think they would take care of their own problems. I had nothing to do last night, so I went to El Dorado to talk to the widow you told me about."

"So?" Andy said. "What does she have to do with the baby George and Ritchie took?"

"Nothing that I know right now. I was just curious, and I couldn't sleep anyway. The interesting thing is that on my way back through Towanda, two deputies beat me and pushed my ugly face in some very nasty gravel. They warned me to lay off the case."

"Sheriff's people?"

"The very same."

"I wondered how you got so pretty. I knew you weren't born that way."

"Those guys went over me like they meant business. They were Sedgwick County boys, and when you add them to the picture, you start to smell graft."

"That is very slim," Andy said. "You got anything else?"

"A swollen arm and two kidneys like footballs."

Andy tugged at his cigar. The shrill legato of a police siren sliced from underground, then faded and stopped. Some lights glowed in the Broadview Hotel above the black river.

"One other thing," I said. "There was an old Indian man in El Dorado, and the widow told me he had some information about the arson murder. If you go to Little Bear's place tomorrow, you'll probably find him hung over.

I think he knew about Little Bear's plan to burn the bingo parlor for George and may have seen George at the place."

"Where has he been? We've talked to the widow up and down."

"She doesn't care for police and was frightened of George anyway. She has a reason to talk now."

"All right," Andy groaned. "We'll give it a try first thing tomorrow. It is a very long shot we're talking about here."

The black desk phone buzzed. Andy grabbed the receiver and placed it to his left ear. "Okay," he said and hung up. "The doctor is through, and he's downstairs with his preliminary report. It's a rough draft, but he's got it. He'll run through it with us before he writes the report for the coroner." I nodded, and we rose together and went outside to the elevator and rode downstairs, the small elevator trembling and shuddering like a broken spine. The basement smelled like a battlefield, rank from cold sweat and rusty blood.

A nacreous livid fluorescence bathed the pea-green walls. One long hallway opened on both sides to operating rooms, and at the end of the hall, a glass door swung to storage areas where bodies lay refrigerated in dark coffins. I followed Andy down the hall. He turned swiftly right into an operating chamber. Cleveland Saunders lay naked in the center of the room under a plastic sheet. His body was rigid on a concrete slab sloped inward to allow blood and slime to sieve and drain through the corpse's feet and collect on the floor in a stainless steel bucket. The body glowed like wet wax, the face a calm, expressionless mask. Red squiggles decorated a toe tag, and when I examined the room, I found myself in a large tile enclosure surrounded by file cabinets and glass cases packed with vials, jars, tubing, syringes, shiny scalpels, and hacksaws.

I studied the body and found a hole the size of a quarter in its stomach. Blue and yellow fluid oozed from the hole.

The police doctor leaned above the corpse and then backed away to place one elbow on a countertop. As he smoked, he flipped ashes into the stainless steel bucket.

The doctor was a small, white-faced man with stringy black hair. His smock was bloodstained and wet. Something about him reminded me of Joe McCarthy, the gray five-o'clock shadow and bulging pouches under his eyes.

"Hello, Doc," Andy said. The doctor nodded, unconcerned. "This is Mitch Roberts, Doc. You two have met?"

"We met," the doctor said.

Once the doctor's testimony at an inquest had placed me in a very tight situation. "Yeah," I said. "Hello, Doc."

Andy walked to the corpse and leaned his face into the waxy mask of Cleveland Saunders's face. He straightened. "Okay, Doc," he said. "Let's have it."

"Dead between ten P.M. and midnight. If I were to guess, I would place it closer to ten than midnight, but that's because I think your nonmedical evidence establishes that. There were no particular lacerations or contusions, no particular bruising, just a nick on the head he probably got while falling down. Knees show some scrapes, but he probably crawled from the porch. His dinner was partly digested, and it looks like he had fried chicken and greens. The body was in good shape for a man in his fifties, slight arterial hardening, enlarged ventricle, eyes going maybe a bit sour. I'd say he was a healthy, well-adjusted man. There was no liver damage, and the other organs were pink as a baby's ass."

"Okay," Andy said. "The cause of death."

"Well, hell. He was shot to death, dammit."

"All right, Doc. You know what I mean."

The doc flipped his cigarette butt into the steel bucket of guts. The butt hissed and went silent. The doctor sighed. "Andy," he said. 'I used to go fishing with my pappy. We'd take a can of corn and a cane pole to a pond, and we'd sit and he'd drink whiskey under a tree while a corn bait floated in that muddy water. When the catfish took the hook, my pappy was usually too drunk to do anything but shout. I'd take the fish for him, even though I was six years old, and I'd clean the fish. It seems like I cleaned fish all my life, and here I am a grown man, still cleaning and gutting things for a living. Only it's three o'clock in the morning, and I've cleaned and gutted a human being. I'm tired, and I smell like green bacon, and my wife won't touch me for the stink. When I walk down the street, dogs wail and mirrors break."

Doc smiled wanly. He rubbed his hands across his stubble and blinked.

"The cause of death?" Andy said.

"Poor bastard bled to death. His chest and stomach were filled with blood. You might say he drowned in his own juice. It probably took him the better part of ten minutes, and most of the time he was conscious but in shock. He was in considerable pain is my guess. He was hurt too badly to get to his feet, and from what I saw out there, it was a deserted place in the fog and cold. It was not a good way to go, and you have to pity the man."

"Weapon," Andy said.

"Unofficially, a twenty-two pistol. I saw the slug, and that's what it looked like to me, but you'll have to wait for Ballistics on that. Ordinarily, a man could survive trauma from such a small slug, but it was fired point-blank through the stomach wall and intestine. You can see flash burns on the lower abdomen. The bullet angled up somewhat, and if not for that, the guy might have made it with a stomach wound. It was the lower intestine that killed the man."

"Meaning what?" Andy asked.

"Take a guess," said the doc.

"Meaning that we are dealing with someone smaller than Saunders."

"Yes. But the doctor was a big man, so our killer could be normal size, even."

"Maybe smaller, if he held the gun straight out."

"Probably so, but you can't be sure."

"But it sounds good for now."

The doc rubbed his chin and straightened himself from the counter. He pulled off a rubber glove. "Another thing," he said. "I was doing the general body search and found a small wound under the right shoulder, inside the armpit. You raise the right arm and look in the pit, and you can see it there. It's hard to spot."

Andy walked to the corpse and raised the arm. I could see a small, triangular wound on the pit. A needle had been inserted in the wound, and where it came out, it raised a small skinflap at the nipple edge. Andy looked at me and then at the police doctor. "This man was shot once from behind before he got it in the stomach?"

'Suppose," the doc mused, "someone had a gun stuck into the doctor's back. Something happens, and he winds up pulling the trigger. The killer would be right-handed and smaller than the doctor. It doesn't make sense any other way."

Andy circled the corpse and walked to a cabinet. He pulled open a tiny drawer and rummaged inside.

"You do the inventory?" he asked the doctor.

"No, of course not."

"Robbery?" Andy said aloud to nobody. He stared inside an envelope and ran his fingers around. "This all?" he asked.

"How do I know?" the doctor said.

Andy found a metal box and emptied the envelope contents into it. The doctor unstrapped his smock and rammed it inside an aluminum waste bin. Andy stopped him with a touch on the arm. They looked at one another.

"Doctor," Andy said. "Did you know Saunders? Did you ever deal with him personally or professionally?"

"No," the doc answered. "You know how it is."

"You never ran across him at medical meetings or at the County Hospital?"

"No, I never get to County Hospital."

"What about a reputation?"

"I don't know what you want me to say. We were doctors, but we lived in different worlds. You live in a different world from him, just like I do. All I know is that he's dead, probably shot when somebody startled him from behind, and then when he turned, shot again in the stomach." The doctor walked to the swinging doors and turned. "Good luck, boys. I hope you find the bastard that did this." The doors whisked closed.

Andy jiggled the metal box. "Here's the stuff they found on Saunders. His wallet was on the grass beside his body, and two pocket linings were out. The cop on the beat told me it might be robbery. Then I found twenty bucks in the wallet and a gold wedding ring on his left hand. There was a cheap watch on his wrist."

"It's not robbery," I said.

Andy scoured the metal box, his voice ticking off each item like a tolling bell. "Wallet with driver's license, medical card, Social Security card, two or three business cards, and nothing much else. Twenty dollars in cash found inside the wallet and a receipt for a vacuum cleaner left at the hardware for repairs. Inside his coat we found a note from his wife to get milk and scouring powder at the store. There were seventy-three cents in change, a small penknife, key ring with three keys, and one toothpick. One small cigar in the shirt pocket, cheap watch on his wrist. We found a birth certificate inside his coat pocket in the liner along with some lint balls. Not much."

I started awake. "Let me see the certificate," I said. The wrinkled black form was a standard photocopy notarized and signifying the registration of the live birth on December third of a baby named Sarah Van Slyke. The delivering doctor was Cleveland Saunders, and the parents were Mrs. and Mr. Harold Van Slyke. I studied the certificate and handed it to Andy.

"Why do you suppose he had that?" I asked.

Andy tinkered with the certificate and put it back inside the metal box. "Well, I don't know," he said. "Suppose we go upstairs and have a drink."

We rode back upstairs on the rickety elevator. We sat quietly for a time drinking small shots of rye and staring at the night fog. Pain stole through my arm in dim bursts.

"Those deputies in Towanda," Andy said. "Did you recognize them?"

"I had a very good look at them."

"We could start with the files. If you could recognize them again from a photograph, I could have a talk with them. I don't need to tell you they'd say nothing and probably talk to the chief about me when I was through."

"Let's forget them," I said. "I don't give a damn about them. I care more about the baby and Cleveland Saunders than two hick sheriffs."

"Okay," Andy said. "What is the point of killing Saunders?"

"Let's start with who."

"Start."

"Saunders was killed by a twenty-two target pistol."

"And?" Andy said.

"Ritchie Polkis owns a gun like that," I said.

Andy swept his elbows from the desk and brushed back an unruly red curl from his face. He closed his eyes and drank from a glass of rye.

"How would you know that?" Andy asked sorrowfully.

"I saw it in the shack he lives in."

"Goddamn it," Andy said. "You broke into his place?"

"Not exactly," I said.

"Exactly what did you do?" Andy asked.

"I used a wire jimmy." Andy frowned. "I found the gun, and for another thing, a picture of a high school kid who is pregnant now."

"Fine," Andy said. "Now I have to compound a felony by concealing it. That's just fine."

"Another thing," I said. "Saunders told me that a doctor named Rolfe attended my client when she was at the Booth Home. Rolfe may be the Polkis brothers' connection to the Home, and they use him and lawyers to make some dough off the kids. Maybe they make enough money to kill somebody for."

"So you think Saunders knew something he was killed for knowing?"

"Or he found something, or he ran into something." I swirled some brown liquor in my glass and looked at the red-smudged dawn through it. The sky was wrinkled purple, thrown above the buildings like a death shroud. My eyes burned from fatigue and smoke.

"Let me get this straight," Andy said. "Your client had a kid snatched by George. You followed them to a lawyer, and Cleveland Saunders gave you the Rolfe connection. You went inside Ritchie's house and saw the gun. Saunders delivered the missing baby. Is that about it?"

"I know it sounds thin, but that's it."

"It's thin if you expect me to tear down the County Courthouse looking for lawyers and judges and sheriffs. Why don't I just stick my head in an oven and turn on the gas?"

"Check out the gun."

"What do I do for probable cause?"

"I can't think of anything that won't land me in a jail cell next to you."

"I'll think of something."

"Send someone to El Dorado."

"I told you I would. But you have to give me the lawyers' names if you expect me to move on this case."

I stood and adjusted my clothes, feeling the dirty weariness around me like a second skin. "What about Saunders's wife? Did somebody contact her?"

"A matron went by at midnight. The widow will have
to come downtown to identify the body, but that can wait.
I'll have to go out to the home myself with his things."
Andy glanced up from his desk, a brave and disconsolate
expression on his face.

"Wait a minute," I said. "What if I go home and clean
up and go to the Saunders home myself? I feel responsible."

"You're not, and it's my job," Andy said.

"I know, but it would make me feel better."

Andy thought, then tugged at his tie. "It's not kosher,
but I suppose it can't hurt anything. Make it snappy,
though. She shouldn't be kept long." Andy stood. "And
you're not responsible. We've been through that already."

"Yeah." I sighed. "That's what everybody says." I
stood and faced Andy. "Let me take the birth certificate
with me, just for tonight and tomorrow. I have a hunch."

"I can't do that," Andy snapped. "The certificate is
evidence in a police case, and I'm in charge of it." Andy
shoved the metal box across the desk. "As for the rest of
his things, take them along. It's little enough left of a
life."

"Trust me, Andy. Let me take the certificate."

"Compounding a felony and ignoring procedure. You'd
ask me to do that?"

"I won't let you down."

Andy rose from his desk and turned to the window. The
dim sun cascaded over his slumped shoulders and broke
to tinted stars. He spoke to the window and the morning.
"All right," he said calmly. "Get the thing back to me
with some answers. We've been friends a long time now,

and I'm going to trust you totally. It's my ass if something goes wrong.'' I picked up the certificate from his desk and slid it into my coat pocket.

I walked through the pea-green halls, rode down the elevator, and went outside. Dawn flicked in the bowers and reeds beside the river, and a confused, lilting chant of sparrows, doves, and thrushes tickled the wind. I walked past the redbrick Forum auditorium, the grease factory, then across the Lewis Street Bridge and skirted the old ballpark walls. A dairy truck roared by and halted in front of an old Victorian near the corner of Sycamore. A milkman in white opened the doors and hopped out and carried a shining load of bottles to a porch.

Francis the cat was hunting robins. He didn't notice as I dragged through the debris of my own life.

THIRTEEN

Cynthia slipped through the screen on sunny wings, her auburn hair scintillant and lush, the skin along her mannered neck tawny and smooth in the hushed morning light. She looked at the tossed mattresses, the pillows and Indian blankets and sheets—like flotsam on a windy, storm-raged sea; she slid to the oak dining table and touched the broken clay vase of a cactus plant and stirred her long finger in the dirt. She looked at the kitchen utensils, pots and pans, and the sugar dumped in the sink. After a long silence, she stooped and picked up a philosophy book, inspecting its broken spine. Then she walked to where I sat in my gray chair, my arm a painful, bloated whipsnake.

"I came as soon as I could." She touched my hand where it lay on the blasted stuffing. "I'm so sorry, Mitch," she said. She knelt beside the chair and placed her denim purse on the floor. Wrens had invaded the porch trellis and from their perches produced a riotous tintinnabulation.

"Thank you for coming. I think I'm going to need some help, and I thought of you."

"I've taken the morning off. Whatever you need, I'm here to help."

"I can hardly move."

Cynthia pushed an ashen strand away from my eye. "Why all of this? My God, what's going on?" Cynthia's green eyes revealed an enormous, puzzled hurt.

"They killed Dr. Saunders, and I'm not sure why. Somebody shot him in the stomach and allowed him to bleed to death in the garden."

"I'm so sorry, Mitch." Faint tears dusted her freckles. One streak caught sun and reflected violet iris. Then she said slowly, "I hate this place. I hate the wind, and I hate the heat, and I hate the long, flat spaces. I hate the way the heat cracks the land, and I hate the way winter lays its dirty hands over everything. Most of all, I hate this disorganized evil that kills a decent man. Why in the world did Cleveland Saunders die, and why do you live like this?" She lowered her head and trembled.

"I only know you have to fight back. I only know that the flat spaces are home, and without a home you are nothing. I don't have much time, Cynthia, I'm sorry. I have to get over to the Saunders home, and I need your help. I don't think I can bathe or dress myself, and I certainly don't feel like driving. I'm counting on you for that."

"Yes, of course," she said smartly. She licked away a tear on her palm. "Who killed the doctor?"

"I think it was Ritchie Polkis."

Cynthia encircled me with her arms and together we struggled across the floor to the bathroom. She rested me against the porcelain tub rail and ran a bath. As steam encased the tile room, gently she took off my shirt and pants, my boots and socks, and finally laid me inside the heavenly water.

"Coffee?" she asked.

"There's plenty in the refrigerator if you can locate it in the mess. The percolator should be under the sink."

I heard Cynthia rustle in the kitchen, then heard the

buzz of my radio and a version of "Moonglow." When she returned, she placed a coffee cup in the soap dish. She lathered my hair and chest and rubbed me with a washrag. Then she soaped and shaved my face. Her eyes glowed green and yellow, like tiger eyes drowned in moonlight. Radiant sweat beads appeared on her skin and shone like jewels.

Finally she said, "I'm going back to Minnesota after the school year."

"For good?"

"Yes. I feel out of place here. The land seems wrong to me. You might consider coming along. It might be your chance to stop living in despair."

"Is that what you think I do?"

"Yes," she said. "I'm not saying that I have any power to help you at all. Women aren't Magdalens, washing and succoring and healing. It doesn't work like that. Men and women are free and individual. I just thought that a change might help you consider your life more fully."

"I don't expect that women have the power to heal. But I think I'm home here, for better or worse."

"And the despair and the murder and the evil?"

"It's no different anywhere. Forgive me for saying this, but you're the color of my grandma's pancakes."

Cynthia smiled. "What a lovely thing to say."

"Help me out. We've got to go."

"I dread seeing Mrs. Saunders. Where do they live?"

"They live in the Ghetto," I said. "You'll learn a lot up there about life as it really is." Cynthia only nodded. In ten minutes we were driving north.

Four roads enter the Ghetto; one road leads out. Cynthia chose Grove Street, driving her red MG the way a panther crouches in a dark tree, alert and relaxed, allowing movement to erupt without effort. I smoked and watched wind drape her auburn hair around her shoulders, revealing a sharp line of jaw, the clean progress of olive

neck disappearing down her white blouse. We rumbled
over a humpbacked railroad crossing and gained a place
devoid of white people, a shabby expanse of tar-paper huts,
pasteboard apartments, weedy vacant lots, mud, trash, and
misery. Scrawny mutts bounced onto wire fences and
yapped as we passed. The sidewalks began and suddenly
ended, broken to chunks. Junk refrigerators and cars labored through the seasons, calcified as bleached bones in
long grass, their hulks rotted in overgrown catalpa groves,
bruised and yellow from time. The dirty snow melted to
gray clumps, and the sun wearied itself in the empty po-
plar limbs. Somehow I saw the wooden face of Cleveland
Saunders collecting dark rain.

The geometry of hatred had squared this land apart from
the land that lay beyond its four invisible boundaries, and
we were strangers in its environs as surely as if we had
come from Mars. I breathed vapor into silvery light and
watched the dilapidated hovels rise and fall like gasps, the
barbecue shacks, tonsorial parlors, and pool halls slide
and fade to memory. The only white presence here was
the rent man, the man who came to repossess the car and
the television and the washer, the cop who arrested and
questioned and pushed. I motioned to Cynthia, and she
turned from Grove to Ninth Street and went east.

"What are these places?" she asked, pointing to a row
of square huts, broken glass in driveways and boarded and
barred windows, pastel walls, and garish painted decor.

"This is the 905 Club and this the Tumbling Dice."
Cynthia gripped the wheel and lost herself in driving. The
gray underbelly of sky darkened. It was suddenly cold,
and rain washed the clouds to slate. Then the wind rose
and washed ruffles in the standing water of the gutters.
Cynthia shivered in her wool sweater, gathering herself
behind the wheel.

"A man gets knifed here nearly every Saturday night,"
I said. "Some poor soul lost in gin and jealousy, maybe

feeling the despair of his poverty and the courage of his emptiness. Cleveland Saunders knew about the rage of his people; he felt the rage as a desire to cure and cleanse. He was a very wise man.'' Cynthia bit her lip. ''Down this street two blocks,'' I said.

Cynthia turned onto Volutsia. I pointed to a blond-brick home surrounded by stunned cedars. Cynthia pulled the MG into a driveway behind an old DeSoto and stopped. Heavy drapes fell behind a picture window of the house. One yellow porch light burned in the gray morning. Cynthia leaned across the seat and opened my door. I tucked the metal box under my good arm and shoved away from the seat, then stood on the soggy dirt yard.

A coal-black man answered the doorbell. Behind the door he stood as if it were a shield, his silent, red-raged eyes gleaming menacingly. His square head held a flat, flared nose, broad cheeks, and short, wiry hair. His ears were tiny and shovel-shaped. His glare would have killed a puppy.

''I'm looking for Mrs. Cleveland Saunders. My name is Mitch Roberts.''

The black man pushed his hand up the door frame, then laid his chin on the back of his hand and bent forward. His flat fingers led to a white palm. His expression simmered to nothing at all, a pure cold stare.

''What do you want here?'' he said. His voice was as searing as coal-mine fire. A woman appeared at the screen and placed one hand on his shoulder.´

''All right, Cleve, honey,'' said the woman. The woman's eyes caught me, and I saw the lonely fear turned russet color and red from crying. She wore a plain black dress. Cleve turned from the door and disappeared into darkness.

''Mrs. Saunders?'' I asked

''Yes.'' Her voice was a rich, burdened contralto.

''My name is Roberts. Your husband was murdered at

my home last night. I'd like to talk to you. I've brought his things. Perhaps there is something I can do to help."

I nodded to Cynthia at my shoulder. Her arm was tucked behind my back, drawn under ribs and elbows. "This is my friend Cynthia Wunderland. She counsels at the high school and knew your husband from the hospital."

"Come in," the woman said. She backed from the door and we went inside to air heavy as pitchblendè. Cleve sat slouched in a tan recliner, his eyes closed. Stale furnace heat doused the room. Mrs. Saunders sat on a faded beige couch and curled her ankles beneath a coffee table. She folded her hands into one another like leaves. I noticed the family pictures on the mantel, fat women in print dresses at church, long-faced farmers in overalls, white-bearded preacher men, hands folded around canes, Cleveland Saunders in bright sunshine, holding his mortarboard and degree. I turnèd to face the widow.

"Mrs. Saunders, I'm terribly sorry. Several days ago I was hired to find a little girl your husband delivered at the County Hospital. I went to talk to him there, and we discussed the baby and the mother and father. I thought that maybe the disappearance of the child had something to do with the Booth Home and a doctor there named Rolfe. Your husband explained the delivery to me, but he didn't know much about my problem at the time."

Cleve stirred and opened his eyes. "Hey, man," he growled. "If you know anything, you'd best tell me."

"All right, Cleve," Mrs. Saunders said.

"All right, nothing," Cleve whispered.

"The police have eliminated robbery as a motive in your husband's death. Did he have any enemies?"

"Oh, please," she said. "My husband would hurt no one. Surely nobody would hurt him."

Cynthia stirred beside me. I went on, "Something must have occurred to your husband. I believe he was murdered for something he knew. I think somebody was staking out

my home, and when they saw your husband arrive, they
held a gun on him. Something happened, and he was
killed. Did he ever talk to you about our conversation?''

"No," she answered flatly.

"Did he ever mention Dr. Rolfe?''

"Nothing like that. Nothing about being crooked.''

"Had he been to the Booth Home yesterday?''

"He was very late yesterday. He came home to dinner
around seven o'clock. I really didn't think anything about
it because he was often late. He was a doctor.''

"Did he seem agitated?'' I asked. Mrs. Saunders wept
gently into a hanky. "I can't help this," I said.

"No," she said finally. "Preoccupied, but not agitated.''

Slowly she unfurled her hands and used them to spread
the folds of her black dress, moving and firming the creases
in the dress until finally she finished and looked away.
Cynthia slid to her side on the tattered couch and placed
an arm around her strong shoulders. The widow touched
her forehead softly. I stood with rocks in my pocket, feeling the sorrow collect like dust in a dead child's room.
Cleve rose and stood with his back to me, his hands draped
on the mantel below the family pictures. His hands played
aimlessly over the molding in circular gestures of grief. I
walked to Cleve and stood for a moment.

"Look, Cleve," I began.

"Don't call me that, mister," he said. The words spit
like viper venom.

"All right," I said. "Whatever you say.''

"Doctor shit," he said. "Just a field nigger done
changed to a city nigger. Pushing the puke bowl around a
goddamn county hospital.''

"Please, son," Mrs. Saunders said quickly. "It won't
do any good to go on with that now.''

I rested the metal box on the mantel under Cleve's

bowéd head. He stirred and one of his hands fell heavily on the box. I could see his chest heave.

"I've brought these from police headquarters. They are your father's things."

"My daddy was killed on your porch?"

"I talked to him early yesterday. We talked about Rolfe and the Booth Home. He must have changed his mind about something, because he wouldn't have come to my home late unless it was important. I don't know what changed his mind, but I owe him for that."

"You owe him, do you?" Cleve asked. The words curdled in clean space. Cleve opened the box and mixed the objects inside with a careless swipe. "That's it," he said. "There's twenty dollars in here, no more than spare change to white folks. Shoeshine boys have that much cash." Cleve closed the box and sobbed angrily. There was nothing to say. Cleve was right and I knew it and being dead was as serious as it ever got.

While Cleve sobbed, as the weary heat drifted to the ceiling in invisible pounding waves, I gazed through a dirty window to a muddy yard, gray sky, a sway of naked elms. Cleve raised his unbearably hollow gaze.

"One thing," I said. "Please look at this." I handed Cleve the birth certificate. He unfolded the form and studied it quietly.

"I don't know what you mean," he said.

"Your father had the certificate in the inside fold of his coat pocket. Everything he carried made sense: watch, wallet, rings. This certificate means nothing to me, but it doesn't make sense that he would be carrying it when he died."

Cleve tapped the certificate against the mantel. He walked slowly across the room and stood above his mother. "Mama," he said. Mrs. Saunders raised her hand and took the certificate as Cynthia left the couch and stood beside me. Mrs. Saunders also rose from the couch. The sound of children playing drifted in the cold wind.

"This is not my husband's hand," Mrs. Saunders said. We were silent together. "Don't you understand? My husband did not sign this birth certificate. Someone signed his name, but it is not his hand. It is a forgery." She sat back down, placing the certificate on the coffee table.

"Did your husband ever speak of this baby or the parents? Van Slyke."

"No, of course not," she said.

I walked to the table and picked up the certificate. "You'll have to go downtown now," I said. "I'm truly sorry."

"I know. I'm prepared for that now."

"I'll find who did this," I said.

"You tell me," she said. "You'll tell us both," she said, taking her son's hand.

"Yes," I said. Then we were out the door into cool gray wind.

FOURTEEN

I bought a paper cup of coffee at a burger stand on Thirteenth Street and instructed Cynthia on how to drive to Maple Grove. She wrapped herself in a brown scarf and found the entrance, a cedar-shrouded portcullis and masonry standard that wound intricately through bowers and stands of stunted cherry and willow to a Civil War memorial. You could hear the crows bleat in the windswept cedars, and far away the cattle trucks shuddered north toward Nebraska on the main line. The sky was slate gray, metallic as mercuric petals on a milky glass mirror, and the brown hillsides stretched away into endless weed lots and ash heaps, carrying their tombstones, memorials, and markers like so many multiformed volcanic boulders. Unhappy plastic flowers dotted the grave sites that sat cluttered willy-nilly in the unkempt earth. I often came here to think and walk and watch the stars, this being one place in the city certain to have darkness and solitude. From the Civil War memorial an overgrown path led downhill to a granite-and-limestone mausoleum, moss-covered and lugubrious. The lachrymose trees tippled in the breeze. We sat on a damp bench, and I drank some coffee.

"I can tell you like it here," Cynthia said without irony.

"I need to think, and I'm tired."

"You didn't sleep all night?"

"No," I answered. "I'll be fine. I just needed some coffee and a chance to think quietly."

Cynthia shivered slightly, then rose and walked to a vast angelic memorial made of concrete and granite, surrounded by a flaking green-painted fence in Victorian style. She studied the legend on the tombstone and looked uphill toward the descending creek and elm grove. The maples of Maple Grove had long since died or been cut.

"I don't find it sad here at all," she said from her distance. The sky threatened rain, and I could feel hot coffee steam on my bruised cheek.

"No," I agreed. "Graveyards have always filled me with a sense of peace, as if all these people have their secrets and are content to rest with them. I don't find it upsetting at all. The restfulness gives me some hope."

"I'm glad," Cynthia said, following the path back to the cold bench. She spread her scarf and used it as a cushion. "What do you think the certificate means?" she asked finally. I sat silently staring at the weathered caretaker's shack, a cedar structure half caved in by time and neglect. My arm struggled against numb pain.

"I know what the certificate means, only it's just an idea. Cleveland Saunders knew it was a forgery, but what his theories were, I can't tell yet. It's part of the plot to adopt babies for profit."

"What makes you think Ritchie Polkis killed the doctor?"

"Yesterday I was trailing Ritchie. I saw him pull a knife on a friend of mine, and the look in his eyes said a lot."

"But murder?" she asked.

"I'm assuming several things," I said. "I'm assuming that Ritchie Polkis was watching my house last night. I saw George Polkis drive by my place that afternoon, so I know that the brothers knew I was on the case. How they found out, I don't know. I'm also assuming that Ritchie didn't mean to kill the doctor, or at least didn't confront him on my porch intending to kill him directly. The evidence of the autopsy suggests that there was a mistake, a struggle, and a shot was fired and Cleveland Saunders died. Ritchie must have panicked before he searched the body for whatever he thought the doctor had. I'm also assuming the something was a birth certificate.''

"But why an adoption? It seems very complicated to sell babies and use adoption as a cover.''

"That's what I thought, too. I spoke to a lawyer friend of mine about the process. Initially, parents are found for babies, and they usually pay expenses and legal fees. The mother and father file a formal consent; then the baby is adopted through the Probate Court with legal documents. After that, the child's birth records are sealed so the real parents can't be located later. Whatever is happening must involve cold cash and lots of it; otherwise murder doesn't make sense.''

"But the complications?''

"When I trailed the brothers, I saw them go into a lawyer's office. The lawyer is related to the Probate judge. My lawyer friend told me that accepting huge expense payments from adoptive parents is highly unethical, and probably illegal, but if this racket were operated by lawyers and judges, that would cut down on the risk. It's usually the Probate Court that investigates the likelihood of fraud in an adoption.''

"But the certificate itself? How does it fit?''

"I honestly don't know, Cynthia.''

Cynthia took my coffee and drank some of it. She put down the cup and pulled on some woolen gloves. A thread of black cumulus towered above the cemetery, and the wind, already cold, steadied to an icy calm.

"Suppose we go to the courthouse,'' Cynthia suggested. "Bonnie's baby is four months old, born last December. Perhaps we could search the Probate records for all the adoptions filed around that time?''

"That's not a bad idea," I agreed. "The mother's records would ultimately be sealed by the state, but the adoption records would probably still be public. If we could find the new parents, maybe we could find the baby."

"One thing bothers me," Cynthia murmured. "Bonnie was so sure she wanted the baby at the end. What made her change her mind?"

"Have you ever been to the Cobb home?"

"No," she answered.

"It's a cold place. But when I talked to Bonnie this week, she wanted that baby. If we can get it back for her, she'll raise the little girl. It won't be easy on her, but she'll try."

I relaxed and stared into my coffee, then drank a sip. It was going lukewarm. The wind skittered again, drawing around the cedars and elms like bones around a heart.

"Do you believe in God?" Cynthia asked suddenly.

"No," I said quickly. "Human solidarity, struggle, goodness, knowledge, luck, and perseverance, but not God. It's much too complicated for that." Cynthia stood and wrapped her scarf around herself, then walked to the MG and opened my door. I hobbled to the car and eased myself into the seat. She started the MG, then turned it in a tight circle and drove out the portcullis gate and down the deserted streets toward the courthouse.

The County Courthouse was a huge, three-story slab of pink granite and limestone covering an elegant block between Pine and Central in downtown. Cynthia parked the car beside a grassy plot beneath a blind lady carrying a sword of justice. There had never been a time when I trusted blind women with swords, even if they made swell pigeon nests. On the corner, a Civil War cannon aimed south. Cynthia helped me from the car, and I stood in the misty atmosphere as she put her arms around me and helped me up the long walk toward a dozen marble stairs and the illumined doors. Cynthia swung open the doors, and we went inside to a rush of official business and refracted images. The elevator doors whooshed open and we rode to the third floor with a janitor who huddled beneath a No Smoking sign, jangling his keys and fingering a wet cigarette. Then we went into the Probate clerk's office.

The office was bright as a Roman candle, the huge room full of monkeys pounding typewriters. A black marble counter divided the room neatly, and behind me sinister judges stared from smoky paintings on the wall. An old woman with pink cotton-candy hair stood behind the marble counter sucking on a pencil. She looked like a broken-down cabaret singer with her cherry lips and high, rouged cheeks. We went to the counter, and I leaned an elbow lazily on the stone.

"Trick or treat," I said. Cynthia placed a toe on my toe and pressed. "What I mean is, we'd like to look at the adoptions for the last six months."

"Certainly," the old woman said cheerfully. "Public files, along the wall behind you. The adoptions are in blue folders from the floor to ceiling. They're not in any particular order as to date, just by case number. But the case numbers are assigned in the order of their filing. The last six months would probably be in the two cabinets on your right. If I can help you, let me know." The woman turned and spoke to a secretary and waddled away.

"Aren't you ashamed?" Cynthia smiled.

"Yes, I'm ashamed. But I'm more ashamed to say I don't know exactly why we're here."

"I don't know, either," Cynthia said. "But you start at the last file and look from the bottom up. I'll start two files down and work my way toward you. We'll look for an adoption of Bonnie's baby, and maybe we'll stumble on a pattern involving children that Polkis and his friends have made. We'll pull all the files that look interesting and make a list and take it home.''

''All right,'' I said. ''It's a good idea, but it might take some time. If we interview all the new parents we find, perhaps we'll discover someone nervous enough to implicate Polkis and his brother. It's just possible I could use the knowledge to get back baby Elizabeth for Bonnie.''

I worked up through the files for an hour, isolating thirty-five adoptions and making a list of the new parents, trying to spot any patterns or unusual bits of information. Cynthia worked toward me, piling folders around herself like Christmas gifts. Lunchtime came and went, and the office workers piled out the doors, leaving us alone with one or two secretaries and a ticking clock. My list had grown entirely confusing when Cynthia stood.

She stretched herself. ''I'll be back,'' she said. I watched her leave through the glass doors and disappear around a corner. I worked another ten minutes until I saw Cynthia return through the glass doors, a nascent smile attending her lips. She pulled me to my feet. Then she gathered the file folders and placed them on the marble counter. ''Come outside,'' she said. I carried my aches and pains outside to a water fountain, where she stopped me.

''I made a call,'' she whispered conspiratorially.

''You made a call,'' I parroted.

''That's right, I made a call.''

''All right, good. You made a call.''

''For God's sake,'' Cynthia squawked. ''Ask me who I called.''

''Who did you call, for God's sake?''

''Brother,'' she hissed. ''I called the Bureau of Vital Statistics in Topeka.'' A small bulb flickered in my head and then went dark. Cynthia sipped some water from the fountain. ''I began to doubt what we were doing,'' she began. ''After all, looking through those adoption files seemed to have little to do with the forged birth certificate. After all, I decided we'd never find a record of the adoption of Bonnie's baby, so I gave that up.'' Another janitor appeared, a tiny cretin dressed in white ducks and navy blue T-shirt. An elevator ate the janitor, and down he went.

"So, what did you say?" I asked.

"I told them I was Inez Tomlinson."

"Inez Tomlinson?"

"You boob," Cynthia said. "Inez Tomlinson is your lady friend behind the clerk's desk. It says so on a plaque. Perhaps you overlooked that."

"Oh," I grunted. The dim bulb filled my head, but refused to ignite properly.

"I told Vital Statistics that the clerk's office was checking on a birth certificate of a baby girl we'd sent from County. I said that maybe there'd been a mix-up and that the certificate hadn't been sent. I asked them to check."

"They'd never tell you the adoptive parents' names."

"I know that. I told them I just wanted confirmation on the birth certificate. That's the point. Nothing but confirmation on the arrival of the certificate."

"And?" I asked.

"They had no record of the live birth of Elizabeth Cobb. It's as if she were never born."

"Of course," I said. I grabbed Cynthia and hugged her, feeling her inside the bulky gray sweater, the sweet, dusty smell of her redolent of peaches and wine. She hugged me, and there was no pain in my back. "It's perfect," I said to her fine ear. "Officially speaking, Bonnie's baby doesn't exist. The baby is born, and then the responsible doctor signs the birth certificate. But somebody at County Hospital intercepts the birth certificate, destroys it, then substitutes a fake photocopy in the file. Cleveland Saunders would never know a false photocopy had been placed in the medical file unless he had a reason to check. When I visited his office, I gave him a reason to check. He found the copied birth certificate and naturally assumed he had signed the original. He must have studied the photocopy and realized that his signature had been forged. He was bringing the certificate to me, probably not knowing himself what it meant.

"This way, when the lawyers locate new parents, they've got a baby who doesn't exist, so they can sell the baby and deliver fake adoption papers to the new parents, who think they've legitimately adopted a child. If they check with the Probate judge, he confirms the adoption. This gives whoever is directing the racket a perfect cover. An investigator could never locate the adoptive parents, because a real record of the adoption doesn't exist. Also, an investigator could never locate the real mother, because there's no birth certificate on file with her name. After a few years, there is literally no trace of anything. The only people who would know for sure would be the mother, and presumably she's been paid. It's ingenious."

"And terrible," Cynthia said.

"There's one way to confirm this," I said.

"How?"

"Drive me to the Booth Home. I think Lurleen Curtis is next on the list. If Ritchie or George has approached her to adopt her baby, then maybe she could tell us the details. It's our chance to catch them out."

"Why don't we go to the police?"

"I've gone to the police. I have a friend on the force who knows what I'm doing. I want to give him the details, along with Lurleen Curtis and Ritchie Polkis in a nice pretty package with red ribbons."

We rode down on the elevator accompanied by a gaggle of feisty lawyers arguing their bank accounts. Cynthia trundled me into the car, and she headed into reedy traffic on Central, driving east across Riverside Park, bucking up the Nims Street Bridge to an eastern fringe of woods and river called Sim Park. The Booth Home lay north of the park in a copse of Scotch pine, fluted sandy hills, and plum.

The car sliced through black elm shadows and fog puffs. Cynthia flicked on the heater, and the car filled with a dry heat. We rode beside the ice-clogged river, then skirted the lion house at the zoo and finally gained the quiet brick-and-frame symmetry of homes that lined the golf course and city water plant. She drove north along an empty fairway, and day dripped to a watercolor impression. I sensed real excitement, and we were silent and expectant.

Then I saw the figures like sodden yellow bubbles on the grassy golf course plateau. The bubbles plotted a solemn Ptolemaic simplicity, moving in the snow fog in twisted, concentric circles. Three police cars were parked in the shadow of a hedge, and farther down the block were two blue Plymouths and a single white ambulance. Cynthia slowed and looked at me, her pure features creased by doubt. A police officer stood in the brick street, his hand outstretched. Cynthia stopped behind a black-and-white police cruiser. We watched as the officers, clad in yellow rain gear, combed the fairway, bending and bobbing with outstretched arms. A big cop in a gray overcoat leaned against the MG, then stuck his face inside the driver's side.

"We'll have to ask you to move it, miss," he said gravely. I opened the passenger door and stood up, hanging above the cloth top of the car. The rain-slick face of Andy Lanham greeted me, black bags beneath his eyes. His cigar had gone out in his mouth.

"What are you doing here, Mitch?" he asked. He voiced the words without expression or intent, the way a violent revolutionary asks a prisoner about his ideology. Beyond his shoulder, through a ruffled Scotch pine bough, I glimpsed the Booth Home, flagstone porch and white portico supported by Doric columns, and above the plinth a line of shiny faces pressed to big windows.

"What are the boys looking for?" I said.

"With you and me it's always a chess game," Andy said. He carried away his cigar with a thumb and forefinger. "Every move is answer and question, nothing clean until the end of the game, and even then you're leaning over my shoulder telling me the move I should have made. What do you think? The guys in slickers are cops, and they're searching the golf course."

"I don't get it," I said.

"Your face brings me bad luck." Andy sighed. He twisted his head in a quick, directional motion. We walked to the rear of the car, and I lit a cigarette. Andy placed a foot on the fender as light rain dripped. A cop inside the black-and-white turned on his wipers, and the whoosh interrupted the thin silence. "A little girl was killed back there in the trees," he said. "She was no more than sixteen or seventeen years old. Her head was busted in like a melon."

"You don't mean an accident?"

"No accident. I'm Homicide, and we don't work accidents. We found a bloody baseball bat down one of the storm drains. The boys are looking around the golf course for some evidence, something the killer may have left behind, anything. Right now we don't have much. Out here it could be the middle of the day and Lucifer could hire a dance band and hold a street dance. You think anybody would hear anything?"

One of the yellow-slickered cops hopped from the trees. "You want us to widen out?" he asked Andy. Andy nodded and the cop left.

Andy stirred and fingered his cigar, rolling it aimlessly in his hand. "She was the prettiest thing you ever saw," he said. "Freckles and red hair, and all that blood. She was skinny, too, couldn't have weighed ninety pounds. We don't even have a clue. Just a little dead girl named Bonnie."

Icy acid violated my soul. I slid around the car and slipped into the seat beside Cynthia. The windshield wipers revolved in whisking half circles, and I saw that Cynthia's face had collapsed into stony sadness.

"I heard what he said," she said grimly.

"Let's go home," I said. Cynthia turned through a U in the brick street, then steered beside the icy river, and we crossed the Nims Street Bridge. The rain drummed through the fog, driving gray tunnels above the water. Tears collected on Cynthia's cheek. The MG rattled to a halt before my Victorian on Sycamore, steam hissing from the tires and the motor, draining upward in the fog. We sat for a time in silence as some ragged crows battled in the ballpark parking lot. I felt alone and deserted in a place beyond the crackling home-place fire, beyond shiny Christmas cards and shiny faces at windows, beyond war and death and human feeling, lodged in a fiery place of cloying stenches.

"I hate this," Cynthia said. "There's no God, then, only murder and loss." Her voice was wracked by angry sobs. "I wish I'd never met you, never been involved in any of this. I just want to go home." I opened the door and stood aside while Cynthia cried openly. Then she drove away down the empty street.

I slumped in the rain, then carried myself haltingly up the old steps to an aching darkness, pausing on the stoop to watch a brown house sparrow with black-banded eyes prance on the rail. My mind returned to Bonnie Cobb, her freckled face radiant in a density of cigarette smoke, her small body perched on a hospital bed, her eyes black-banded by plain uncertainty. A searing resolve struck through me then, and I walked inside the old house.

FIFTEEN

Francis the cat curlicued beside my piled clothes and hopped to the base of the bathtub. He pulled himself into a tight pretzel, extending a brown leg, and sat running his tongue between each pink-padded toe, then drawing it in long, gooey troughs through his prickly fur. For a time he watched himself reflected in the hot water. I flipped a drop onto his nose and he bolted to the top of the clothes hamper, where he sat watching me with deep and abiding suspicion. Francis curled onto his stomach and pulled out some more cockleburs, contemplating probably the wild evening he had had with the lovely Persian next door. I soaked my back and arm and teased Francis with the end of a dirty washcloth. I had been thinking and soaking in the tub for an hour, allowing the pain and exhaustion to seep from me, allowing ugly ideas to flood my mind, following my intuition and reason on a long, terrible trek into an environment of misery and greed. My thoughts had centered on the Cobbs and what I had decided was not pretty enough to bury on midnight during Halloween.

The gray wind banged against the windows and eaves, ruffling the one ragged awning out back, a sound morose and disturbing as a woman's crying. It was now the middle of the afternoon on a bad Wednesday, and two people were dead and my arm was black and my back hurt. The front screen slammed.

I unplugged the bath and wrapped myself in a tattered blue housecoat, rubbed a towel over my stringy hair, and opened the door a crack. Jack Graybul stood inside a blue topcoat, surveying the damage and ruin of my room, the broken-spined books, upturned plants, turned mattress, and scattered dishes. He was smoking a cigarette, and some of the ashes dotted the blue of his coat. His socks were mismatched, as usual. He saw me emerge from the bathroom and nodded.

"Door was open," he said.

"I've got some coffee," I said. I poured some from the percolator and we sat in the living room, Jack poised on one side of my footlocker, while I took a place in an oak chair in the alcove.

"I read about the doctor somebody killed. I'm sorry, Mitch, I really am. Does all of this have something to do with the adoption you asked me about?"

"I need your help," I said. "That's why I called."

"Who tossed your room?"

"The cops. The doctor was killed out front, and they used probable cause to wreck my place."

"That's typical," Jack said. He took smoke down deep and creased the cold air with his exhalation. Tiny crystalline snow spit through the air outside as cold wind drove southward in a straight line. The barren trees clacked as if shivering. "Some things never change. But how did the doctor figure into your adoption business?"

"I'm going to tell you something fantastic," I began. "Your lawyer friends Kunkle and Reid are selling babies. The Probate judge is involved. The doctor somebody killed had come to my place with some important evidence. He was shot for his trouble."

"Jesus." Jack whistled. "That's rough. What can I do?"

"Just listen," I said. "My client was killed in Sim Park just now. I'm not sure why, but it was her baby that is missing, the baby I'm trying to locate."

"You'd best go easy. Who killed the doctor? Who killed your client?"

"My best guess is a punk named Ritchie Polkis. He's kind of a good-looking, greasy psychopath."

"Can you prove it?"

"I've got a plan. I don't have a way to prove it, but I think I can cause enough trouble to flush these birds into the open. I don't know if I can ever get a clear shot at them, but I've got to try."

"Polkis is a name I know," said Jack. "These guys are very mean. I wish you'd give what you know to the police and let them handle it. This is a job for Andy Lanham; you know that."

"I feel very personally responsible for the doctor and the kid. I wouldn't stop now if the Polkis gang had me cornered with pitchforks. I couldn't stop."

Jack nodded and pitched his cigarette into an ashtray. "What can I do?" he said finally.

"I'm trying to get the baby back, today, maybe tomorrow. Can you help me find a home for the baby? Someplace with love that goes a long way?"

"Aren't there some grandparents involved?"

"You don't need to worry about them. They'll release the baby. I've been thinking about that all afternoon, and I'm sure they would consent."

"All right, Mitch," Jack said. "I work all the time with the people at Lutheran Social Service. You'd wouldn't believe how many decent, loving couples have been waiting years for a child of their own. I know a couple in Kansas City now, and I think they'd be perfect."

I dug in my footlocker, riffling through the fishing gear, tackle, chess books, guns, knives, war souvenirs, and letters until I came to my small Montana ranch–money stash.

I unfurled five hundred-dollar bills and handed them to Jack.

He waved them away. "No way," he said. "This is on the house, between you and me."

Christian's old Nash pulled to a stop in front of the house, and I watched him lumber through the slush and wind to the screen. He came inside and said hello to Jack. "I found your Indian and her boy. I gave them the money, like you said, and put them on a bus this morning for Omaha. They'll transfer tonight for South Dakota. She couldn't really believe it was happening, but once she understood, she didn't ask many questions. For what it's worth, she looked happy as hell."

"That's great," I said. Spud walked to the kitchen and returned with a cold beer. Jack had known Spud since the war had ended and since we began regular Sunday poker at my place.

"So," began Spud, "is anything happening with our good friend Ritchie?"

"He killed a doctor on my front porch, and I think that this afternoon he killed Bonnie."

"Christ," said Spud. "I'm really sorry. What the hell is he doing?"

"I've seen his look before, and its sociopathic. I think he enjoys the killing, because none of it makes much sense. He killed Saunders over a scrap of paper, when he could just as well have knocked him out and found it. I don't know why he killed Bonnie, but it was near the Booth Home, and so it probably had to do with one of the other pregnant girls."

"Do we have a plan?" Spud asked.

"I have a plan. You're out of it now." I took one of the hundreds and handed it to Spud. He waved it away. Spud could be a rough character: One night in a shabby snooker hall outside Kechi, Kansas, I'd seen him sink an eight ball in the corner pocket and in the same motion shove a pool

cue through the upper bridge of a farmer's teeth. The
farmer had been sitting in a theater chair spitting tobacco
juice onto Spud's shoes while he shot snooker, and Spud
had adroitly avoided each slobbery pile until the end of
the game. Spud said nothing, sank the eight ball, and
knocked out seven of the farmer's teeth.

"This is something I have to do on my own," I said.

Jack rose and we shook hands; then he shook hands
with Spud and stood in the open screen door, wind buf-
feting his topcoat and swirling in his gray hair. "I'll line
up the couple in Kansas City through Social Service. We'll
do the adoption legally and honestly, and the child will
have a good life. I promise you that, because I know these
people. You have my word on it."

"Thanks, Jack," I said to the back of his topcoat.

Spud looked at me. "I don't really have any idea of
what's going on here, but if there's anything I can do, you
let me know. I'd kind of like another crack at Ritchie Polkis, especially now. And besides, I don't want anything to
happen to you. You don't play poker very well, and I really
need the extra Sunday money."

We smiled and shook hands.

"When this is finished, I'd like to talk," he said. "I
know you've been saving that money for your ranch, and
I know it hurts to spend it like that. I think it's damn
fine."

"Forget it," I said. "A week from now we'll be sitting
inside a fine spring, playing chess on the front porch. Winter never lasts, and like the Scandinavians say, it teaches
you patience. Hell, where would we be without the hope
and anticipation of the four seasons?"

"In the tropics," Spud said.

"Get out of here." I laughed. Spud shuffled through
the screen door. I heard some rain spit against the rotten
roof and the porch. I sat still, thinking about the sweet
body of Cynthia Wunderland moving along the shiny axis

of the Milky Way, fading and moving farther and farther
into the swelling stars and black gasses at the end of the
galaxy. Then I put on some gray wool slacks, a Pendleton
shirt and leather vest, and boots. I cleaned my gun and
put it inside a leather pouch and tried to put some order
back into my room. I put the Van Slyke birth certificate
into an envelope and sealed the envelope and put it inside
the mailbox with the flag up. The postman would be calling later, and the certificate would be on its way back to
Andy. I fed the rabbits in their hutch and washed their
water dishes and put clean water in their pens. Thirty-six
blocks of snow and ice lay between me and the death
house on Lorraine, where I knew the Cobbs would be
waiting.

I drove to the Take-Homa-Burger on Maple, ordered
two hamburgers with chili, and had wolfed them by the
time I crossed into the warehouse district on Waterman.
Some lombrosians hustled scrap metal and used cars, rising steam obscuring their backs as they worked. The day
lay in a gunmetal-gray coffin as I drove to Washington
Street, then turned south to Lincoln and cruised along the
old brick. I slopped snow and mud onto neatly manicured
lawns maintained by the lower-middle class. I reached
Lorraine and stopped in front of the Cobb house to smoke
a cigarette and gather my ideas. I opened the car door and
walked to the front porch, waiting there in the rushing
silence, hearing the hum and swirl of cold wind in cedar,
the sound of children's voices faint in a distant schoolyard,
the occasional honk of a car horn on Kellogg Street. The
white frame houses and picket fences stood lonely as a
dead man's false teeth. There was a crack in the veneer
and a sudden rush of heat.

Her face advertised pain and guilt. She had been crying:
red lines of grief trailed on her cheeks like rivers. Still,
through the tears, the deadly scent of anger and pettiness
escaped, something dreadful and dreary as the sympathy

of a professional mortician. She wore a black dress and gray wool sweater, black shoes with holes in the toes, and a mauve shawl. She looked as if she had just stepped out of the Brown Decades with Grover Cleveland Alexander as an escort. She spoke above the steady incantations of a television soap opera.

"Can't you leave us alone?"

I put my foot in the door. "I'm coming in. There aren't two ways about it."

She had tied her face into knots, anger and grief taut in her plain features and mean eyes. I pushed against the door and fell into the fetid heat of the living room. The television cast livid shadows on the fuzzy couch and chairs.

"Sit down," I said tersely.

She sat, and then she cried, subtly at first, choking a little as she tried to hold back. She shuddered with the effort. "They've killed her," she said. The effort of saying it shook her, too, and the words flew from the cage her life had created and fluttered there in the heat. A cresendo of organ music cascaded from the television, some silly jingle about processed cheese, dreadful and absurd as the Bach played by prisoner orchestras at Dachau. I lit a cigarette and threw the match on the floor. It was a gesture I would later regret, one drawn from pure revenge and hate.

"I'm sorry your daughter is dead, Mrs. Cobb. I liked Bonnie, even though I only talked to her once. She seemed like a decent kid to me. I'm here to get some answers, and I want them quickly because her baby is in danger now. I've got a plan to straighten out this mess, but it calls for you to tell me the truth. If you don't, you're playing with Elizabeth's life. There are two people dead. Don't allow it to continue, Mrs. Cobb. Isn't that enough?"

Maud looked up at me from the couch with hard, mean eyes, bright black points in red outline.

"Can't you leave me alone? Can't you see I'm grieving? There is nothing anyone can do now that will bring back

Bonnie. Besides, they've threatened us, too, and they mean it. I don't want to talk to you. I'm sorry I ever hired you in the first place. It was a big mistake. Leave us alone.'' Maud pushed gray and black hair away from her brow. She was a study by Whistler, without the love.

"All right, Mrs. Cobb. I'll do the talking. I want you to listen very closely.''

"I hate you,'' she said.

"Good,'' I said. "That makes us square.'' I crushed the cigarette on the floor. "You came to my office on Saturday. You told me a story about how a tough kid named Ritchie Polkis took his own baby away from Bonnie and how you wanted me to get her back. It sounded like he might have wanted the baby for his own, even though the Polkis clan isn't known for its charity. One thing bothered me right away, though. I looked around your house, and I didn't see any of the things you'd expect to see where there was a new baby. There was no crib, no dirty diapers piled around, no cute pink rattles with Daffy Duck on the handle. I thought that was strange. I couldn't believe that Polkis took all the baby clothes and toys, so it bothered me that the child was here and then gone, and there was no trace. Still, I was being charitable and trying to account for the differences among people.

"So, I talked to Bonnie. She told me that Ritchie is indeed the father of the baby and he had come here one afternoon, threatened her, and had taken the baby. Right away I decided that something was strange. Neither you nor your husband were in the house, and in the middle of an afternoon, I knew that at least you should have been here. After all, there was a baby and a daughter in the house alone. You wouldn't leave them like that. I know people like you, and you sit around in the afternoon watching television. Still, even if my worst thoughts about you were true, I couldn't believe you'd intentionally leave the house so George and Ritchie would be alone with Bonnie, so you'd escape the blame. I didn't think you'd go that far just to get rid of the baby, but it did cause me some concern. Are you following me so far?''

Maud shook her head, as if to ward off the words.

"I worked on the case without worrying about these details too much. Then on Tuesday night something happened that shook my confidence in you, something I couldn't ignore in a million years. I drove up to my house and a maroon Ford rumbled by, going slow, the driver looking me over. Behind the wheel there was a big man, dark felt hat, black striped suit with wide lapels. I knew then he had been following me. I also knew it was George Polkis in person cruising down my street. I asked myself if that could be another coincidence. I had trailed him to his lawyer's the day before, and I wondered if he could have spotted me. I didn't think so, because I was way behind them all the time. Ritchie didn't know who I was, either. There was only one logical idea that came to me. You put George onto me, Mrs. Cobb.''

"Are you finished?'' she said. She wrapped her shawl around her shoulders and glared at me. I had to admit she was tough, deep down vicious as an alley cat.

"I'm not finished,'' I said. "That night out on old Highway 54 it was a nice night with rain and mud puddles. I was driving down the highway when I was stopped by two sheriff's deputies. They got me down in the gravel and beat the hell out of me with their clubs. They told me to lay off the case, just like that. I knew George had spotted me that afternoon, and then that evening the deputies stopped me. It seemed pretty clear that George had sicced the deputies on me then. Are you following me?''

Then I saw Robert at the entrance to the basement steps, his stooped form huddled on the edge of a black abyss. His blue work shirt was streaked by sweat, and there was excelsior in his hair. His face was the ghost of a face. He stood there silently, his features drawn and gaunt.

"Here's what I decided, Mrs. Cobb. Bonnie had told me the truth. She didn't know what was going on around her; she just knew that she wanted her baby back at all costs. Something underneath told me that she was decent and wanted that child. She wouldn't come out and admit it, probably because she was afraid, but that's what she wanted, all right. She acted tough, but she wasn't so tough as she made out. The one thing I think now is that you hired me to satisfy Bonnie that you were making an effort to locate the child. You consulted a lawyer and hired an investigator, and that was supposed to satisfy Bonnie. I have to think she wanted to go to the police herself, and for some reason that must have scared you enough to go through the motions of hiring me. As soon as you hired me, though, you tipped George, and he tipped the deputies and they were supposed to scare me off the case. If that happened, you'd have done your duty to Bonnie. Then, maybe she'd keep quiet about the child. I think you hoped this whole thing would go away. Now, why the hell would you do something as complicated as all that? What could have prompted you to try so hard to keep Bonnie quiet?"

"Five thousand dollars," Robert Cobb said from his darkened perch. He deflated and sagged against the door. His eyes darkened, and his shoulders drooped. "Dear God, we sold the baby."

"Shut up," Maud hissed. She folded the pleats of her black dress, then casually flicked at the tears that streaked her face. It was a hidden, futile gesture.

"Ritchie offered you five thousand for the child. I suppose that was supposed to be expenses and legal fees."

Robert stumbled, half-dreaming, into the living room. His face held a tragic aspect, as if at any moment it would dissolve and break. "Why did we do it?" he said to his wife. The television rose and buzzed in the wavery heat. Maud's face was a tough, lined, minor-seventh of a face. She shook, gathering strength.

"You fool," she said. "Did you think that Bonnie should raise that baby? The sin was one thing, and we're not the ones to forgive it. Leave that to God. Where there's sin, there's damnation and fire. Can you see Bonnie raising that baby in God's word? Can you?"

Robert walked to the stairwell.

"You really think you can justify this?" I asked.

"The money was for expenses, and they said the baby would have a good home, a far better life than Bonnie could provide," Maud said. "We tried to convince her, but she wouldn't listen. Then, we had to do it on our own. It's easy for you to criticize, but there was no earthly way to keep that child here. You wouldn't be so quick to judge if you were in my place."

"But you didn't get the money, did you? Ritchie kept the money and took the baby."

"No," Maud said. "He lied. He wouldn't give us the money."

"So Ritchie kept your money and threatened you if you told anyone."

"Yes," she said quietly.

Robert turned from his dark corner. He spoke quickly, his small voice hurt and choked. "Ritchie has been here today. Bonnie wanted to go to the Booth Home to talk to Lurleen. If she talked to Lurleen, she'd find out the whole story. I think Ritchie must have killed her before she got to Lurleen. Christ, what have we done?" He broke and sobbed, his face buried in the darkness of the basement stairs. I heard him creak down the steps. Then I was alone with Maud Cobb. The furnace poured hot, dry air into the room.

I walked outside and down the broken stairs and across the wet grass and got into the car. I smoked five cigarettes, watching the silver March air stir in cloud shadows. The street was quiet as an empty church, white frame houses and picket fences, swaying cedars and empty elms stretched like burnished pews. Sunnyside Elementary loomed from the strange darkness, three stories of red brick in a black sky, huge classroom windows burning like rows of fiery teeth. I sat while the north wind cursed the flat landscape, smelling blood and gas from the rendering plants north of town. The wind bumped clouds through fog, fog and cloud in disarray. A bell in the schoolyard rang and children boiled from huge doors and bolted to the playground, gathering themselves with molecular unconsciousness into groups for tetherball, three flies-up, pepper, and ring-around-a-rosy. I watched the children play, then drove away to my fate.

SIXTEEN

The lanes smelled of oil and beer and old smoke. An ageless fat man grabbed his black ball and stepped to the line, adjusting his glare at the ten shiny white pins, wiggling his thumb and popping it into place, then walking deliberately toward the line. The ball made a solid sound as it struck home. Dark shadows flooded the lanes, and the old pin spotter clanked as it scraped away the fallen wood. I finished my pinball game and dropped a nickel in the pay phone. The lanes were empty save for the fat man and a small, hairless cashier. The telephone rang twice, and the lawyer's secretary answered.

"Wilson Kunkle," I said quickly and with authority.

"He's with a client," she chirped.

"Who's the client?" I said.

"Please, sir. I can't divulge that information."

"Give it to me straight, Millie."

"Oh, my," she said. "Who's calling, please?"

"I've heard this line before from lawyers and bankers. I want you to tell Kunkle that Mitch Roberts is holding. I'll hold for a few minutes, then I'm hanging up and going to the police. It might interest you to know that this deal could be worth big money to your boss. He won't appre-

163

ciate it if you don't give him my message. It wouldn't surprise me if he'd flail your ass, too. Get with it.''

"This must be a joke," she said. Then she said, "I'll give him the message, sir.''

I waited in the acrid, aromatic confines of the small phone booth. I could taste cheeseburgers and greasy french fries. The hairless cashier unwrapped some chewing gum and tossed the silver wrapper on the floor. Wind banged against the glass doors, and I could see fog through the glass, a hazy, indefinite smudge on gray litmus.

"This is Kunkle," someone said. "You've got three sentences, smart guy, and that's it." Kunkle's voice was a pleasurable growl.

"This is Mitch Roberts; you probably know the name by now. I understand how you sell the babies. I want Elizabeth Cobb back.''

After a moment Kunkle said, "Wise guys like you are very cheap. You know what they say, don't you? Money talks and bullshit walks.''

"Fine, Mr. Kunkle. This stuff might work with impressionable girls at a local dance. Let's say I can crack you wide open with what I know, and I'm smart enough to know that cracking the County Courthouse could be tough. I'm willing to deal, so what's it going to be?''

"Why not go to the cops, smart guy?''

"I want the baby. Nothing else interests me much except her well-being. In the ordinary case, I don't give a damn what crooked lawyers do for rich clients.''

There was a dense, frosty silence. Somehow I heard nuts and bolts rattle in the lawyer's head. "Thirty minutes," he said finally. "You be here in thirty minutes. I want you to bring a clear story, or you walk.''

"Thirty minutes it is," I said. "I want you to have Rolfe, Randolf Kunkle, and George Polkis there, too.''

"No dice.''

"They have to be there or it's no deal. There is no other

way. I want to talk with everybody concerned. You really have no choice except to face a major investigation, whether you think you can beat it or not.''

More nuts and bolts rattled on the line. ''All right,'' Kunkle said. ''But you get your ass over here, and you make this good and clean.''

I bought a beer from the cashier behind the sandwich counter and walked back to the pinball machine. I shoved a nickel in the slot and played the shiny contraption. I lighted all the electric palm trees and buzzed the grass skirts on a dozen hula dancers. The machine plocked five times before the last silver ball disappeared into the mouth of an alligator near my right flipper. I sucked some beer and left the bowling alley, leaving also the five free games, food for thought, and some other sucker's faded dreams.

I parked across from the Brown Building in downtown Wichita. A gauzy darkness hovered in the plate glass windows. I hopped into evening traffic, dodging an Isadora Duncan type piloting a pink Thunderbird. Some haggard businessmen followed their flowing topcoats down the sidewalks, and one blind man in a blue engineer's cap hawked evening newspapers, shaking his tin cup like a tambourine. The purple-shaded sky exhaled a particularly eerie, pale breath; the refracted glimmering of a fading day collected in glass and metal and melted snow. A city bus gushed exhaust onto the face of an imitation Big Ben attached to the city bank. The clock was wrong, and all the clocks downtown were wrong in their own ways. I went inside the office building and took the elevator to Kunkle's office upstairs. One secretary sat behind a blond desk and a collection of silk flowers, her face a rictus O of surprise. She said almost nothing, just emitted a sigh, and ushered me to a door marked PRIVATE. I slammed the door proudly behind me after I went inside.

Where most people sprouted ears, Wilson Kunkle grew two red cabbages. His hair was serenely white, full of switchbacks and plastered spots. Bushy eyebrows circled his tiny, birdseed eyes and crashed together like surf above a pier. Translucent fat dripped from his chin and disappeared inside the slightly grimy collar of his expensive English linen shirt. He may have had a neck, but from where I stood, you couldn't quite tell. He had the red-mesh, broken face of a hard drinker.

The offices were strictly Charles Laughton by way of *Mutiny on the Bounty.* Kunkle hunched forward in a black captain's chair behind an expensive mahogany desk. Seascapes, yachts, and pictures of sunsets studded the walls, a regular bounding main. One wall held the standard oak bookcase filled with statutes, case reports, treatises; on another wall hung what appeared to be a barnacled anchor salvaged from a sunken ship. Kunkle glared at me with a Phineas T. Bluster; then sweat beads rolled from the cranny below his nose. The window behind him gave forth on the brick Forum and the Arkansas River. The sky was like a bluejay's powdery wing.

"All right," Kunkle said. "You're here. You'd best have a decent hand." His voice struck forcefully as a hammer on a baby's head.

Two leather chairs fronted the mahogany desk, and there was a leather couch catercornered from the bookcases. Nobody else was in the room.

"Where are the other boys?" I asked.

I stood still while Kunkle hawked phlegm into a white hankie. He thumbed a buzzer on his desk, and the sound echoed inside another office. Then an oak side door opened, and a short man with a round head and watery, unfocused eyes walked inside. His florid face swam lazily on a flabby neck, and his body looked held erect by string. He wore white rumpled pants gone gray from overwashing. He walked around Kunkle's desk and stood in the pale light with his arms folded nervously.

"Nice you could make it," I said. "You must be Dr. Rolfe."

Rolfe shifted his weight and ran a stubby finger along his nose. "You've got nothing to say," Kunkle said, looking at Rolfe. Rolfe sagged against the desk.

The others came inside together. George Polkis barely fit through the door frame. His shoulders under the padding of his black pin-striped suit were the width of college goalposts, his jaw square as a lantern. Fluffy black and gray hair billowed from an open black sport shirt. The Probate judge was behind Polkis; they strode in quick, rigid formation.

The judge was a thin monster with a beak nose and jagged cheekbones. His off-white hair swept back from a frosty forehead. His blue eyes pierced a well-defined skull, and he wore an impeccable brown suit and an impeccable red tie and an impeccable red kerchief in the left pocket of his impeccable coat. His shoes were buff, shiny as new money and hand stitched. Waves of expensive cigar smoke trailed the judge to a spot near the office window. Polkis leaned against the door behind me. Stares clanked around the room like infantry on Bosworth Field.

Polkis stiffened and pulled a cigarette from his suit pocket. His ruddy face was pockmarked, his eyes like steel-blue ice. "This guy is a joke," Polkis said without anger, enunciating the words like a scientific theory. His voice was rough and cogent, with a touch of gravel. The Probate judge smoked his cigar and pursed his lips, enjoying the tension and the taste of the cigar.

"We'll hear him out," the judge said. "Joke or not, we'll hear him out. Then we'll put it to a vote. Naturally, my brother and I will have the only votes, as we agreed." The judge looked at me. "We'll listen carefully. This is just business. We've done nothing illegal, you understand."

Polkis leaned against the office door. He sucked his cigarette viciously. "It's all in a day's work to me, but from the look of this guy, we ought to take him off right now. Our operation has been damaged enough already without this guy poking his head in. Suppose we stop the bus and let him get off."

"That's fine," said the judge. "We've heard your opinion. We'll let this gentleman have his say, then take a vote."

The judge smiled at me with his best, most authoritative smile, slightly condescending and fatherly. The pennies in my pocket turned blue, and my hands shook slightly. Outside, a few scrawny stars twinkled in the southeast.

"I want to make a deal," I said. "In the first place, I could have gone to the cops. We'll call it good faith that I didn't. I've told you that I don't want to ruin my chance of getting the baby back by making unnecessary trouble. I don't see any virtue in making a case out of your business arrangement, when all I want is the baby. I'm not stupid, and I know what kind of clout you guys have. But I have some information that could hurt you seriously, and I want to trade it in on the assurance you'll give me back the baby. It's a risk for both parties, I suppose, but it's a risk I think we can both afford to run."

"He's loaded," Polkis said aside.

"Patience, George," the judge said. He waved with his hand. Wilson Kunkle swept a steeple from his stomach and ran two greasy hands through the sweaty strands of hair pasted to his head. "Let's hear your proposal," the judge said. "You haven't got much time, as far as I'm concerned."

"Ritchie Polkis has to fall for two murders. I don't care how you arrange it, but he has to fall."

The room was suddenly as quiet as Hiroshima on Sunday morning. Polkis launched onto the balls of his feet, color draining from his streamlined face, the edges purple with anger. The judge paced to the window and stared outside at the evening star.

"Let me have him," Polkis growled. I remembered with fondness my gun stashed in the Ford.

"Ritchie Polkis killed Cleveland Saunders," I said. "He killed Bonnie Cobb this afternoon in Sim Park. If we play this straight, then I go to the police with everything I know, and they sit on Ritchie for a while and maybe he cracks and spills the beans. I don't know how tough he is under spotlights, but he might ruin everything for you guys. Even if they don't believe my evidence about your business arrangement, those two murders look bad for you boys."

"He's bluffing, Judge," Polkis said. "Take him off."

The judge turned from the window. His thin face was satanic in the purple glow. "Suppose you make it clear what you know," he began. "It seems this is the only way you can inspire me to continue to listen. What you've proposed already is outrageous."

"All right," I said. "I know that Rolfe spots girls who might be willing to give up their babies. I suppose Wilson here provides the wealthy clients, perhaps through his contacts in high places; it doesn't really matter. You use George and Ritchie as muscle, to make sure the undecided don't stay that way, and to give the reluctant a runaround. Rolfe substitutes birth certificates at the County Hospital. The Probate Court files a phony birth certificate, and the real birth disappears because no record of it is ever made in actuality. The Probate judge arranges for the adoption of a child who never really existed in the first place. It is very tidy and maybe not that illegal, like you say, but I wouldn't take it to the Bar Association in a silver wrapper."

The judge turned slowly from the window. "And why would Ritchie Polkis go so far out of line as this?"

The quiet increased and drained indelibly through the

room. Rolfe broke a fancy sweat and rubbed his hands mechanically.

"I suppose everything worked smoothly for a time. The state is satisfied because the birth is registered, and consent forms appear as if by magic. Rolfe substitutes the certificates so nobody can be touched if something happens years later to arouse suspicion. After all, what good would it do to find a baby who never really existed? But Cleveland Saunders came to my house with one of the forged certificates. I don't know what made him search his records, maybe something I said to him when we talked. But Ritchie Polkis was watching my house, saw the doctor, and killed him."

"You can't think we ordered that," the judge said. "That would be purely foolish."

"I think you might kill a man for enough money. Besides, if the forged certificate ever turns up, then you're tied to the Booth Home and Rolfe and the nonexistent babies. The police wouldn't take two days to turn up dozens of fake adoptions, and even if they couldn't tie you boys to the scheme, that would be the end of your business arrangement, the end of all that lovely money, and the beginning of some very nasty explaining."

Rolfe turned lime-green. He leaned over Wilson Kunkle and placed his sweating hands on the lawyer's shoulder. "I don't want anything to do with this," he squealed. "That girl was killed in front of the Home. My God."

"Shut up, you fool," Kunkle said coolly.

"Fool? I'm a fool?" Rolfe shouted. "I told you about that cretin. I told you." George Polkis pushed away from the door. The judge wheeled and pulled Rolfe away from the desk, and Polkis shoved him against the bookshelves. The two men stood huffing and puffing.

"Gentlemen, please," the judge said. He looked back at me as Rolfe panted. "You've given me no motive for Ritchie to actually kill Saunders. After all, you can't prove he even knew Saunders had the certificate on him when he died."

"Ritchie didn't pay the Cobbs the five thousand dollars you boys promised. He embezzled from you. His motive to kill Saunders was as much to hide that fact as to stop Saunders from talking to me."

Color drained from the judge's face, and as he looked at his brother crouched behind the mahogany desk, some uncertainty seeped into his eyes.

"He wouldn't do it," Polkis said. "This guy is running a scam. My brother wouldn't take such a risk on account of me."

"The family hired me because they didn't get paid," I said.

The judge said, "It's a possibility, George. You have to really see it as a possibility." He walked across the plush carpet and puffed some cigar smoke into my face. Then he placed a bony hand on George's chest and George fell back to the door. Rolfe shook himself and stiffened.

"What is your proposal in concrete terms?" asked the judge. "My friend Mr. Polkis is ordinarily a rather calm individual. I also presume he is willing to assume responsibility for his younger brother, a man prominent in this arrangement because, shall we say, of his fecundity. I think we all agree that he was temporary. George here will do what we decide. Isn't that right, George?" The judge said it to me, but he was talking to George. George waved a hand.

"This is going to be rich," he said.

"Like I said, I want you to arrange for Ritchie to take a fall for the murders. I don't care how you do it, but I want him to go down for it. Then I want you to deliver the baby to me at my place on Sycamore on Saturday morning, along with five thousand dollars that was supposed to be paid to the Cobbs."

The judge stared at me with his flinty eyes. "And so you expect to make a profit of five thousand dollars."

"We both make a profit," I said. "The five thousand shouldn't matter to you. It was already spent."

"And the certificate?"

"I return it when the baby comes back."

"Why this concern with the baby?"

"It will keep the Cobbs quiet. Otherwise, they go to the police. They don't know the scheme." This was a lie, and I told it with utter seriousness.

"You want me to believe you're in this for five thousand dollars?" asked the judge.

"I'd sell my mother to Mao Tse-tung for five thousand dollars. It's more than I make in a year."

The judge looked over at George Polkis. I could hear him breathing behind me. "I say the kid delivered the five thousand," George said.

"You propose we continue our enterprise?" the judge said.

"I don't care," I said.

Wilson Kunkle leaned forward above his desk. "I think it is going to be hard to trust him, Randolf," said Wilson Kunkle. "Blackmail isn't a viable alternative for us."

"What do you say to that?" the judge asked me.

"No blackmail, just business. I want to live too much to go back on my word at this point. I don't doubt George and his ability to take me off. I just want my money."

"You're selling us back the certificate."

"If you want it that way. I also want Ritchie."

The judge smiled an insouciant, self-regarding smile, his narrow face opening like a nut. Behind him, Wilson Kunkle flipped on a brass lamp, flooding the office with an organdy glow. Cigar smoke drifted ambiently.

"Randolf?" Wilson said.

"Wilson?" the judge said.

"You know Ritchie is crazy," Rolfe said.

"Shut up, Rolfe," Wilson said. "I vote we give this guy one chance."

"I agree," the judge said. "We'll leave the details to George." He turned to George. "I want you to investigate what our friend here has to say about your brother. I think you know what this means to all of us. If he didn't pay over the money, then we've got a very serious problem. May I trust you with those details, George?"

George took three steps forward on the carpet. His shoes were black loafers with tassels, shiny as a postcard cover. He stood staring into my eyes with a fierce hatred.

"You know, Ritchie has done some crazy things in his time," George said. "You're wrong about the money, and when I find out, I'll hurt you so badly you'll wish you were never born. You'll curse your mother for having you. We have a very nice proposition here, and my brother would never cheat the family." George grinned and tapped me on the chest. "Hey," he said. "Don't worry, punk. Meet me at Eddie's Bar on Maple Street downtown tomorrow night at six. If there's a problem with Ritchie, we can discuss it over beer like men. Deal?"

"I'll be there," I said.

"That's settled, then," the judge said. "I'll leave it for you two to work out."

George smiled and eased into a corner. I slipped out the door and went down the elevator and outside to a dark, cold night. Beyond the old hotels and saloons downtown, above the eastern verge of trees and apartment houses, blue and orange stars burned on the horizon, Spica sapphire, Regulus red and orange. I drove home and parked beside the rabbit hutch and spent two hours cleaning house, washing dishes, ironing shirts, and picking up books. I made some chili and drank three or four beers and read chess books until the thought of sleep appeared in my window. I tossed in a tangle of sheets and remembered

what Nimzovitch had said about chess: It's not who makes
the most mistakes, but who makes the last mistake.

⁻I dreamed of Cynthia Wunderland, but the dreams were
remorseful and sad, a landscape ruined as wheat after hail.

SEVENTEEN

My rooms floated in foggy silence, amber lambence of cigarette smoke and sunshine. I had showered and had pulled on a blue Shetland turtleneck, a pair of woolen trousers, and a battered leather jacket my father had worn. In my dreams there were no oranges or lemons, no jackpots, no pair of silky legs to kiss, and so I sat drinking coffee in the silence, fading myself into an ordered and somber loneliness that passed for life.

I leaned into the fuzzy warmth of my gray overstuffed chair and thought—there was a lot to think about. I thought about the occasional rattling wind, imagining it wild in the barren elms, in the one forlorn catalpa, hearing the wind as it moved through the vagrant limbs as if through the skeletal remains of huge animals, the elms screeching and shuddering like ancient fingers. I thought about the brown, squat image of the buildings of all Wichita poured out beyond the sluggish wintry river, wavery and stolid in late afternoon, a poor stack of weatherbeaten tombstones plopped accidentally onto the endless dun prairie. There was the Wichita of trailer houses, tenements, saloons, and gaudy cinemas, the endless, pathless stretch of brick and mortar and wood arranged in anonymous row upon row to the purlieus and beyond to the horizon, where the town's body outdistanced itself into train yards, junk lots, and garish nightclubs until nothing remained but the endless whispering grass.

There were the Quaker and Mexican neighborhoods as well, and the Friends' clock tower bathed in purple sun, the sun sinking through the vast waving elm limbs. There were the lovemaking, whoremongering, and drinking; the beatings and the caresses, all the strange and marvelous contradictions of life; and there were the ballpark and the orange boxcars; and, suspended above in the pale, winter-washed sky, some child's red box kite flying, delicate and threatening as summer rain. And there was George Polk-is.

I knew how it would be at Eddie's Bar. George would wear his gray suit and black shirt. He would have on his shiny, dangerous black shoes with leather tassels. His meaty fingers would be clean and perfectly manicured and very strong, and he would sit hunched over the bar sipping beer, neon bleeding into the sharp jaw, smoothing itself along the boneless features of his forehead. His eye would be the steel color of the flank of a shark, and it would glide silently as if underwater. He would ask me what I thought I was doing. I would have no answer.

I rose then and scrambled up the back stairs of the old house and pounded on the door to Mrs. Thompson's upstairs apartment. She scuttled to the door and pulled it open slowly.

"Mr. Mitch, Mr. Mitch!" she yelled in her deafness. She stood there unsteadily, surprised and pleased, bundled in her tattered housecoat, her face an aged wad of wrinkles and uncertainty. I went inside the apartment, into the dry heat and closeness. She peered over my shoulder as I wrote a message in big letters on a Big Chief tablet:

I NEED YOUR HELP, MRS. THOMPSON. IF I
DON'T COME BACK TONIGHT FOR ANY REA-

SON, PLEASE GIVE THIS MESSAGE TO MY
FRIEND ANDY LANHAM AT THE POLICE DE-
PARTMENT: ANDY, I'VE LEFT TO MEET
GEORGE POLKIS AT EDDIE'S BAR ON MAPLE. I
MET WITH THE LAWYERS KUNKLE AND REID
AND THEY ADMITTED THE BABY SCAM. I'VE
MAILED BACK THE CERTIFICATE, AND IT'S A
FORGERY. DR. ROLFE AT THE BOOTH HOME
FORGES THE CERTIFICATES. START WITH HIM
AND YOU'RE HOME FREE. YOU'VE BEEN MY
BEST FRIEND IN LIFE. WHAT THE HELL.

Mrs. Thompson took the note in her small hands and
she read, her head bobbing like a cork on a windy pond.
She looked up, and in her eyes I saw a frightened question.
I pecked her cheek and smiled and squeezed her hand,
and she smiled back and folded the note into the pocket
of her housecoat. I went down the back stairs and got into
the Ford and headed for Eddie's. Long shadows hung in
the empty streets. Here and there orange and blue neon
popped. The sky seemed clear and pale as a woman's silk
handkerchief. Spring was somewhere, somewhere. I
steamed to a halt in front of a flashing beer sign, lit a
cigarette, and walked inside the bar.

In the 1930s and 1940s Eddie's had been a cheerful
baseball bar. Later, it became a workers' hangout when
the airplane factories began to churn out planes for the
war. Soon, foundry workers and grease factory employees
made it their home. Now, however, it was just a sloppy
dive for punks and toughs, for gamblers and squalid small-
timers, grifters, and weasels. I stood there in silhouette,
surrounded by rainbow outbursts of Wurlitzer light, smoke,
hushed murmurs, and the curious disembodied swish
common to taverns and beer bars everywhere. A row of
dark oaken booths stretched to the rear of the old building.
On my right, a big mahogany bar was backed by a huge
mirror. Black domino tables littered the place, some filled

by old men, their heads bent above beer and bones. Some
high school toughs clutched a pinball machine like sailors
on a life raft. I knew that somewhere in the dim recesses
of the back rooms, rooms where poker and dice were
played, where heists were planned, would be George Polkis. I angled to the bar and sat on a stool at the end, a wall
on my right, the door on my left.

The bartender needed a shave. He was a half-pint guy,
the type who would carry a big chip on his shoulder from
being small. He had thinning gray hair and ragged,
splotched skin and a fleshy gooseneck. He hitched at the
white smock he wore, then leaned a tatooed arm on a
gallon jar of pickled eggs.

"What's your pleasure, pal?" he said. His watery eyes
were bland as Tuesday night's wrestling card. Behind his
shoulder an ancient waitress chopped blood sausage on a
white plate. I sat Jesse James style, protecting my view of
the bar against danger.

"Beer and an egg," I said.

"If you want to eat, we've got ham, corn bread, and
beans." The beer clock on the wall read six-fifteen. The
sweat inside my turtleneck had turned to steam; nervous
mist probably rose from my body.

"Thanks, just the beer and egg." As the bartender
walked away, the front door opened, allowing a shaft of
purple and a sandy-haired tough guy dressed in jeans and
cowboy boots inside. The tough guy had big arms and a
big belly. He walked past the bar and the domino tables
and disappeared into the back rooms.

"Here you go, pal," the bartender said. He slammed a
beer bottle on the bar and popped the top with a church
key. The beer fizzed, bubbles pouring over the sloping
mouth of the bottle. He dug inside the gallon jar with a
fork and stabbed an egg, placed it on a paper plate, and
slid the plate to me. He flipped the fork onto the plate and
walked to the far end of the bar and stood with his arms

folded on his smock. The Wurlitzer sang Bob Wills in raspy tones.

As usual, there was nothing to do but think and drink. It seemed to me an even chance that the judge and his men would see fit to put the pressure on George to finger Ritchie. It was reasonably certain that Ritchie had never told George about his five-thousand-dollar mistake, and that George didn't know about the murders of Bonnie Cobb and Cleveland Saunders. If that were true, then there was a good chance that George would cooperate and turn Ritchie over to the police. In any event, I intended to pull the plug on the whole gang as soon as the baby was returned, and take my chances with George Polkis all alone. I hoped that George was weighing his alternatives, and deciding to preserve the lucrative baby trade, hoping that cold cash would make the difference, that George would weigh all that cold cash against the evil stupidity of his brother, and decide the cold cash was worth making a deal with me. I was ready for a double cross, but didn't have any idea where it might come from. I wanted the baby back and five thousand dollars and a chance to break the gang. If George didn't kill me instantly, then I would stand a chance. Blood and money are hard to figure, and so I gave up thinking and drank beer.

I had no gun and I had no knife and I had no blackjack. I knew it would do me no good to bring any of that to Eddie's Bar, where George had a dozen friends with guns and knives and blackjacks, and where they would search me anyway. My only insurance policy was the missing certificate and my knowledge of the forgery. I hoped I could ride that knowledge and George Polkis's love of cold cash. If not, then I'd have a broken skull and a small bullet wound in the back of my head and they'd give me a cheap funeral, and my mother and grandmother would cry and a few of my buddies would get drunk. It was little enough and better than some I'd seen.

A pay phone woke me from these lovely musings. The barkeep spoke into the black phone, then walked my way. He wiped his nose with the shoulder of his smock.

"There's a message for you from the back. I guess you're going through the back door and into the first room on the left."

"I guess I am," I said. I ate the egg and drank some more beer. Some sweat boiled away, and I gained courage.

The doorway in back led to a smoky hallway, cobwebbed by darkness. I felt a belly touch my back as the sandy-haired cowboy took my arm. Light exploded from the door on my left.

"Just take it easy," the cowboy said. His voice had an evil, easy lilt, probably from Oklahoma. He moved me against the dark wall, then patted me down. "He's clean," he said to the doorway. I walked into the light.

Polkis wasn't wearing his gray suit, but he wore the black sport shirt. A dirty jeans jacket covered his muscled arms and thick chest. His bulky, square face hovered in a netted shadow mesh, harsh glare coming from a single lamp descending upon a green felt poker table. He sat slouched and relaxed above the table, his hands and fingers spread evenly, motionless, floating above the surface of green felt as if levitated there by magic. The small room was perfectly square, every inch of the walls covered by photos of nude women in obscene poses, filthy calendars, and clippings. There were snapshots of whores and girlfriends. George puffed smoke into the lamp, then picked up a bottle of beer and drank deeply. The ugliness bore in on me like sniper fire.

"Sit down," George said.

I sat across from him at the green table. George flipped me a cigar and it rolled to a stop in front of me. I smelled the cigar and put it in my coat pocket. George smiled, and

I fingered a book of Eddie's matches. The silence and tension did doughnuts around the room

"Beer?" Polkis asked. I nodded. "Taylor, boy, get Mr. Roberts here a beer." The sandy-haired cowboy appeared, carrying two dark bottles. He set the bottles on the table and went away. We were alone. "Play poker do you?" Polkis said then. He relit his smoldering cigar from some Eddie's matches.

"Nothing serious," I said.

"You always gamble serious. Otherwise, you're pissing the wind. You lose, what fun is that?"

"My game is blackjack and craps."

"You can't back down a crap table." Polkis looked straight into me and smoked his cigar. His face was broad and flat as a shoehorn. There was five-o'clock shadow and razor scars on his cheek. Gray hair swept from his forehead, slick at the ears. He seemed a blue block of frozen ice, dangerous and unmanageable as an iceberg can be. "I like the feel of poker, making guys seriously sweat. Tables and dice, you can't make them sweat, now. I think maybe you're gambling right now."

"No way. Your brother is the gambler. He gambled he could swipe the five thousand intended for the Cobbs, and he gambled you wouldn't find out. You probably never would have if I hadn't stumbled onto the certificate."

George leaned into the glare. "I can't believe you, you know that. I can't believe you at all. What makes you think I won't stuff you down a water well?"

"Did you check the five thousand?"

"I checked it out," he said. "Maybe Ritchie did get a little carried away about the money. He lost sight of business, and it made his ideas a little crazy." Polkis relaxed and smiled. "You goddamn turd," he drawled. From his jeans jacket he extracted a barber's razor. He unfolded the silver blade and creased the green felt. "When this is over, I'm going to advertise your balls in the funny papers."

"What now?" I said.

"Now, you're going to get your wish. Ritchie is taking
a fall. Maybe he did the nigger and the kid. I could give
a damn about that. But he took the money from my business, and he let shit like you inside. For that we're going
to nail Ritchie. Nothing you said means a thing to me.
I'm doing this on account of business and nothing else. It
may be you should leave town tonight."

It was strange, I thought: He operated on his own level,
using integrity in a way I'd never thought about before.
George Polkis burned buildings, ran women from hotels
in Kansas City, and hot-wired expensive cars. He sold
some dope and gambled. But he paid his gambling debts,
and he didn't beat up hitchikers. He killed only for money,
and probably the people he killed had it coming anyway.
It was an integrity that separated him from some cops and
all politicians.

George said, "You know where Axel's Steak House
is?"

"Twenty-ninth and Broadway," I said.

"Yeah. You be in the parking lot of the lumber yard
across the street tonight at midnight. Don't be fucking
late. Sit there and be quiet. I'll be along, and then you'll
see Ritchie take a dive. Don't bring any brass bands and
don't bring any cops, and don't bother to bring a gun; it
won't do you any good. I'll tear out your heart if you do.
You ever kill anybody before?"

"Plenty," I said.

"Yeah?"

"Mostly Germans. I didn't mind that at all. I killed
some Italians, and didn't like it."

"You were in the war, huh?"

"All of it."

Polkis stood, looking in the wavery light as if he were
twenty feet tall. "Some smart guy," he said. "Tonight
will be a treat for all of us, then. Maybe we'll even have

us a wiener roast.'' Polkis walked out the door and was gone.

Something small crawled to the back of my brain and nested. I remembered talking to Andy about Polkis and about his fondness for arson. I remembered the trick at the bingo parlor that had left Little Bear a scorched hunk of meat. I smoked a cigarette and listened to cowboy music seep through obscene pictures. Glaze from the naked bulb flared on the photos' glossy surfaces. The small thing in my brain shuddered, then shook its filmy wings, eyes aglow, vulgar neck craning, two spiked shoulders green and garish orange.

I stood with my cigar and matches and shoved them in my coat for later. I walked into the penumbral hallway. The sandy-haired cowboy was leaning against the back door.

"Just leaving," I said.

"Be my guest," he said. I walked into the hallway, and the cowboy shook his thumb toward the rear exit. "Shit goes out the back," he said. I fell through the back door into a clear, starry night. My breath frosted the air, and the small thing in my brain screeched and soared away.

I drove home and made fresh coffee and sat in lamplight reading a volume of Rubinstein's chess games. I lost myself then in the mystical lushness and freedom of the master's play, the slowly enveloping density of his ideas, the inexplicable and ultimately corrosive subtlety and baroque sensibility. For a time I imagined the Ukranian Jew, a short, intense man in a black suit, his beard a coiling gray expanse, his cigar a black smudge pot. I imagined the incredibly frail old man bent awkwardly above a shining chess board in a high-ceilinged, cold tournament hall, some old hotel in Carlsbad or Riga, the smell of apple orchards and oak and cigar smoke in the air, the hall quiet save for the steady hiss from gas lamps. I imagined, too, the densely forested river slope slashing across the coun-

tryside, falling suddenly upward from a cold river, and in
the rolling fog, dark carriages clattering on cobblestone.
And, for Rubinstein, there had been the horrible torment
of the First World War, a tumult that led to his starvation
and his death, a man whose only thoughts were of chess
and God, killed by a war made from money and madness.
I set my alarm for eleven-thirty and tried to sleep.

At ten minutes before midnight I was in the car driving
north into the wasteland of Broadway, cruising past railroad yards, refineries, cheap Mexican restaurants, and junk
stores that clutter the North End, dotting it like pox on a
whore's face. The night was unusually clear, the truck
stops noisy and crowded. The car bounced over the brick
street, and I felt the sweat return to collect under the neck
of my sweater, fear and uncertainty rising through me,
invading the subdued yellow gleam inside the car. I found
Twenty-ninth Street and turned onto a drab dirt road lined
by old cottonwoods.

Orion descended the western horizon, glittering in the
deep sky. There were no streetlights and no houses, just
shacks, some vacant lots, warehouses, horse pastures, and
barns, verging onto the sandy mush of river bottom. I
drove a mile along the dirt lane, spotted the lumber yard
and the squatty white form of Axel's Steak House.

I parked in the rocky lot of the lumberyard and looked
across the street at Axel's, forty yards away through hedge
and cottonwood. Axel was a Lebanese from the old
school—pinky rings and nosehair and dollar bills—who
ran a clean steak-and-seafood place. There had been some
slot machines in the back once, but the steaks were honest
and lean and always cooked rare. The drinks were honest
too, and that was saying a lot in Kansas. The building
itself was a square luminescent barn with a sloping roof:
I knew the place inside: a dance floor surrounded by tables
and a line of big booths, raised dance bandstand in one
corner, bar and kitchen near the front door. The place was

dark as coal, and someone had painted the walls garishly with shiny portraits of hula dancers, bullfighters, and airplanes. The juke had plenty of Rosemary Clooney and Vaughn Monroe.

I sat there in the dark car, smoking cigarettes.

In time, a maroon Ford rumbled to a stop, clouds of invisible dust rising in the white corridor of headlight beam. Polkis cut the lights, stepped from the car, and stuck his head inside my Ford.

"You ready?" he said. Polkis wore black gloves and a black felt hat.

"I'm ready," I said.

"Get in my car," he said. I sat and he swung the maroon Ford into Twenty-ninth Street and bumped across the dirt road. A faint moon illuminated the cottonwoods. Polkis parked the car in deep shadow, and I looked across an open pasture at the tiny, twinkling lights of another world.

Polkis drew a revolver and aimed it at my stomach. He smiled and the moonglow ignited his face. My heart raced as I stared at the muzzle.

"You know," Polkis said, "something tells me Axel forgot to lock his back door tonight." Polkis waved the gun and I opened the door and he motioned me to the trunk of the car. Polkis handed me the keys. "Open the trunk," he said. I did and saw two gallon cans of gasoline. "Grab them," he said.

"Don't do this," I said.

"Grab them," he said. I walked ahead of Polkis to the back door of the steak house. The only sounds were miles away on Broadway, big trucks chugging north and south with beef and oil and pipe. Polkis put the gun in my back and we went inside the building.

We stood in the kitchen. I felt one of my legs against the cast-iron leg of an industrial oven. The oven was as large as a Ping-Pong table. Cabinets circled the room, and there were deep-fat fryers, some smaller bread ovens, worktables, and heavy cutting boards. Polkis pushed me through some swinging doors, and we walked onto the darkened dance floor. The only light was some blood red from exit signs. Polkis stopped me with an arm.

"Drop one of those cans by the side entrance. Spread the gas around."

"Don't do this. You don't need to do this."

"Get busy. You wouldn't want to go with him, would you?"

"You wouldn't kill him for five thousand."

"You got the idea?"

"A wiener roast," I said. "Why don't you just finger him for the arson. That's all I want, anyway."

"What you want doesn't count. The kitchen is going up like a bomb. We don't want anyone to get out the other doors, do we? Not if we're going to do it right."

"I can't," I said.

"I'll kill you right now if you don't."

I poured out the gasoline and Polkis shoved me across the room and motioned for me to pour gas on the drapes which covered a fire exit. I doused the drapes and watched for a chance to jump Polkis. He stood ten feet away, the gun leveled. Then he motioned me back to the kitchen and handed me some Eddie's matches.

"Light the oven," he said. Polkis turned on the gas and I poked a match in a hole. The oven exploded into fire. Polkis kicked closed the oven door. "The son of a bitch who pours gas under that oven is going to burn." Polkis lit the other stove himself, and some of the fryers.

"You can't kill your brother," I said.

"I got three brothers," he said languidly. "I only got one sweet racket like this baby thing. Nobody steals from me, not even my own brother. This is strictly business, strictly a money proposition. "Let's go," he said.

We went out the back door and got inside the maroon

car and Polkis drove across the street to the lot. He stopped
the car beside my own Ford and we sat in darkness.

George lowered the gun to his lap and we sat there
staring at the night. "You're not half-bad," said George.
"Still, I'd leave town if I were you. You return that certificate to me, and then you leave town. I can't help but
like your style, but it wouldn't do for you to stay in town."

"Sure," I said.

"Fine," George said. He unfolded some bills from his
jeans jacket. "Five thousand dollars," he said. I took the
money. "The baby will be at your place tomorrow morning. Rolfe will bring her. I don't know what the hell you
want that kid for. She's worth fifty grand on the open
market. But, it's your party."

We waited then, silently. There was a beer bottle in the
front seat, and I worked my thumb into its open mouth.
At two o'clock in the morning a green Chevy pickup truck
descended the sandy lane and turned into the dark treed
lot behind Axel's. I watched Ritchie Polkis drag a ten gallon gasoline can from the bed of the truck, stuff rags in
the pocket of his pants, and move away to the back door.
Minutes passed and I watched George stare out the window of the car, the gun leveled at my side.

The explosion funneled black night. An impossible stink
rose as red flame erupted from the steak house chimney.
The blast shuddered and died. George Polkis leaned across
and opened the car door. I got out, and he gunned the car
and drove away down Twenty-ninth Street.

I drove across the street and through Axel's parking lot
as the building gushed flame. I dropped the beer bottle,
the cigar, and a book of Eddie's matches in the parking
lot, then drove quickly to Broadway, then south into downtown and home. I could hear fire engines clanging. The
dark thing flew behind me all the way.

EIGHTEEN

Night hugged a southbound Santa Fe. The freight hugged the night back, the throb of its slow progress like an echo across the prairie. I sat in a swamp of pipe smoke and yellow lamplight reading E. A. Robinson, allowing the song of each verse to surround me and my overstuffed chair as the pain, surprise, and exhaustion seeped away. A few dark sounds intruded, the bleat of a night hawk, the whoosh of a kite hunting insects, the ragged yowl of alley cats. I made some coffee and later studied some games from the great New York tournament of 1927. Before dawn, Rolfe brought the baby.

Rolfe mounted the stairs, a vacant shadow huddled at the screen door. An orb of lamplight enfolded his knees, and he stood in the doorway panting.

"All right," I said.

Rolfe stepped inside the cold room holding a bundle in pink blankets. The bundle was quiet.

"I've got her," Rolfe said nervously. Rolfe wore checkered pants and a bulky gray sweater. His face glistened from sweat and fear. He walked slowly to the brass bed and deposited the bundle at the foot of the bed on an olive-drab blanket. Then he stumbled a few steps back toward the door. "Now, you keep your part of the bargain." His voice twitched.

"Get out of my sight," I said.

"I'm telling you," Rolfe stuttered, "if you don't keep quiet, you know what will happen to you. We've made a deal."

Rolfe faded another flutter step toward the screen. Some morning doves cooed far away and the sparrows chirped. Rolfe formed a noose with his hands, then twisted them together the way I had seen him twist his hands in Kunkle's office.

"Did you know Cleveland Saunders?" I asked.

"Yes. I'm sorry it happened. It wasn't meant to happen that way."

"Saunders thought you were trash."

Rolfe went out the screen door and down the steps. Then I sat on the edge of the bed and phoned Jack Graybul. I studied the wrinkled baby face, beet-red and simply formed, the face of an old man or a saint, a face that didn't know the world and all its pain, a face that would never gaze upon its natural mother's own face, a sad, lost face, an orphaned face. I walked to the kitchen and found a large box and stuffed the box with blankets and put the baby softly in the box. I heard Jack's car pull in the leafy driveway and stop in some evergreen shadows. Jack walked up the stairs and came inside.

"You've got the baby," he said.

"She's asleep. She looks fine."

"You'll maybe tell me about this someday."

"Read the papers tomorrow."

"It sounds serious."

"I'm afraid it is serious."

"I don't want to do anything illegal or shady. You know that. You know I trust you on this, trust you not to lead me down the primrose path. I need my ticket to practice law."

"You know I'd never do that, Jack. The baby's mother

is dead. Her name was Bonnie Cobb, and she was murdered in Sim Park yesterday afternoon.''

"I heard about it on the news. The cops don't have many leads, I guess.''

"The grandparents are alive, but they won't give you any trouble with consent. I'm sure of it.''

"They'd need to consent. They're the natural guardians now that the mother is dead. What about the father?''

"He's dead, too.''

"That's tough,'' Jack said. He wandered to the box and looked inside. "Hardly born, and already an orphan. That's very tough.'' Jack lifted the box from the bed and cradled it under his arm. "I talked to that couple from Kansas City I told you about. You don't need to worry, Mitch; they'll take good care of this baby. She'll make it. They're awfully good people.''

"I'm glad to hear that, Jack.'' I took the five thousand dollars from my jacket pocket and handed it to the lawyer. "That's five thousand, Jack. Don't mind where it came from, but it belongs to the baby. I want you to put it in trust for her and manage the investment. Whatever the adoption costs, I want you to take your fee from the money.''

"There's no fee, Mitch. This one is on the house.''

"When the baby is eighteen, the money is to go to the kid, wherever she is.''

"Check,'' Jack said. "She'll be fine. I know she will. I'll keep track of her for you. I'll bet you'd like to meet her one day when you're old and gray. It would be a fine thing.''

"That might be a fine thing at that. It doesn't look like I'll have any kids of my own.''

"Never say die,'' Jack said. He walked through the screen door and down the steps and drove away. Gray had tinged the black sky, and from the backyard I heard the sounds of rabbits sputtering in their cages, the neighbor's chickens clucking. Some wrens warmed up for morning with scales, trills, and warbles in stacatto descent. I walked to the backyard and watered the rabbits and then stood looking at the sky—thin pink strands tracing the eastern horizon where a few stars winked out. The morning promised a new warmth, and from the black fecund earth there issued spring's promise, new birth, greenery, hope. I walked around the silent, sleeping house and stood by the droopy porch. A scent of cigar smoke drifted in the somber light, and as I ascended the creaky steps, I noticed the big form of Andy Lanham. He sat in shadow with his elbows on his knees sucking a cigar. His dark suit hung around him like limp barbed wire. A felt hat was pushed back on his head, revealing a miasma of tangled red hair. He looked like an old man waiting for the bus.

"Andy?" I said weakly.

"Mitch," he answered. "I haven't been home in two days. My kids think I'm a salesman or an uncle come to visit." Mauve-and-coral arms snaked in the morning sky. The cardinals and jays joined the wrens in song. Just as suddenly, the night crickets ceased.

"Do you want some coffee?" I asked.

"I could use some coffee," Andy said. I went into the house and returned to the porch with two mugs. Andy leaned against the porch rail and dropped his hat into a rocker. He sipped coffee as in the gray light some cars rumbled past on Sycamore. Andy lit a cigar and sucked it to a red circle. "We picked up the old Indian in El Dorado yesterday. We sobered him up, and he was scared and babbled a lot, something about leading his people home. But later he said enough about the Little Bear fire that we can use it on George Polkis. In fact, we were going to pick George up on suspicion, but we never made it. I guess you heard about the fire at Axel's this evening?"

"I heard."

"You heard that Ritchie died in the explosion?"

"Now, how would I hear about that?"

"Maybe you just heard."

"Maybe the Cubs will win the pennant this season."

"More likely you heard about Ritchie."

"What about George?" I asked.

"Damn funny about George," Andy said. "The Arson boys covered Axel's parking lot and found a beer bottle with George's prints all over it. They found a pack of Eddie's matches and one of George's cigars. Everybody knows the brand he smokes. You wouldn't think George would leave his calling cards all over an arson job. You wouldn't think he'd make a mess and wait for the cops to find it."

"It's nice luck for the cops," I said. I drank some coffee and leaned against the porch balustrade. Dawn broke fully above the ballpark, sending cerise tentacles into the sky. A dairy truck parked at the end of the block, and a chunky fellow in a white suit began his deliveries.

"We arrested George on the bingo parlor job. We charged him with murder. When we arrested him, we charged him with arson, too. We also searched his car and found a twenty-two target pistol. It went through Ballistics already, and the gun we found is the gun that killed Cleveland Saunders. That's another nice piece of luck. Now that we can put George on the scene of the Axel fire, we can really put some heat under him." Andy laughed grimly. He sipped some coffee and rubbed his raw face. "There's another problem in the case, though. I wonder if you'd like to make a guess about what it is?"

"I'd rather not guess."

"Fine. I'll tell you, then. I can imagine why George killed Little Bear in the bingo parlor fire. Axel was in debt and the business was going, so I can tell you why Ritchie Polkis was torching the place. But, Mitch, when we found Ritchie, he wasn't anything but roasted meat. The job somebody did on Ritchie is just like the job George did

on Little Bear. I just can't figure out why a man would
kill his own brother. Give me a motive, Mitch.''

I drained my coffee and sat down in a rocker. Andy put
on his hat and sat down beside me.

"Bonnie Cobb's parents called me last week.''

"The little girl who was killed.''

"Yes. She'd had a baby by Ritchie Polkis, and the Polkis boys had taken the baby from her. She wanted it back.
I followed Ritchie around a bit and flushed him to a meeting with Wilson Kunkle. I told you I searched Ritchie's
house that night and caught a look at his pistol. It didn't
mean anything to me until I heard Cleveland Saunders was
killed with a twenty-two target pistol. I couldn't help but
wonder why George and Ritchie would go to Kunkle's office.''

"This the Kunkle with a brother who's Probate judge?''

"Yes. Later I went to see Cleveland Saunders because
he had delivered the baby. It was a long shot, and he didn't
really help me much. When Saunders was killed that night,
I knew it had to be because of the certificate he had in his
coat pocket. I decided then that Ritchie had killed him,
but I didn't know why. I'd seen George cruise by my house
that day, so I also knew that someone had tipped them that
I was on the case.''

"This makes me very unhappy,'' Andy said.

"I went to El Dorado on a hunch. I found the old Indian
drunk, and his woman told me he knew something about
the bingo fire. I told you about that.''

"Go on, damn it.''

"On the way back, I told you those deputies beat me
up.''

"You told me.''

"They were working for the Probate judge.''

"Randolf Kunkle,'' Andy said.

"The very same.''

A resigned look haunted Andy's face. "It had to be,''

he said. "It just had to be. It's probably the whole damn courthouse."

"I took the certificate to Saunders's widow, and she told me that the signature was a forgery. Saunders's name was on the certificate, but it wasn't his signature. A Dr. Rolfe at the Booth Home created a false birth, and signed Saunders's name to it. He knew Saunders delivered hundreds and hundreds of babies and probably wouldn't remember anything about any of them after a time."

"Why the fake certificate?"

"With no real record of the baby, there's no real record of its parents, either. It would make tracing the false adoptions almost impossible."

"Who is in on the cut?"

"The Probate judge, his brother, Rolfe and Polkis."

"What's the take?"

"Fifty thousand dollars in some cases."

Andy whistled. "So Ritchie killed Saunders and panicked before he found the certificate."

"Yes. He was out of control."

"That can't be why George killed his brother. It's too thin."

"Polkis was to pay the Cobbs five thousand dollars for 'expenses.' Ritchie took the money and threatened the Cobbs."

"Ritchie stole from his brother. And the Cobbs sold their daughter's baby."

"Yes. I'm afraid that's how it was. I confronted the boys at their office downtown yesterday. I told them I wanted Ritchie to take a fall. They took me quite literally."

"I don't want to hear it. It doesn't matter."

"Thanks, Andy."

"If anybody wants to know, you were with me last night when the explosion took place. We were here playing chess and drinking beer, listening to the radio."

"You don't have to do that, Andy. I'm not asking."

"You don't have to ask. We stick to that story."

"Thanks, Andy. But if George beats this rap, I'm in bad shape."

"I suppose that's right," Andy said. He thought for a while. "I'm surprised George didn't take you off."

"They knew I had the certificate. I told them all I wanted was the five thousand dollars and I'd forget all about it. I told them I was only interested in money, that I didn't care a damn what rich lawyers did with rich clients."

Andy smiled. "You lied," he said.

For a time we sat drinking coffee. I lit a cigarette and drifted smoke into the pearly morning air. A sun slice peeped above the riverbank. Already I knew, the grounds crew at the ballpark would be hanging bunting on the grandstands. They would be mowing the green grass, and vendors would be readying their tickets. There were already a few cars in the parking lot of the ballpark, early birds for the big game.

Andy stood and leaned against the porch rail. He looked at the ballpark and sighed. "Dodgers and Braves," he said languidly. He looked at the ground. "I'd like to go home and take a long shower. Then I'd like to take off my wife's clothes, piece by piece, and just look at her. Then I'd like to lie down with her all morning. Then I'd like to have a big breakfast and take my kids to the game and eat a hot dog and drink a cold beer. You know what I mean?"

"I know what you mean."

"I never thought I'd say this, Mitch, but maybe you should think about getting married." Andy put on his hat and walked down the steps and stopped in the yard. The soft day had become blue. Mrs. Thompson scuttled around the driveway, pecking at paper and weeds. Francis the cat followed her, flicking his tail, a drowsy grin on his face. Then the ballpark scurried alive, cars and kids and vendors arriving in waves, getting there early for the big game, waiting for the teams to arrive. And that was the way it is in a minor league town. You sit and you watch the grass grow and the stars wheel and you wait, all for the glorious moment when you glimpse Duke Snider or Eddie Mathews, that magical instant when life glows and you know you'll have something to talk about for the rest of your life, the time you saw Pee Wee Reese play baseball in Wichita, and then you know on your deathbed you won't say something stupid like "more light," but you'll say something smart instead, something like "God, wasn't that Campanella some kind of catcher?" And in that last moment of your life you hope God allows baseball in heaven, and that you're going there and they'll have grass and peanuts and cheering fans.

"You'd better give me the certificate," Andy said from the yard.

"It's in the mail."

"This is going to be tough," Andy said. "We have to take on a Probate judge and a rich lawyer and George Polkis, not to mention that doctor what's-his-name."

"Rolfe."

"Yeah, Rolfe. We have to take on the whole court system. If we don't make this bust stick, Nome, Alaska, won't be too far away for us to run and hide." Andy slapped his thigh. "If we don't make this stick, Polkis will have our hide. Are you ready for that?"

"I am," I said. "Are you?"

Andy looked away, studying the blue sky. "Where should we start?"

Mrs. Thompson hobbled up the porch steps and sat in the porch swing, smiling. We always sat together in the morning, Mrs. Thompson quietly humming to herself while I petted the cat and watched children walk to school.

"Rolfe is ripe," I said. "Tap on him and he'll crumble. There's also a kid at the Booth Home named Lurleen Cur-

tis. I think the Polkis boys had their hooks in her. Bonnie Cobb was going to see her when she was killed.''
"Ritchie, too?''
"Yes,'' I said. "Ritchie, too.''
Andy pulled down his hat and walked toward his car. "Andy,'' I said. He turned and looked up at me. "You didn't answer me. Are you ready for this?''
A slow smile knotted his lips. Slowly he said, "You bet your ass I am.'' Then he got in his car and drove away.
Francis hopped to my lap, and Mrs. Thompson shouted "Good morning,'' and smiled. I smiled back and went inside the house for coffee and milk. I thought for a time about the ten-round donnybrook to come, about the blood and the broken teeth and the popped ears, wondering who would be left standing when the final bell rang. I hoped the winners would be Elizabeth Cobb and Robert Cobb and Andy Lanham and Cleve Saunders and all the people who got hurt and didn't deserve it. I threw off my clothes and put on a dirty bathrobe, poured some coffee, and went back to the porch.
The morning turned rosy, the ballpark alive with crowds of kids, moms and dads and boys and girls. My back and arm ached where the deputies had struck me with their clubs. I felt sad and alone, but steady, too. I rocked with the old woman and the cat.
Toward noon a red MG whirled into the driveway and stopped behind a lilac bush. She walked around the lilacs and I watched her swaying walk. A bus pulled into the ballpark lot, on its side a sign that said: Brooklyn Dodgers. She reached the top step and stood looking at me in my old bathrobe, the cat in my lap, the old woman dozing at my side.
"Your friend Christian told me,'' she said. I left the swing and stood next to her. The yellow sun glanced at her silken hair and made circles in it. Her eyes were deep

jade and she wore blue jeans, a crisp white blouse, with a bulky pink sweater tied around her neck.

"Cynthia," I said.

"I want you to forgive me," she said.

"There's no need," I began.

"There is. You were right, Mitch. There is a place for struggle and a place for happiness. You can't ignore the real evil any more than running away will make it disappear. Please forgive me."

"All right," I said.

She smiled. "These Dodgers and these Braves," she said. "Are they good?"

Somebody inside me was crying for joy. "Bach and Handel," I said. "Just like Bach and Handel." I put my arms around her and squeezed. She squeezed back hard. Over her shoulder I saw a red box kite soaring in the clear March sky.

"You could use a hot bath," Cynthia said.

"Just like the other bath?"

"Well"—she laughed—"there may be some variations."

I held her and smelled her hair. And in front of God and the Brooklyn Dodgers, I kissed Cynthia Wunderland on her soft and lovely mouth.

RAINMAKER

In tornado season
when the late, hourless
afternoon tenses
and each static elm
is exactly unreal,
a skinny
sparrow of a man
is making rain,
knee-deep in ochre
praying simply,
abandoned as a Nazarite.
He plays pennywhistle,
twisting hymns,
windblown,
lilac-scented
adrift
in the tremulous
darkening sky
above the old hotels
downtown, the imperious
avenues, the one
last salesman
hiding in a battered
Plymouth, smoking,
rigid, regarding his own
scream, the recurrent
looming siren
and sudden rain
as magic
altogether unknown.

—A fragment discovered among the effects of Dr.
Cleveland Saunders after his unfortunate death.